RAINBOW GAP

What Reviewers Say About Lee Lynch's Work

"Author Lee Lynch offers readers so much: written with a gentle, almost stream-of-consciousness voice, [*An American Queer*] is partly memoir and partly LGBT history with a personal touch. Lynch's essays are approachable, comfortable and enjoyable to read, and how she writes about the past is more relatable for casual readers, I think, than are similar books by academics."—*The Washington Blade*

"Lynch, whose novels, such as *Old Dyke Tales* and *Sweet Creek*, have won numerous awards, deserves to be in the pantheon of legendary lesbian journalists since her columns straddle the literary and the journalistic, always contemporary in their look at queer women's culture and beyond"
—*The Advocate*

"*An American Queer* follows the tradition of 'the personal is political' in an accessible quick read, both heartfelt and gentle, that stays in the reader's thoughts. It is recommended for all public and academic libraries."—*GLBT Reviews*

"Lee Lynch has not only created some of the most memorable and treasured characters in all of lesbian literature, she's given us the added pleasure of having them turn up in each other's stories. *Beggar of Love* ranks with Lee Lynch's richest and most candid portrayals of lesbian life."—Katherine V. Forrest, Lambda Literary Award-winning author of *Curious Wine* and the Kate Delafield series

"Lee Lynch reads as an old friend, and in a way she is."—Joan Nestle, Lambda Literary Award-winning author and co-founder of the Lesbian Herstory Archives

"I've been a fan of Lee Lynch since I read her novel *Rafferty Street* many years ago. Her books—especially her deeply human characters—never disappoint. *Beggar of Love* is a story not to be missed!"—Ellen Hart, Lambda Literary Award-winning author of the Jane Lawless Mystery series

"*Sweet Creek* is Lynch's first book in eight years, and one that shows the maturing of her craft. In a time when much of lesbian writing is more about formula than finding the truths of our lives, she has written a breakthrough book that is evidence of her unique gifts as a storyteller and her undeniable talent in creating characters that move us and remain with us long after the final page is turned."—*Sacred Ground: News and Views on Lesbian Writing*

Sweet Creek "...is a textured read, almost epic in scope but still wonderfully intimate. Lynch, with a dozen novels to her credit dating back to the early days of Naiad Press, has earned her stripes as a writerly elder—she was contributing stories...four decades ago. But this latest is sublimely in tune with the times."—Richard LaBonte, *Q Syndicate*

"...the sweeping scope of Lynch's abilities... The sheer quality of this work is proof-positive...that writing honestly from a place of authenticity and real experience is what separates literature from 'books.'"—*Lambda Book Report*

"[Lynch's stories] go right to my heart, then stay and teach me...I think these are some of the most important stories in the dykedom."—*Feminist Bookstore News*

"Lee Lynch fills her stories with adventure, vision and great courage, but the abiding and overriding concept is love. Her characters *love each other* and we love them for caring."—*This Week in Texas*

"Lee Lynch explores the elements of survival, the complexities of defining community and the power of claiming our place..."—*Gay & Lesbian Times*

"[Lee Lynch's work] is a salute to the literary and bonding traditions of our lesbian past, as well as the acceptance we continue to demand and achieve within a larger society."—*The Lavender Network*

"Lee Lynch is a mature novelist who retains the freshness of outlook of a young writer. Her independent, self reliant women…are ever ready to face the challenges that all lesbians meet."—Sarah Aldridge

"[Lee Lynch's] writing is a delight, full of heart, wisdom and humor." —Ann Bannon

"The highest recommendation I can give Lee Lynch's writing is that you will not mistake it for anyone else's. Her voice and imagination are uniquely her own. Lynch has been out and proudly writing about it for longer than many of us have been alive.…A good book can make the reader laugh, feel desire, and think, sometimes all in the same scene."—*Queer Magazine Online*

By the Author

From Bold Strokes Books
Beggar of Love
Sweet Creek
The Raid
An American Queer: The Amazon Trail
Rainbow Gap

From Naiad Press
Toothpick House
Old Dyke Tales
The Swashbuckler
Home In Your Hands
Dusty's Queen of Hearts Diner
The Amazon Trail
Sue Slate, Private Eye
That Old Studebaker
Morton River Valley
Cactus Love

From New Victoria Publishers
Rafferty Street
Off the Rag: Women Write About Menopause,
Edited with Akia Woods

From TRP Cookbooks
The Butch Cook Book, Edited with Sue Hardesty
and Nel Ward

RAINBOW GAP

by

Lee Lynch

2016

ISBN 13: 978-1-62639-799-6

THIS TRADE PAPERBACK ORIGINAL IS PUBLISHED BY
BOLD STROKES BOOKS, INC.
P.O. BOX 249
VALLEY FALLS, NY 12185

FIRST EDITION: DECEMBER 2016

CREDITS
EDITOR: RUTH STERNGLANTZ
PRODUCTION DESIGN: SUSAN RAMUNDO
COVER DESIGN BY MELODY POND

Acknowledgments

Rainbow Gap has been many years in the making, and I have a multitude of people to thank for sustaining me in any number of ways.

No one, of course, more than my treasured wife, Elaine Mulligan Lynch. Also Radclyffe, who I hold in the highest regard. And Ruth Sternglantz, an outstanding editor and my own personal Yoda.

The late Cate Culpepper for the honor of using, with her permission, both her name and Kirby's.

My trusted early readers and listeners: Sue Hardesty, Nel Ward, Jane Cothron, and Elaine Lynch.

Allison Mugnier, for her support of the Golden Crown Literary Society.

Bold Strokes Staff: Sandy Lowe, Connie Ward, Toni Whitaker, Cindy Cresap, Stacia Seaman, Kathi Isserman, Paula Tighe.

Shelley Thrasher, my teacher.

Ann McMan, my literary cohort.

Kiddo and Ally.

My ever-supportive friends: Mercedes Lewis, Lori Lake, M.J. Lowe, Liz Gibson, Sandy Thornton, Patty Schramm, Nell Stark, Liz McMullen, KG MacGregor, Mavis and Heather, Karin Kallmaker, Mara Witzling, Mary Davidson, Mary Jane Lynch Hackler, Marilyn Silver, Katherine V. Forrest, Paula Offutt, Carol Feiden, John D. Bartola, Bobbie Weinstock, Sue Dart, Wendy Richardson, Rachel Spangler, Jackie Brown, Ellen Lewin, Mark McNease, VAB, Anne Laughlin, and Diane Anderson-Minshall.

My family Dave, Betsy, Carolyn, and Chris Lynch.

The Golden Crown Literary Society, Saints and Sinners Literary Festival, Lambda Literary, Recovering Hearts, and Womancrafts of Provincetown.

And thank you every reader, for your emails and letters, for introducing yourselves at gatherings and for thanking me for writing our stories. I thank you for reading them.

Some sources: Donald L. Bentz Collection, University of South Florida; MCFilm.co, http://www.mcfilm.co/bars-that-were-new/; Hillsborough County (FL) Public Library Cooperative; Tarpon Springs (FL) Public Library.

Dedication

For Elaine Mulligan Lynch
You are
My little bit of deity,
All the love
And all the light
I can imagine.

And

In homage to the Spirit of Marcia Santee
She wanted the Powers, the Great Spirit, both of which
were Good/God, to help her find her own goodness.

Prologue

They started courting as schoolgirls in that fall of 1959, when they were eight.

Berry and Jaudon held hands on the sandy path from bus to school, wearing thin, fresh-washed little girl dresses homemade for the Florida heat. They dilly-dallied in and out of the shade of oak and palm, past red hurricane lilies risen that very morning after a downpour.

By then, Jaudon Vicker already worked at her family's new business, The Beverage Bay. It wasn't usual at the time for a girl of any age to work at a drive-thru beer and pop store, but Jaudon was far from a usual girl. Quick-tempered and scrappy, blessed with ungirlish strength and form, she'd also inherited her father's talent for joshing, which kept the customers returning, the bullies mostly at bay, and masked her sore, bewildered, uncomfortable, different young self.

Berry Garland was a poster Southern Christian girl, mild-mannered and polite. She was an eager student at school and had a sweet smile for everyone. She played as hard as a tomboy, but loved her Sunday go-to-church dress. Before she'd moved to Florida for good, she'd followed her ma and Grammy Garland through the house in Georgia, learning to fix meals, sew, and clean. She'd also followed her pa and Gramps around the yard and the garage and was taught how to change tires and shoot. Every night she recited her prayers.

Berry's last memory of her ma and pa was watching them drive down Stinky Lane away from Gran's place on Pa's motorcycle, Ma waving, dust rising between her and them. She couldn't wait till they got set up and sent her an airplane ticket to join them. An airplane. California!

Berry and Jaudon met on the bus that carried them to third grade.

"*Jaw-dun*," Jaudon told Berry. "You say my name *jaw-dun*. After Momma's family."

Berry noticed that Jaudon always said *Momma*, not my momma, as if hers was the only mother in the world.

Berry spent her first years on the Florida border in Georgia. Her speech was so muddy with drawl it took Jaudon months before she stopped asking, "What? What?" Slowly, Berry sounded more like the other kids. Though they lived close, they didn't wait at the same bus stop, because the school didn't want children walking over the railroad crossing on Eulalia Road.

Berry's hair was old-fashioned—dark, wavy, and thick. In the humidity it frizzed out and stayed out, resembling a living helmet, but beautiful. Her church wanted girls to wear their hair long even in the heat. Under the helmet was a pale, pale face, as if it was masked in powder. Makeup was against the church rules too. They hadn't outlawed freckles yet and in the Florida sun they blossomed on Berry.

The Vickers' house was on the dry side of Eulalia Road at 12 Pineapple Trail in Rainbow Gap, Florida, where Jaudon grew up during country-and-western singer Tennessee Ernie Ford's heyday in the 1950s. The house was set on a post-and-block foundation. Pops and Jaudon's brother Bat connected the original two rooms, or pens, by enclosing the dogtrot, although Momma complained of missing the breezes that used to blow through. This enlarged the living room on one side and gave them space to install an indoor toilet and tub on the other.

Up in the Vickers' tree house, Jaudon and Berry giggled, imagining a hurricane sliding the old outhouse, barrel and all, far into the swamp to rot.

The men connected the kitchen out back to the main house with a windowless, skinny hallway. The fireplaces and chimneys remained at the gabled ends of the main building. They put on a new tin roof and attached rails to the sun-bleached wood porch. The four wings added to the original structure, one square room at each corner, were the bedrooms. The ceilings were grayed pecky cypress. Home, to Jaudon, smelled of new wood and wet cement as much as it smelled of the red trumpet honeysuckle by the porch, cool air after a thunderstorm, and a pot of Pop's swamp cabbage with bacon.

The Garland family used to move back and forth between grandparents, so Jaudon and the tree house in the old live oak became constants for Berry. Her pa had a best friend named gambling. When he wiped out, Pa, Ma, and Berry returned to Grammy and Gramps Garland up in Georgia, or came down to stay with her mom's mother, Gran Binyon, in the travel trailer behind Gran's manufactured home. The small homestead was set in forested, swampy wetlands on a dirt road called Stinky Lane after the smelly mushrooms that thrust up through the soil by the hundreds around there a couple of times a year.

Berry's Binyon and Garland kin were connected way back when. Cowmen, including some Garland boys, came down from Georgia to let their cattle graze on grassy flatlands. They were called Georgia Crackers. In the early 1800s, the Binyons left Wales for America, migrating south over time until two grandsons found Rainbow's Gap, as the settlement was first called, rowdy enough for their tastes.

Jaudon and Berry spent a good chunk of their childhoods on the Vicker property in the tree house whose branches had a sixty- to eighty-foot spread over the long pond everyone called Rainbow Lake. Despite an occasional sulphur smell, Rainbow Gap kids dove to a hidden freshwater spring and a small underwater cave. Berry and Jaudon wouldn't go in because of alligators. Instead, they played card games on an old wood bench half swallowed by reeds. There they heard the burble of the spring and watched ospreys and eagles follow their submerged prey, swoop and clutch large fish—or several small fish—in their talons.

Jaudon made up stories of what might be hidden in a fissure of the cave, and of a secret swim path all the way to the Gulf of Mexico. She claimed there were manatees down there, nosing into warm spots. Berry said she didn't believe a word of it, but she reckoned how it could be possible.

When the Garlands were in Florida, Berry and Jaudon played, imagined, read, napped, laughed at the strutting peacocks and scurrying hens, cried over unfair punishments—and they were all unfair. In season they gobbled strawberries up in the tree house out of sticky reddened hands. Strawberry farms lay everywhere in drained fields. The girls were often covered with calamine lotion to treat the poison sumac they ignored as they played.

Bat hid his transistor radio in the tree house when he joined up to drive trucks for the army. Jaudon happened on it, so they were able to listen to Mel Tillis, a country singer from their area, and to JoAnn Campbell and Pat Boone from North Florida. She also found Pops Vicker's favorite station, with all the old big bands and singers. They listened so often to such tunes as "Some Enchanted Evening," "White Christmas," and "On the Sunny Side of the Street," they knew the words.

It wasn't quite a tree house—more a shack on stilts leaning against the forty-one-foot oak: high stilts, twelve feet off the ground, reinforced by struts and camouflaged by the huge leaves of an elephant ear plant. They used a homemade ladder and pulled it away from the tree at night to keep varmints out. More than once Jaudon, who always checked before Berry went inside, found snakes and took a hoe to them from the top of the ladder.

Bat, officially Batson, their mother's maiden name, painted the outside of the tree house black before he enlisted, but only patches of the paint remained on the weathered gray wood. Stains on the inside walls could be maps of the world. There was a warped door that almost closed, and outside plywood window covers were hinged at the top, with hooks to shutter them. Jaudon, at age ten, built a narrow railed platform over the pond, big enough to lie on, and sawed out a pint size dormer window under the overhang of the roof so she saw more of the sky. There was an old window in the garage which she used to cover the hole—too big, but she hammered it down tight.

She nailed screening across the windows for the bugs, but the bugs were clever. One year the mosquitos got so bad she had the bright idea to soak the floorboards with citronella from Momma's stash at the Beverage Bay office, but it stank to the high heavens and Berry wouldn't visit at all.

After every storm she checked the tree house first thing.

The freight trains came howling across Eulalia Road towing gondolas of oranges, limes, lemons, and grapefruit. Hopper cars moved tons of phosphorous from the Bone Valley mines. Momma commented it was a wonder some train didn't shake the tree house apart. Jaudon's granddad originally built it for a young Pops who, some months after inviting Momma to visit the tree house, married her. He kept it in good shape for Bat.

Jaudon wanted to do whatever Bat and Pops did.

By the time Jaudon was three she was climbing the ladder. Pops seemed to know she would be as much of a son to him as Bat. Pops dragged her off the tree house ladder and smacked her on the behind time and again. For her fourth birthday, he stood at the bottom of the ladder and watched her climb it over and over, propping her up when she started to fall, until he saw she did it safely. At that point Jaudon planted herself in front of him, fisted hands on her hips, and he gave a roar of laughter. "You, Daughter, inherited the true Vicker spirit!"

Jaudon, proud, stood as tall as she could and never forgot his words.

Pops also laughed when Jaudon, age eight, over Thanksgiving dinner, announced to a houseful of relatives that she planned to marry Berry and live in the tree house. She went back to gnawing on her drumstick. When she became aware of the silence and Pops's laugh faded to a cough, she looked up to see the family watching her. She excused herself, drumstick in hand, and jumped off her chair to run to the pond bench and cry. She never forgot that incident either.

CHAPTER ONE

Berry insisted Jaudon finish high school with her. She would help Jaudon catch up and take leave of those hallways the first second possible.

Early on, Pops had told Jaudon, with true merriment, that she walked like a sailor late from shore leave, knees hugging air, leaning forward into the wind to rush up a gangplank. At school she was called a circus freak. The bullies grabbed her books and scattered them. They pinched her behind and teased her more for crying. Humiliated, uncomprehending, emotionally scorched, at school she found no help. The teachers looked the other way—Berry never did.

By their junior year, Jaudon didn't get any more girlish, but she made a good-looking boy, Berry thought. Jaudon was so energized, so excited, so much fun when they were alone together.

"Is it okay, Berry, that I get a funny pitter-patter in my heart when I see you? And how I'm feverish, but I never felt better in my life?"

"If it's okay that I want to cuddle you into my lap and pet you till you purr loud as Toby. Or that I want to be in your lap so you can pet me till I purr."

The school bus was still a trial. They agreed to ride it like statues to give no fodder the bullies could use to further torment them. Both of them endured name-calling, shoving, and—one day—a dead rat tossed onto Jaudon's lap. She grabbed Berry's arm to stop her from reacting, dumped the rat to the floor, and used her foot to push it under the seat in front of them.

Every weekday they escaped the school bus and dawdled through a sandlot of sad-looking grass to reach their redbrick high school. When the other pupils were far ahead, Jaudon sometimes looped around the smooth gray palm trees and leapt out at Berry for no good reason but pure silliness. School smelled of chalk dust and Pine-Sol.

Those were the best days. On the worst days, home at the tree house, Jaudon would cry and Berry would hold her, praying this cruelty would someday end.

Their classmates' words were soon carried home to the adults in the small congregation of the church Berry, with reluctance, attended.

One Saturday she saw the pastor talking with Eddie Dill, the man-friend Gran took up with a few years after Grandpa died. As soon as they walked into Gran's house on Stinky Lane, Eddie took hold of Berry, slapped her hard across the face, and slammed her against a wall. He pulled her to him, turned her around, and slapped her from the other side. He threw her into an armchair.

"Is it true about you and that Vicker girl?"

Berry held her cheeks. Her face stung. Her head throbbed from the nasty blows. She said nothing, her ears filled with noise, as if her skull was a bell Eddie had rung. She tried to find her inside place, her peaceful sanctuary, her time with Jaudon.

Eddie's voice turned shrill. His breath stank of rotting teeth, his body of dead animals and swamp water. "Is it?"

It was true she loved Jaudon, but the other truth was no, what people said wasn't true. Brought up to wait for marriage, they did no more than hold each other, to staunch tears, and out of affection. If it was her gran asking, she'd have said more, but not to this loathsome, depraved predator. He deserved lies or silence.

Eddie raised his bony hand again, his face misshapen with what looked like disgust. She rose up quickly, lifting her arm to ward off the blow. The side of his hand hit her wrist like a hatchet chop. She screamed in rage and pain.

Gran rushed at him. He swatted her away. Berry fled to her bedroom, the former laundry room. They'd moved the washer outside under a thickly fronded palm and the dryer into the living room. There was no other place for it, or her. She was scared stiff. With one hand and her legs, she rammed her bed against the door and her dresser against her bed. She jammed her rear to the wall and used her feet to reinforce her blockade.

Jaudon called her a girly girl; but there was no rule saying a girly girl couldn't take care of herself. She wanted to run across the railroad tracks to 12 Pineapple Trail and ask the Vickers to call the police, but that would cause Gran to suffer and Berry suspected she suffered enough from Eddie Dill. Instead she recited the names of the trees she knew: pond pine, loblolly pine, sweetbay, redbud, grand oak, live oak, chickasaw plum, sweetgum, holly, cypress, bottlebrush, myrtle, magnolia, cedar, palm.

The stabbing sensation in her wrist was so bad she was about to sick up. Her head was swimmy. *Help me God, or the Great Spirit that Gran talks about or some, any, powerful Thing.* Her pleas came out in whimpers and she covered her mouth to hide the sound from Eddie. What did she know about Gran's swamp vagrant? He seemed to have no history, no family. For all Berry knew, Gran took in an escaped prisoner. Lots of them fled to Florida. A hobo? A man who saw too much war? Her hatred was a torture to her, but she would not turn her cheek after this.

Another girl might run away from home. Berry knew she was lucky to have a home, what with no ma and pa. She ought to give up putting herself to sleep at night burbling *MaandPa, MaandPa* into her pillow. She often woke with a stuffy nose and red eyes. Gran put her hand on her forehead and concluded, each time, that Berry suffered from allergies. Berry would lie there asking herself, did Pa land in hot water with illegal gambling on their way to California and were they serving out jail terms? Did he gamble away the bike and try to resume the trip ever since? Get robbed and left for dead or lose their memories like in the movies? Were they too ashamed to come home after a losing streak?

No, Berry was a wicked child and drove them away. Was there something that made them suspect she was inclined to love a girl?

Other than loving Jaudon Vicker, she was a regular person. She stayed and waited out Eddie's anger. Gran knew how to bind a hurt wrist. No, she refused to answer Eddie Dill or be even a mite close to him again.

Gran wanted her to go to college, teach children like Ma—she dropped out early on and ran wild. With fair and conscientious teachers, Gran told her, she might have been comfortable enough to stay in school and get on in the world. It stung Gran when the teachers claimed the Binyons spoke as if they were gargling mush. Not all Floridians had deep accents, but the Binyons and the Vickers did. Gran didn't always understand Berry, who occasionally sounded like her pa's relatives. So Gran encouraged Berry to talk right if that was what it took for someone in the Binyon family to make a better life.

She heard Gran's calming murmur and Eddie Dill's grumbling, with the occasional loud, "Out!" Who was he to think Gran was going to let him send her away? She wished she could get her hands on his gun, or one of her own. She pictured herself shooting holes in him, over and over, cutting him down, one bullet at a time. The fantasy was soothing and conflicting. She shouldn't want to harm a living thing, but outrage took her places she didn't want to go and trapped her there. Who wouldn't want to run her out if they saw far inside her head?

Where would she go if he got his way? To Georgia, where the last of the Garlands lived? The Binyons, but for Gran, were every last one gone from Rainbow Gap, chasing employment or being chased by the law. If she left, Jaudon would never finish high school and she might never see her again. Pain was clouding her thinking so she switched to prayer and became lost in conversation with her faith. What was her faith? Gran had schooled her a bit in what Berry's Seminole great-grandparents believed.

Some Seminoles took up Christianity, Gran told her. The original tribe believed there was a Great Spirit and that critters and objects have their spirits set free when they die or break. The Seminoles hunted for food, but knew nature needed to maintain a balance, so they apologized to the animals they killed by a ritual of sweating and bathing after the hunt. Rainbows, the moon, and the sun were supernatural spirits too.

She listened to Gran, and took on those Seminole beliefs. The tribe's words and notions held what she believed. She came by vegetarianism and the rescue of small animals naturally.

Her ancestors' Great Spirit would guide her if she learned to listen. She was self-conscious about saying *the Great Spirit*, even to herself, when everyone she knew said *God*.

Gran tried to open her door.

Berry, without the adrenaline of terror, wasn't strong enough to push her furniture from the door. Between them, they made a passage big enough for Berry, who had meager flesh on her fine bones.

Eddie Dill was in bed. Gran said Berry's arm was too swollen to fix at home. "We'll see the doctor tomorrow if you can wait. I don't know how we'd pay for an emergency room visit. Take two aspirin every couple of hours."

Gran rigged up a sling to keep the wrist motionless. One minute sweat seeped from Berry's every pore, the next chills made her shake. They sat close together on the couch and Gran pulled the floor fan near so it blew on Berry.

"No, Gran. I'm colder than the deepest well water."

She didn't dare move her arm for the pain of it, but Gran had enough worries without a big bill. The doctor always let her pay over time.

"We best not send you to school tomorrow, pet. They'll busybody us to death." Gran looked toward the bedroom. "He's too mean to live. If I thought he wouldn't go into hiding out in the swamp forest, I'd tell the authorities."

Never before had she heard Gran say a word against Eddie Dill. She never put up with him harassing Berry, but was otherwise meek with him.

Her hatred threatened to spill out in a slurry of words that would bury Gran in guilt. She dammed away her ill will. "Why do you stay with him, Gran?"

"He's part Seminole, pet. He's almost kin. A woman like me needs a man."

Berry didn't think she needed a man herself, didn't think so at all. It was 1967 for crying out loud, a long time since Gran was young. Berry knew she would do fine with Jaudon.

Gran looked abashed, but her eyes smiled. "He doesn't know I took out an insurance policy on him. I'm in the dark about where he gets to or if he'll show up at all."

She wondered if it would be as much of a relief for Gran to lose Eddie as it would be for her. She gave Gran a half hug. "You're the smartest person I know."

Gran scrutinized her eyes. "Thank you, pet. You're so smart, never mind nursing, you'll be a doctor. You have my grandmother's eyes, so dark. She was a healer. I wish I'd had the interest to learn her secrets. I loved her, but she kept the old-fashioned ways. I wanted to be up-to-the-minute."

She hugged Gran. "I'd be content as a healer, but a doctor?" She pondered the idea. "That's not the road I'm on. If I'm a nurse, I can be closer to the people I help. You've said yourself, doctors like prescriptions and tests. They forget how to talk to their patients. I guess I wouldn't mind someday running a clinic respectful of patients."

They watched TV for a while. She dreamed about the future to keep her mind off her arm. At the advertisement, which was for Aero shaving cream, she came right out and asked Gran how come Jaudon had conspicuous hair on her face and arms, like duck fluff. Gran told her most women found themselves with hair they didn't want, in places they didn't want it, but they went on to marry and have kids.

After a while Berry said, "Can you imagine a man marrying a woman and waking up the first morning to find her in the bathroom shaving?"

"Does it seem so bad to you, Berry, your wife having whiskers?"

"She doesn't. And Jaudon's not my wife."

"Of course she is."

"Women don't have wives, Gran."

"Yes they do, and men have husbands. It happens all the time, everywhere. People fall in love, some people fall in love with people the same as them, some don't. It's human nature. After your Grampa Binyon's death and your ma and pa going missing, life is too precious to quibble about the manner anyone lives. Your ways may be peculiar to me, and I know you think I don't belong with Eddie. It's beyond me why some people judge other people in matters of personal choice."

"You think there are more people like Jaudon and me?"

"I know there are, my pet."

Gran continued to call her pet despite knowing what was between her and Jaudon. The thought soothed her. She looked forward to telling Jaudon.

Berry didn't sleep much that night from the pain. She was at the bus stop before Jaudon, wearing the unbleached muslin sling. She pleaded with Jaudon to go to school without her, so they wouldn't miss anything.

Jaudon looked over her shoulder for the bus. Their driver never stopped the other riders when they spit and teased her with hateful, injuring words while she fought to hide her tears.

"I'm going to the doctor with you, Berry."

"No, Jaudon, you can't." Gran didn't want anyone to know Eddie Dill hit her and why, but this was Jaudon—it made sense to tell her.

Jaudon slammed her book bag to the ground. "We're not safe at home anymore." She scrunched up her forehead. "I guess we never were. Momma isn't very nice to me either. She used to wrap a scratchy rope around my middle to keep me in place so she didn't have to bother watching me while she sold cold drinks and strawberries at our roadside stand, before the first Beverage Bay opened. The rope stretched as far as I needed to go to dump melted ice out of the cold drink washtubs. When I was strong enough to wiggle free, she used a switch to keep me in line, the same one she had for Bat. But at least she was my mother. That son of a biscuit Eddie Dill isn't even your grandfather. He better not show up at my family's door. I'll stay home too, in case."

Berry gave her a reproving look. She might not agree with the church on everything, but prettied-up cuss words bothered her.

"Sorry." Jaudon tried her best not to curse.

Berry prevailed over Jaudon, as usual. The school bus driver waited for her to follow Jaudon onto the bus. She displayed her sling. As the driver pulled the lever to shut the door, a football player from one of the new showboat houses on Lake Suggens called out, "Did you break your arm fighting off the weirdo?"

Berry surveyed the ground around her, picked up a broken piece of asphalt, and flung it at the football player with all her might. It would have hit him if she hadn't been hurt. She yelled, "You better shut up or I'll knock your teeth down your throat till you spit them out in single file."

The bus pulled away and Berry wrinkled her nose at the puff of diesel. She imagined, as if she was praying, the Great Spirit protecting Jaudon and herself. She was lucky not to have hit that ignorant child with the asphalt but also wished she had. Her ugly words repeated on her like nasty burps. She sat on the ground until the dizziness and sweating passed.

Gran's doctor pronounced a clean break and put her wrist in a cast. When asked how it happened, Gran reminded the doctor, in a long story, about the day Berry's pa, as a kid, broke his leg. The doctor didn't ask again. He should have been retired, or stopped drinking—she smelled the liquor. His hands shook while he wrapped padding around and around. She needed to take care to keep the kids at school from writing anything evil on her cast.

The visit to the doctor cost enough, but Gran took her afterward to buy a short, boxy, lightweight white jacket at McCrory's, never asking anything, never talking about Eddie Dill or Jaudon. This was Gran's favorite store out in Plant City, far from any big shopping center. It was the very first department store in the area and served non-whites, but the salesladies were all white. Berry shopped there twice before in her whole life. It was a wonderland with a little bit of everything, a big, plain building made magic by goods in cases of dark wood and glass. When they passed the furniture section she squirmed onto a red leather easy chair. She bounced once on a mattress, which irritated her wrist. A saleslady hurried over.

"Ida, it's you!" the woman said. Gran had once worked with her in a packing plant and they did some catching up. She asked Gran about Berry's arm and Gran blamed the injury on a fall from a tree.

"She's a lively looking one, all right." The woman patted her on the head. "Take after your grandmother, don't you?"

They drank thick strawberry milkshakes at the fruit and vegetable stand on the way home. Watching the customers poke around the bins was as entertaining as a movie, they joked.

"You can tell the Northern women," said Gran. "Look at those floppy sombrero hats." Berry and the ladies from Lecoats County went bareheaded or, at most, tied a scarf around their hair like Gran.

They poked fun at the visiting men's brightly colored porkpie hats with contrasting bands. "You won't find our men in anything but straw or truckers' caps." The local men bought boiled peanuts and ate them out of brown paper bags while they waited for their wives to get the melons or mangoes, potatoes and fresh pea greens in the pod.

In strawberry season, every roadside stand sold, besides the milkshakes, individual strawberry shortcakes, strawberry soft-serve sundaes, and strawberry bread. Gran had shown Berry how to freeze the berries along with stalks of rhubarb to make pies year round. A church woman Gran knew came over and exclaimed how Berry was a young lady now.

It was one of the best days of her life, despite the pain and knowing she'd have to keep living with despicable Eddie Dill a very long time if she planned to go to college. Jaudon always said no place was safe for them.

The next time Eddie took off, she got into his shed, scared herself silly when her head brushed against a croaker sack full of frogs, found his pistol, loaded it, set the frogs free in the woods, wrapped the pistol in the empty sack, and took it into the house with her.

Go ahead and womp me again, Eddie Dill. Go ahead and try to womp Gran.

CHAPTER TWO

They started at Cloud Christian College directly out of high school, summer semester. Berry was in a hurry to make them independent. She wanted a four-year RN degree. Jaudon studied business.

The Vickers were able to foot the almost $2,000 a year for Jaudon's education.

After Ma was born, Berry's grandfather Binyon bought a life insurance policy from a church friend. The same friend stepped in to advise Gran on investments when she became a widow. Gran invested, but otherwise never touched the money and it grew substantially, enough so she could mostly pay for Berry's college. Berry earned scholarships. She supplemented them by working at Jaudon's store. Better to save the investment money, what she could of it, for Gran or a rainy day.

"Eventually, Jaudon, I'll look for an after-school job like nurse aide. For the time being I'm going to enjoy working by your side."

Berry looked around her. Momma had updated the Bays' lighting, added shining stainless steel coolers, stark white ice chests, and shelving that made it faster for employees to snatch products. Model airplanes, all painted silver, glittered and swayed overhead. In her store, Jaudon kept the glass surfaces so clear they mirrored every ray of light—starbursts everywhere. Momma outfitted the Bays with white bell-shaped hanging lights. Jaudon bleached the concrete floors regularly. "This must be like one of those light shows so popular out on the West Coast," Berry told Jaudon as she admired the ceiling from below.

Her whole life lately was a starburst, ever since the night she chose between Jaudon and her school friends and despite Eddie's attack. Berry loved being at the tree house, but the girls at school asked her to their homes and taught her how to use makeup. She ran with them and their boy hangers-on till the night their little gang went to the movies and stopped at Jaudon's Beverage Bay afterward. Her new girlfriends were rude to Jaudon and made fun of her. She'd recited the line from the Bible she associated with Jaudon: "People call you an outcast: Zion, no one cares for you." She'd closed the car door behind her and shut the girls out of her life. God bless them, those school friends were a waste of good time.

An excited pleasure filled her whenever she saw Jaudon. She helped Jaudon close the store on the nights she worked and Jaudon drove Berry to Gran's mobile home, up Stinky Lane. At graduation Pops Vicker presented Jaudon with the heavy van he once used for deliveries—he switched to a three-ton truck. The van had a bench front seat so she sat close to Jaudon and held her hand even when Jaudon maneuvered the stick shift.

Those last days of high school had been intoxicating. Their plan to ignore the bullies had worked—the bullies lost interest. A new freedom awaited them, but she'd relished their last school bus rides, sitting side by side, lagging behind the other kids as usual, dallying close together from the bus stop to school, stretching out the minutes under the tall royal palms that lined their path like an honor guard.

Berry thanked the powers that be for leading Jaudon to graduation. On the last day of school Berry wore sandals and a new pinafore-style dress Gran had sewn. Jaudon was in one of her shapeless skirts; her short-sleeved blouse was half tucked in, her tennis shoes were worn through at the left little toe. At Berry's suggestion Jaudon had finally given up wearing Bat's old shoes. Jaudon held her hand for a few furtive feet. Berry's heart sped to a crazy pace. Jaudon scuffed her shoes along the sandy ground, leaving a trace of Berry and herself.

In June, Berry celebrated her eighteenth birthday. After dinner Berry walked over to Pineapple Trail and climbed the ladder to the tree house. She brought some of the eighteen birthday cupcakes Gran made her. She knew she was now old enough to make up her own mind about things.

It was ten years or so since Ma and Pa left. It weighed on her about them not being at her high school graduation. What did she do wrong to get under their skins so bad? Pops Vicker was there with Gran, though. Pops had carried on about her graduating as much as he did for Jaudon.

Jaudon heard Berry's steps on the ladder the night of Berry's birthday and turned up the transistor. Ella Fitzgerald was singing a moony song. Jaudon's grin stretched her mouth so wide her eyes were forced almost shut. In the tiny tree house, Berry's kind, calm bearing filled Jaudon up with what must be happiness.

"They didn't cost much," Jaudon said of the two gold bands she'd found, after much searching, in an antique store. There, in the catawampus tree house, in the dusky light, she gave one to Berry. Her voice was as raspy as a teenage boy's. "Happy birthday, Georgia gal. Will you marry me?" She showed Berry the matching ring. They'd already agreed to marry; the rings were to make it final.

Berry went so pale Jaudon feared she would faint. She held out her hand. Jaudon set down her own ring box and worked Berry's ring onto her finger. They both admired it. Berry did the same for Jaudon.

"When do you have to be home?"

"I'm eighteen now. I told Gran I'm sleeping over tonight."

They kissed and drew away, Jaudon's eyes wide, as if she was surprised all over again at the pleasure of it, or in fear; Berry wasn't sure. The boy she'd kissed had pushed at her mouth until her neck hurt. She kissed Jaudon again, gentle as she could. She touched Jaudon where her breasts should be and found slight swells of flesh around firm nipples. Jaudon was so familiar; she refused to imagine being without her.

Tears outlined Jaudon's eyes.

She stroked Jaudon's cheek. "You scared?"

Jaudon shrugged.

"What are you scared of?"

Twisting away, Jaudon wiped the tears from her cheeks with the hem of her faded polo shirt. Her voice hoarsened. "I don't want to be a man."

Berry didn't know what she meant. "But you're not."

"I must be, I married you. I'm kissing you. I want to do it more. The kids know it's true, I'm not a girl. Your gran's boyfriend said so."

"Eddie Dill? It's cruel to say, but he's as dumb as those kids. Why would I want a man? I want to be with you and you alone. Forever." The fear in Jaudon's eyes was receding.

Berry sat on the old twin mattress they'd long ago lugged up the ladder and kept under the table. "Come and sit," said Berry, patting the spot beside her, studying Jaudon's shirt. "Guys don't have breasts."

Jaudon's tanned face flushed pink. "Do you for a fact want to be married to a queer?"

Berry smiled. "If you do."

Jaudon's hands were tentative as they touched Berry's braids. Her fingers were nicked up and there was a small wart on the back of her left thumb. Whenever she thought Berry was looking, she folded her thumb under her other fingers.

Berry admired Jaudon's hands, big for her wrists and as sturdy looking as Jaudon.

A man's hands, Jaudon thought with disgust as she unbraided the hair she'd so often braided.

Berry embraced Jaudon and clasped her to herself, imprisoning her arms until Jaudon calmed. She pictured one of their many nighttime campfires in a space under the live oaks Jaudon cleared by the pond bench. The last time they made a fire, they held hands in the dark, listening to the voices of the swamp: crickets, alligators, water birds, a dozen kinds of frogs, heard the animals grunting, croaking, whistling, rustling, flapping wings, splashing—a glee club of them making repetitive, rhythmic sounds increasing in volume and thundering in the night.

In the tree house, Sinatra sang "Almost Like Being in Love." Berry ran the tip of her tongue lightly over Jaudon's upper lip. Her memory of the campfire burned hotter, its crackling leapt into the roar of the swamp. Jaudon carried the smells of campfires and earth, milky sweet coffee, and strawberries, always strawberries.

Horrified and embarrassed at first, Jaudon little by little got stirred up. Berry's tongue was rolling along her lips, moistening them. Jaudon opened her mouth to take a breath and Berry, excited, dipped inside.

Berry never knew anything as soft as Jaudon's mouth. Should she stop? The church would want her to. It didn't strike her as wrong, what they were doing. No, this was good and befitting and the Great Spirit wanted her to love the world and everyone in it: the birds and frogs and her own little outcast.

Jaudon was awed. This wasn't the same as the tickling and touching they did. They'd never kissed before today; she'd never kissed before at all. How did Berry learn?

Berry was glad she'd gone out with a boy once and learned to do this. It was so much more delicate, sweet, close, tender with Jaudon. "Begin the Beguine" came on the radio. Jaudon's arms closed around her and she let herself go without hesitation into them to be closer to those lips that did so much more than touch. She wished herself a sweet warm syrup, always coating those lips.

A mosquito came near. Eyes closed, lips against Berry, Jaudon stretched out an arm and, surprising herself, caught the bug, crushed it, flicked it away. She wanted nothing to intrude, nothing to interfere, nothing to distract them from these light-headed sensations, from the pleasure flowing through every inch of her flesh, better than delicious sleep and delicious awakenings.

On they went, kissing the night away while Rosemary Clooney, Jimmy Rushing, and Dinah Washington serenaded them.

Jaudon's lips were impossibly sensitive. Berry's were bruised with continuous arousal.

I'm kissing Jaudon, she thought.

"Berry, Berry, Berry," Jaudon spoke against Berry's lips.

They collapsed together on their mattress under the table, two swamp saplings taken by a hurricane.

Jaudon squeezed Berry to her, more aware than ever of the immoderate strength in her arms. She wasn't a freak in the circus if Berry liked kissing her. Or maybe she was because she liked kissing Berry. She was a cauldron of excitement, remorse, desire, despondency, and a euphoria she'd never known before. This body of hers was not all torment and trouble.

Berry said, "Take off my clothes, angel?"

Jaudon tipped their table against the door for privacy. Self-conscious, they giggled at their shaking hands as they undressed. Berry managed to light a citronella candle, though the worst of the pests left with darkness. When they lay facing each other, she wasn't sure what to do. As they kissed she looked with a finger for Jaudon's spot, the spot she'd discovered on herself, and brushed over it. Jaudon started.

"Did I hurt you?"

"No," said Jaudon. "I didn't expect—"

"Relax, my angel. Everything is as it should be."

Jaudon's was different, fuller and bigger, but very womanly. It infuriated her when Eddie Dill walked around in skimpy underwear. She'd never looked at him after the first repellant time. Gran would tell him to dress himself. If he answered at all, he muttered, "My home, Ida. I'll do as I please." In fact, it was Gran's home and property, not Eddie's.

Jaudon tried to relax. "Where you're touching, am I the way I'm supposed to be?"

"Of course you are."

"I was afraid, because of the rest of me—"

"You're not so different from me, silly. Didn't you ever do this yourself?"

"No. You're not supposed to."

"Why? Because you'll go blind? I'm not blind."

"You do that?"

Berry kissed her. "Yes."

"But your church—"

"Remember? It's not my church anymore. This is another reason why it isn't. What's wrong with enjoying our bodies?"

"And there's nothing wrong with me?"

"Nothing I can tell, honey."

They kissed more.

Berry was excited, touching Jaudon, giving her pleasure. She shut out everything but Jaudon, Jaudon's lovely pleasure. Jaudon didn't get wet the way Berry did. No matter, Jaudon was shuddering against her. Berry wanted to shout in triumph. *This is beautiful.*

Jaudon somehow knew to put her fingers inside as Berry went over her edge and Jaudon's was receding. It alarmed her when the walls around her fingers contracted and then opened wide once, twice, again. She hoped Berry wasn't irritated by the calluses on her hands when they touched her sensitive places.

"Lord have mercy. Don't ever stop what you're doing, Jaudon." The unexpected exquisite sensation of Jaudon inside her blocked every other awareness. When her mind was clear, Berry whispered, "We're two halves of the same person."

Against her belly, Jaudon's lips stretched into another big smile. Make this last, she thought.

CHAPTER THREE

Summer 1969

Pops brought his proud daughter a nameplate: *Jaudon Vicker, Store Manager*.

As of that day, Jaudon hired her own helpers. She required them to be flexible because she needed to schedule around school. Berry had long since taken a part-time job as a medication aide at a rehabilitation facility. Her Aunt Lessie covered odd shifts to relieve Jaudon and her cousin Cal.

Cal came in one day with his draft notice.

"Gosh damn. There's no way I wanted to go. Guys are getting killed right and left in 'Nam. Can't you tell the army you need me here?"

Jaudon squared her shoulders, filled with patriotism. "Bat's done a couple of tours in 'Nam. Your country needs you more than I do, Cal."

Her cousin was a motorcycle enthusiast. When he wasn't putting in hours at Beverage Bays, he fixed cycles, raced, and was friends with guys in a motorcycle club. He was a burly, hairy kid who seldom took off his prescription aviator glasses and had accumulated a wardrobe of motorcycle club T-shirts, though Aunt Lessie forbid him to join one.

"I knew what you'd say, Cousin Goody Two-Shoes."

Jaudon said, "Ha-ha." Cal came off threatening, but growing up they'd played at each other's houses. She knew he'd messed around with dolls as a youngster. She'd hated playing dolls, even paper dolls.

"You can't shirk that easy, Cal. They'd know I was lying."

Cal's shoulders slumped. "Find me a way to serve, but let me do it alive and whole. What if I'm released with no arms to steer my hog? And for what? Someone else's civil war?"

She pumped a fist in the air. "To keep the Commies in line, Cal."

"I guess." The poor guy pouted as he always had. "If I don't have to kill anybody. Hey, I have to do this quick. I don't want to spend my last days of freedom selling cigarettes and beer, and I already asked my mom if she minded taking my hours."

"Aunt Lessie told me a long time ago she never wanted to work regular hours, but I always get a few people stopping by to ask if I'm hiring. One lady in particular I've taken to. We josh each other no matter how many cars are waiting. Momma will have a conniption, though."

"The lady's not from our family?"

"And then some."

"Don't tell me you're hiring a colored lady?"

"Afro-American is what we say nowadays, Cal. You better practice saying it for the Army."

"Your momma's going to have a fit."

Jaudon jutted out her jaw. "By the time it's done, Momma won't be able to undo it. Mrs. Ponder used to come through every day with her youngest boy, Emmett, and his older sister. The boy's busy playing sports and studying to get into college, and the sister is married with her own baby. Mrs. Ponder tells me she's bored and lonely. We jaw about every subject on earth and she teases me about my delusional Southern white girl opinions. She wants to make money to send her boy to college, but wanting and getting hired are two different animals around here if you're Afro-American."

Cal put on his Beverage Bay jacket and went to wait on a customer. Jaudon called Mrs. Ponder to ask if she was available. She arrived the next morning for training.

Jaudon leaned, elbows on the counter, eye to eye with Mrs. Ponder. "There's one thing I need to tell you."

"I know what you're going to tell me. It's your mother, isn't it? You're going to be in a heap of trouble."

Jaudon held up her hands in peace. "She won't make a scene in front of you, but don't be surprised if she inspects the store and finds things to criticize while you're on duty."

"I have to hand it to you, Ms. Vicker. You're a brave child to hire me on. People like your mother have been rude to me longer than you've been alive, but I know my worth. Mr. Ponder works at MacDill and I worked at the BX there for years. The budget cuts came and I was laid off. I am honest, reliable, hardworking, and know how to follow instructions. If it would help with your mother, I can go after a written reference spelling it out."

"Sure, if it's no trouble. Not so much for me as for you if you ever need to stick up for yourself. I don't expect it to come to that, Olive, but I understand if you're disposed to give this job a pass."

"I think I can give Mother Vicker a run for her money at least as well as you, sugar. She didn't raise me."

"Lucky you."

"Poor and black, coming up in a tar shack?"

"I take it all back. Lucky me."

They worked together over the next weeks. Olive was steady and deliberate in her duties, seldom making an error, good at catching them and asking for help. She was nimble with heavy or light cartons on the dolly and neat in her shelving. The vendors asked for Cal, but Olive put them at ease. She knew how to cash out the register and volunteered to replace a high fluorescent bulb because she was taller than Jaudon. Olive was eagle-eyed at rooting out old stock which she left in the cooler for Jaudon to deal with. Some items smelled so rancid Jaudon gagged. Olive Ponder went from part-time to running shifts without a hitch.

"You're so capable I'd vote for you for president," she told Olive.

As much as she commended herself for hiring such a gem, Jaudon picked a time Momma wasn't in her office to drop off the references Olive provided. She girded herself for Momma's reaction and skittered away. It was bad enough Momma kept asking her what she and Berry got up to in the tree house and why they spent so much time there.

One night after she and Berry came down from the tree house, and she watched Berry go up Stinky Lane, Jaudon went into the kitchen with the stump of the candle they'd used. Momma was standing by the stove with folded arms. She'd expected Momma to be in bed by this hour. Jaudon quailed at what was to come.

"You better not burn down the woods," was all Momma said before turning and walking to her bedroom.

Jaudon bit her lip to keep from showing a reaction. She was relieved not to be given Hail Columbia over hiring Olive. She and Berry would never be careless enough to start a fire, though they might rock the tree house or break through the floor. Theirs was the lovemaking of two slight, innocent young women, whispering and falling into fits of laughter and sharing touches light as the breeze from a handheld fan. As Berry said, "How is what we do wrong?"

Momma showed up at the store the Friday after Jaudon delivered Olive's paperwork. Olive said Momma parked outside and entered while Olive was hustling to serve two customers. Olive never saw Momma up close before and said she hadn't expected her to be so much taller than Jaudon.

From pictures of Momma and Pops, Jaudon knew Momma was never the prettiest girl in town. She had those furry, dark eyebrows—two upside-down *L*s over her eyes—their tips not quite touching. When she started wearing wire-rimmed glasses, Momma's countenance turned all the way stern. Her hair looked like she was struck by a lightning bolt that flattened and scorched a path, gray as ash, front to back over the top of her head, dark hair frizzing the rest of the way to her earlobes.

"Yeah, I'm the runt of the Vicker litter, Olive, no getting around it."

"You don't resemble your momma one bit, Jaudon. For one thing, I can't see you in a feathered black hat perched on your head with hat pins." They laughed. "Oh, my, she was a surprise. In black head to toe, down to her low heels. I assumed she was a poor lost widow woman looking for directions."

"Pops says she wears black to downplay her hip size."

"You could have knocked me over with a feather when she introduced herself, nice as pie. I kept on working while she watched me. She asked if I needed help with anything and I told her I was fine. She left without another word. You hear from her yet?"

"No, and that's unlike her. I'm leery," she told Olive, looking over her shoulder. "I sense a black bear stalking me, out of earshot."

Olive tittered at her. "No, honey, you mean a big white bear dressed in black."

"Aw, heck. I put my foot in it, didn't I? I regret my words, Olive."

"Thank you, Jaudon. But I wish I had a mirror to show you your once-white face. You're redder than some apples I've sold."

"It's bad enough we have to go up against other people's prejudices without having to root it out of ourselves." She didn't know if Olive had figured out yet about her and Berry, or if Olive needed some rooting out herself.

CHAPTER FOUR

Jaudon liked to study at a particular carrel in the Cloud Christian College library. Most of them were set at the open ends of aisles, but this one was blocked from view. She saw nothing to distract her and she was hidden unless someone turned that corner.

"Studying isn't my greatest talent," she'd once reminded Berry.

They were on their mattress at the time, enjoying a freshly laundered velour bedspread from Goodwill. Berry pressed one of Jaudon's hands against herself. "I know what your greatest talent is, angel."

Jaudon tried not to turn vain when Berry said this sort of thing. She did admit to having a talent for making Berry happy that way.

She massaged where Berry placed the heel of her hand. "I don't care about being a great student. I have a job waiting for me once I graduate. I want to learn everything I can to run the Beverage Bays someday. Momma's paying for my education and she always demands her money's worth."

Berry came again, holding tight to Jaudon. When she caught her breath she said, "I'm not a natural A student, Jaudon. I work myself hard for good grades because I want to be able to keep my scholarships and grant. I also need to stay on the honor roll to pick and choose my specialty and my employer."

Business and math were what Jaudon wanted to learn. Days when she was preparing for those classes she let her mind travel where it wanted, which was usually to the tree house and Berry and what they did up there. She called Berry her sweet swamp flower, thinking of the peach-colored hibiscus blooming by the house. Berry was like the hibiscus, petals open wide. When she touched Berry with her fingers and eyes, no thoughts, no worries, no mockery—nothing existed outside their elevated lair. She imagined a lifetime of pleasures for them both: work they loved, a real house of their own someday, and each other in the warmth of Florida.

At the carrel she was having trouble concentrating. She ran through some homework calculations and drifted to a memory from last Sunday when they'd walked the two miles to the town center for fun. A train came and they watched the old box cars stop at the two small shacks which constituted a depot where Lemon Street met Eulalia Road. Rainbow Gap's downtown consisted of an Elks Lodge, the small but active community theater that housed a one-room branch of the Lecoats County library, an insurance agency in a tiny old stucco building, a semiretired dentist, and a store that sold bait, fishing gear, pop, candy, a bit of hardware, and anything else that would turn a dollar. Mudfoot's Fish Camp Restaurant sat off by itself, and across the tracks was a hairdresser in a private home. A white woman in curlers smoked a cigarette on the hairdresser's front porch, talking to someone who leaned out the doorway. The post office was a converted 1930s vacation cottage, painted plain white, up on stilts.

Berry said, "The way the population's growing, with so many Northerners buying summer cottages and investing in retirement land, the county will soon have to build a new post office and sell this."

The town itself was smack in the middle of marshy lake land, but it was cleared and more habitable than where they lived. Some owners kept up lawns and personal orange, lime, lemon, and avocado trees, swimming pools and garages. The whole town flooded in heavy rain.

What was it about Florida, and Rainbow Gap, she loved so much? It was tangled up with Berry, with loving her and being loved—and possessed—by her. It was something to do with the hot sogginess of the land, the mysterious overgrown, intertwined, thorny underbrush, the yellow bouquets of glowing daisies offered from the earth. For Jaudon, the heat was home itself. While others complained, she prided herself on her endurance. She hoped never to be cold. Everyone thought hell was hot; any hell she went to would be bone cold.

The air got so heavy you swam through it like in a dream and an hour later the same air turned dry and seared your throat with every breath. Berry thought Florida should be inhabited by the Eddie Dills of the world, the ones who hunt and are hunted, as well as by prehistoric bugs, birds of impossible colors, massive plants, and Banyan trees with grasping roots.

Berry told her that bush hogging to clear land and pour cement over the Florida wilderness was suffocating evil. She said the evil would not die and predicted wild growth breaking through with concrete chunks for teeth.

They lay together after studying in Jaudon's room one night, listening to the house sounds. Berry said Vicker-style Cracker homes were fragile, built with boards stolen from struggling trees that groaned and creaked in misery to this day. It was true, the trees were dried and swollen by turn in the torrid heat and soaking rains. Jaudon told Berry she had a vivid imagination and was a poet; Berry shushed her.

Shushed or not, Jaudon had asked why Berry loved a place she described as she might a nightmare. Berry looked away. It had become a habit, this covering up the evil in herself and in her outlook, believing she drove off Ma and Pa.

"To me," Jaudon told her, "it's not a nightmare. It's a mystery."

In the college library, she refocused on her textbook, but no more than a minute later she just about leapt out of her skin.

"Ah!" Jaudon squawked, starting up from her seat.

"I didn't plan to frighten you to death." A husky guy with a head full of long loose coppery curls which should have been on a girl's head stopped in front of her. "I wanted to introduce myself. This is my favorite spot too."

She stood and held out her hand. "Jaudon Vicker. Do you need the seat? I can move."

His handshake was more like a leaf falling into her outstretched palm than anything she'd call a grip.

"No, no, darling. It's sweet of you to offer. For a moment I took you for a handsome boy. Just my luck." He hurried to the next carrel, his arms cradling textbooks.

"Me? A handsome boy?" She was confused for a moment—shouldn't she be upset? *Why no, he's a fairy*, she realized, amazed. A real live grown up sissy boy. She picked up the package of M&M's she was nibbling to keep herself awake and offered them. He practically bowed when he thanked her.

"Say, what's your name?" She bent toward him in her chair, legs wide, hands splayed flat on her thighs so he didn't take her question the wrong way.

He lowered himself to his chair, crossed his ankles, and seemed to search her face. "Even your name could be a boy's. I'm Rigoberto Patate— Rigo. Do I know you?"

"Not really. I remember you because you got teased at least as much as me in grammar school."

He looked at her more closely and arched his eyebrows. "You're the she-male they told me I'd grow into. I have to tell you, darling, I'll take your looks over mine in a heartbeat."

She laughed. "That's a deal if you give me your hair."

"You can have it. I'd rather be blond like you."

Blond would look as striking as red against his skin color, which she knew would be called olive, but not any olive she ever saw.

They were whispering because they were in the library, but someone told them to hush anyway.

"Can you take a break?"

She looked at her watch. It was Pops's big Hamilton from the Korean War. Momma gave him a new fancy watch with an alarm when they opened the fifth store. He liked to socialize and tended to run late.

"Let's give it an hour and meet out on the front steps. I have a report due for a five o'clock class."

Berry was late to the tree house in the evening, harried from studying. Jaudon greeted her with the open-armed enthusiasm of her discovery.

"His dad is Cuban," she told Berry, bouncing on her toes in excitement. "Rigo's mother was a performer in Miami. She refused to move to Cuba. Rigo visited his dad's sugar plantation summers when he was a kid, but one year when his dad came to Florida for a visit, he got word the Commies took over his plantation and would kill him if he ever got in their way."

"You like this boy?" Berry's face was no longer harried, but blank, the way it looked when she was upset.

"You're kidding, aren't you? He's one of us, Berry. He mistook me for a cute guy—it's why he stopped."

"You are my cute schoolboy." She kissed Jaudon on the cheek. "Tell him hands off—you're all girl. My girl." Berry surprised herself with her zeal; no one was taking Jaudon away from her ever.

Rigo, Berry, and Jaudon took to going to art movies on campus together and having sodas at the student café. Rigo's presence gave them the freedom to be seen in public, which they were timid about. His humor left them with tears in their eyes. His father, who had always kept his money in American banks, supplied Rigo with a red Camaro convertible. They went for rides along the Gulf Coast at twilight. He showed them certain spots where men sought one another out. Jaudon and Berry insisted on speaking to Rigo in Spanish, which they were all studying in school, Rigo for easy As, the girls because they expected to need it for their jobs.

They showed Rigo Rainbow Gap. He rolled his eyes.

"Swampland? Orange groves? Strawberry fields? Phosphorous pits? Train tracks next to your property? You girls need to move into town."

"Why?" Jaudon demanded. "We love the bellowing whistles. The long trains going by at night have lulled me to sleep since I was a baby."

"And oranges," cried Berry. "Strawberries too. In season there can't be better perfumes on this planet."

Jaudon thrust her head between them from the backseat. "Schools around here used to run on a strawberry schedule, open July to December when the farm kids picked strawberries. Now the farmers hire migrant workers. When the berries are ripest we go out at night to a field up the road. They're warm from the day's heat."

"We come home with red faces"—Berry licked her lips—"dripping with luscious strawberry juice."

"The farmer has known me since I was not much taller than those noisemaker stakes in his field. He told me he'd rather I got the overripe berries than critters that tear up the plants. You should see the heaps and heaps of starlings that will cover an acre of ripe plants."

"We leave plenty for them. Critters need the food more than us."

Rigo imitated Berry, licking his lips. "Look at the luscious berries outside the feed store. Do farm boys always hang out here?"

Jaudon hit him on the shoulder. "Those are Harold's boys. He hires high school kids to stock the store and load customer rigs. Always uses yellow-haired football players."

"Tasty. I have a yen for some fertilizer."

"You're so bad, Rigo. You know there's three boys in the nursing program?"

"Oh my God, Berry. You waited to tell me this—why?"

"I don't know if they're our kind. The one in my class went to elementary school with us, Jaudon."

"Who?"

"Jimmy Neal Skaggs."

"A bully going into nursing? Those poor patients."

"I adore male nurses," Rigo said.

"Rigo, you adore anything male."

"Jaudon, I must admit truer words were never spoken."

Berry was happy as a lark. Rigo was great fun, Jaudon was great fun and sexy. Watching a playful Rigo and Jaudon together was even greater.

On another of their drives they tried to convince Rigo this area, called Hanker Pond a century earlier, was once known for its cotton plantations and, later, its celery fields. He scoffed at them.

"But I would have loved to be mistress of a Southern plantation." Rigo ran his fingertips through his shining hair. "Servants to fan me in the heat, cooks to feed me, a master to dominate me. That would be the life. As soon as I get my inheritance, I'm going to Sweden for a sex-change operation."

"How much would that cost?" Berry asked.

Jaudon gave her a sharp look. Berry had once wondered aloud if Jaudon might have an easier life if she was male or pretended to be. "I don't want to be someone I'm not," she'd replied. There was no pretense in Jaudon.

Looking at Rigo and Jaudon together, she realized they had similar builds, short-legged and rugged, and could be brother and sister if their hair and skin tones weren't different. Jaudon already passed for a guy, of course, but Rigo would need more work to get by as a woman.

"Rigo," Jaudon said, "if you want to take that road, more power to you, but I'd miss your sissy ways."

"I'd love to know how it is to be normal."

"Why in the Sam Hill would you want to be normal?"

"Doesn't everyone?"

Jaudon was unable to tone down her fierce reply. "Not me. I don't want to be normal if it means I can't love Berry."

"You've got it, Jaudo. When I'm a woman, I can marry the man I love. Never in a thousand years will you be able to do the same."

A cloud of dust coming off a fallow field caught Jaudon's eyes. "Look." She pointed to a number of grayed wooden sheds, some small, others long, with plank loading docks, leaning toward collapse. "See the dozer? Looks like it's tearing down the old packinghouse buildings."

"Probably putting up more housing." Rigo looked around. "Where are these people coming from?"

"Up north, I guess."

Berry always teared up over the subject. "God bless the developers. They're filling in the swamps, cutting down the orchards, chasing the birds away. I want to stop it."

"It'll be okay." Jaudon reached to pat Berry's shoulder.

Berry placed a hand over Jaudon's. "This area also used to be known for its plant nurseries, dairies, lumbering, sawmills, turpentine stills. I wish for those days."

"Oh, pooh," said Rigo. "Life used to be a lot tougher. Today we have air conditioning—well, not you and Jaudon—and insect repellent and decent places to live."

Berry said, "I wish they built some of it for the poorer people. I feel bad for the Publix cashiers, the office cleaners, the caregivers, the motel help, the fruit pickers and packers. Most of the buyers are retired white people. There should be a law requiring a certain number of homes be made available for people who do the work."

"Does anybody work out here? Are they too poor to drive into Tampa?"

Jaudon was proud of her birthplace. "We have people making decent money, like anyplace else. They might be Lecoats County employees or railroad workers or teachers, bankers, construction guys, well-to-do farmers. There's some mansions here too."

"No one but the darned real estate agents and Northerners can afford those mansions."

"You're envious, Berry."

"No, sir, Rigo. Gran's place is perfect for me. I just can't stand to watch the countryside beat all hollow."

"Progress can put us in reverse, can't it, Miss Berry? I'm heading home to Tampa. The city's built up. Different things to bellyache about."

"Drop us on home, buckaroo," Jaudon said. "I need to memorize some biology for my science requirement."

Rigo raised his eyebrows. "Nurse Garland can help you out with that."

She saw Berry cast her eyes down, the corners of her lips twitching into a grin.

"Sorry, darlings. I forget how modest you two are."

Jaudon jumped over the car door when they stopped at Pineapple Trail. Jaudon stood gripping Berry's door while Berry leaned an arm on her hand. They never hugged or kissed in public though her whole being wanted the one last close contact. Instead, they watched the sunset. Lazy-fingered palms were dark against shades of pink and yellow.

Berry told Rigo to drop her at the start of bumpy Stinky Lane, but he insisted on saving her the walk in the buggy twilight. She gave him a kiss on the cheek for it, and hoped Eddie Dill was out hunting, not here to watch her every move or to inspect Rigo.

Oh no, she thought at the sight of Eddie, parked in front of Gran's house, hauling a dead five-foot alligator from the rear of his Scout. Zefer barked and lunged from the end of a stout rope tied to the steps in front of Gran Binyon's mobile home.

Her stomach turned, as much at the sight of Eddie Dill as at the poor dead alligator. How would Eddie Dill like it to have his skin turned into a purse?

Rigo watched the man. "What is that?"

"That's a genuine swamp vagrant hobo and my Gran's boyfriend." On top of Eddie's other crimes, he was shaming her in front of Rigo.

She saw him through Rigo's eyes: a dense ungroomed gray and white beard tucked inside green bibbed waders, a habitual wide-brimmed hat over his last straggles of hair, and a long-sleeve shirt streaming with mosses and sweat.

"You know about skunk apes"—Rigo stared—"those smelly apes people claim to see in the swamps?"

"They're bigger than him." She opened the car door and tried to reassure Rigo with a smile.

Rigo coughed. "Forgive my lack of manners, but he smells of skunk ape."

"He smells worse. You're noticing the mushrooms. Stinkhorns pop up from at least May to October."

"How do you stand it?" Rigo inched the Camaro in reverse. "I need to move my car out of here before the stench soaks in."

Rigo had once shown them where he lived, in a big white colonnaded house near the water in Tampa. A gardener had been at work. Berry had no doubt he was keeping out offensive fungi.

Eddie Dill, the gator under one arm, grabbed her with his other hand. "Must be your beau." He leered.

"No. He's my friend." She pulled away from him, but felt his eyes watch her walk toward the house.

Then, with no warning and a whoosh of sound, Eddie Dill, the Scout, and the alligator fell into the earth.

She sprinted to the trailer. "Gran, run! Sinkhole!"

Her grandmother turned off burners on the stove and grabbed her hand. The cat, Toby, was trying to squeeze under the couch. She let her grandmother go and pulled Toby out by the scruff of the neck, grabbed a croaker sack, stuffed Toby in, and cinched it. "Come on, the house is going down with Eddie."

Gran followed her, only stopping when she saw the Scout's bumper visible in the hole.

"Eddie," she called.

A hand appeared. It was Eddie Dill hauling himself up out of the hole, covered by damp, sandy dirt.

Gran turned to help him while Berry untied Zefer and tugged her away.

"You can't do any good," Berry yelled. Toby yowled and scratched through the bag, Zefer barked nonstop. "You'll add weight to the edge of the hole, Gran. He knows best what to do."

Was there a rope to throw Eddie? But no, he was a secretive man. Ever since she'd stolen his gun, he kept his equipment and tools padlocked in the shed, the key in his pocket. He never said a word about the gun going missing.

She guided her grandmother toward Eulalia Road, trying to run. There was no telling how long a sinkhole would turn out to be or how deep. Gran looked around and pulled her to a stop.

"We can pray for him, Gran." She laid a hand on Gran's gray curls. Prayer might neutralize the conviction that her own hateful thinking caused this catastrophe. She never wanted Gran hurt, yet everything Gran owned, and her companion, were about to be lost.

Gran had escaped in her apron. She used it to dab at her eyes. "I don't know," she said. "He's had this coming for a good long time. A good long time, the way he loved to kill the animals and some people's spirits."

Without rancor, she agreed with Gran. "I imagined the animals or the trees or Mother Nature herself taking him sooner or later." She was too unsure of herself to tell Gran about believing in the Great Spirit of their ancestors. She squatted to calm Zefer, imagining them all in a spotlight of protection. Nothing but images of jagged-edged colors came to mind.

They stared into the night which was ripe with mushroom smells, loud with the sound of earth, in clods, falling into the hole swallowing Eddie Dill.

Eddie's elbow was on the edge of the hole. Somehow, he held onto the gator under his other arm. The hole grew larger yet. The Scout sank deeper; Eddie's elbow slid off. The murdered gator came flying up out of the ditch—Eddie was taking no chances on allowing what was his to sink.

There was a loud creak as Eddie Dill leapt from the half-buried hood of the Scout toward solid land. The Scout sank deeper and more earth fell away when Eddie launched. He'd waited too long: his hands and feet, arms and legs scratched, dug, kicked, and tore as sand and dirt and limestone crumbled beneath his weight.

Gran watched with both her hands in front of her mouth. Eddie's fingers grasped at every root, trailing plant, clump of damp sand, anything, but he was losing ground. Mercifully, one of the dismantled lawn mowers he'd planned to work on crashed into the pit, a sharp metal edge hitting square on the back of Eddie's head. It happened very fast, and she saw blood come through his thin hair, saw the angle of his neck, saw his arms go limp. They watched him slide farther down, oblivious to the sandy soil seeping in his wake into what was becoming an abyss.

No, she wasn't asking the Great Spirit to save this man who respected no living thing, including herself.

Now there was a new sound, a rumble where the sinkhole spread under the trailer's cinder block steps. They went next. The house sat, untied, on a foundation of more concrete blocks. As the blocks closest to the sinkhole slipped, the house, with a crunch, buckled at its front door, began to fold in on itself, and leaned forward over the hole.

Gran watched with a hand over her mouth, as if she wanted to hold in a cry. "He's taking the house with him." The earth crumpled under the front cinderblocks. "My home. The house your grandpa left me when he died. My plants! All my beautiful plants."

"But this remains your land, Gran."

"How can I live on it without Eddie? He brings in pure drinking water and he keeps the generator going. He hauls the propane for heat, the block ice for the swamp cooler. He keeps the place sprayed so we have some peace from the skeeters and roaches. Men have their uses if you can keep them fed and satisfied, child. My eighteen acres. Full of sinkholes and that stinkhorn smell of rotten meat. Even so, there's not a better piece of land on earth. It's so alive and thriving. It'll be me, the wild birds and the gators, the coons, the possums and frogs. I'll never sell it to the developers. It'll be yours someday."

Berry kept leading them away. Toby was no longer mewing. His furry body panted through the bag and she opened the zipper again to keep him from overheating.

Gran's eyes lost their darkness. "You'll keep it the way it is, won't you? Promise me you won't sell it to the developers. In my lifetime I won't turn out the wild animals for commuter houses or a trailer camp or a gas station. Promise me and I'll get through this horror."

"I love this land, Gran. I won't let it go." How else would Ma and Pa find her?

Gran cried, "The propane. My God, the propane and his truck."

They fled to the road, the explosion not far behind.

Gran was out of breath. "Poor Eddie. He was a bad man in so many ways, but such a horrible death…"

The smell of it was sickening from the stinkhorns burning. Flames rose skyward.

Toby in his tote was lifted from her arms. Jaudon was there with Pops, taking Zefer from Gran and urging them toward Rigo's car. So Rigo hadn't left after all. He'd alerted the Vickers and brought them.

She managed to pray it was quickly over for Eddie, and the earth would be kinder to him than he ever was to it.

Gran, her cheery Gran, turned her face into Berry's shoulder while Berry held her with a firm arm. Gran said, as she cried, "Despite all his wickedness, he didn't deserve this."

Berry met Jaudon's eyes over Gran's head. In the light of flames as tall as the tallest palms, she reflected, with an unforgiving wrath like a demon inside her, *Yes, he did.*

CHAPTER FIVE

Of course the Vickers opened their home to Berry and her gran immediately.

Jaudon, Pops, and Bat, with an army buddy John, who came home with Bat on leave, hauled Gran Binyon's twenty-foot camper, which survived with outside smoke damage and one melted tire, to Pineapple Trail and set it behind a hammock that sloped up the back of the Vickers' property with a stand of slash pine for privacy.

Berry expected the heat of the night and the fire, the sickening satisfaction of Eddie's death, and the loss of the manufactured home Gran hadn't been able to insure, would haunt her forever. Jaudon comforted and distracted her overtaxed mind, but Berry had become a more serious and purposeful young woman.

On the porch early one morning while Bat was still home, Berry tried to be calm, but found herself spitting bullets about more than Eddie himself. "The hellfire and brimstone of his church, Jaudon. The church Gran and I go to, where she met him, what they preach proved true. What else would you call what happened to him if not going to hell? The church says what you and I are doing is a willful transgression, but not what Eddie did in his lifetime. Yet Eddie was plunged into hell. What does God have in store for us?"

"Do they tell you love is bad?" Jaudon spoke in a hushed voice. Berry was so seldom mad, it was always unsettling. She was intimidated by Berry's cogent, ladylike way of expressing anger.

Zefer seldom left Gran's side—Gran who was so fragile and unsure of herself since the sinkhole. The dog sat leaning against Berry's calves.

"I don't believe that church comprehends love. If they think an action isn't approved in the Bible, you're subject to church discipline, but who are they to judge us or anyone?"

"Aw, heck, Berry. What can they do to you?"

"It's pitiful. They counsel you and have these whole big sessions with a lot of people. They can throw you out."

"We better find you another church. Why in the world would you go to a church Eddie Dill believed in? A church that's stingy about love and preaches you can only love the way they say?"

"It's Gran's church too, Jaudon. It's where they met. And what church is going to say it's okay to be the way we are? Better to do without. We don't need a building or the judgment of strangers. Whatever's out there is for us and loves us all." Berry spoke with a vehemence Jaudon never held for any church, any religion.

This was a subject they often talked about. Berry confused her, both complaining about the church and making excuses for it. The Vickers had no time for church, but she often heard Momma call people *good Christians like us*. She guessed she was a Christian, but without those discouraging regulations.

Berry played with her ring. "Maybe there is a God and maybe there isn't and maybe God is a power inside everybody, a soul, maybe to lead us toward wholesomeness and keep us from killing and robbing and doing a lot of other harm."

Berry might be changing some parts of what she believed, but she held tight to her faith. She believed God would bring her ma and pa home eventually. Jaudon didn't understand faith, but if that was what made Berry who she was, Jaudon was all for it. Were people born believing or was it taught? What the heck, if it made them happy.

"I want to be good," Berry said, drumming her fists on the seat of the swing. "It's frustrating—folks get in the way of good in this world."

"I wish you would step out of the fight ring and see you're already a champ," Jaudon told her, stretching Berry's arm up in the air as if declaring a winner. "Nothing can take away from the good you do."

Moments like this scared Jaudon; she was on the edge of Eddie Dill's sinkhole, or sin hole. Would Berry's spiritual needs lead her away? Would she be happier with someone who had faith?

Zefer got up to greet Bat, who yawned and stretched in the high school football shirt that didn't reach to his wrists these days.

"You awake, lazybones?" Jaudon teased.

He lit a cigarette. "You know, I don't want my trip home ruined by you ladies fussing over the what and why of a swamp geezer about as useful as a stump full of granddaddy long legs. I'm losing more buddies in 'Nam than I care to count."

Jaudon nodded. "I guess we have to put the sinkhole in perspective."

"This is why I'm home and not doing R and R in some Asian cesspool. The army can either lose us or give us a break."

Berry started to clamp a hand over her mouth. "Of course you don't want us harping on Eddie's fate. I'm sorry, Bat."

Bat reached into a pocket in his fatigues for his US Army money clip and took out a bunch of twenties. "Why don't you and Berry's gran get away for a day? How about going on the boat ride over in Tarpon Springs."

"On the Gulf?" Jaudon got jittery about straying far from home, even when they went with Rigo.

"The boat goes down the channel out toward the Gulf, but not into it. I took a girl there once. We watched a guy dive off the boat for sponges, like they used to when the Greeks first settled that area."

Jaudon tapped her foot to a rhythm of her dread. "Tarpon Springs is a long ways from here."

"Do Berry and Gran a favor and get out of your rut, Jaudo. Eat at a restaurant. Go to the beach. Come home late. Have some fun. I'll watch lazy Zefer sleep. You only live once, girls."

Berry's cheeks dimpled up. "It's a fine idea, Jaudon," said Berry. "You work so hard." She turned to Bat. "Your sister is always ready to cover shifts in other stores if your momma needs her. She works doubles and triples if I don't stop her. Your momma's lucky Olive Ponder's always ready to pitch in when Jaudon's needed elsewhere."

Jaudon remained nervous and delayed the trip as long as possible. Bat wasn't far off the mark—she grew fractious when her routine was upended, which she liked to limit to home, school, and work. Stepping out of her familiar circle made her jittery.

"Okay, I'll take my best girls to the beach," Jaudon told them.

Berry leapt from her seat and hugged her, Gran, and Bat.

Gran owned a pampered red Corvair she swore she'd drive until it fell apart. Saturday the car was filled with a delicate gloom as Jaudon navigated it toward the sponge docks.

Berry never got to the coast much growing up and she became upbeat at the first sight of a bright blue canal. "It amazes me people can dock their boats outside their homes."

"Would you want to be rich enough to have a yacht, pet?" asked Gran.

Berry considered what to say. "It's appealing, but I don't think I'd spend my money on boats, Gran."

They passed a plain trailer park filled with discolored vehicles and trash. Someone had a colossal burn pile going which looked unsafe to Jaudon. "You'd buy everyone in that park new Airstreams."

"Oh, you," Berry chided her with cheerful humor. "I'd give them a chance to learn how to build decent homes and I'd lend them money for construction."

"She'd throw in land on a bayou too." Gran patted Jaudon's shoulder. "You know my granddaughter well."

Jaudon said, "And you know what? If we could put up the money, it might be a sound investment."

When they crossed US 19, Gran surprised them with wistful talk not about Eddie, but about her husband.

"Your grandfather and I honeymooned on Santa Maria Island, Berry." She pointed south. "It took some time to get there in those days, over a rickety wooden bridge. We rented a one-room cabin. Every day we went out on the pier fishing, and at night your grampa fixed what we caught for supper over a pit fire on the beach. It was an extravagance, but he was known for his champagne taste and beer wallet. He always showed me a good time, till the day he died."

"Tell us about more good times, Gran." Jaudon called her Gran, as her own had long since passed on.

"On the way home, kids, if I'm not too worn out by these big happenings."

Gran's voice was at its strongest since the sinkhole misfortune, either from happy memories or this adventure. Jaudon found a parking space on a side street at the Tarpon Springs sponge docks. White sand shone in patches on undeveloped lots.

Berry put on a horrified face before she laughed. "Can you imagine how much sweeping we'd be doing if we lived this near the beach?"

"True," Gran said. "But we'd have these delicious breezes."

Two retirement-age men sat at a table, selling tickets to the sponge boat. Jaudon led them on as it was almost filled. Gran's stories had livened them up.

"Walking the gangplank, Gran?" said Jaudon, kidding, and offered a hand to help her board.

The ramp led them into a boat painted bright white, with mahogany trim. They sat on the hindmost of the long benches under a wood canopy. Two little kids in front of them craned their necks to look at Jaudon, whispering and giggling until their mother looked too, smacking the one closest to her and yanking the arm of the other child. The mother turned back to a conversation with her neighbor. After the boat left the dock, the children snuck frequent quick looks. "Is it a boy or a girl?" one of them asked. The mother swatted the air without interrupting her chat.

Berry squeezed closer to Jaudon.

This was why she feared outings. The comments were hateful to her, and she imagined Berry and Gran must be embarrassed half to death. *What does it matter what I am?* Jaudon railed to herself, trying not to cry in front of these spiteful strangers. *Why are people so desperate to pigeonhole every living being?*

Berry glared at the two kids. She wanted to bawl them out, but feared cross words would draw more attention to Jaudon. *Would people always raise children like these to pester Jaudon to her grave?*

"We don't have to take this." Gran leaned forward and tapped the mother on her shoulder.

The woman turned with a grimace.

"Your children are being rude to my granddaughter. You need to teach them some manners."

As upset as she was, Jaudon wanted to jump for joy at Gran claiming her.

Berry was as tense as a cat stuck in a tree.

The woman turned her back and cuffed both kids in the head. "Shut the hell up, you two, or you're going overboard." She looked at Berry, let her eyes linger on Jaudon, and told Gran, "Why don't you teach your granddaughter how to be a lady?"

"My granddaughter isn't badgering your brats."

The mother gave Gran an angry look and turned her back. She made some loud, rude comments about Gran and Jaudon to her friend. The kids sat face forward for a while.

Berry smiled and, under cover of her flared skirt, touched Jaudon's hand, unsurprised it was in a fist.

Retirees took up much of the seating with more preschoolers and mothers scattered among them. Jaudon left the bench and rode silent and backward for a while, leaning on the stern rail, the purr of the boat's engine vibrating up through her body. Nature was spectacular here. The banks of the Anclote River hosted skinny-legged birds while frogs dodged the birds' long beaks. Dolphins played in the boat's wake; more birds roosted in the tops of mangroves and bay trees and fished amidst the green and yellow saw grass. The air was warm, but the canopy shaded them. She breathed in the earthy, fishy smells of the river and simmered down.

As the captain steered farther out into the bayou, he gave a running commentary about the history of the Tarpon Springs sponge industry. The diver was pulling on a suit used to this day by sponge divers. Jaudon went back to her seat, tensing up again.

Berry took Jaudon's hand between her own and rubbed it while everyone watched the diver sink into the water from the weight of his iron shoes. There was quiet suspense while he was down there, but he soon surfaced with an object on a long two-hooked pole. Everyone applauded.

"Goodness, I never saw a sponge so dirty." Gran made a face, but touched it when offered all the same.

Berry balked about putting a hand on the thing. "Didn't the captain say they're animals, not plants?"

"This is an animal?" Jaudon didn't touch the sponge either, afraid to bring attention to herself.

"Nowadays you can't find real sponges in the stores."

"Best news yet, Gran, because they were killing harmless animals so we could wash dishes."

"Come on, Berry," Jaudon told her. "We're supposed to be having fun today. Don't be talking about killing things unless you want me to go after the group in front of us."

"Can't say as I blame you, Jaudon," said Gran.

The ride lasted about thirty minutes. On the way back, Berry named the wading and diving birds: a kingfisher, an osprey. A flock of red-winged blackbirds flew from branch to reed and back. A gator slipped off a bank. Turtles, necks stretched upward, sunned on flat rocks.

Berry said, "It smells so fresh out here." She leaned on the arm Jaudon stretched along the back of their bench. The children had at last lost interest in Jaudon.

"Those clouds look to be out of a movie." She caressed Berry's back with a furtive thumb.

Berry craned her neck. "They're shooting straight up in the air into a long lazy sky river."

Back on the dock, Gran pretended to work at getting her sea legs. "That was very peaceful. Short and sweet."

Berry smiled at her happiness. "Our ocean cruise, Gran."

Jaudon was overwrought from the encounter with the kids. She watched them debark and steered Gran and Berry in the other direction. She swept a hand toward the boat, bowed and announced, "The Queen Elizabeth of the sponge docks."

"We didn't have to ride in steerage like some of our ancestors," said Gran.

Jaudon rubbed her hands. "I'm starving. Where are we going to eat?"

"Let's look into a few shops. We can drive back to Pappas's Restaurant," Berry said.

Jaudon dashed across the street. She met them as they crossed at the next corner. "I was too hungry to wait." She danced in place with edgy excitement, tearing off pieces of a sesame bread ring for them.

Berry, with her trace of a sashaying walk, led them into a gift shop. She looked at the dead sponges lying in bins, but didn't say anything this time. Jaudon and Gran were showing each other souvenir ashtrays and spoon rests, shot glasses and nail files, having a good old time as far as she could tell. Berry was relieved there were no more confrontations with poorly brought up children. She pretended not to see Jaudon take a tiny glass bird to the cashier. She went along with the idea and picked up a few stocking stuffers for Christmas while alone in the next shop.

Jaudon spotted a blue cement mermaid statue holding a bird bath bowl. She found some chips and stains, but insisted she'd buy it if she got a discount. She wanted Berry to be able to watch her birds.

Berry said no because of the expense.

Jaudon said, "Uh-uh. Look at your face charged up like Broadway, New York City. We're getting it." She plunged inside the store with her sailor's walk and asked the man behind the counter, "How bad do you want to get rid of the mermaid out front before the tourists figure out it'll chip worse in their frozen backyards than it does here?"

The guy looked at her for a long moment, stared at the moisture-stained ceiling, peered out the door, ran a finger over the keys of his cash register, and asked where she was from.

"Over to Rainbow Gap, about an hour east on 60."

"Not one of those Northerners?" He came down eight dollars. Jaudon said twelve, he said nine, and they settled on ten dollars off. Once they got the birdbath stowed in the trunk, she hopped up and down, reveling in her victory. When she looked up, a short dark-haired woman was swaggering past them, carrying a small bouquet of pink and purple flowers.

"Tante Genevieve," called a small child.

"Hold up there, Sis."

The woman turned to her brother and opened her arms to the tiny girl, presenting her with the bouquet.

Berry looked at Jaudon. "Are you thinking what I'm thinking?"

"She's family, like Rigo would say."

"Or she's from France."

"We get Canadians vacationing here."

They heard the woman speaking English. Simultaneously, they said, "A New Yorker," and laughed at the woman's accent.

"She looks like a miniature James Dean."

Jaudon shaped her hair into a pompadour and imitated the woman's strut.

"What are you gals up to?" Gran asked.

With a start, Berry gestured. "Where do you think that woman got those hollyhocks?"

"There was a driveway stand back a ways selling flowers. She must have stopped."

Berry followed Gran into a store where she found a tiny model of a sailing ship with *Tarpon Springs* hand painted on it. She presented it to Gran as a souvenir of their outing. They drove to the restaurant and tried everything: gyros, dolmades, keftedes, and shared a plate of loukoumades for dessert.

"Oh my gosh, I'm full." Jaudon used her index finger to scrape up honey residue and lick it off.

"Brim full of joyousness." Gran patted her tummy. "I haven't eaten Greek food in an age."

"You haven't eaten much of anything recently, Gran. We need to have fun more often. We're like tourists."

Gran nodded. "It's not Paris or the Bahamas, but look at these out-of-state cars come to explore what's an hour from us. Plus we have a beautiful birdbath to remind us of today. I had no idea you knew how to bargain, Jaudon."

"Jaudon is first-rate at everything she does."

She was pleased to hear Berry brag on her. "I can't say as I've negotiated before. It'll come in handy if I'm someday buying for the Bays."

"Oh," said Gran, "you will be. Not a doubt in my head."

CHAPTER SIX

Spring 1971

Momma Vicker rose to treasurer of the chamber of commerce. She decided she needed something newer than a Cracker house, something more suited to the Beverage Bay revenues and her growing position in the business community. She wanted room for an office, an area for entertaining, a house that was closer to town, for certain in an all-white neighborhood, and larger, not a hodgepodge of add-ons perched in swampy wetland.

Pops rounded up the male relatives and moved into a new stucco house with pretend white columns and a screened-in porch called a lanai across the back. The house came with a regular green lawn, budding Southern magnolias, shaped crepe myrtles, palms without a yellowed frond in sight. Momma hired a landscape company to take care of the property. There was an oversized two-car garage to hold Pop's newest big pickup and the baby blue Cadillac de Ville Momma bought herself.

Pops told them they could find him Sunday afternoons smoking a cigar with other businessmen. They served mojitos on the lanai.

"Aren't they overdoing it?" Jaudon asked Berry.

Berry smoothed Jaudon's cowlick down. "This is your momma's dream house, angel. She's worked hard for it."

Jaudon didn't begrudge Momma, but a niggling foreboding filled her. This wasn't the momma she knew.

Once Pops and Momma were gone, Berry moved out of Gran's trailer into the old house with Jaudon and—when he was on leave—Bat, neither of whom wanted anything to do with Momma's palace, as they called it.

Berry was naturally handy and Jaudon had learned a lot from Pops, so they picked up tools and, day off by day off, framed, roofed, and otherwise did the work of adding a bathroom and fixing up the southwest bedroom with a bay window and window seat for Gran. A cousin from Momma's Jaudon side plumbed the bathroom. Toby the cat stayed with Gran in the trailer for the months it took to finish the project. Zefer moved between house and trailer, anxious to be buddies with old Muddy, reluctant to leave Gran.

Although Jaudon and Berry each had a room, Berry caught on that Jaudon paid no attention to the old sock and wet dog blend issuing from her room. They slept together in Berry's bed.

Rigo regularly fought with his father and showed up at their door to find sanctuary in Jaudon's empty bed. He borrowed Gran's nightgowns. Gran found him a hoot. Bat found him ridiculous. If his army buddy came home with him, Bat gave Jaudon Hail Columbia at any sign of Rigo's dress up inclinations. Rigo quit visiting when Bat was home.

"Hey, Sister," said Bat during a trip home. "We should turn this place into a plant nursery when I'm cut loose for good. I'm thinking Bat's Royal Palm and Plants."

"What about the Bays?"

Bat looked at her, one eyebrow raised.

Of course he doesn't want to work for Momma, she realized. *She bosses him around worse than any ten armies.*

"What do you think, John?" Bat's buddy, John Lau, was an intense, serious Chinese American with old world manners. When he and Bat went out on the town, poor John took a lot of guff—strangers assumed he was Vietnamese.

"Why not turn this place into a nursery?" Bat said. "Veteran or no, if I can't find a damn job except for the Beverage Bay, my druthers are to drive trucks or work outdoors. I wouldn't mind selling trees to the damn Yankees and charging to plant them. There's plenty of sabal palms, lantana, and daylilies in every color to dig up around here to give us our seed money, Johnny boy."

John nodded his head, as if he didn't know Bat was full of stillborn ideas. "I've thought of a business along those lines, home in Oregon. Not palms, but a Christmas tree farm."

"Maybe I'll move out there to help you. Great minds, hey, John?" They cuffed each other's knees.

Berry pursed her lips. She knew better than to start a discussion so tried to skirt around her real message. "I wish you two didn't have to go back over there."

John and Bat chanted in unison. "Look Sharp, Be Sharp, Go Army!"

"How sharp do you look in the jungle?"

"We do okay driving stores to the troops, Berry, don't you worry."

"I do worry, Bat. I worry why we're in Vietnam." Berry put her hands together, as if in prayer. "There has to be a better way. Why get our boys killed by Vietcong artillery?"

"Are you a peace nut, Berry? 'Cause if you are, I would kindly ask you to remove yourself from my home. Meaning this house and my country."

Jaudon was distressed by the conversation and worried Bat and Berry would go off on each other. "She's asking questions, Bat. It's a democracy. We're supposed to be able to ask questions."

"We're supposed to stand up for the United States of America."

"Right or wrong?"

Bat held up his hands and looked at John as if John knew the answers.

"We're not brainwashed, Berry," said John. "We may not know the ins and outs of government decisions, but I trust our leaders to do the best thing. It's my job as a citizen and a soldier to back them up. I also trust you to back us up."

"How can anyone back up war, John?"

Bat's face was hard. Jaudon saw the soldier in him.

He turned to her. "Where do you stand, Sister? Do you insult American soldiers on the street?"

"Heck no, Bat." Jaudon put away her annoyance at Berry and gave the smile Bat said always lit him up. "You know better. Berry doesn't believe in killing anything that isn't a spider."

"They needn't die because of my fear," Berry said. "Jaudon catches and evicts them."

John cracked up. "We need you to keep watch over us in 'Nam. Florida has nothing on ten-inch centipedes—"

Bat, bless his heart, grabbed the chance to clear the air. "Mosquitoes carrying malaria and dengue fever, cat-sized rats, dog-sized—"

"Come on, Bat. They'll think we're bug exterminators, not military."

"We are exterminators, John. Our vermin is human." Bat grabbed his cap and jacket and waved a V sign at them. "Peace and love. Come on, John, let's go find some women who like men in uniform."

Jaudon smiled and held her hands palms up. "I know, you'll be at your favorite beach dive bar." She hugged Bat before he left.

"Don't wait up, Sister."

The house went silent. She looked at Berry, vexed. "Why did you start talking war?"

"I didn't. I wished he'd stay home and sell plants. I don't understand what makes anyone hurt other people. I don't believe they're trained—they're indoctrinated. Somehow, we turned a group of people different from us into the enemy. I believe in the Golden Rule and the Ten Commandments. Our society believes in both—why do we go to war?"

"Because of the Communists, Berry. Don't forget, Bat's my big brother. You don't have to agree with him, but, jiminy, Berry, we do have to be nice to him when he's home."

"I'm sorry, Jaudon. He's my brother-in-law and I care about him if for no other reason than how devastated you'd be if anything happened to him. Don't you wish he wasn't putting himself in danger?"

"I don't want to think about Bat getting killed over there. It's nothing you can stop, men going to war. They graduate high school and sign up because it's their bounden duty. They think it's manlier than waiting to be drafted."

"And being manly is more important than being humane."

Jaudon stomped a foot. "When it's us or them, it is."

"Someday we'll have a peace march around here. I'll join in and help end war forever."

"Where's your priorities? These guys are risking their lives to protect us, Berry. You know the Commies don't believe in religion. And they can take away our business and jobs and put us to work in the fields."

"You're afraid?"

"You bet I am. Especially the way I look. Especially who I love. They'd as soon kill a girl like me as squash one of your precious bugs."

Berry reached to Jaudon with both hands. "Let's not fight about fighting. There's got to be a better way than going to war."

"I agree, but that's what we've got." She was too churned up. It helped holding Berry's hands.

"The world's not a safe place, Jaudon. Can we be each other's safety?"

Berry was such an innocent sometimes. As if it was possible to win against such powerful forces. Her girl needed caretaking. Jaudon pulled her tight against herself.

CHAPTER SEVEN

"Yoo-hoo," Rigo called as he came through the door. "Everyone decent? We have com-pany."

Bat was long gone. Berry and Jaudon were in the kitchen, cleaning the shelves of the unfinished white cedar cabinets. Rigo hugged them both. With a lordly gesture, he presented his prize.

"This is Larissa Hand. I brought her home because she doesn't know one gay gal out in the sticks and she lives down the road from you a couple of miles."

"Call me Lari." It sounded more of a command than a cordial overture.

Toby, as a rule too lazy to move for any reason, took one look at Lari and left the room. Zefer never moved her eyes from Lari. Muddy slept on; her muzzle was white, she was failing. It wouldn't be long.

"Lari, this is Jaudon Vicker and Berry Garland."

Lari examined the two of them. "Berry Garland? Did your mother name you Berry on purpose?"

"She said an angel told her what to name me." She counted on her name being unique enough for Ma to find her.

Jaudon said, "I love how Southern it sounds." So this, she thought, was another example of who they were, who gay girls were.

Berry gave her a warning glance she took to mean, *Be nice*, and said, "Well, look at you. You'd have to stand up twice to cast a shadow."

Jaudon was jarred by Lari's abrasive manner and strange speech. She folded her arms. "You from up north?"

Lari was medium height, skinny, slow footed, soft voiced, and had the narrowed red-rimmed eyes of someone on alert all night and day. She smelled of cigarettes. Her black jeans and long-sleeved black shirt matched black straight hair cut in a straight line across her midback. She wore gray eyeliner and her ears were pierced. The peace sign on her shirt was gray.

Jaudon looked from Lari to Berry. As Berry had matured, she'd developed a heart-shaped face with wide-set eyes. Jaudon found her ten thousand times prettier than Lari, but, to her shock, a part of her responded to Lari's rebel girl look. She wanted to growl or howl or carry Lari into a cave.

Rigo sounded proud of his find. "Lari's been kicked out of more schools in Minnesota than I've gone to in my life."

Lari looked at her boots, black and pointed under the tapered jeans. Her hands were in her pockets; a black leather jacket hung from her elbow. She nodded, an angry pride showing in the set of her shoulders, the squinting eyes. "They're making me live with my religion-happy great-aunt in her gated senior trailer park and go to college here. I'm supposed to be her caretaker." She pulled cigarettes out of a pocket.

Berry didn't know why she had her hackles up. She was almost too quick to stop Lari. "I don't do well with the smoke or the smell."

Lari glowered at her, but stuck the cigarette behind her ear.

Rigo said, "Lari goes to Cloud Christian too."

"They picked it because it was founded by a Minnesota native on Christian principles. I'm sick of the freaking cold anyway. I'm not going back north."

Berry laid eyes on Lari's black-painted fingernails. What sort of girl was this? She might be in a Halloween costume or from a monster movie. Her glasses were old-fashioned: round and gold-rimmed. Even Gran wore more stylish frames. Lari swayed as she stood, the smile on her lips close to a sneer, red-rimmed eyes unfocused. She told herself not to judge Lari, but she knew she didn't trust the woman at all.

Jaudon was curious and eager to study Lari, despite her attitude and strange as she looked. "Aren't you hot in those clothes?"

"Hey, it's how I dress." Lari looked Jaudon up and down, from her short hair to Bat's torn olive T-shirt, to her baggy, below the knee shorts, her leg hair, white gym socks and sneakers. "You ought to know, Magilla Gorilla."

At first, Jaudon wanted to drop through the floor. A second later, she was ready to clout the woman on her thin-lipped mouth. Berry and Rigo stared at Lari.

"The college is threatening to expel me if I don't dress like the rest of you." Lari gave a snort of laughter. "The last thing I want to be is Southern respectable. You're all but segregated for one thing. I was revolted by the shacks and outhouses and tattered laundry hanging on clotheslines as I traveled south."

Jaudon held her fists at the ready, fingernails pressed into the heels of her hands. Magilla Gorilla. This woman didn't care whose heart she trampled on. She was in the business of showing the world how mad she was at everyone and everything. Was she angry because she was different? Was it because she didn't have a Berry of her own? She better keep her hands off Berry.

Behind Lari, Rigo said, "We're working on it. At least the public schools are sort of integrated."

"That's why private schools are so popular down here."

"We're not that bad, not how they are in the Deep South," Jaudon said, apologetic.

Jaudon, Berry saw, was a puppy dog, nodding her head in agreement, yet at the same time teeth bared, ready to lunge. Lari was about as open as a folded jackknife, while Jaudon, when not under attack, was good-natured and eager to please and be liked, above all at the store. At the same time, Jaudon turned challenging to the point of truculence in a heartbeat. Today she appeared to find a hasty forgiveness for this stubborn piece of work who was slapping at a mosquito on her cheek as she surveyed their primitive homestead.

"Your family's into their colors," said Lari. Both chairs Momma left behind flaunted cushions of faded green bark cloth with a yellow pineapple pattern, the edges stiffened with age. Rigo gestured to the windows. The closed curtains were thick nubby cotton to keep out the heat. Huge bubblegum-pink hibiscus and green palm fronds, small mango-colored parrots, and brown sticks of bamboo lay against their blue-gray background. On the shady side of the house where the curtains were open, the neighbors' peacock, displaying, walked by. The room was bright, while the squeaky ceiling fan and curtains kept the sun from overheating the room.

Berry winced at the ongoing sounds of a Batson uncle in Gran's bathroom, hammering and cursing as he installed a green-tinted jalousie window Gran found at a flea market. No doubt Lari believed they were all Crackers, and they certainly were.

Jaudon, gesturing and pointing, went off with Lari to give her a tour and the history of the house.

Berry lit a tarnished brass floor lamp, white swan end-table lamps, and settled on the long orange Sears sofa. Rigo chose one of the colorful rattan chairs. Between them was the coffee table that had served as a scratching post for several generations of kittens.

When they sat, Zefer lay at Rigo's feet, panting, and continued to eye Lari. Berry picked up her knitting.

"What are you making?" asked Rigo.

"A new afghan for Gran."

"You don't mind sharing with your grandmother? I mean, honestly."

"Her room is on the other side of the house, Rigo. Besides, she knows about us."

"Well, yeah. But knowing and hearing are two altogether different experiences in close quarters."

"Don't be such a worrywart. Gran doesn't hear as well as she used to."

"God, my dad would outright disown me. Mom was in showbiz so long she'd be surprised if I turned out straight."

"You found out about yourself because you were around show people?"

"Kinda sorta, Berry. The men had eyes for one another and I was their pet, or their communal son, because I did my homework at the theater. Or didn't do it. I knew about options a lot earlier than other kids. I knew I wasn't alone."

She saw Lari and an animated Jaudon through the window, out toward the road, where Lari was smoking. "She talks fast, doesn't she? Should we be more like her?"

"Berry, you and your woman are without a doubt marvelous as you are. Gay girls come in scores of varieties. You should join me at the bar sometime. I'll show you."

"We don't drink," Berry said.

"You can have Cokes. And dance."

"I never learned to dance to rock 'n' roll."

"One of your church's rules?"

"They threatened dancing would lead to worse sins."

"Such as being gay?"

She laughed and clapped her hands. "They were right."

"I say it's time for you to learn to rock and roll along with your thing for ballroom music. "

Berry kept her doubts to herself and wanted to end the conversation. "I'll talk with Jaudon about it."

Rigo followed her back to the kitchen. "Why not come with me? You're already sinners."

"Oh, you, stop. You know we're not." She opened one of the cabinets to get the fixings for sweet tea, remembered the canister was empty, and hunted through everything on the counter before she found a new supply atop the refrigerator. She boiled the water as she listened to Rigo tell tales of bar life.

Jaudon led Lari back in. Lari played with some wallpaper curling along its seams and sat at the table, stretching out her legs. She took a sip of the tea and made a face.

"How about ice water?" Jaudon asked, popping up to get some.

Rigo poured Lari's tea into his own emptied glass. "Jaudon, I'm trying to persuade your girlfriend to come to the gay bar."

"At least the bar's integrated," said Lari. She traced the yellow butterflies and red skeeter hawks printed on her placemat. "Gay people are so much more advanced than the rest of the world."

Jaudon immediately rejected the idea. "A gay bar? When hell freezes over. They'd run us out of college so fast you'd think we weren't white people."

Rigo scoffed at her words. "They haven't caught me and I spend half my life there. Plus I'm only half-white."

"They haven't caught on yet, Rigo. Besides, I might bump into a customer."

"The customer would be yours for life, hon," said Rigo. "Do you have no inkling how famished gay people are for the companionship of our own kind? If we find a store or a restaurant where we can be comfortable, we flock to it, like swallows to a buggy pond."

Jaudon gave a quick sidelong glance at Berry. "Uh-oh, I feel hell getting frosty. I know that rascally look of yours. We have to go, don't we?"

"I wouldn't want to risk my scholarships." Berry looked at Lari. "If we did go, would I need to get gussied up?"

"Not in your Sunday school clothes." Lari's tone was quick and scornful. She gestured to her own outfit. "I'm always ready."

Rigo was wearing his hair longer than ever. He indicated his pristine white shorts and fitted polo shirt. "It's come as you are, kids, if you dare to join us. Guaranteed, there's no question you'll blend in."

CHAPTER EIGHT

It took them until September to agree to meet Rigo at the bar. Jaudon drove, but a glance at Berry's tight lips and knitted brow confirmed the persistence of her concern.

"We don't have to go, Berry. I'll turn around anytime you want." She sorely wished Berry would tell her to go home.

"It's not just what we're doing, Jaudon. You know I hate going out in the van after dark. It's hard to see animals crossing the road."

Jaudon ticked her bright lights on wherever possible and drove in moderation. She was used to Berry's night vigilance, but tonight suspected the bar boosted her concern.

The nights had been cool all that week and her headlights picked out an occasional tree with a headdress of yellow leaves or a purplish-red Japanese maple starting to go orange. A fog of baking smells from the Wonder Bread factory passed all too soon. They met Rigo and Lari by a school in St. Petersburg.

She parked with great care—it wouldn't do to get a ticket tonight. They checked to be certain every door and window was shut up tight. It would be worse to have the van stolen over here.

When she hugged Rigo hello, Berry hung on to him a little too long.

He said, "It's okay, hon. Your Uncle Rigo's here for you. Would I let anything bad happen to my favorite couple?"

"You think anyone would actually steal your rust bucket?" Lari said from where she leaned on the schoolyard fence, one hand hanging from a chain link, her gloomy smirk in place. Berry wondered if Lari thought everyone was beneath her, that she was some omniscient being practicing the Zen she professed to believe in.

"It's safer to park at a distance," Rigo said as they left for the bar. Jaudon wore white ducks and a wrinkled Hawaiian shirt, looking, to Berry, more than ever like a sailor boy on shore leave. Berry was dressed in coral-colored clam diggers with earrings to match and a gray V-neck top. She wore the Coty brand pink lipstick she favored.

Berry knew that alcohol had taken hold of her mother and father young. Pops Vicker drank beer at ball games, but didn't keep it in the house otherwise. She wanted no part of it, yet she and Jaudon needed a place to belong. Where better than a hidden gathering place filled with kindred spirits?

They hurried without words along the dark uneven sidewalks. Though half closed for the night, patches of fleabane—small white-petaled, egg-yolk weeds—bloomed like floodlights in neglected yards and vacant land.

Jaudon longed to take Berry's hand, both to protect her and to bolster herself. At the sight of a small neon beer bottle sign, she increased her distance from Berry. It didn't make sense to her, sneaking around to have fun, but she followed Rigo into a small room in an old factory building partially converted to a tavern where two old guys slumped over a bar and a row of three booths sat empty. This was it? This was the big bad gay bar they feared?

There was a rhythmic pounding beneath their feet, but there was no music in the barroom. Rigo went to a door. A small wooden panel opened at ear level. Rigo whispered and the door opened. The hefty Afro-American man minding the door gestured to the staircase.

They'd brought their birth certificates, but no one questioned their ages. Digging them out made Berry think about why Gran, and not Ma and Pa, had hers. It couldn't be they never planned to fly her to them, could it? She told herself not to be silly. Gran said they'd adored their baby girl and she'd adored them. On a motorcycle you needed to leave all those official scraps of paper behind was all.

They went inside a bare-bones room tarted up with streamers and beer signs and packed with women and men of different ages, sizes, and colors. Most were dancing to the loud jukebox.

Every eye appeared to Jaudon to be, briefly, on the newcomers, some twice, as if making sure they were a same-sex couple and Jaudon was not a man.

Berry observed this too. She whispered to Jaudon, "There are dopes everywhere."

Jaudon was disappointed—she was expecting to feel welcomed.

Rigo got Jaudon and Berry colas; Lari came back with a long-necked bottle of beer. They passed through the ebb and flow of the crowd into a corner of the room, where they huddled together. Lari lit a cigarette, one of dozens smoldering around them. Berry coughed. A very tall man in makeup came over and kissed Rigo on the cheek and motioned to a young man who shook their hands solemnly as they yelled their names over the music. Berry looked at Jaudon, but Jaudon didn't seem to recognize Jimmy Neal Skaggs, grown into a big-eared giant of a boy with hair in a monk's tonsure and a blunt nose. Nor did Jimmy Neal give any sign of recognition when he saw Berry, but he was first-year nursing and she was second so they shared no classes.

Jaudon caught Berry's eyes to telegraph her incredible relief at the sight of a whole room of people like them, despite the initial stares. Okay, she wasn't ever going to be womanly, but her differences fled at the sight of women their age or in their thirties and forties—even a couple who looked to be Gran's age—holding one another, sneaking a kiss here and there, sitting in groups the same as real couples out in the rest of the world. She looked on enchanted, smiling, and at last belonging somewhere besides the tree house.

Lari pushed and pulled her onto the dance floor and left Berry to hold their drinks. "You come across too happy. I'm going to make you dance in this mob."

Confused, looking back at Berry, Jaudon at first let herself be led across the sticky floor between the dancing couples. She balked. She should have asked Berry for this first public dance. *What a backwoods numbskull.* Maybe she could learn rock 'n' roll steps and teach them to Berry.

She watched Lari, who danced like a Halloween skeleton jouncing in a breeze. Jaudon shrugged her shoulders and leaned left, leaned right, jiggled her arms as if trying to amuse Berry. She repeated the moves over and over, in time to the music.

Berry covered a smile—Jaudon looked like one of those wooden stick men that flapped its limbs when a string was pulled. From the intent watching look on her face she could tell Jaudon was serious about studying how to dance to this music, but she was much smoother alone, at home, dancing to their swing records.

Berry stared at the two grown men as they danced in each other's arms. Although Jimmy Neal towered over him, Rigo held him tight and led him to the theme from *Valley of the Dolls*. Rigo gave Berry a wave with his fingers as he passed. Distracted, she lost sight of Jaudon for a minute. Her heart pounded as it had when Eddie Dill went under. Hell took a lot of shapes, and losing Jaudon Vicker would be one.

She was changing. Once she would have mouthed a desperate prayer, but lately she stayed inside herself, trying to summon her Whatever with silence and the deep breathing she read about in her comparative religions class.

Summoning anything in such loud music was taking a lot of breathing tonight and the cigarette smoke was foul. In this packed, blighted basement, her foundation of strict religion collided with the lives of these people, herself included, condemned by creed and country. Yet, if not for the alcohol, her cough, and the close dancing, she could be at a church social. The women and men—how were they so different? How did they— *who* did they—harm, crowing and posing and greeting one another like long lost family, yet banished from any society beyond the barroom doors?

She recalled the words Lari once used: *My head exploded.* Tonight she thought she knew what Lari meant. Images of people in front of her merged with memories of preachers and congregations. The darkness of a chapel lit by candles had become less sacred to her than this space with its bar-long mirror, Old Milwaukee clock, and neon beer signs on the red brick walls. The booming music moved through her like the resonant voice of an inspired sermonizer. She was in both realities, breathing herself above the scene.

If only she was an angel, gifting the whole world with clarity, so they saw the truth of their interconnectedness: people, plants, air, every living creature. Even, she thought to herself, spiders, and smiled despite herself. Smiling dimmed the orthodox images in her mind, but she was uneasy. Was there a more dramatic entrance to this gay world than once and for all rejecting Eddie Dill's religion?

The conflict was exhausting. They would leave as soon as Jaudon came back. Jaudon? Was that Jaudon? She was dipping and skipping to a song, "People Got to Be Free." Jaudon never before moved with such abandon and it made Berry smile. Jaudon saw her, smiled back and, when the next song began, left Lari to escort Berry out on the dance floor.

A tall man with a shaved head made his way through the crowd taking drink orders. He quipped "Pay to stay, pay to stay," in an unnaturally high-pitched, horror-movie voice.

But Jaudon was stepping high, jumping in a circle, taking Berry's elbows and manipulating her back and forth. Berry pulled away and moved on her own. The music did tow her every which way. The beat through her feet guided her legs, her arms and, she noted with surprise, her hindquarters. The people in motion seemed galvanized into one connected dance.

Her face hurt from grinning so hard. Oh, the beauty of this moment, of every moment with Jaudon who was her revelation angel, complete with rainbow around her head, leading her away from darkness inside, leading her into both her body and the glory of her spirit as well, better than any prayer or holy deed. The menacing atmosphere dissipated. It had come from her fear of the bar patrons and theirs of her.

The Great Spirit was in this room with her, with Jaudon, with every one of these people. They no longer frightened her because, she rejoiced to think, her dance birthed light; she was a holy ray.

She laughed aloud, as silly as some unbalanced person who thought a deity spoke to her or through her. Wasn't it true though? What was prayer or meditation if not a conversation with...whatever each human believed? She looked at Jaudon, her strong, smiling mate, giving herself over to the music without these quandaries, and matched her raucous moves.

When they stopped, several songs later, they were pouring down sweat, out of breath, holding hands here, in public. They ran out of money for the exorbitant Cokes. The waiter glared them to the door. Lari and Rigo stayed behind, Rigo dancing with that Skaggs boy. It was hard to let go of Jaudon's hand outside; they should always be hand in hand. It would do the world good to see their happiness.

Instead, Jaudon hurried Berry the blocks to the van and they locked the doors behind them with the quickness of criminals.

CHAPTER NINE

Fall 1971

Jaudon moved between her accounting and her business classes, grateful for their calm predictability; her emotions got enough of a workout outside school. At the same time, she always watched over her shoulder, expecting to see someone from the bar—they'd gone back a few times— hoping for discretion.

When the business ethics teacher pointed at her to answer a question, he called her young man for about the third time. She worried that he did it on purpose, out of disapproval. He was, after all, nothing but an accountant who taught evenings to make ends meet at home. She averted her eyes as she left the room later; she didn't want to see his expression if he realized she was in the college-required skirt. These episodes left no question she was a freak. She tried to lighten her step, to move her arms like other girls, to unclench her fists at her sides. She wore skirts with pockets. She dared to wear culottes to classes and no one stopped her. She longed to wear shorts at school.

The TV news was flooded with signs of change. She had hopes the future would be less restrictive for her, for nonwhites, and for people who immigrated because they believed in the freedoms promised by the United States. At times she despaired. Berry once asked, "What's wrong with this world we live in that marks time by deaths? First the president, then Martin and Bobby."

In her next class, the principles of business instructor echoed Berry. "Look at what happened in the last decade. Americans killing our leaders: another Kennedy, Martin Luther King. Drug music by the Beatles winning respectable American awards. Homosexuality brazenly rhapsodized in sick bestsellers like *Myra Breckinridge*. Crazy women, lesbian predators, protesting the Miss America pageant."

No one outright insulted her in college—instead they stared—but this guy was teaching them to despise who she was. Why? How did her love for Berry harm him, or anyone? Thinking of Berry reminded her to breathe deeply.

The teacher ranted from his podium way down at the bottom of the slanted lecture hall with its sprinkling of students sprawled on thin wooden pull-down seats. The backs curved slightly in an uncomfortable academic embrace. Jaudon watched out the window above him, imagined leaping to it, breaking the glass, sliding her wrists along its jagged edges. She was going to jump out of her skin if he kept on this way. A great blue heron glided by, smooth as a dance with Berry. From the high open side windows she heard the brassy rattles of Monk Parakeets, free of their cages.

Enough was enough. She didn't need to listen to this hogwash. She would clear out of Cloud Christian where she was seen as a predator, a monster, a sinner with a capital *S*. Straightforward business classes would do the trick, the heck with liberal arts and science and the heck with religion classes and chapel attendance. The heck with a school which limited its students to people with white skins and prejudiced minds.

Momma would stop paying for school if she quit. Working the hours she'd need to, it would take her more than four years to get the degree and all the credentials she wanted. The more passionate the teacher got, the more attractive she found a business college. What did she need with liberal arts and what was so liberal about them? Cloud Christian refunded money if a student withdrew within so many days. She would concentrate on business and accounting so Momma would stop threatening to fire her—she'd need Jaudon more.

Berry was such a believer in a four-year piece of paper. Would she go for Jaudon taking longer? Because the more Jaudon heard, the less she wanted to come back and be insulted and indicted her entire junior and senior years.

"Where are you going, mister?" the teacher called out as she gathered her books, slammed the writing tray back into its armrest, and headed for the door. "I mean, miss."

She was filled with fury, resolution, and trepidation, but she kept walking. At the door she turned back. "Someplace where they'll teach me how to run a business, not how to run down people different from themselves."

Through the door she left open she heard some tittering and a quick tattoo of applause which ceased, she assumed, when the teacher turned back to the class.

After work as she sat at the kitchen table with a glass of sweet tea, Berry discovered the pleading in her eyes. Her hands fidgeted with a pencil, her leg jiggled, and she was sweating. Outside, the jar flies were the loudest sound in the world, warning of, reveling in, shouting down the heat. Gran had started dinner early that morning and the room smelled of andouille sausage browned with onions and garlic.

Berry saw the sheen of sweat on Jaudon's face. She got up to open windows and get some cross-ventilation going. She also pulled the chain on the ceiling fan till she got it to high speed.

Jaudon was so earnest as she outlined her plan to be a certified public and business tax accountant, Berry threw her arms around her.

Jaudon repeated the titles several times in the course of her prepared speech, which she gave from notes in her lap. Advanced accounting, auditing, cost accounting, federal tax accounting, business math and law—

Berry tried to interrupt the bumper crop of words.

Jaudon still read from her notes. "A school in Tampa has my courses. I already talked to the Beverage Bay accountant. He agreed to be my mentor and verify the experience requirement based on what I've been doing in the stores all along." She looked up. "I'm not wasting more time on weirdo Christian Cloud teachers."

Berry's hug stopped the words and toppled the notes. "The only reason you went there was because I did, my angel."

"It's okay with you? Honest to goodness okay?" She grabbed Berry, got them into a dancing position, and sang the words to "I've Got a Gal in Kalamazoo," one of the swing songs they'd loved when dancing to Bat's left-behind transistor radio up in the tree house.

They crooned together and broke out laughing.

No wonder Jaudon had been playing so much of her beloved Nina Simone on their stereo, Berry thought. She was upset about school and was struggling to come up with a plan. Jaudon had no problem with Nina Simone's politics either—Berry once saw her raise a fist in solidarity when Simone sang "Old Jim Crow."

"If your momma gets another bee in her bonnet and hounds you out of the company, you'll have a great skill to fall back on, angel. This is why I love you: your ambition, your enthusiasm, and the way you come up with solutions to problems. You've gotten a lot from your liberal arts classes. Junior year on up you'd concentrate on the technical courses anyway."

"Cloud Christian will refund three-quarters of my tuition, enough to pay a business college. Come on, I'll treat you and Zefer to a cone."

There was a dairy stand not far from them on Buffalo Avenue. It backed up to a small lake—or, as they joked, a large sinkhole. "Who can tell the difference?" they asked, as always, in unison. At a picnic table with a sunshade they watched each other drip ice cream between licks. Jaudon wanted so bad to hold Berry's hand again. Wonderful Berry who never let her down.

"You're prettier than a Florida sunset, and they're awful pretty."

Berry puckered her lips at Jaudon and kissed the air.

The late afternoon downpour came while they ate. They made for the overhang around the side of the building. The van was in sight and Zefer's head poked out the window, snout in the rain, tongue hanging, eyes on their ice cream. Muddy had passed away some weeks ago and they'd buried her in high ground, crying as they shoveled.

"Thank you," Berry called to the skies.

"Who are you talking to up there?" asked Jaudon. "The rain god?"

"Meaning Baal in the Bible? He started out as a rain and fertility god, I think. The Seminole myth has medicine men gathering by a spring and communing with a snake to bring rain."

"Berry, you amaze me. How do you remember this stuff?"

"It's important to me." She crunched her cone and saved the tip for Zefer. "I need to believe in something."

"But what?"

"It's the question that keeps me seeking, my angel."

"I believe in us, Berry."

The rain let up and they dodged puddles on their way to the van.

"So do I. Some energy brought us together, Jaudon. We didn't happen for no reason. It made each of us who we are."

The cracking vinyl seats of the van sparkled with drops of rain. Jaudon fished dry rags from the back and tossed them to Berry. They persuaded Zefer to move over for them with the ice cream.

"You don't think you'll end up in one of those religions that hates us, do you? I worry they'll convince you to reform." She knew she blurted the words out like a loony.

"Nothing will reform me away from loving you, Jaudon. No religion in the world would suit me if it didn't love us for who we are."

"I don't think there is such a religion."

"If so, I don't need any of them."

"I have to tell you, Berry, I don't understand religion at all. It loves rules to keep us in line and only men get to make the rules. "

"The sheer reassurance of faith keeps me believing there's a force of some sort to believe in." Berry laid the rags flat behind their seats to dry.

"I don't intend to be dumb, Berry, but didn't you say you needed to believe in something? And other times you said you didn't?"

"I'm beginning to understand faith and religion are two very different ideas."

Jaudon drove out of the lot. "You know I don't have a religious bone in my body. I'd rather be up and doing stuff, not sitting on my bottom and listening. This is beyond my smidgeon of a pea brain."

"Your way of worship is action, Jaudon. Mine is stillness."

"If I did believe in someone, it would be Mother Nature."

"I've thought of that myself."

"Call whatever's out there anything you want—Mother Nature suits me. Nothing earthly is capable of coming up with one of those."

Berry followed her pointed finger. Two sandhill cranes, in all their ungainly bulk, lifted from the lakefront into flight.

"Aren't they magic?"

"The Wright brothers would be embarrassed, my little swamp flower."

"But, you see? What religion would practice its faith by sitting at a dairy stand and enjoying the wildlife? It would be nice to have friends who believe what I do, but organizing would spoil the faith pouring out of my heart at this sight. I fit best with you."

She drove, silent while Berry did her deep thinking.

"Jaudon, I can't do anything but suppose. I don't want to worship anyone or anything. Be grateful, yes. Celebrate, yes. Be humble before these miracles—that I can do. Worship a creator? We humans are so limited we can't imagine a being other than ourselves, so that being looks human: an aged man in a white beard. What's out there is unfathomable, Jaudon. It doesn't need us to understand or worship it. People are the ones who need a divinity."

Jaudon couldn't help it; she chuckled. She looked at Berry. "In that case we're the creators, aren't we? Because we created the white-bearded being."

When Berry smiled it took over her whole face and raised her ears. "The thought never occurred to me."

"Why not invent a religion of your own?"

"Could be I am inventing one."

"Soon people will worship you." As they pulled into Pineapple Trail, Jaudon reached for her. "You know I already do."

"Oh, you." She pretended to flee from Jaudon's outstretched arms.

Jaudon and Zefer pursued Berry into the house. Berry checked that Gran was in her room. Then, and only then, did she let Jaudon catch her.

Afterward, Jaudon said, "The best way I know to appreciate you is to give you this."

"And to let me have my way with you."

Jaudon made *tsk*ing sounds. "I'm serious, Berry. You have a perfect body, as smooth and creamy-colored as the petals of our Southern magnolia. At the same time you can bang a nail into a two-by-four like nobody's business or whip up a meal and go for ice cream to celebrate the surprise change in my plans. Nobody knows how to love as wholly as you do."

"Are you sure, my angel? Why don't you come close again and show me how capably you love."

Chapter Ten

Whenever Lari walked into the Beverage Bay, the lights seemed to flicker and dim. After a hectic day registering for winter classes, her second term at the business school, Jaudon was worn to a nubbins and completely off balance.

"You don't live anywhere near my Beverage Bay. How come you spend so much time here, even on school nights?"

Lari shrugged. "I'm close enough," she said. "I have a car."

"But the store is so busy with the airport and the industrial park, don't you have more available friends?"

"You interest me."

Most nights, Lari would arrive at the Buffalo Road store in her black clothes and heavy white makeup, buy some cold Mountain Dew, and read aloud from Jaudon's textbooks when business was slow. A raw plant smell clung to Lari. Periodically, she moved outside to have a smoke and returned with the smell heavier on her. She was helping Jaudon study and, in truth, Jaudon did remember more of what she heard than what she read.

She knew she should be grateful; instead she was suspicious. "Why are you doing this for me? Don't you have your own homework?"

She wanted to talk to Berry about Lari, and mentioned the frequent visits, but was at a loss to find words that described her discomfort, which consisted of excitement, vexation, and a not unpleasant apprehension. She'd told Berry, "You should come around when Lari's there. It's creepy she visits when I'm alone."

But Berry never did. So Jaudon invoked her presence by talking about her.

"Berry's okay." Lari's tone made it clear she was holding back her real opinion.

Another night Jaudon said, "I wish you'd talk about yourself sometimes, Lari. We're not having much of a conversation."

Lari leaned on the counter in silence a while. "I came out with a girl on the high school swim team."

"You played a sport?"

"Hell, no. Sports? I met her in the locker room after the stupid phys ed class they made us take."

Jaudon scoffed. "PE's my favorite class. I'm taking fencing this term." She jumped and lunged toward Lari, her arm the sword. "When I pull the mask down over my face, I can be anybody."

"You can have their games. I could care less."

Lights shone into the hangar and a car pulled up. Jaudon ran for a six-pack of beer and a bag of pork rinds. Two more customers arrived, one looking for milk and a box of animal crackers; the next wanted hard liquor, which they weren't licensed to sell. Was he a cop testing her? The secret hooch stock was Pops's responsibility and his alone; sales were by referral only.

"Why are you watching every move I make?" she asked Lari, although she found the attention flattering. She was at the top of the store's tallest ladder, changing out a lightbulb.

Lari called up, "It's a free country."

"I haven't heard that phrase since third grade." Lari was downright childish at times.

"Doesn't mean it's not true."

"Quit your pouting. You'd think I was trying to cut you down. You going to answer my question?"

"You're unique. I like unique."

Keeping time to a song on the jazz station, Jaudon wheeled a handcart filled with stock out on the floor. She was proud of her strong thighs and muscular arms. As she brought the cart to the back office, she remembered dancing with Lari at the bar. What could she learn, making love with a different woman? Her heart sped up and her breathing changed. She shut the idea out of her mind. She blamed Jack Teagarden's trombone, bluesy and buoyant at the same time. The big bands always stirred the cornball romantic inside her.

Lari grabbed Jaudon's hand and yanked her to the storage area next to the office. Backed up against the dry goods, Lari drew Jaudon to her until they were too close not to kiss.

"Stop it." She shoved back from Lari before their lips touched.

Lari hung on, eyes fixed on Jaudon's mouth, lips parted and appealing, hips moving suggestively to the music.

Jaudon's sense of right and wrong rolled over and died. She wanted her hand in Lari's britches as soon as Lari undid her own big belt buckle. Jaudon reached down and eased her fingers to the pliant, plumped up part of Lari, beside herself with lust for this stranger who wanted her and who quickly reacted to her touch by digging her fingernails into Jaudon's shoulders.

Jaudon didn't know herself. Shame joined desire. What about the store? What about Berry? Jiminy, heck, darn, where did this come from?

"More," whispered Lari. Jaudon was trying to comply when Lari pushed her away with such force Jaudon crashed against a stack of boxed cereal and saw the tower land on Momma's shoulders and head, knocking off her glasses.

From the concrete where Jaudon stopped her fall with the heel of her hand, she watched the second row of cereal topple. Momma scuttled to the office. Lari's britches were buttoned and she was working on her belt. Jaudon levered herself up along the doorjamb with her other hand. Momma thumped her purse on the desk and tied on an apron with the store's picture printed on it.

"You are not my daughter," Momma intoned. "You are not my employee. From this moment, you are not welcome on my property. Any of it."

"But, Momma—"

Momma turned to wait on a VW idling in the lane. As she dug under the counter for a pack of cigarettes, she spat, "Out, Daughter. Out this minute. I'm ashamed I gave you my family name."

Lari slunk past Momma and disappeared into the dark night in her fancy sports car. Lari didn't offer to drive her anywhere. Better this way, Jaudon thought. Who knew where they'd end up? Berry was at the library studying for another two hours—no way to get hold of her. Momma wouldn't hesitate to bring someone in to finish the shift. If Momma saw her waiting around, would she call the cops?

From the hangar's doorway she hollered, "Let me talk to you."

Momma turned her back to Jaudon.

"I know I did wrong in there," she called.

"That's your howdy-do."

Momma picked up the phone. Whoever she was dialing, it wouldn't be great news for Jaudon. Her own mother ought to at least listen to her side.

"Momma," she keened one last time before she wormed out of sight behind the store. When Berry came for her she'd flag her down before Momma saw the van.

There was no option but to tell Berry, and tell her tonight. It was a mistake she'd never repeat. She wasn't sure what happened to her in there, but those Ten Commandments Berry talked about didn't give such terrible advice after all.

She wiped sweat from her face and realized her fingers smelled like Lari. Where would she get soap and water? There was a gas station out on the highway. She hiked until she spotted a van racing toward her. Berry? What the heck?

She stepped into the street and waved.

Berry braked. "What happened?"

She picked up a handful of dirt and scrubbed with it as she walked to the passenger side. She opened the door, but didn't go in and averted her eyes from Berry.

"Are you all right?" asked Berry. "Your momma called the college and they paged me. She told me to get out here quick to cover your shift."

"I made a mistake," she told Berry. "A big one, but I'm not injured or anything. You better go on to the Bay and do what Momma says. Once she's gone, I'll come in and talk to you."

She was taking a chance Momma would be too ill at ease to describe to Berry what she saw, but Momma did have that vicious streak. She hoped Momma's agitation would be stronger than her wicked side and she'd keep her mouth shut up.

Momma didn't blab. Jaudon told Berry the whole story baldly, rapid-fire, softening nothing and laying the blame on herself. As she spoke, they worked to fill the shelves, count the till, cut the lights, and close the store for the night. She jumped at the sound of any car, ready to flee if Momma came back. When she finished speaking, tears rose up in her eyes and, one by one, fell like the errant spatter of a perpetual fountain.

Berry was confused. Or jealous. No, hurt. Jaudon had broken an unspoken covenant they had. She didn't know what to say, what to do. Her mind repeated and repeated, *But Ma and Pa left me too.*

They sat in the van after closing the store and she wanted to be home, lying in Jaudon's arms, but Jaudon had scarred her heart, why seek comfort from her? Because it was always Jaudon who comforted her. Always Jaudon for anything she needed.

She should be angry. She should threaten...what, a breakup? She didn't want to break up, she wanted everything to be the way it was before tonight. It was crystal-clear that if her loved ones abandoned her, it was her own fault.

"Oh, Jaudon. What did I do? We were so perfect." She tried not to cry, as she always tried not to cry.

"You?" said Jaudon. "You didn't do a thing. This is every bit on me. Don't be brave, Berry. Go ahead and cry too. I did a terrible thing and I know it." She was horribly regretful. "I don't know why I did it. Lari is nothing to me. She's pesty, to tell you the truth, and she smells funny."

She knew Jaudon's transgression didn't deserve an extravagant response, but she did cry, over at the far side of the passenger seat. Whatever emotional dressing she wore over the gash left by her parents was ripped away and she was bleeding tears.

Berry started the van when Jaudon said, "I need you to move us. I don't want Momma calling the cops if she sees me here. She doesn't want me on any property she owns. Where can I go? "

"Go back to yesterday. Undo it all."

"I wish. I hate myself." She could hardly breathe from crying so hard. "I might as well be a wild animal. I never wanted to be hot and bothered about someone other than you. It's bad enough I look like I do, but to act like what Lari called me—a gorilla? I belong in a zoo."

Without thinking about it, Berry drove to the Cloud Christian parking lot, both of them wordless through the warm, dark streets.

Jaudon's guilty hand, scoured in dirt, hung swollen and heavy outside the window. She wished some speeding semi would tear it off her arm.

Berry was too torn up to think. Jaudon needed her. They had to figure it out together. Or perhaps she shouldn't take it on at all, given what Jaudon did. There was no guarantee she wouldn't do it again; Jaudon might truly be sick in the head or damaged. How would they know?

It was the time of night frogs kick up a fuss. Normally she loved their songs. Not tonight. Thousands of them joined together with their guttural or shrill or sharp or lazy croaking. The galling sound assaulted Berry's ears.

"Say something, Berry." She loved this girl with her quiet, thoughtful ways, such a contrast to her own loud, gravelly voice and rough manner.

"Make them stop! Shut them up," Berry pleaded. Her hands were over her ears, but she was trapped inside an echo chamber with the singing frogs and this abrupt, searing heart and soul pain.

"Shut who up?" Jaudon looked out the windows. "No one's out there, Berry. You're scaring me. Calm down, would you?"

Berry turned on her. "Calm down? You want everything to be sweetness and light after your mother had to stop you from acting worse? How could you do such a thing? How can I ever trust you again?"

The frogs went silent, waited a moment to break into a cacophony that seemed twice as loud. Berry's head felt hot enough to light a fire. She was thinking of Eddie Dill's gun, hidden in her room, and how she wanted to use it on Lari.

Jaudon never saw Berry so soppin' mad before. It made her think about walking away, walking away from everything. "What good is love when it can scorch and burn like napalm?" she asked.

Berry's anger settled in her belly, sickening her. She needed Pepto Bismol formulated for fury.

Jaudon realized they were bombing each other with words. She stopped speaking, taking a break from their storm. Ahead, the moon was caught atop some branches, a balloon about to puncture. The parking lot was empty of people, and Jaudon knew they better get out of there before security came by.

Berry pleaded with the Great Spirit for a sign, a direction, a hint. She was lost in a wilderness of new emotions. "What are you going to do?" she asked Jaudon.

Berry's word—*you* not *we*—reverberated within Jaudon's head like a death sentence.

"Do?"

"I won't let Gran get evicted," said Berry.

"Why would Momma evict her?"

"Same reason she'll make you and me leave."

"She's not kicking you out. You didn't do anything."

Berry sounded cynical and world-weary to Jaudon. "The woman made it perfectly clear she doesn't care for what we are to each other."

"Momma doesn't know about us."

"You mean before tonight."

"Why would she call you in to work if she fired me?"

"You know she can be meaner than a snake."

"It doesn't make sense, Berry."

"One way she's punishing you, pure and simple, is by favoring me over you and tattling on you. Why else have me paged at school?"

"Punishing should be your job."

Jaudon held her gaze and Berry saw the sadness there, the regret and self-blame. She bowed her head and imagined her anger burning out, an incendiary consuming its own fuel.

"Oh, Jaudon. I guess you're no more than human. Lari is too, for wanting you. Isn't hurting me the worst possible punishment?"

"You know it is, Berry. There is nothing on the face of this earth so scalding as thinking of the suffering I brought on you. If we could be married in the eyes of the law, I'd promise to be faithful till the end of time."

"I'm not sure I care to be married to you after this, Jaudon."

"I swear it, Berry. I will always be faithful to you. I can't believe what I risked. I promise. I—wait. What did you say?"

Berry wouldn't be over this anytime soon. "Are we too young to be making such promises, Jaudon? Do you need some wild oats time? I hope not, since I don't guarantee my survival."

"Berry, you're my wild oats, my settling down, my everything."

Berry looked sideways at her. She wasn't smiling. "Let me go see what I can do about your momma taking away our home. As if I'd take her side against you. Maybe your pops will volunteer to talk to her for us."

As she drove toward Momma and Pops's house, Jaudon imagined Berry's thoughts in a dark swirl above her head.

Which was how they seemed to Berry: dense, sticky confusions where she needed calm. Anger, disgust, disappointment. Her best tool was prayer so she prayed for the grace she'd need to forgive Jaudon, her Jaudon, and the strength to keep loving her. She understood Jaudon was different, almost like boys were different from girls in behaving themselves. In truth, it had nothing to do with Berry, it came from some loveless urge Jaudon needed to control. If she was able. That's where the fear came in. Berry wasn't going to live this way even for Jaudon.

It was late to be visiting, but the big brick house was lit up, like Momma couldn't spend her money fast enough.

Winter blooming sweet peas were planted along the edge of the lawn—what did the Vickers need with a lawn. Sweet peas were flowering so profusely Berry feared she would never smell that fragrance again without evoking this terrible night.

Berry rang the bell and, despite the late hour, Pops Vicker's voice boomed out, "Come on in."

She peered into the overdecorated, overstuffed living room. Momma must have been impressed by Gran's plants, because she had huge planters: an indoor tree, a snake plant, and another with oversized sharp leaves she'd only seen at the dentist's office. She went into the den, where Jaudon's father was in his favorite worn recliner, a sweating beer can beside him and the TV weather reporting highs, lows, drought, and the high dry winds that fed fires. Berry bent to give him a kiss on the top of his head and smiled— she bet Mrs. Vicker wanted to replace Pops's ratty chair something awful, but it appeared that Pops stood his ground and banned plants from this room as well.

"We were expecting you," he told her. "I hear Daughter got herself into a speck of trouble with some girl. Her momma is burned up. She always swore Jaudon was off in the head or body and I've been telling her for twenty years she's ours, we made her, and whatever her nature, it's our job to love her harder than ever. I bet you agree. So don't worry your lovely head about Momma's fool ideas, I'll take care of her. If my daughter's outside, tell her to get her tail in here. I want to give her a big hug."

Berry hadn't said a word, but she gave Pops a hug herself before sending Jaudon in.

Jaudon trembled as Pops banged his recliner down and reached for her. She flinched.

Pops mashed her to him. "Daughter, your momma's going to come around. Leave it to me. She can run a business like a thoroughbred runs a race, but when it comes to understanding human nature she's a dumb Dora. Go on home, home is where you need to be, but if I ever hear you stepping out on Berry again, I'll come after you with my spanking belt."

She cried in his arms. "What's wrong with me, Pops?"

"Not a thing, baby girl, not a thing that isn't wrong with every human on earth. Every one of us is a bit better and a bit worse. Take care of your own, you hear? Life's going to throw enough curveballs at you without you bringing trouble down on yourself."

He wasn't answering her question, but she knew why: Pops had no idea how she got to be the way she was. She needed to know if her response to Lari was related to her boy body, her bold facial features, her heavy blond eyebrows, her preference for, say, gadgets over ruffles, and her refusal to wear one of those tight bra things.

She turned to leave. Momma stood in the doorway, arms folded.

"Daughter? Have you apologized to Berry Garland?"

"I have." As comforting as Pops was, that's how petrifying she found Momma.

"I hope I put the fear of God in you. I don't know what you see in that rank woman in black. If I ever hear of you hurting Berry again, or if I find out you're carrying on in my store, driving away customers, Daughter, I will take away everything I ever gave you. As it is, I'm docking you a week's pay. I expect losing income will make an impression."

She wasn't able to look away from Momma.

"I hear what the customers say about you, Jaudon Vicker, how they avoid the store where the strange girl works. I'm not telling you Berry's too good for my own daughter, and I do not approve of these goings-on, but you're darned lucky to have her affections, such as they may be between young girls. If there isn't going to be a man in your future, I can't hope for a more decent match for you, so I want to see you work to keep the girl, not throw her away."

She found herself in the van as if she was blown there by a funneling windstorm. She was by turns enraged and relieved. Berry drove.

"I'm so, so sorry, Berry."

"At least one positive result came of it: we're out in the open."

"Yeah, I'll write Lari a thank-you note."

Berry pushed at her thigh. "You're such a card." Berry was smiling, a wavery, brave smile.

"You're saying you'll try to forgive me?" Jaudon asked.

"It's painful being upended like this. I'll work toward forgiveness, but you'd better sleep in your bed for a while. And swear to me you'll never again do anything to crush me like you did tonight."

"I do swear. I swear with all my heart and soul. I'll sleep in the tree house if you want. I'll do anything to stop your pain."

She couldn't look at Jaudon. "Just give me some time."

CHAPTER ELEVEN

It seemed every day brought some new crisis into Jaudon's life.

Not long after her mistake with Lari, Jaudon drove through Tampa and passed a small pack of peace marchers going up and down the sidewalk outside the US Courthouse Building. Through her open windows, she heard them chant, "Hell, no, we won't go!" They wore bandanas around their necks and waved poster board signs on cardboard tubes. People called insults from passing cars.

She was madder than a wet hen. It was their duty to stand up for American soldiers.

It was winter and cool enough for jackets. She remained churned up about the marchers, and Lari, and Momma. There was ongoing unquiet between herself and Berry.

On their way home from work one night, she said, "It made sense for Bat to join the army. He's proving his independence. Momma lords it over me. What does she think, that if not for her, I'd be homeless, jobless, and loveless?"

"The army? You want to help kill more of those poor people over there?" Berry was driving, but reached to slap Jaudon's thigh. It was the first time Berry had touched her since that night with Lari. "Wouldn't you be afraid of getting injured?"

"Me, afraid? You know me better than that."

"I can't stand the thought of you going away, Jaudon. Tell me you won't enlist."

There was icy terror in Berry's voice, but Berry had been pretty icy for a while.

"I'll solve a lot of people's problems. They need soldiers in Vietnam. Those peace demonstrators aren't helping anyone. Bat hasn't got a scratch on him. I'll learn a skill besides running a store. Momma and Pops won't be embarrassed about bringing up a freak. You'd get on with your life and not have to protect me anymore. I bring you all kinds of calamity."

Berry drove the van under a canopy of low-hanging Spanish moss outside the closed Rainbow Gap general store. Eyes shut, fingers locked around the thin plastic steering wheel, weak from fear and anger, she breathed herself calm.

Had she been too hard on Jaudon? Did Jaudon want to leave what they had? She wouldn't hold her back if she needed to see the world. Or try other loves, though it would about kill her. She imagined Larissa Hand instead of Jaudon at war, going through the ordeals Bat told them about. Too bad women weren't allowed in combat. She stopped herself and, without words, apologized to the Great Spirit for wishing capture and torture on Lari.

Jaudon was so tense she trembled. She knew Berry had a knack for soothing anyone, fixing any mess Jaudon made. She wasn't giving up on Berry, but they still slept separately and she didn't dare approach her about making love. "I would. I will, if it would make you happier to be without me."

A car with no muffler idled at the one stop sign and revved onto Front Street.

Berry stamped a foot on the van floor. "Go on—there's a recruiting poster with the phone number on the store's window."

Jaudon stared at Berry. She wanted to swallow her words. Her response was weak. "But you don't believe in fighting."

"Sounds to me like you do, Jaudon. I'm not here to control you or pass judgment on what you set store by."

"I guess you don't need me around."

When Berry didn't answer, Jaudon put a hand on the van door. Her insides twisted up as she walked to the poster. What was she blowharding about? She didn't want to leave home. Like Berry said, why pester people in another country? She did believe in America, though, and that meant going along with what the government decided.

She went to pull the poster from the wall, jerked her hand away, and got in the van without it.

"I forgot," said Jaudon. "How can I show this body at the physical exam? They'd reject me for being a werewolf."

"They see all sorts of bodies, but they'd make you wear a bra."

"I don't want a soul to see this body but you. If you ever want to again."

Berry took Jaudon's hand in hers. "I hope you know I'll never stop you, but I don't want you to go."

She looked at their hands and caught her breath. She repeated one of their childhood catchphrases. "Cross your heart?"

Berry gave Jaudon's ear a quick kiss. "And hope to die. Together. Peacefully. In Rainbow Gap, Florida, USA."

"For real?" She leaned forward and tugged Berry closer.

Berry allowed her. They held like that until Jaudon let go.

"I don't ever want to leave your side, Berry. But I still want to help our soldiers."

"Let's send them a care package. One a month until this is over."

"It's not much, but at least it shows them we care, Berry."

"What do you want to put in it?"

"Oh, candy bars, comic books, crossword puzzles."

"Real books too, Jaudon. We'll send them paperback books."

"Socks and foot powder. Beef jerky—"

Berry drove them toward home, thinking. Jaudon was an action type. If she had a conflict, she'd fret and fume. Give her a task to do and she was happy as the day is long.

As they jounced along Pineapple Trail, Jaudon said, "I bet we have leftover fried chicken. I can almost smell it from here."

She was confounded by Jaudon's fickleness with Lari and her hasty impulse to run away to war. Was she asking too much to want Jaudon all for herself? For the moment she would work on forgiveness and send the last of her misery to the Great Spirit, but couldn't resist bedeviling Jaudon. "The way you're always hungry, she wouldn't cook fast enough to keep you satisfied."

"Who?"

"Larissa the kisser."

"I didn't kiss her. I never kissed anyone but you. If I think there's ever a chance of it happening again, I'll run like heck. I'll call the cops on her if she comes near the store again."

"No, you won't. I'll call your momma. Bless her heart, she'll be a lot better at chasing away all the girls who'll want you. If you went into the service, goodness knows how you'd fend them off."

Berry acted cheerful enough, but it was obvious she would never forget that night.

Jaudon woke up well before dawn the next day to find her arm wet where Berry lay beside her.

"Berr?" she whispered. Berry was crying in her sleep again.

This happened once in a while, the crying; at times Berry called out for her ma and pa. She mumbled in her sleep too, and said, *I'm sorry, I'm sorry*. Jaudon didn't understand why Berry's folks left. She wished she was enough to replace them. She kept to herself a suspicion they crashed their motorcycle and died or got amnesia. You saw such stories on TV—why not in real life?

Was she crying this time because of what Jaudon did? It must have brought back the hurt her ma and pa had done. She was a trial to this woman she loved more than anything, yet who declined to be left in peace. Once again she considered military service. If she was brave enough to risk going to Vietnam, she ought to have the courage to stay faithful to Berry.

"It's okay," she whispered, taking Berry's warm hand under the covers. "I'll always be here."

Love was the best thing and the worst thing in the world. She wanted to tear Lari limb from limb, eradicate from the face of the earth anyone who got between them. Herself included, if need be. She told the sleeping Berry, "Nothing and no one will come between us again. I promise."

The next day, Rigo stopped by the house early. "I asked Lari to come with me," he said. "She dropped an armload of books and practically fell backward down the stairs trying to catch them."

"Give her a push next time, won't you?" Berry said, tossing her braid in lingering resentment. She wasn't about to try forgiving Lari too.

"Am I hearing our Berry Garland talking? How unlike you. What did you girls do to Lari?"

"She got herself in trouble with my momma, for one thing," Jaudon said.

"Heaven forbid. Who in this county hasn't?"

Berry told the whole story, with an apology for her bitterness. Jaudon looked nowhere but the floor.

"Darn pothead Yankee. I brought her to meet you girls because she seemed so lonely."

"Pothead?" Berry and Jaudon said in unison.

"Can't you tell? She's stoned most of the time."

Jaudon's fists went to her hips. "Is that what I smelled on her?"

Rigo's eyebrows went up. "Didn't you ever smell marijuana before?"

"Jaudon and I don't know any dope fiends."

"Look at you, the two Miss Innocents. It's a good thing you have me to protect you."

Jaudon punched him in the arm, clowning. "You ought to introduce Lari to some straight girls. You'd be doing girls like us a big favor."

Berry indulged in another vile image of Lari Hand: she pictured her in jail for dope. Serve her right.

"I'm confident you're here for breakfast, Rigo. Berry's planning to cook up a mess of sausage gravy and biscuits."

Rigo never turned down a home-cooked meal. He set his book bag under the kitchen table. "What's the matter with you, Jaudon, letting yourself get lured into Lari's trap?"

"Hormones," said Berry. She was relieved to be her reasonable self again. "I'm learning about them in one of my courses. At our age, they take over our brains when they're stimulated."

Rigo fanned himself. "I didn't know girls had urges."

"Jiminy. I almost lost Berry because of some science thing? I was walking a tightrope of fishing line. Thank you, Lord. It was more than hormones, though. I was flattered. I didn't think anyone would be interested in me besides my Berry."

Berry squinted at the top of Jaudon's head, spit into her hand, and patted her cowlick down. "I'll have to remember to flatter you more in the future."

"Look at Jaudon and me, the opposite of hunks, or whatever you call girl hunks. I'm a complete hairy chunk. An endomorph, speaking of biology class."

"He hit the nail on the head, Berry." She was stammering in front of Rigo. "I'll never understand why you want me. I walk like an ape and I acted like one."

Rigo tried to talk, but laughed through his nose instead. Zefer got excited and made to jump in his lap. "Come up here, you monkey-haired doggie."

Berry set down a bowl of biscuits and pointed to them. Rigo put two on his plate. She realized Jaudon's eyes were glazed with tears and ladled extra gravy over her biscuits. She held the full ladle over Rigo's plate. "No gravy until you tell us what you're laughing about."

Rigo used a paper napkin to wipe his face. "It shouldn't be funny at all. People may think I'm a red-haired ape-man with a perm. It cracked me up to hear Jaudon say the same. I'm sorry, I wasn't laughing at you, Jaudo. We need to remember we're vibrant, sexy people, which should be a turn-on for anyone."

Berry touched his curls. "These aren't permed."

"Haven't you ever seen an ape with curls before?"

"We're not seeing one now. Neither of you."

Rigo pretended to eat with his fingers and made grunting sounds. Jaudon swiped Rigo's cheek with a finger full of warm gravy. Rigo put gravy on his spoon and catapulted it at Jaudon. Berry swatted them both with her napkin.

Gran came out of her room to see what the commotion was about. "When your plates are empty, I'm going to shoo you three away to get to school. I'll clean up here."

Rigo squinted at the kitchen clock. "I'm off to the teach-in." He pulled a comb from his book bag. "Jimmy Neal invited me."

"Jimmy Neal Skaggs from the gay bar?" Berry asked.

"He's been asking me to go out with him. I told him he's not my type, too gentle and shy, but beggars can't be choosers."

Jaudon sing-songed, "Rigo's got a boyfriend."

"Teach-ins don't count as dates. It's more like sharing a ride to class."

"He can at least carry your books."

Berry said, "I saw signs for the teach-in on campus. I'll see if I can join you for part of it after my pharmacology class."

Jaudon said, "Watch out, Berry, three's a crowd. What the heck is a teach-in anyway?"

Rigo explained to Jaudon. "A number of local professors are against the war. They canceled their classes and invited students to learn about Vietnam in the lecture auditorium in Desoto Hall."

"And you're both going?"

Rigo was at the door. "Why not?"

"The darned Communists will try to brainwash you."

"Well, hello, Ms. Joe McCarthy," said Rigo. "This is about information, not persuasion. No need to get paranoid. You'll be leaping at your shadow next, thinking it's subversives."

Jaudon speared her last biscuit so hard it slid from her plate. She retrieved it from the pine floor and picked at the dog and cat fur until it was clean. "It's no skin off my nose if you want to go. Mind you, be careful of those types against our government."

Rigo looked at Berry who smiled and nodded. "We're learning so we can decide what to believe, Jaudon."

Jaudon scowled. "I have all the information I need from our Constitution and Bill of Rights."

"Do you actually believe Berry and I are incapable of making up our minds, Ms. Paul Revere?"

"Aw, heck, Rigo. 'Course not. What do you take me for? If you believe the president and Congress have our best interests in mind, you don't need to learn anything else."

"I don't know about the president, but I bet what Congress has in mind is its own pockets. War brings in big profits. I wouldn't be surprised to hear the politicians have shares in every munitions manufacturer in the country."

Jaudon feared there might be some truth in what he was saying. Hadn't Pops mentioned he was losing his trust in government? She didn't want to think about it anymore. "Go on, you two. Even a blind hog finds an acorn now and then. If you find out anything worth knowing, you better tell me."

Berry kissed Jaudon good-bye. "I'll take notes on the brainwashing."

They left in high spirits, Berry in the van, Rigo dropping Jaudon at work.

"Don't you lead Berry too far along that path," Jaudon said by way of good-bye.

Rigo honked his trick car horn as he turned onto Eulalia Road. It sounded to Jaudon like a sick cow.

CHAPTER TWELVE

It was taking a long time to get back Berry's trust. She was pretty sure time was the only cure there was.

Jaudon's new classes were filled with men—and with a few women who said they planned to keep the books for their husbands' small businesses. For the first time her teacher was Afro-American.

Her life was a blur of lectures, studying, and preparing for her license. She wasn't aware of world events or that Berry wasn't home much either. She ate at the Bay, studying between customers and stocking the shelves. Olive Ponder always came in to work for her when she needed more study time and sometimes gave her a wink and shooed her home to spend a few hours with Berry. She met weekly with her mentor, who taught her about real world retail beyond what she learned at school. Often, Berry was in bed asleep under a light sheet, ceiling fan going, when Jaudon lay down for the night. Berry caught rides to school with another student rather than add to Jaudon's feverish schedule.

Two or three weekends a month they managed time alone at home. It was short, but rich.

"Jaudon, how do you keep up this pace and still manage to send me over the rainbow?" Berry squeezed her legs around Jaudon's strong thigh, the pleasure contractions going on and on. It was a muggy Sunday and she wanted to stay in bed all day under the breeze of the fan, with the scent of climbing roses outside her bedroom window. Gran was at her new church. Toby hung out at the bottom of their bed until they drew apart, then climbed on Jaudon's stomach, twenty pounds of him, and claimed their attention with loud purring.

Jaudon stretched her arms over her head. "As long as we have close time together, I'm dandy."

Berry snuggled against her. "Time's going to get shorter as I get closer to graduation. When I start my practicum, who knows what hours they'll assign me."

"Someday I'll finish up the licensing exams, and be able to arrange my schedule around yours." Jaudon curled her body around Berry. Toby arranged himself across both of them. "Are we nuts to work this hard?"

"Of course," said Berry, "but it'll make life easier in years to come. Gran said it's why we're given heaps of energy when we're young."

Toby decided to clean himself at that exact moment, lost his balance, and fell between them. "Pretend you didn't see that," Jaudon whispered when Toby swiveled his head as if to see whether they picked up on his indignity. They stifled their laughter and soothed him with petting.

Jaudon said, "He looks like a college break kid on a drinking spree."

"Are you seeing many fake IDs this spring?"

"The usual dribs and drabs. I want to know how they afford the trip. We live here and don't have time or money to take a week off."

"Why? Are you dying to spend a week drinking and getting sunburned?"

Jaudon rolled away on the wrinkled sheet and made a face. "Can you see it? You and me and thousands of girls chasing boys and boys chasing girls?"

"It's a mating ritual. Spring festivals go back to the Greeks and Romans, orgies and fertility."

"Now, they should teach *that* in Sunday school."

"Oh, angel, they hide the details of pre-Christian religions. Eddie Dill's church didn't observe Easter because it came from Paganism."

"Well, well, ban the bunnies and the baskets," Jaudon teased. "Bunch of jerks."

Berry gave her a soft slap.

"Tell me more," Jaudon said. She wanted to show Berry she cared any way she could, even if their interests were different.

"You mean the way the priests invented the Virgin Mary to give people a substitute for their goddesses?"

"Where are you picking up these tidbits? Are they true?"

Berry scooted out of bed and came back with books. She stopped and admired Jaudon, propped on an elbow, her hair more unruly than ever, her shoulders wide as a competitive swimmer's, her breasts tiny, stomach flat. She loved being held by those strong arms and getting Jaudon's muscled legs to slacken and fall open, the hairs on them like gold threads. Berry saw herself as the other end of the feminine spectrum, each part in curvy proportion to the next, her hair, not yet braided for the day, a bit wild from the sex and the weather.

She sat on the bed with her books and pushed to lean her back on the wall. "I take my breaks with a few of the other nursing students. We've been talking about religion and feminism."

"Bra burners?"

"Bra burning stories are made up, Jaudon. To make feminists look bad."

Jaudon made a snarky face. "Who needs to make up stories to make feminists look bad?"

She swatted at Jaudon with a book. "You're impossible. But I love you anyway. See this book? It talks about the harm men do to women. How they beat up their wives and girlfriends, how husbands and boyfriends rape and wound women. I pictured nasty Eddie Dill when I read it." Berry shivered remembering his white-stubbled face, his stringy arms reaching out of the sinkhole for life, Gran's life and her own.

"Pops doesn't harm anyone. Bat neither."

"The writer is talking about the rotten apples, the greedy pigs who can't help themselves because their biology drives them to reproduce."

"How does reproduction explain Rigo?"

"Nobody told his biology he's not trying to make babies."

"But—" Jaudon tried to puzzle it out. Her momma hurt her, not Pops. The girls at school ridiculed her as much as the boys. Didn't Rigo go after guys like other men went after women?

"You can't say every one of them is bad, Berry."

She handed a book to Jaudon. "This is about women's spirituality, goddess worship. I'm starting to understand religion came about for humans to explain life to ourselves."

Jaudon shied away. "What's wrong with just living life?"

"Not a thing, angel. It's a shame religion became about power, about dominating everything and everyone, especially women. Control our bodies and you control the present and the future. Reproduction is the biological reason for being male."

Jaudon scrunched up her face to show this was over her head.

"Judy, one of the nursing students, loaned me this." She handed an oversized amateurish-looking book to Jaudon. The title was *Our Bodies, Ourselves.* Jaudon leafed through it with suspicion.

Berry put an arm across Jaudon's shoulders. "A group of women in Boston wrote it. According to them, men control medical research, treatments, availability of care. This tells us how to take care of ourselves. The medical profession limits itself to teaching what men think. We lost a lot when men took medicine out of women's hands. Women were the early healers."

Jaudon was shocked by the drawings in the book, recognizing what resembled Berry's private parts or her own.

"My nursing coursework doesn't cover anywhere near this much about women. We're working with the department head to add the book to our curriculum."

Jaudon made the mistrustful face again. "You're getting involved in this feminist stuff for real?"

"It makes sense to me, Jaudon. Did you ever think about why being like us gets everyone so angry?"

"'Cause we're different."

"Yes and no. Men want women for themselves. They always kept their power and land by having sons to carry on the family name and keep the property. Women were possessions, the same as cows or horses. Fathers once paid other men dowries to take daughters off their hands. The daughters were used for breeding. It's still going on in some parts of the world."

"The Vickers are upside down, aren't we? Momma runs things and I'm the one studying to take over the business."

"And you're the one with big plans to expand."

Jaudon was glad about the change of subject. "Can't you see it?" She sat up and used her arms to embrace a gigantic make-believe empire. "Look at the hordes of people moving to Florida. I think we can go beyond the idea of drive-thrus. Put in a pump or two and while the cars are being gassed up, customers talk into some sort of two-way radio to order a quart of milk, a six-pack of beer, Holsom white bread and a bottle of RC Cola. It's better than the convenience store trend."

"Does your momma know what you're thinking?"

"I haven't brought it up. She'll tell me it's silly or would never work. But I know we have to start moving in the direction of convenience stores or lose business."

Berry imagined a glowing trail of light emanating from the heat of Jaudon's animation. She said, "I want to stay here with you until tomorrow morning, but I need to get into the garden before the heat of the day." She drew on the one-piece blue playsuit she wore for working outdoors. "I'm determined to grow a vegetable garden this spring and use all that compost we saved through the winter to fertilize it."

Jaudon said, "I better hit the books. I'll vacuum the house first." Gran did a lot of their housekeeping, but vacuuming gave her a headache so Jaudon did it.

Cleaning allowed their earlier conversation to whistle around her brain. Jaudon suspected those feminists wanted to convert Berry to their man-hating ways of thinking; she'd see to it they never got the chance.

Berry tackled the purple and green crabgrass and spiny bull thistle, worrying about Jaudon's plans. If the Vickers expanded to convenience stores, pushing their way into the competitive world of men's big business, would every bit of honesty, principle, and fun be smothered out of Jaudon? She resolved not to allow that to happen.

CHAPTER THIRTEEN

Berry never talked about the sinkhole experience with anyone but Jaudon. It preyed on her mind. Were sinkholes everywhere? Would the earth swallow them up someday? She continued to believe the evil in Eddie Dill brought him disaster, but wasn't she evil at times, with her secret rages and hateful thoughts? She combated them, but was concerned they didn't make her any better than Eddie.

The group of nurses she spent time with didn't believe in evil; they weren't religious. Instead, they called themselves spiritual and used the term goddess, which didn't fit her vision of a universal spirit. Why would it have to be female or male? A mini Vietnam continued to wage in her soul, between what she was taught growing up and what she learned and saw as an adult.

Starting with love. The churches got themselves in a tizzy about her and Jaudon, but, she thought, reviling us? What good did it do to throw mud at anyone? Religions seemed to need someone to pick on, to look down on, like Jaudon's school bullies did. The church's punches and insults were directed at souls and minds and hearts rather than bodies. She knew how deep Jaudon's scars went and respected her ability to live with the amount of pain she must have. It made her sick to think of it.

Berry's idea of evil, aside from her own, was much closer to what her friends called social problems. It was plain to her that greed was very evil: the rich had more than enough money and others went hungry. The other deadly sins were obvious too; she tried to be aware of them in her life. The Ten Commandments—she was thinking on those, starting with the first one. God was made more in man's image, not the other way around, and she kept coming back to one question: Who said, if a deity had a gender,

God was male? *Our understanding is so limited*, she thought. *We can't imagine anything outside our own experience.*

The summer after high school she had been determined to get through a book her senior English teacher challenged the class to read, *Walden* by Henry David Thoreau. Thoreau wrote about living in nature, but, Lord, she thought it would never end. Berry read it aloud to Jaudon in the long afternoons of days off. Jaudon whittled. The book tended to lull them into naps. She never finished the book, but almost hidden in the tedious detail, one of Thoreau's thoughts resonated. "*What the Powers had made here*," was one of them. The Powers—another way of saying God. She reasoned that the Powers made the world and the Great Spirit took care of it.

She told no one, not Jaudon, not her friends, about the Great Spirit. She was still sheepish in her certainty, and not certain enough to declare it. There must be truth to some greater presence because, when she reached out, it soaked up her sickening anger and left her limp with relief at the departure of her upset feelings. She wanted the Powers, the Great Spirit, both of which were Good/God, to help her find her own goodness.

To remind herself, she placed fat little Buddha statues around the house. She was most fond of the grinning figures and collected them at thrift stores and rummage sales. One sat on each side of her dresser.

Her new friends believed in civil disobedience. In between memorizing for pharmacology, human nutrition, sociology, and history classes, she read about Mahatma Gandhi, draft resisters, and the civil rights movement from abolition on. This was new to her, not history she learned in any school, including Sunday schools where moral responsibility should be taught. Come to think of it, she never saw a non-white person in her church. Why had it taken her this long to realize their absence?

The group took turns meeting in one another's homes. They came to the house in Rainbow Gap for the first time in the middle of a thunderstorm. Three small cars splashed through the sudden sandy mud and stopped short of the front porch. One after the other, five women rushed the front door. Berry gave them all hugs.

"Rain wasn't in the forecast," said Judy Fish, crowding onto the couch between Mercie Lewis and Samantha O'Connell. Donna Skaggs sat on Jaudon's recliner, while Berry and Perfecta Maldonado took the wicker chairs. Mercie was a dark-skinned, sumptuous woman who was always changing her hairstyle and, along with Judy, was the smartest of the group. She tended to wear women's dashiki shirts in bright colors. Judy, Samantha, and Donna were white. Perfecta was Puerto Rican, compact and sprightly with pinkish-tan skin.

"I love all the plants in colored pots on the porch," said Judy Fish. "And everywhere in the house."

"My gran does that," Berry explained, looking around at the greenery. Trailing small-leaf ivies and white streaked philodendrons, tiny green cacti, some flowering, and swollen succulents, hanging plants—all thriving. "She believes it brings a place to life."

The rain came to a sudden stop. As they chit-chatted, a tall, robust non-nursing student, Cullie Culpepper, arrived, dry as dry could be, tanned to a color somewhere between Mercie and Perfecta, her thin arms as gnarled as Jaudon's by muscles and veins. Judy introduced her.

"I met Cullie at Publix. You know me, klutz that I am. I knocked over a display of—canned refried beans, wasn't it, Cullie?"

Cullie laughed. "They were everywhere. Half a dozen of us were on our knees chasing the things along the aisles."

"I was flustered and kept dropping the cans I picked up. Cullie was so gallant. She helped me to my feet and said something hysterical."

"We met again in the parking lot and started talking."

"Such a feminist. I had to invite her."

A pool cleaner by profession, Cullie wore big smudged glasses. She'd carried her oversized West Highland terrier in with her. They sat on Grandma Vicker's hand-braided rag rug. The dog squatted and left a widening dab on it.

"Dog pee washes out in a jiff," Cullie said. She jumped up and lifted the drippy rug. "This is my little coconut, Kirby. She's sorry she made her mistake and wants to know where your set tub is."

"Out back," said Berry, pointing to the screen door as she set down a cooler of ice and cola by the plates of dishpan cookies she'd baked last night. The women, she observed, went for the sweets as if they hadn't eaten in a month of Sundays.

Donna Skaggs announced they wanted to ask Berry a favor. Donna was a big soft-looking woman, until you saw her face, which was long and narrow with a fringe of bangs at the top. She scrunched up her eyes and pursed her lips like an earnest fish. "What do you say, girls, wouldn't this place be perfect?"

In unison, Judy and Mercie said, "Women!"

Donna slapped her own wrist and repeated, "Women."

Berry was puzzled. "Perfect for what?"

"We have a favor to ask of you, Berry." Perfecta's Spanish accent was thick and smooth as the best salt water taffy.

Judy wriggled on her chair as if unable to contain herself. "A woman came and talked to us about what's happening in Puerto Rico."

"Forced sterilization," said Perfecta. "US doctors going in and trying to secretly keep the population down. Big greedy companies are behind it, though I don't know why. Allison can tell you more."

"The woman's running around exposing a government program and you're bringing her here?"

"Not exposing, educating," said Donna.

"Who is she?"

Perfecta said, "Her name is Allison Millar. She's about twenty-five and already she's an experienced public health nurse from Atlanta. Very passionate about, well, everything, but on fire about this issue. And Florida—she's loco about Florida."

"What's she got to do with me?"

"She must have an out-of-the-way place to stay for a while." Donna was domineering to the point that Berry was hesitant to protest.

Cullie came back with her dog. "I hung the rug on your clothesline. It should dry by—"

Samantha interrupted. "Do you live alone here?" Samantha had a husband and was expecting a fourth child. Berry assumed they lived in an apartment too short on space for a guest.

Cullie tilted her head, her eyes on Berry.

"No. There's Gran and my…housemate. Sometimes her brother too."

Cullie was grinning across the room and nodding.

Donna's voice was deep and demanding. "Reliable people?"

She tried not to, but she got sharp with them. "Why are you quizzing me? Are you looking for a rental for this woman? Because I'm happy to talk with Gran about the possibility of renting out her travel trailer. How much trouble is she in?"

No one replied.

Cullie was grooming Kirby with her fingers and raised her head. "Don't be looking at me for a place to stash the woman, I'm nothing but a poor little pool boy."

Berry chuckled, thinking Cullie, unfolded, must be at least five foot ten inches and agile for her weight.

Donna looked annoyed. "Allison has no money for rent. She's an incredibly brave woman and deserves our support."

"No money? Needs an out-of-the-way place to live? You're not bringing trouble into our home."

Mercie Lewis wasn't a big talker, but everyone paid attention when she spoke. "Allison's a fugitive. And she's trying to get support to sue the US government."

Perfecta said, "She was in PR, passing out flyers to warn women who went to the hospital for childbirth that the doctors had a history of tying tubes after delivery. People were simultaneously protesting at every public hospital, but Allison was the only one arrested and charged with conspiracy to incite and other bogus accusations."

"She is showy," said Samantha. "You'd think she's a Southern Belle at first. Making a speech, though, she waves her arms around, not a bit ladylike, and prances in front of her audience like a preacher at collection time."

"Or Mick Jagger." Cullie played Kirby on her lap as if the dog was a guitar.

Berry suspected Cullie's sense of humor could keep the group—and the world—from taking itself too seriously.

Judy Fish sank deeper into the couch, arms folded. "Jagger is such a pig."

Cullie threw her head back and laughed from someplace so deep it had to start in her heart. Rigo would say she was fabulously butch.

"I've got nothing against men except they're men, and nothing against straights except they're straights," said Cullie. "They both think the world was invented for no one but them and the rest of us are interlopers."

"Allison has Jagger's energy. I wish I did." Judy, who was a tiny, thin fireball, waved her arms over her head, barely avoiding Mercie and Samantha. Her hair was dark and springy. She'd told Berry she kept it straightened and constantly fought the rain and humidity.

"She made bail, thanks to the PR nationalists who agreed the sterilization program was genocide. Which it was," added Donna. "By making it public and suing, Allison's group is trying to ensure it won't happen again in any third world country. Our government wants to shut them up, of course, and they're trying to make an example of Allison."

"She flew into Tampa. It was the first flight the poor woman found," Mercie said, her compassion overriding her shyness. "Now she's in hiding, moving from place to place."

"She can't hide forever," said Berry. She fought off the sympathy that crept into her heart.

"Your help would give her time to clear her legal troubles."

"What about any of you?"

"You're the most secluded," said Perfecta.

Cullie's face was serious for once. "Like I said, I can offer, but my cabin just about fits Kirby and me. The woman would have to share my bed and you know, gay or straight, she wouldn't be able to resist my body once under the covers. If that's the case, thanky, thanky, I'll take the mystery woman."

Samantha shushed her.

Berry stared. Cullie was like them? But Jaudon would explode if Berry brought an antigovernment person home. Gran might be perturbed and want to move out. She needed one person in her blood family to stick around. She looked at the women. "I will not hide the truth from my family."

"Isn't there any way they might not know?" Samantha said. "How about saying she's a school friend?"

"Now you're asking me to lie for some stranger?" She was annoyed. "Would you lie to your kin?"

Samantha circled her pregnant belly with one hand. "When I think it's better for them, I might."

"I won't put mine in danger. I won't go to jail for harboring a fugitive in a cause that isn't mine."

The women looked at one another. Cullie plucked a flea from her dog, studied it, and cracked it dead.

Donna declared, "It *is* your cause, Berry. You're a woman like her, like us, aren't you?"

This made her think of Jaudon, who was so often not recognized as a woman. She and Jaudon didn't have to worry about children or getting sterilized and they expected the state wouldn't let them adopt.

Yet, a desire to help came naturally. "Why does the gosh-darned government do these things to people? Wouldn't it be smarter to sterilize the men?"

"Exactly Allison's point," said Perfecta.

Mercie said, "You're willing to meet Allison, aren't you?"

"Of course, but…"

"We'll talk more." Donna changed the subject.

Samantha got her aside as they readied to leave and asked how she could be a nurse and not want to help Allison. Berry escaped outdoors.

On the porch Perfecta lifted her graceful arms to the sky. "Look at this sunset, burning yellow with pink around it. Like it's pulling a blanket over the sun to go to sleep."

Berry touched Perfecta's arm. "You should be a poet."

Perfecta made a soft *tee-hee* sound. "When the kids are in school, I do housework and make up a few words." Perfecta indicated Mercie beside her. "Mercie puts the words to music on her guitar."

"You'll both play for us sometime?"

"Oh, I hope you will," said Judy Fish. "And, Berry, I love the bottle tree out there. So colorful." She was pointing to a sun-silvered cedar snag left standing, its shortened branches adorned with all manner of bottles.

Samantha said, "So pagan."

"The Vickers always have bottle trees," Berry said, trying to ignore Samantha. "The bottles capture any evil spirits that might come their way."

Samantha gave an exaggerated shudder and backed away. "Why think about evil spirits?"

Cullie stayed on the porch and whispered, "I spotted the other bottle trees out back. I wouldn't live in a place without one. Growing up, our driveway was lined with three. That's my favorite." She pointed to a tree Bat had adorned with beer bottles and, separately, their caps.

"My housemate's brother was only twelve and claimed he took the beer bottles from someone's trash."

Cullie winked. "Yeah, I'll bet."

Kirby made a mess down on the ground. Cullie kicked it under the porch on her way to a worse-for-the-wear Chevy pickup. *This woman is pure country*, Berry thought.

Cullie blew an air kiss and said, "Smooch!" The dog sat on her lap as Cullie wrestled the steering wheel, backed out to Pineapple Trail, and crept onto Eulalia Road, forcing a man in a station wagon to brake behind her. The driver, in his wide-brimmed hat, looked so much like Eddie Dill, Berry thought it was him for a second. He needed to get shut up in a bottle.

Berry was late to studying so put off talking to Jaudon and Gran about the Millar woman. Would the Vicker property be at risk if a federal fugitive was caught on their land? Could Bat be forced out of the military? Would she, Berry, be arrested and denied a nursing license?

She considered avoiding the group outside of class, but that wasn't her way. She owed Allison Millar, a braver woman than she was. The question was, how much did she owe her?

CHAPTER FOURTEEN

Jaudon hadn't been around enough that week for Berry to talk with her about the fugitive, and the women were pushing for an answer, so she agreed to meet this Allison person with the group.

Between classes one day, Berry made room for herself in the front seat of Cullie's pickup. Cullie was in the truck bed. Donna drove them over the trolley tracks into the Ybor City section of Tampa. They were spiriting Allison out of the redbrick boarded-up cigar factory where she was hiding.

Berry looked at the truck seat, wondering where they would put the woman.

"We have it covered," Cullie said through the open rear window from the canopy. "You stay put and act innocent if we get stopped and you'll be okay."

"Where's your dog?

"My precious coconut? I didn't want to put her in danger."

Berry considered the danger they wanted to put her family in.

Cullie seemed to read her mind again. "People can take care of themselves when bad stuff happens. What would my helpless animal do without me?"

"Heck, I'd take her." Berry had no doubt the handsome Westie was trainable. Zefer would help. Better Kirby than a radical.

"I'll hold you to that," Cullie told her.

Donna's voice was small and tight. "Here we are." She pulled into an alleyway and stopped on the far side of a loading dock.

Cullie looked at Berry, her eyes, for the moment, humorless. Forehead wrinkled, Donna nodded. Without unnecessary sound, Cullie opened the canopy and dropped the tailgate. "Stay put, you two."

"You'd think she was talking to her dog," Donna said.

From the extended side-view mirror she watched Cullie run, bent at the waist, and vault to the metal door of the loading dock. She raised and lowered it real quick. As soon as Berry looked away the truck bobbed down. She heard two thuds and the tailgate latch. Donna accelerated to the end of the alley and kept to the speed limit as she left the city.

Donna drove east up and down numbered county roads, making sure they weren't followed, all the way out to Salem Church Road, north onto Old Lecoats Road. Berry fretted they were heading for Pineapple Trail. They didn't go near it, yet ended up two miles away at the fancy manufactured home park south of Gran's land. Donna punched in some numbers at the gate, drove through, backed into a driveway, and stopped at a triple-wide manufactured home on July Lake. "Look at these lawns," said Berry. "Do they measure every stalk of grass and cut the blades with scissors?"

Cullie grunted. "Northerners are so wasteful. Do you have any idea how much water the lawn must suck up?"

The garage door opened. Three wood storks took flight at the sound, black faces a stark contrast to their white feathers.

A grim Donna drove the truck inside. The small, insubstantial-looking fugitive jumped out of the back, followed by Cullie.

"We should be filming this. It's like a *Mission Impossible* show," Berry said.

Donna was already out of the truck. "Oh, sure. Let's bring attention to ourselves so the authorities can arrest us all."

Startled by its loudness, Berry turned to see the garage door rolling down behind her. "Well, shut my mouth. I've never seen one of those electric garage doors in a private house before. These folks are living in high cotton." It seemed fitting for a hideout; she expected they wouldn't need the Vicker place.

The living room was enclosed by windows on three sides, with views of the lake. What did they do in hurricanes? She answered herself: they paid someone to cover the windows with heaps of plywood. The fancy place was intimidating and she was as nervous as a long tailed cat in a room full of rocking chairs.

Allison sat with her back to the panorama. Her eyebrows were drawn together and her eyes were on Cullie. She wore makeup. Cullie introduced her to Allison with a bow and a flourish of her hand.

"You'll be staying here until Berry opens her home to you," Donna said.

Berry couldn't believe the nerve of Donna. "That hasn't been decided yet. You couldn't pry me out of this picture-perfect home if you sent in the Marines to get me."

"My aunt will be back Thursday. Allison has to leave before she gets home."

She looked toward the nasal voice. It was Larissa Hand, Larissa the kisser, smoking in one of those high-backed rattan armchairs. Her heart rate shot up and she forced herself to breathe again. This was where Jaudon's brief temptation lived?

Mercie said, "Berry, you haven't met Lari yet. She's been looking for a women's group."

Berry was fit to be tied. She'd worked hard to forgive the treachery of this vixen, yet she could not deny the bile of fury and hatred that filled her heart. She clamped her eyes shut and squeezed the pillow she held, afraid she would throw it at Lari. She eyed the table lamp next to her, a bigger temptation.

And was this what Lari called a trailer park? It was an estate-like manufactured home community. The house was modern, elegant, the grounds kempt. *Lari must think we're bottom-dwellers.*

They glanced at each other. Donna asked Allison to tell her story. Cullie had disappeared.

Allison sat back in her chair and looked up at Berry. There was a fierce, strong, and exhausted air about her, in her cheerful skirt of white and yellow checks, an embroidered white blouse, and a yellow headband holding back her straight, waist-length brown hair. Berry wondered how the woman kept so clean and neat on the run. She looked more like a young church mom than an agitator.

Allison smoothed back her hair. "Did you know parts of Canada have forced sterilization programs today? Sweden and some US states too." Her accent was in fact Georgia, thought Berry, but not country. "It's the Native Americans, the people of color, the poor and undereducated who are targeted."

"The United States?" Berry didn't believe her.

Allison adjusted her hair band. "It's one of the worst ways women are oppressed. I needed to start somewhere to educate the public. Puerto Rican women were once targets of compulsory sterilization in their own country and who knows if they still are." She paused as if anticipating an argument. "Not for mental illness or birth defects or criminal behavior, but to keep the population down. I wanted to start by exposing what went on in Puerto Rico."

Berry was again by turns angry and hugely sympathetic. She didn't understand why Allison hid. She resented sitting in the same room with Lari. She admired what the others called *clitzpah*, but she preferred the idea of changing the world quietly.

"Can't we make any decisions for ourselves? I don't want to have kids, but that's my choice." Allison jabbed her own ribcage with an index finger. "Mine alone. Nurses in PR were trained for a while, as standard procedure after childbirth, to tie the tubes of any woman with two or more kids. A second physician checked to verify it was done. What an obscenity."

This wasn't making sense to Berry, "Did you go into hiding to get support? Why not face the charges? They sound weak."

Allison looked at Donna. "Didn't you tell her?"

Donna looked flustered. "I wanted her to meet you first so she wouldn't think you were some crazy radical."

"Are you leading me down a garden path?" Berry asked. "I don't like this one bit. Cullie, you drive me home. Or I can walk from here."

"No," said Donna. "The last thing we need is one of us getting raped out in an orange grove. Won't you listen to Allison?"

"I didn't commit any crime, Berry. They started out charging me with impeding pedestrian traffic and I'm not big enough to impede anything by my lonesome." Allison held her hands out, palms up, a hapless look on her face. She saw why Allison was admired: her passionate convictions and full-throated ardor cloaked her feminine slightness. "They're trying to silence me by pinning a real crime on me."

As Berry listened, she caught Lari checking Allison out. The new woman did have a compelling combination of demure prettiness and adamant talk. Did she take drugs too?

"The apartment I was crashing in was raided. The cops found bomb-making materials. I didn't know the people and they were out of town. Yes, they're nationalists and I sympathize with them, but I wasn't one of them and armed struggle is not my thing. Armed snuggle is more my style."

The other women, never taking their eyes from Allison and her look of delight, chortled as one.

This was very foreign to Berry. "You're willing to spend the rest of your life hiding?"

"Y'all won't catch me going to jail for handing out educational flyers and sleeping on the floor. I'm a feminist and a lesbian, not a mad bomber."

"A lesbian?" Cullie was back from smoking a cigarette with a surprised smile on her face and in her eyes.

"Didn't I tell y'all? Is that a problem for you?"

"Heck, no," Cullie said. "Why didn't you say so in the first place? I've been the state lesbian long enough, amiga."

Donna was squinting at them with what appeared to be horrified interest. Lari moved into Berry's line of vision. Berry realized much of her anger came from Lari's presence and this made her both hostile to and protective of Allison, who was such a small woman with such a big mind and heart, but also the reason she was in this uncomfortable place.

"How long will you need to hide?"

"To be honest, Berry? As long as it takes my lawyer to separate me from the bomb makers' cases. The cops think I can lead them to their hideout. They don't believe I know nothing."

"No timeline?"

"More's the pity, no," Allison said. In a flash, her eyes got brighter and she spread her arms in excitement. "But if you'll take me in for a while I'll be so good to you. I'll clean your house and feed your pets and mow your lawn if you have one. I'll wash your car, your dishes, your dog. I am so tired of moving and moving. And so bored. I'm a nurse—I can write your school papers for you."

Berry raised her hands in amused surrender. "Enough of your monkeyshines."

No, Allison wasn't a mad bomber, and she might be fun to have around. Allison made her want to smile and learn and talk about all this. She'd failed to awaken Jaudon's interest in women's rights. Allison was capable of converting a pack of good ole boys to feminism.

"Do you have any idea how very much I miss the South?" said Allison. "Being back here is a relief that flows through my whole body."

Cullie's arm was around Allison's shoulders. "I think I love you, Little Miss Clitzpah."

Berry paused. Out of nowhere she found herself wanting Cullie to think she was a Miss Clitzpah too. She promised, "I'll knock this around with my family."

CHAPTER FIFTEEN

Jaudon was in pajamas when she got to the kitchen. Zefer leapt to greet her. The dog had made a fast transition from life tied to a rope to a love hound, as Berry called her. Jaudon pointed out that anyone would become a love hound around Berry. It had been hard on Jaudon when Muddy died of old age, but Zefer was the perfect cure.

"Come on, Jaudon." Bat pushed her down into a chair. "Berry made us blueberry pancakes."

She smacked his hands off her shoulders and gave Berry a big grin. "Now this is worth missing sleep for—my big brother's home on leave and your special pancakes." Berry had insisted on a family breakfast. Jaudon set two alarms to get up by eight after studying until three a.m.

The pancakes steamed on her plate. She spread butter and poured too much syrup out of the yellow Steen's can. "Nothing better," she told Berry and filled her coffee cup a second time.

After she finished she went to take her dish to the sink. Berry stopped her.

"You are so tuckered out, and there's no rush to get your license, Jaudon. Let me clear up here. Don't go anywhere—I need to talk to you all."

Now she had come of age, Berry had a delicate toughness about her. She was a very deliberate person, always weighing pros and cons and looking for the wisest choices. She'd almost never dashed up the tree house ladder as a little kid—Berry always fixed her clothes for modesty and to protect them from tears and soil. If Jaudon had never met her before this day, she'd recognize at first glance a woman who got the job done, whatever it was, and handled the personalities and obstacles with persistent, sensitive determination.

Yet the last few nights had been close to sleepless for Berry, thinking about putting Allison up. Would Lari be hanging around smoking illegal drugs? She concluded Lari's presence was a bigger risk than anyone ferreting out Allison. After she dunked the last dish to soak she explained her thinking to them.

Gran said, "For pity's sake, bring her on over, Berry, as far as I'm concerned. This isn't my house, but we need to help these people who speak up about what's wrong. If they'd done the same thing to poor farm workers here, there wouldn't be a Gran Binyon."

"I don't know," said Bat. "I work with plenty of Puerto Rican soldiers and they're great guys, but PR's a teeny scrap of an island and if they keep going the way they are…"

"Bat." Berry stood at the stove, spatula in one hand, the other on her hip. "Think what you're saying. If you get married, what if you and your wife want a big family?"

"This is the US of A, Berry. Like Gran was saying, nobody's sterilizing us."

"But they are, Bat. They're doing it to people they don't think are fit," Berry told him.

"You're talking about retards?"

"Oh, Bat," said Gran. "I think you're a mite tetched yourself, thinking such backward thoughts."

Berry was annoyed at this dumb cluck of a man. "What if you were born, say, deaf, and the people in Washington, DC, were afraid your kids would be deaf too and they passed a law to sterilize you?"

"Don't be a ninny," Bat said, mopping syrup off his shirt. "They wouldn't, not to folks like us."

Berry took the sticky napkin from Bat and gave him the wet dishrag. "What if some man gets into office in Washington, DC, and decides the whole state of Florida is contaminated from the fruit bug sprays so our kids might have birth defects. Would you take a chance of having kids?"

"I might."

Berry scowled. "Would you want to make that decision or let them?"

"But—"

"No buts, Bat." Jaudon let a fist fall hard to the table. Berry was surprised, but she should have known Jaudon would speak up for her; she always did. "You know you'd want the decision if it was your parts they were cutting up which they wouldn't be because the lawmakers are men."

"Hush your mouth, Jaudon. I get what Berry's saying and no, nobody's going to keep me from being a daddy if I want to be. I'm worried harboring a criminal at home will get me kicked out of the service."

"I worry about not being able to get my nursing license for the same reason."

"It's not worth your license, Berry. Or Bat losing his military career." Jaudon's tone was uncompromising. "I agree with backing her up, but the woman can hide somewhere else."

Berry breathed deeply, hands out, palms up, an unwilling supplicant. "Allison Millar isn't the point. It's about government men bossing us around. They decide if we can have abortions after they rape us, they make laws to keep Jaudon and me apart. We're not out there fighting to protect ourselves, the least we can do is help someone who is, for heaven's sake."

Gran sighed. "Some things about life you can't change, young 'uns. Men are always the bosses, and they always will be."

"Maybe so, Gran, but we should stand up to them."

Bat threw the sticky dishrag at her.

"Bless your heart, pet. You'll learn. Look at how much room we have here to give someone sanctuary. We can always say we didn't know she was a renegade."

Berry was tickled by the renegade description. "When you meet her, you'll see Allison's a reasonable rebel. She's trying to do some good."

They fell silent, as if picturing themselves falling into a renegade life with the best of intentions. Berry thought she might tell Lari, if she visited, to go directly to the trailer and bypass the house. What a mistake it was turning out to be, getting to know other women like themselves—Lari Hand, Allison Millar, and livewire Cullie Culpepper were disrupting their lives. She reminded herself to be grateful for their circle of acquaintances even as she wanted to lock the door against them.

"Life is as good as your pancakes, Berry," said Jaudon. "Why risk everything?"

"Yeah, tell those weak as dishwater feminist types to come at us all they want, Sister," said Bat with a teasing grin. "We can take it."

"You be careful, Bat. Someday you're going to be answering to a lady general."

Bat affected a lisp and a raised pinky. "Oh, yeah, that's me. Taking orders from the ladies."

Jaudon burst out in laughter. "You hush up, Bat. You'll get us both in hot water."

Berry went back to the sink. Jaudon joined her with a dry dish towel.

"Go on," Berry told her. "You have to study."

Jaudon looked over her shoulder at the table. Gran and Bat might have been lifelong pals the way they were chatting away at the table.

She kept her voice low. "I'm not going anywhere when you're mad."

"I'm not mad, but I don't see why you think it's so funny when Bat puts down our kind of people."

"When did he put us down?"

"The nurse comment and his pinky in the air."

"He doesn't mean anything by it, Berry. You know guys."

"Jaudon, he knows what we are to each other. Can't he be a teensy bit sensitive?"

"He was making fun of fags, not us."

Berry didn't understand how Jaudon missed the connections between enforced sterilization, keeping women down, and targeting Puerto Ricans.

For her part, Jaudon didn't know what bug bit Berry. Why did she hang out with these feminists?

Gran scraped back her chair and Bat helped her up. She was bulkier than she'd been on Stinky Lane because the kids insisted on doing the heavier housework. "It's time for my TV shows," she explained. "You're welcome to use my trailer for the girl in trouble if y'all want. I believe the Lord would have us give her a place of refuge, a place where she can be innocent until proven guilty."

Bat went outside. At the kitchen window, Jaudon and Berry saw him using a machete to cut back the horseshoe of wild growth encroaching on the house. Every visit home he went at the dwarf live oak, the saw palmetto, wax myrtle, swamp dogwood, and the rest of it as if he was clearing a way for his resupply truck through the war zone. Mockingbirds complained at the top of their lungs while blue jays tried to drown everything out.

"I bet Bat would appreciate Pops's machete overseas."

"Why doesn't he come home, Jaudon?"

"He doesn't say."

They looked at each other across the chasm of their differences. Jaudon knew Berry didn't even hold with fighting the War of Northern Aggression. There were situations when you have to fight. Did Berry want those Communists getting the upper hand?

"You're sounding like a hippie peacenik, Berry." She covered Berry's hand with her own. "These feminists are changing you."

"Not much. I've always been for peace. And after living with Eddie Dill, well, there was no mistaking who was in charge, who got what he wanted and took what he wanted."

"They're making you hate men."

Berry turned to her with a frown.

Jaudon reared back, ready for a tongue-lashing.

"Aside from Eddie Dill," Berry said, mildly, "no. I hate what some men do to women. I hate their senseless wars. I hate them running everything. The one way a woman gets into office in this country is if her husband dies and they stick her there as a place marker."

"Your own gran told us it's not going to change."

"But, Jaudon, imagine if we can make it change."

CHAPTER SIXTEEN

Jaudon didn't have it in her to deny Berry anything; Allison Millar came to live in the trailer.

They waited until the weekend after Bat shipped back out to Vietnam. He decided that the Army wasn't about to accuse any urgently needed soldier of a situation he knew nothing about. In any case, Allison would be gone in a few weeks. It wasn't safe for her to stay in one place longer.

Bat always promised to come home once each enlistment was up, but this trip he told Jaudon he looked at the figures and decided it would be better for him to finish out his twenty before working at the Beverage Bays. Jaudon was okay with Bat staying in the service, but in her bedroom, Berry pitched a fit.

"You're putting twenty years of work into the Bays when Bat isn't lifting a finger?"

"Who's fighting in Vietnam protecting our country so we can have stores and run them as we please?"

"Who? They're emptying out the inner cities and the backwoods to send poor kids to war because they're giving exemptions to well-heeled white boys. As for protecting our country," said Berry, "you heard what Bat's army job is. He loads the mail, food, and materials into his truck and drives. He brags about avoiding combat and hard work. You're going to let him waltz in and take over the company? Bat will run it into the ground."

"You're so hog-wild about peace, it's a wonder you're not glad he's safer than some of the other soldiers."

"He'd be safer if we kept our noses out of other people's battles. Those folks have no beef with us. You know I believe we don't have a lick of business fighting over there, getting our boys killed and crippled."

"And we're hiding the Allison woman because we have business in Puerto Rico?"

Berry was on her high horse. "Our business there is with women. They should be able to have kids if they want."

Jaudon was so superheated from agitation she reached up to pull the chain and start the ceiling fan. "They're not going to have any rights if the Communists win over there."

"Don't be thick, Jaudon." In nothing flat she regretted using the word thick to sensitive Jaudon and tried to redirect her attention. "You don't believe such a teensy-weensy country is going to take over America."

"If the Commies win there, they'll be taking over Puerto Rico next. They already have Cuba."

Jaudon hated fighting with Berry. They didn't do it often and this was the worst since her mistake with Lari. Arguing with her was far more upsetting than any subject they found to argue about. She always cried when they fought and she did so now, embarrassing herself.

"I'm sorry, Jaudon. I pushed Allison on our household. If it bugs you so much, I'll tell the group to find someplace else."

"It's not Allison. I know she thinks she's saving the world, Berry. It's you. You never cared about war and peace or women versus men. You were my own sweet beautiful Berry. You cared about your gran and me and making a life together."

"You're a business student, Jaudon, and I take care of people. I'm learning so much about how harsh the world is out there—I have to do my bit to make it better."

Jaudon spoke through tears, runny nose and all. "Well, I have to do my part to keep the Bays running so I'll always be able to support us. I can't have my head in some cloud thinking flower power can right the wrongs of the world."

Berry was out of words. Jaudon looked like her heart was broken.

Jaudon blew her nose into a paper napkin thinking she'd broken Berry's heart again. She was the first to start a twitchy smile. Berry pressed her lips together, but her eyes were loving. They moved into an embrace without brakes and held tight.

"I do hate war," said Jaudon, "and I wish Bat would come home to drive for the company."

"I love Bat and your Pops. Pops's big laughs get me going. Guys are okay when they treat women well."

"And I hope Allison doesn't have to go to jail. She's a peach when you get down to it." She squeezed Berry at the waist. "Another Georgia peach."

"She claimed she used to be a carefree Southern girl until she got serious about health policy in college."

"I guess her family is rich to get her a master's degree."

"Silly," Berry said, giving Jaudon a soft push with the heel of her hand. "What difference does it make to be from a comfortable family?"

"You just said it yourself, poor people get sent to war." She didn't want to start arguing again. "My real problem is, I don't know what to expect from you these days."

"I don't know what to expect from myself, Jaudon. My eyes were opened. I can't close them. You live in a bubble where your momma calls the shots and whoever does the best job gets the work, man or woman—as long as they're white. The rest of the world is different. Look how few women doctors there are. Wouldn't it be great if more women like us went to medical school?"

Jaudon looked pensive. She veered back to their argument. "Do you really think I'm thick?"

She made a show of wringing her hands. There was no avoiding Jaudon's thin skin. "Oh, angel, you know I don't."

"If medical school is what you want, we'll find a way, Berry."

"No. I don't want to be a doctor. I want to open an affordable clinic for women, where they learn about birth control, and where women like us and migrant women and black women are safe." The image of a childhood friend's living space was burned into her; she had sad dreams about the crowded, neat room. "I want an all-female staff and women doctors. Learning to doctor takes a big chunk out of a person's life. I'd be paying back student loans so long I'd never get around to what my heart wants to do."

"I'm all for the affordable and safe parts. But who cares about women who want to be with men? That's their problem."

"Exactly what I said, angel. You can't see outside our bubble. Do you think those migrant mothers want to have a passel of children they can't house decently? How many of them could afford to live better if they controlled their pregnancies? No one would have to think about tying tubes if birth control was available."

Jaudon was determined to keep her voice civil. "What's wrong with sterilization? There are too many people in the world already. There aren't enough jobs, people are starving, and they fight with each other to keep whatever they have."

"Don't you see, Jaudon?" Berry gave a gentle stamp of her foot. "If women called the shots, we wouldn't have so many starving babies. But population control is not taught in nursing school and it's one of the most important subjects there is. Another one is abortion. Would I have an abortion? No. If I did I might regret it for the rest of my life, but it should be my decision to make."

"Jiminy, Berry. Being pregnant would make me feel lower than a snake's belly in a mud hole. Getting into that state would be worse."

"Allison says there are ways to have babies without sleeping with men."

"I'm happy with Zefer and Toby. And a talking bird would be nice, one those big bright ones down at the pet store."

"I don't like the thought of caging a bird."

"Oh, it would have the run of the house. See why I love you, my Georgia girl? You are the gentlest of creatures. When you're not mad."

"I try not to let you see me mad. I know it scares you."

"I try not to get you mad, Berry. I know I don't always make the smartest moves." She wrung her hands.

"Talk like this makes you fidgety." Berry again ordered Jaudon off to do some studying before her shift started.

Someone from the group would be by soon with a hot meal for Allison. Berry's job was to pick up news from Allison's attorney at a box in the Rainbow Gap post office. The letters came through Allison's mother in Atlanta. The group decided this many layers would hold off the hunt for Allison until the lawyer did his magic. Allison was a minor miscreant, after all. Berry envisioned her free to return to the West Coast by the end of the month, though she anticipated that Allison would sooner or later come home to the South. Who wouldn't? In the meantime, Allison and trouble were fated to travel together.

An unease pervaded the household after Berry's disagreement with Jaudon.

A few weeks later Gran asked Berry, "Do you want to move to a trailer park with me, pet?"

"Goodness gracious, no. Jaudon and I are for life, Gran. I thank you for your kindness, but divorce is not for us."

Gran asked Jaudon if she was happy with them there.

"As long as you and Berry are okay with it, I'm happy as a june bug."

"Not everyone is lucky enough to find her true love at such an early age."

Jaudon was putting up the living room curtains Gran had washed. Gran handed her another panel.

"She's gotten so different, Gran."

"Has she? Or has she found new ways of being herself?"

"I don't catch your meaning."

Gran was quiet for a moment. Jaudon was having trouble holding the brass curtain rings open to attach the fabric. "There's got to be a better way." She stretched to her full height atop a red metal stepstool.

"Look at you, Jaudon. You sold colas out front here before you started school. You manage your own Beverage Bay and you're studying business so you can take on more responsibilities, more stores. You're the same Jaudon Vicker, you always go in a straight line. My grandchild follows her spirit, or spirit guide, which leads her on a winding path, through her very own maze. Berry always had the softest heart: for animals, for you and her Gran, for the sick, and since she's grown, for the whole world. She's ambitious like you, but in different ways."

Jaudon was quiet while she threaded the last panel onto the rod. She backed down the ladder and sat on the wing chair, thinking about what she'd done with Lari and how strong Berry's attachment to Allison seemed to be. She looked over at Gran, who was on the couch with her sewing kit. She wanted their lives to be smooth sailing, or at least an easy row, but watching Gran made her think again. Was anybody that lucky? Gran lost two husbands so far and she was normal, not shunned by the world.

She'd enjoy Berry while she had her. But their differences worried her to pieces.

"I don't know, Gran. Can Berry and I get too far apart?"

Chapter Seventeen

Allison was in the trailer much longer than planned. The lawyer explained that her case might not be weighty itself, but it carried implications for the federal government as well as the Puerto Rico law enforcement community. He counseled patience and said he needed to tread carefully.

Berry and Jaudon were outdoors scraping moss off one side of the house. They'd cleared the roof the week before. It was a balmy winter's day, palms waving in the breezes, a day made to lure tourists and retirees to the area, and to send the locals outside to do upkeep.

Lari came up the driveway in her shiny black Cougar. Through the mishmash of palmettos and high weeds bordering the yard, they saw the car was stacked high with grocery bags. Lari slowed as she passed them and gave a lame smile, which Berry saw, as Jaudon continued scraping with a typical doggedness which allowed no interruption.

This intrusion got Berry's goat. Never mind the pot, Lari was bound to smoke cigarettes in Gran's trailer though she'd been told not to. When Cullie visited, they saw she always stepped outside for a cigarette. Berry took a break to sit on a porch step and dab at sweat on her forehead with the clean corner of a rag. She was incensed Lari would think it okay to come on their property. Incensed, but guilty. Allison was the lure and Allison was her fault.

"I'm sorry, Jaudon." Her voice sounded very small.

"About what?"

"Bringing temptation to our home. Allison and Lari, I mean."

Sweat rolled down Jaudon's cheek, not so much from heat as from how upset she became at a glimpse of Lari's car out of the corner of her eye. "She's no temptation to me. Not for nothing, but she's a pot addict. I wouldn't be surprised if they smoke pot together." She mopped her face with the bottom of her T-shirt and dared suggest what was on her mind. "Is Allison a temptation for you?"

Berry never once thought of Allison as a lover. With a finger pressed to her nose, as if pondering, she teased Jaudon. "She's okay, for a city girl." She paused briefly before kissing Jaudon's cheek. "I love you, my angel. I'm not interested in being Allison's girlfriend."

Jaudon's quick, "I didn't think you were," was unconvincing even to herself. She'd seen Berry's fascination as Allison told them tales of life on the West Coast, which Jaudon imagined was nothing but a degenerate Florida.

When she'd first arrived, Allison had told Berry and the rapt nurses in the Vickers' living room, "I live in Oregon, on women's land." Jaudon heard bits and pieces as she moved around the house after a long day of school and work. "Atlanta is a pokey little city, though with the big companies bringing young out-of-state employees it may change. I suppose every city was pokier in the 1950s. I thought the West Coast would be more exciting and I found a highly rated nursing school out there. It didn't take me long to get into the rural scene. Hippies moved north to get in touch with nature, dropping out to save the world. I worked part-time in nursing, the rest doing art."

Samantha had asked, wide-eyed and a little breathless, "Are you a hippie?"

Allison pushed her hair back and resettled her headband. "I love the music: Joplin, Grace Slick. The art is cartoonish and too psychedelic, there isn't much depth. There were so many artists trying to make it, the lessons I took were cheap. I almost changed my major to art. In my school years, with the counterculture people, I was able to find my own style. I call it drawing with light. I ignore the object I'm reproducing and try to draw the light around it. Am I making sense? Without light, we don't see the outlines of objects. When we look at an object, its details are created and emphasized by where the light touches."

Allison had looked around the room, making eye contact. "But helping people is my thing, so I got a fifth-year certificate and a master's in public health nursing, which was an offshoot of the school of social work. Art got me involved with the hippies and back-to-the-land lifestyle. After living so freely, the thought of nursing in a hospital or doctor's office gave me claustrophobia. Public health took me out to underserved communities and health advocacy. I always carried a sketch pad when I went on rounds or to community meetings. I can draw in jail if I have to."

Jaudon had seen Berry's lifted face, her mesmerized eyes and deep contemplation of Allison's words.

Jaudon had been in the kitchen when the group took a break. Donna Skaggs emerged from the bathroom and said, "You have one of those chain-pull high-tank toilets. My mother told me she grew up with one."

Jaudon said, "Be darned grateful my folks upgraded from the outhouse."

"You don't have another bathroom?"

Jaudon remembered getting prickly. "We've got this one and the great outdoors."

"You use the woods?" Jaudon hadn't answered, but that was no deterrent to Donna. "I love the tin tub, but there's no shower."

"Sure there is." Jaudon gestured to the window. "See those two rain barrels over the plank stall? Get under it and you have the softest shower water in the world."

"You must be kidding."

Mercie Lewis stood nearby, removing her guitar from its case on the kitchen table. "This is how my family lived before the housing authority bulldozed our house and put up the projects. You're lucky to be able to keep some of the venerable ways, Jaudon."

Her mood had lifted at Mercie's words until Samantha came down the hall and peered into the kitchen. "Bless my soul. Look at the porcelain and cast iron sink. This whole house is an antique."

Donna said, "It's so quaint, I bet they clean their clothes in a set tub with a washboard."

Jaudon ignored them and told Mercie she was welcome to use their shower anytime.

"Thank you. I'll come by some extra-hot day as a treat to myself and pay you a visit," Mercie said.

Jaudon had watched Donna herd Mercie and Samantha back to the living room. They stopped to admire Grandma Vicker's sunburst pattern quilt.

Watching them, she'd concluded that Mercie Lewis was the only one worth a plug nickel, and maybe also that pool cleaner Cullie and her dog. Jaudon had gone out back and let the screen door slam. She was doing a lot of slamming lately. These women reminded her of the girlfriends who took Berry away from her in high school. She bit down on her fear and refused to let it get hold of her.

Since then, she and Berry'd been so busy they got sparse time alone together.

It was because of their schedules, they told each other. They worked, studied, slept. There was meager energy for play times, as they took to calling their intimate encounters. Childhood toys were gone—each had become the other's toy.

Alone in her bedroom, studying, Jaudon played her blues records over and over. She loved Nina Simone in particular, despite the singer's anger—or because of it. Her own harassment and rejection must be nothing compared to what black Floridians went through. Under her breath, she sang along with Nina because she shared her sadness and sorrow, bewitchment and bliss.

One night, Jaudon went to Berry's closed door, Zefer's claws clicking on the wood floor behind her. She heard voices inside and retreated to her own room. She tried to study, but the murmuring went on and on. At least, she told herself, if they're talking they're not playing. The memory of her sudden lust for Lari returned, a lust without love or friendship or history. Berry deserved her own experiences. As long as they went no further than Jaudon's. As long as Allison, who didn't hide her very active love life, kept her hands to herself.

The next time Berry's group met at their house, Jaudon leaned in the doorway to the living room, listening. Allison talked about a group of women in Arkansas who were trying to impress on their police department the urgent need for domestic violence training.

From her perch, Jaudon said, "You ain't whistling Dixie."

Every head but Berry's turned to her. Why did they stare at her with repugnance? She was agreeing with Allison. Later she heard Mercie play her guitar. She guessed it was Perfecta singing along in Spanish.

Another night as Jaudon went in to study after supper, the door to Berry's room was closed. Jaudon knew Allison's voice. The two of them were talking well past Berry's normal bedtime. She went to the kitchen and used the yellow wall phone to call Rigo. She hadn't seen him in a while. Berry complained Rigo wasn't respectful to women. True enough; he was always telling degrading stories about women he knew and celebrities. He didn't listen when Berry insisted he use the term *women* instead of girls. It was the way Rigo talked—he called his male friends girls too.

She met Rigo every few weeks at a luncheonette which served Cuban sandwiches and *batidos*, mango milkshakes. The place offered a sweet rice pudding she loved.

On the phone, she told Rigo what was going on. She fingered the beaded wainscoting, a habit from growing up. Running from dip to dip with her fingertips settled her. Rigo had already been privy to news of the unwanted, unnamed guest in the trailer, but the closed-door visit to Berry's room outraged him.

"Walk in on them, girl," he told her. "What are you, man or mouse? Get that groper out of your house."

"I don't want to turn Berry against me, Rigo."

"You won't, you won't. She's a sensible girl. She'll understand."

"I'm so afraid the door will be locked. She might tell me to go away. Allison is as fetching as a movie star and then some, not a sorry excuse for a girl like I am."

"Berry wants you smack dab the way you are. She's a femme, so's Allison, they don't want each other. Do this and end your misery. Do it now."

"Better I end me."

"Do I have to drive out there from Tampa to do this for you?"

"No. I'll die a mite more every minute I wait—I'll go to Berry's room. Stay by the phone?"

"You bet your sweet bippy."

She'd been grasping the phone so hard she had to force her fingers to uncurl. *Heaven help me. Please don't take her away.* This was her punishment, she decided, for her moment of temptation with Lari, for the boyish way she dressed, for refusing to shave where other women did or wear a bra.

Now she was outside the door, she heard the voices start and stop with a strange rhythm. Were they doing some form of chanting? Feminist chanting in a made-up language?

Warm relief cascaded from her head to her toes. She wanted to kick herself.

Back at the phone, she told Rigo, "I forgot she borrowed Allison's tapes to learn Spanish. She's listening to our tape recorder and repeating words. What is wrong with me? I am such a suspicious creep."

"What did you say to her?"

Toby jumped on her lap. "I called through the door to say I was fixing to make a tomato sandwich and did she want one."

"So Uncle Rigo was right on the money as usual?"

"You should be a headshrinker when you grow up."

"What a coincidence. Shrinkology is what I'm studying, as you well know. But tell me seriously, Jaudo, what in the world got into you?"

She scratched Toby's neck until he purred. "I'm always nervous Berry will have a lapse like mine."

"Don't be silly, missy. I may not be a therapist yet, but I don't need a textbook to tell me we all have those fears. You never know where the mind—or life—is going to take you."

"Aw, heck, Rigo, why would anybody want me in the first place? Bat says when the stork brought me, he dropped me on the ugly tree and I hit every branch on the way down to Momma."

"He was trying to get under your skin, Jaudo. No one's as gorgeous as me, of course, but remember I was about to make a pass when I thought you were a boy."

"You need glasses. I'm a bearded lady from a circus sideshow. I saw one when I was a half-pint. She had a full beard, moustache, long hair and wore a dress. She was built the same as I am. Scared the living daylights out of me. Pops says I walk like a sailor and the doc says I can't have a young 'un. Not that I want to. He says it's my endocrines. He'd give me shots, but needles scare me silly, and besides he told me it's too late at this point. Plus, I'm not about to mess with what's natural to me, but one hint my looks bother Berry and I'll stand aside."

"Be careful not to worry your love life to death. Berry knows her mind and you are what's on it—along with Spanish lessons."

"I don't know, Rigo. Ever since she got in with those feminist nurses she's forever woolgathering, as if she's trying to unlock the secrets of life."

"Is that a bad thing?"

She heard him light a cigarette. "I don't appreciate her doing it without me."

"Aha. Go ahead—do it with her."

"I worry her feminist nurse pals take a dim view of Berry and me loving each other."

"Isn't Lari running with those feminists? She doesn't speak to me anymore. Forget staying friends with that no account hussy after she came between you and Berry, but is there a rule they can't have men as friends?"

"Seems like it. I hope Berry can tolerate me."

"If she can't, I can. What are you doing tonight? I might go over to the bar for a while."

She needed to let off some steam and discourage another attack of nerves, though going to the bar created its own tumult inside her. "I'll meet you there."

CHAPTER EIGHTEEN

Allison met with Berry's group of nurses in the living room one night when Jaudon was working. She'd taught women's self-help clinics when she lived out West. The group took her up on her offer to teach them cervical and breast self-exam techniques. They used the Boston self-help book. Allison brought three new women with her, nursing students from a different college.

Samantha acted like a timid kid despite all the babies she'd had. The rest were guarded, except Cullie, who cried out, "I'm as excited as a heron after a frog. This is the first step in creating our women's clinic."

Berry invited Gran to join them, but Gran preferred staying put in her bedroom with two hours' worth of saltines, stewed prunes, TV shows, and her needlecraft project.

The women pushed back the furniture to make room.

Allison instructed them to lay out white paper from a roll she produced and to place the pillows they brought from home on it. Donna supplied each of them with a clear plastic speculum from a medical supply shop. Allison handed them small mirrors and the others brought their own K-Y Jelly. They were going to see what the insides of their bodies looked like.

Nervous goose bumps on her arms, Berry's hands shook as she sat on the paper across from Cullie. There was giggling from the twosomes around them.

"You know I'm not a nursing student," said Cullie. "Please don't think I'm a pervert for being here. I mean, I am, everyone knows"—she poked Berry on the elbow—"but it's not for the thrill or anything, honest, amiga."

"I may be eager to learn, but I'm as twitchy as you, Cullie."

"This is a procedure you need to know to do your job. It's related to my job because…" Cullie wrinkled up her forehead. "It doesn't relate to my job at all." With a thoughtful look she added, "But it might make me a better lover, neener-neener."

Cullie's silliness in the midst of their earnest probing made the whole procedure brighter for Berry.

Berry tilted her head. "They should teach this in school, like Allison said. Instead, we learn about what equipment to lay out for the doctor, what notes to take. The doctor is almost always a man."

"Honest? I better learn to do this self-exam stuff because no man is ever poking me with any instrument down here." She took her shorts off. "Let's quit shilly-shallying."

"Okay, I'll go first because I learned this part of it at school." She unwrapped the speculum and slathered K-Y on it. Cullie wiggled her pillow under her bottom. Berry placed the speculum, but told Cullie to insert it, which she did with an unexpected swiftness. Berry winced. With the exception of Samantha O'Connell, the other women were complaining about discomfort and telling their partners to slow down.

She switched her flashlight on and looked through the vagina into Cullie's cervix, which was close to identical to her textbook. Allison told them the act of demystifying and studying this part of a woman's body was liberating. It was not an idle exercise; the purpose was learning about their bodies, ending the taboos, enabling them to say the forbidden words, name their secret parts, and claim their bodies for themselves.

"Are you okay, Cullie?"

"As okay as I can be having intercourse with a cold medieval torture device."

The skin around Berry's freckles prickled and, she knew, reddened.

Cullie apologized. "You still want me to do this to you?"

"*For me* sounds nicer. But not till you look in this mirror." She gave Cullie the hand mirror.

"We are going to change the world by taking care of business ourselves." Cullie positioned the mirror as Berry shined the flashlight. "Well, bless my girly soul. Who'd have guessed I'm pink and creamy in there?"

"What did you expect?" Berry tried to keep a professional face, but lost it with Cullie's answer.

"Something coarse and damp and bumpy, like toad skin."

Berry laughed out loud. Someone said, "Shh," but Allison cut her off. "It's okay to have fun doing this, women."

This clinic was, as Allison kept saying, empowering. Nonetheless, Berry wasn't comfortable exposing herself to anyone but Jaudon and she saw she wasn't the only squirrely one. She was in a skirt, so needed only to remove her underwear. Cullie performed the procedure as Berry had, but in complete silence, her face red. She wondered if Cullie was even able to see through her steamed-up glasses.

All the while Berry worried. She wanted to kick herself for not warning Jaudon the nurses and Cullie were coming over. With more women than she expected, the whole situation was out of control. Jaudon was with Rigo at the bar tonight. There was always the chance Jaudon might come home sooner than she planned. Cullie was there; telling Jaudon the clinic was for a class was not going to work.

Next to them, Mercie cried out. "I am so sorry. It came on early." She had her period.

"No, no, don't apologize. This is our lucky day." Allison asked Mercie if she would be willing for others to look. "Fact, sisters: we menstruate. I know the word sister sounds corny, but we are sisters in the struggle."

Not Jaudon, Berry thought with some sadness. How mortified she'd be if she were here. Donna Skaggs, as put off as she was by lesbians, would have a cow if she was partnered with Jaudon. She swallowed a laugh at the idea of Donna having a cow while they watched. They all took turns viewing what they looked like when shedding blood.

By that time, Mercie was crowing about being the one to offer their first view of the curse, as she called it, and the atmosphere was warm and victorious.

"You see why this is important?" Allison said. "We know more about our bodies. Just as good, we can run across one another anywhere in the world and recognize sisters. We have a bond much greater than a cigar-smoking Bubba club."

Allison was inspiring. They applauded with excitement as she urged them to say words they'd never used before: mons, labia, vulva. Berry recognized a sense of accomplishment new to her, and a glowing pride she tried to tamp down, as she was taught to do in her church. It wasn't so much a personal pride, as a tribal certitude. The women were doing for themselves. It seemed so natural she wondered why they'd let go of their powers way back when.

What was that? She plainly heard a key in the two sticky front door locks. Bat! The others heard it too and looked as one toward the door. Someone whimpered.

Jaudon called out in her raspy voice, "Hey, how come you locked me out?" The front door slammed behind her as she, mouth open on her last word, scanned the half-naked pairs of women on the white sheets, frozen in the act of examining their own or one another's breasts. Plastic instruments shiny with clouded jelly and, next to Mercie, a bloody paper towel lay discarded.

"What in the Sam Hill...?" She backed out, bumping the door ajar with her bottom and pulling it closed with an arm, her book bag catching on the knob.

The eyes of one of the new women, round with horror, shifted from the door to Berry. Pointing, the woman asked, "Who was he?"

In a soft, deliberate voice, refusing her annoyance, Berry answered. "Who, Jaudon? Her family owns the house."

"Jaudon is a *her*?" said the same woman.

She was trying to think of a scathing response when Allison cleared her throat and said, "Jaudon is one adorable strutting rooster." Berry wondered if she should worry about Allison. Free love was the rage these days and she could imagine some of these women diving in without a moment's hesitation. "Let's get back to what we were doing."

Berry, with gentle earnestness, examined first herself, then Cullie, using a chart in the book. No one found any threatening lumps. The students pledged to buy and carry the book to their classes to show their teachers and other students its wealth of information. They picked up their equipment, their paper towels slick with jelly, finished cleaning themselves, and gathered the stained exam table paper. At the door, they reached across shoulders and around waists in a group hug. Donna carried out the garbage bag of medical waste.

Cullie gave Allison and Berry extra hugs. "When do I get to spend time with you and the mysterious butch in the doorway?"

"Oh, I don't know." Berry was confused. Butch? Did Jaudon have to carry that label around with her on top of all the rest? She swore she liked gay men at the bar better than Berry's friends. "Anyway, Allison met Jaudon."

"She's cute as a bug, but I make her nervous," Allison said, with an open smile.

Again the uneasy feeling tackled Berry. *Keep your mitts off my Jaudon.* She declined to rassle her meanness this time.

Cullie told Allison, "You don't make me one bit nervous, teach."

"Bless you for saying so. I thought I scared away every last one of you rural butches."

"It's true y'all talk awful dad burn fancy. Do you do everything so fancy? How about some lessons in how we do things here in the country, teach?"

They looked at each other with face-stretching smiles.

"Why don't you come visit with me tonight, Cullie?"

Here we go, Berry thought, annoyed and nervous. Allison was supposed to be in hiding, not dragging people to Vicker land and attracting attention. "You two get on out the door before some frog gets a mind to jump inside," Berry replied with an attempt to sound hospitable.

Cullie said, "Smooch!"

The nearest frogs went silent as Cullie and Allison stepped along the wooden floor of the side porch. Berry went to give the all-clear to Gran and put the sheets in the wash. She saw a light under Jaudon's door. She must have come in the back door.

Should she knock? Jaudon didn't drink when she went out with Rigo, but she and Jaudon were changing so fast, she wouldn't be surprised if that changed too. She wished they were changing together. Every day another barrier grew up between them and she didn't know how to break through. She raised her hand to knock, hesitated, realized she was too faint-hearted to face Jaudon. How to make sense of the living room scene for her? She walked on by Jaudon's door.

"You going to tell me what went on in there?" Jaudon sat on the edge of Berry's bed after a wakeful night, wearing her pajamas and a put out expression.

She *was* put out. Berry ought to have told her there was going to be a…whatever went on last night. This morning, she awoke to the sound of a big pickup truck starting outside. One of those girls from yesterday afternoon was driving. Cullie? Did she stay the night with Allison?

Berry massaged Jaudon's chest where the pajama top opened in a *V*. She explained, watching the incredulous expression on Jaudon's face.

"I have leftover speculums. It might not be a bad idea for us to get familiar with our bodies. We might be able to spot trouble down the line."

"Aw, heck, Berry. You want to do *that* to me?"

"If you're willing. Practice on me, angel?"

After some arm twisting and a lot of instruction, Jaudon held a mirror for Berry. After that, she looked herself.

"How do I tell if what I'm seeing isn't what it's supposed to be?"

"That's why you're looking, so you'll have a baseline for comparison."

Jaudon gave a noisy sigh. "Okay, go ahead and do it to me. Better to know than die, I guess."

Berry expected Jaudon to agree, but gave her one more surprise. "First, your breast exam."

"What?"

"It's another place we can head off trouble."

"Jiminy," Jaudon said as she took off her pajamas.

"No one but my Jaudon can combine self-exams with a Walt Disney character."

"You have to admit, this is downright Goofy."

"Hush up, and do what I'm doing. You're probing for lumps or anything new or strange."

"Mine are too small to grow extra bumps." Jaudon was proud to be small. "I never asked for these things anyway."

"They're so soft," said Berry and caressed them.

Jaudon swept Berry's hand aside. "Quit fooling around. Or is this part of it?"

"With you, angel, yes. Okay, on your back and position your legs the way mine were."

"I guess this won't be the first time."

"Hush. I'm greasing this up good so it shouldn't hurt you, okay?"

A peacock shrieked outside and Jaudon recoiled. "Get it over with."

"No need to rush. You have the mirror?"

Berry pushed the speculum.

Jaudon yelped. "I can't, Berry. Take it out!"

"I'm so sorry, so sorry," Berry repeated and repeated as she slowly, slowly withdrew the tiny bit of speculum she'd eased in. "I honestly could not have been gentler, Jaudon."

"Oh, sweet Jehoshaphat. I must be all tore up." Jaudon's tears dripped onto the bed.

"My poor angel, you are so tiny inside. No wonder you don't care for me going in there much."

"See, I can't be a regular woman if I wanted to. Men, babies, forget it."

"Can you imagine what it's like for women who don't know how they're built until they marry men?"

"Did any of the other girls have trouble last night?"

"Nothing was mentioned. There's no shame to it. We're every one of us built different."

"Some of us more different than others." Jaudon *was* shameful that yet another characteristic made her peculiar. If Berry was seeing how real girls looked, she might change her mind. "How come I don't get as wettish down below as you?"

She cuddled Jaudon's head against her breasts. "Wettish? I flood you out and you think you're strange? I don't know how to convince you, Jaudon, we're all different."

Jaudon had her lips pressed together hard. Berry was wiping gel off herself with tissues.

"If you were different? I'd adore you more. There's not a soul on earth better than you, and I get to keep every special bit of you forever."

She looked up at Berry. "You mean it?"

"'Course I do." She kissed Jaudon and stroked her hair. As their love matured they continued to share long exciting kisses while listening to their big band music, but this wasn't the time of day for music.

Jaudon continued to be shook up, but she bet Berry was in the mood for more today.

They continued kissing as Jaudon guided Berry onto her back.

"Jaudon, you're going down under the sheets again?"

"Down under? You have Australia in mind, don't you?"

"You are Goofy."

Jaudon walked her fingers along Berry's stomach. "Almost there."

Berry was slick with that Vaseliney stuff. She was always smooth and silky wet, but this was nicer.

She loved Berry with every inch of herself. On impulse, she moved downward and kissed the part Berry called the outside labia. Berry gasped and let her legs fall open. Jaudon kissed the inside, the inner lips. She always imagined Berry pink and pretty there and was taking her time admiring her. She wanted to worship the hidden glory of Berry and used her tongue and lips to do so. The other tidbit, she forgot the name, was tiny on Berry; when she kissed it, Berry acted as if she lit her on fire. Jaudon had never heard those kinds of sounds from Berry in all this time. She stuck her tongue inside to taste her.

Berry lifted herself up to press against Jaudon's tongue. These were not things you learned in nursing classes, but she'd read about oral lovemaking. She wanted it to go on forever, this melding of Jaudon with the new sense of herself. She was connected to, and part of, everything. She wanted Jaudon to experience this. The release was indescribable. About now the house could fall apart around them for all she cared.

Jaudon reached an arm up to muffle the noises coming from someplace way inside Berry. She wanted to give Berry more, but Berry made her stop and got her head between Jaudon's thighs. She concentrated on her building tremor. Yeah, it was good—Berry loving her enough to give back like this was the best. She wasn't one to make sounds herself, but this sensation, she had to let off steam somehow. She pulled the pillow over her face and tried not to remember afterward what sounds she made.

Berry scrambled up into her arms. They held on until Berry's alarm went off. Jaudon was going to miss half a class as it was.

"Go bang on Allison's door to see if Cullie will give you a ride," Berry said after they kissed, their mouths tasting of each other.

"That's her filthy tank of a pickup?"

Berry nodded as she slid off her bed. "Probably."

"She woke me starting the truck. She's long gone, whoever she is."

"Cullie's one of the feminists helping with Allison." Berry hesitated, remembering Cullie got as wet as she did during the self-exam. There was no narrowness inside Cullie. It was interesting, how different from each other two tomboy types could be. Not an observation she'd share with Jaudon. "I guess Cullie spent the night with Allison."

"Helping?" Jaudon suggested. "The way I *help* you?"

"Get out of here." She gave Jaudon a playful push. "I'll be ready to go in ten minutes."

"That'll be the day." Berry's nightgown made a surprise landing around Jaudon's neck. "Nice throw," she called.

Predawn frolicking was an excellent idea. She never wanted to take Jaudon for granted or be guilty of neglecting the light of her life. The recent strain between them eased.

CHAPTER NINETEEN

Berry and Jaudon weren't home much. The nurses were finishing their clinicals, required humanities, med-surg, and medical ethics classes. Jaudon studied at home, on the job, during classes to get her credentials sooner rather than later.

Gran, who'd come back stronger than ever once she wasn't under Eddie's thumb, kept an eye on the property, visitors, mail, slick salesmen, lost varmints, and the revenuers—as she called the tax assessor and his cohort functionaries. Since Allison's arrival, she took on guard duty in case the law came asking about a young woman fugitive.

Gran loved Allison, and described her as a fine young lady. Allison teased her about taking in a radical lesbian feminist activist, but Gran visited the trailer each day to chew the fat and give Allison advice about how to live her life.

"The Culpepper gal is over yonder quite a bit," Gran told Jaudon and Berry one Sunday evening. Berry looked at Jaudon and knew she was thinking the same thing: Allison chose Cullie over Lari.

Unsullied white clouds took the shape of vapor trails. Palm fronds leaned motionless against the last graying blue in the sky. With each infrequent breeze came a leisurely rustling sound.

"And her white Westie. Cute as a bug's ear, the three of them." They were on the porch, citronella candle burning steady in the hushed night air. Gran was on the rocker they'd managed to save from Stinky Lane. It had belonged to Gran's mother. Jaudon and Berry shared the porch swing. "Cullie takes Allison out places."

Jaudon slammed a fist into her palm. "They don't have the good sense God gave a goose, do they?" She turned to Berry. "Your friend is supposed to stay put. What do we know about Cullie? Or Allison? Do we know Allison's last name?"

Gran was resolute. "Don't know it, don't want to know it. The less said, the less I have to tell the law."

"Her name is Allison Millar," said Berry. "She's like us—she craves her Cullie time. Cullie's nothing but a regular person."

"What concerns me," said Gran, "is them leading the law back here. And I'm going to talk to both of them about it. I'm very partial to Cullie, she's funny as a gator on ice skates, but I suspect the dog is leaving puddles in the trailer."

Jaudon pushed off the swing and stomped down the wooden steps. "It'll smell to high heaven after a while. Allison's overstayed her welcome, as far as I'm concerned." She wrenched a weed from the ground.

Berry didn't plan to sound as sharp as she did. "I never wanted Allison here in the first place." She tried to practice the habit of consulting the Great Spirit. A few deep breaths did the trick, but half the time she forgot. "I'd like to give sanctuary to everyone who wants to patch up the world, but yes, Jaudon, I agree her time is at an end here on Pineapple Trail. It's for Allison's sake too—she knows she needs to keep moving. I'll talk to the group tomorrow about finding the next place."

"Allison won't fight moving," said Gran, "but I'll miss her. She tells me she's apprehensive out there. She believes someone's watching her."

Jaudon said, "Bless her little pea pickin' toes. If the law was chasing me, Gran, I'd think I was being watched too."

"Oh, Jaudon, Allison's a good woman. She's given up a lot to do what she thinks is right."

"For your information, Berr, Cullie's truck wasn't out there this morning. It was Lari's sporty foreign number. Again."

Berry smiled as if she was swallowing a secret. "Lari might be delivering groceries, might not. Allison doesn't believe in monogamy."

Gran wrinkled up her forehead. "Monogamy. Like the Mormons do?"

"The opposite. Monogamy is sticking with one person till the end of your days. Allison wants variety."

Gran nodded. "I'll tell her to quit while she's ahead and not make my mistake. You can see her and Cullie enjoy each other's company. That Larissa Hand, she has an untrustworthy manner about her."

Jaudon cringed at Berry's comment about Allison and variety. When Jaudon met Cullie they hit it off like long lost pals. She even took Cullie up to the tree house. Cullie, of course, climbed the ladder with her dog under one arm. Zefer had whined on the ground as she watched them climb without her. Jaudon was none too pleased to hear Allison might be misbehaving on Cullie. "You're saying Allison sleeps around."

"I don't know what she does, angel, only what she tells me she believes."

"I hope her morals aren't contagious."

"Not in this household they aren't," Berry said.

"You girls are smarter than I was. Eddie turned into a real Dill pickle as soon as I told him to move in. But your grandpa died of the flu a month before your mother was born. Life was very hard on my own. I needed a man."

Not that man, you didn't, Berry thought with some viciousness. She didn't dare look at Jaudon, who must be thinking the same thing. If Ma and Pa stayed, Gran might never have needed to take up with someone like him. *Eddie's my fault too*, she thought. *It's a wonder I don't drive Gran away along with Ma and Pa.*

"Now I have no idea what I did need a man for."

Berry got up and hugged Gran. "We'll always take care of you."

Gran patted her shoulder. "I know, pet, and I'm ever grateful. Life gets topsy-turvy at times and makes someone think. One day your life is all ahead of you and the next you're nearing the end. As soon as I feel up to it, I plan to make hay while the sun shines, but don't you worry, I won't shame your momma and get you tossed out of your house and home by drinking and gambling and carrying on, though I wouldn't rule out a bingo game on occasion."

Berry laughed, but Jaudon was on a different channel altogether. "Is Allison one of those fools who want to let Vietnam go Communist?"

"No. She wants to get Americans home safe."

"Well, we can't stand by and let the Commies take over." It burned Jaudon up how Allison, with every freedom in the world, didn't appreciate what Bat was doing over there. If she was a man, and didn't have Berry, she'd go kill as many Commies as possible.

Berry was taken aback by Jaudon's anger. She suspected it wasn't all about Vietnam, but more about her own war with the world over being different.

"She's not a Communist, Jaudon. Allison talks a lot about protecting democracy."

"Why is she hiding then? America stands for fair trials."

Gran spoke up. "The girl prefers to be on the lam than locked up for a crime she didn't commit. Wouldn't you, Jaudon?"

"I'm not about to poke my nose into government business. Sterilize away. This whole planet is getting too crowded."

Berry looked at her grandmother, whose eyebrows were raised high.

Gran said, "Jaudon, Jaudon. You're so angry."

"No, I'm not. Miss Feminist is more trouble than a houseful of hornets. And this unfaithful business. How do I know she's not going to go after you, Berry?"

Gran *tsk*ed. "Jaudon, don't look trouble in the mouth."

"She might talk you into believing we shouldn't be together."

"I have a mind of my own, Jaudon. Not Allison, not anybody's going to come between us."

The distance between Berry and Jaudon yawned wider. They watched an armadillo amble across the front yard.

"You're in quite a sulk, Jaudon," said Gran.

Am I being dim-witted, thought Jaudon. *Stubborn? Don't I have a claim to be uneasy?* Why were they looking at her like she was too dense to live? She scraped back her chair. "Hey. I'm getting ready to run a chain of stores and to make some money at it. I don't have time to live with my head on Allison's cloud."

Gran slapped the table. Berry jumped. It was clear Gran was going to educate Jaudon. Instead Gran made a suggestion. "Why not put her to work in one of the Beverage Bays? To earn her keep."

"And get shut down by the FBI?"

"Allison has false ID. You wouldn't be to blame. In one of our afternoon gabfests she told me she worked in a natural food store out West, so she won't need much training. And she wants to help out. Says she's going stir crazy, but doesn't know how she'll get a job until she clears her name."

"Someone will recognize her from wanted posters. Cops often come into the Bays."

"They won't know it's Allison when I get done with her." Gran planned aloud how she'd color Allison's hair, cut it short, and have her wear glasses. Allison was known to wear short skirts and alluring tops, so Gran wanted to switch her to slacks and polo shirts—and a bra.

"This could work," said Berry. "They won't expect to see her directly under their noses."

"You'll pay her wages in cash to help her move on, help her go home." Gran wasn't asking anymore, she was giving Jaudon orders.

"You want me to pay her to leave?"

"She'd be working off her rent."

"Would not. What if Momma found out? It's bad enough we're hiding her here."

"Your Momma won't know anything more than you do. Remember Allison will be transformed. She'll be whoever is on the fake ID. Employers don't look any further than that."

Jaudon looked at Gran. "Do you think it's safe?"

Gran took out her cigarette purse, undid the clasp, and fished around inside. She kept a book of matches in there for infrequent smoking. Both Berry and Jaudon wrinkled their noses and waved away the smoke. "At this time in my life, young 'uns, I don't know if anything is safe. I'm more concerned with what's good, what I'll bring with me to judgment."

"I need to weigh the same thing, Gran—what's good for my family, as much as for Allison."

"And all women," Berry said.

Jaudon bent over and slapped her knees in mirth. "Now that's more than I can take on, Berry."

"The way I see it, Jaudon, the government is just trying to quiet a very public activist."

Jaudon decided she was being thick-headed and was puzzled about what. She decided to back off, calm down. "Talk about taking risks, Berry. Can we trust her in the store?"

Berry's eyes had a teasing look. "She might go for you, Jaudon."

"She better not try anything. I'll bean her with a wet string mop."

Gran weighed in. "I trust Allison. She's not one to steal from the people who help her. Or anyone."

"If she has to be so gosh-awful public, can we at least hustle to tell her to find another place to stay? We can't deny knowing who she is if she's living here. How about Cullie's place?"

"I'll check. Cullie said her old rental is too small for the both of them, but Gran's trailer may be smaller. More to the point, Cullie said no to the idea before the two of them got so close." She looked through her eyelashes at Jaudon, trying to be coy. "I'll tell Cullie if she wants to keep playing with Allison, she's in charge of putting her up, shuttling her to and from work—and keeping her hands off my girlfriend."

Jaudon said, "We're getting in deeper and deeper. You know, in a horror movie, this is when the audience starts screaming, *Don't go in the basement. Don't open the door!*"

There was no laughter.

CHAPTER TWENTY

Jaudon needed a night clerk and stocker, so she put Allison to work. Thanks to Gran, Allison sported dark blond hair in a poodle perm out of their childhoods. Jaudon hee-hawed as boisterously as Pops at the sight of her. Gran outfitted Allison in slacks with a slight flare and a ladies' Western shirt, with a yoke and pearl-style buttons to take the last of Atlanta out of Allison, who was trying for a Texas drawl when she spoke because the ID Rigo got her was from Texas. Jaudon forbade her to make conversation with the customers beyond *How can I help you, please?* and *Thank you, ma'am.*

"What does Cullie think of your getup?" she asked.

"She says it's a real turn-on."

Jaudon was skittish around Allison. She avoided touching her and skipped away when they were in the office area at the same time. The idea of going with more than one woman at the same time was foreign and disturbing. The thought crept into her mind whenever she was in Allison's company.

Over the weeks, Allison didn't complain about her situation. She worked hard enough, but was inclined to talk and ask personal questions when they were alone in the cavernous steel building.

"I'm not too nosy, am I?" Allison said with that eyelash-fluttering way she had. "I like to know everything."

Jaudon had already told her how she and Berry got together and how the stores came to be and her ambitions.

"Don't you want more experiences?" Allison wanted to know. "See the world or be with other women? Florida is a captivating state, but there's so much more beyond Rainbow Gap."

"What would I do out there? The same thing as I do here, plus being cold. As for Berry, she's all I want." She made no mention of her fear of travel or that she was too self-conscious to relax in new places.

"I don't think I ever met anyone as small town as you before, Jaudon. I can't imagine living a life in one place with one person."

"I'm sorry for anyone who can't. I've got everything I'll ever need: family, a house, a job for life."

"And that's all you want? My father is like you. After his service overseas, it's enough for him to drive to the same office in the capitol building every day. Other than vacations at the shore, his life is one long routine. My sister takes after him. She teaches at the state university. She's inextricably tangled up in departmental politics and getting tenure so she can work there her whole life. She doesn't dare push for women's studies courses, no matter how much I nag her. I'm the opposite: I rushed out into the world."

"I don't get it, Allison. Cullie's head over heels for you and you'd step out on her?"

"You're asking the wrong question, Jaudon. Am I her property? Who has the final say about what I want?"

"When you love someone, you want to be with her and her alone."

"I think you're equating love with possession, Jaudon."

"What if I am?"

"Do you think Berry is yours, not her own person?"

"Forever. And that's a fact."

"No, you're talking romance and romance is a product manufactured by male minds to seduce and enslave women."

"Not my romance with Berry. If it's manufactured, it's made by us."

Allison looked pained. "The concept of romance is taught, Jaudon. It's not innate."

"Hogwash. It comes from my heart, not some man's."

"We live in a money-based society. We have to own things. Romance is a coin of the patriarchal capitalistic realm."

"What?" Jaudon wasn't even going to try to follow. "Bottom line, Allison? Break Cullie's heart and you'll have me to answer to for it."

Allison closed her eyes and drew a long satisfied sigh. "There are too many fascinating women in this world for me to turn my back on every one of them."

"Why not be friends instead of intimates?"

"I like sex, that's why. Do you see anything wrong with that, Jaudon?"

Two cars drove in and interrupted the heat of their discussion.

Jaudon wanted to know what made this woman tick. After another flurry of customers, Jaudon asked, "What is women's studies? Does the class at our house fall under that category?"

"Oh, God, no. That class was a special women's self-help clinic. Women's studies teaches about the slavery and disenfranchisement women."

"Why? We don't have to sit in the back of buses."

"You're so cute. You don't have the faintest idea, do you? Too many of us were formed by 1950s America."

Was Allison making fun of her? She didn't hardly mind; Allison was becoming a pleasure to look at and listen to, like visiting royalty. She tried to get a rise out of her. "I'm a Florida Cracker. I need to be schooled in these things."

Allison was not ruffled. She was pulling cartons of cigarettes from boxes and filling rows with single packs. Jaudon ripped open a carton and handed it to Allison.

"The inequities between women and men are endless, starting with wages."

"We pay everyone the same here at the Bay."

"And if the big companies ever do, we'll be okay. But, other than your family, tell me the last time you saw a woman bank president, a woman running Ford or Chrysler, a woman managing a Burger King. Women can't get to the top. We work the bottom jobs: bank teller, receptionist, cashier. If we do get proper jobs, we're paid less because men have to support their families."

Allison ripped open a case with her bare hands instead of the box cutter. Jaudon feared she was aggravating her.

"Cullie is living proof, Jaudon. The guys started out at almost twice what she was offered."

"And she took the job anyway?"

"She enjoys the work. There aren't many outdoor jobs a woman can do. At two years they gave her basic health insurance after she signed a document absolving the employer of responsibility in case of injury."

"Do the men have to sign too?"

"Cullie was told she was more of a risk than the men."

Jaudon leaned on her push broom. "I never knew."

Allison moved to the small stock of health and beauty aids the Bays carried, sorting them. "What about women who support families, women living together, or widows, or divorcees, don't we have families to support?"

"My mother used to employ married cousins who lamented the whole shift about everything they left undone at home."

"And politics." Allison was growing more animated. "When will we get a woman president? Or a mayor?"

"You're going to start a revolution."

"I wish. Did you see the speech Fannie Lou Hamer gave on TV several years ago? She talked about what women of color in Mississippi face, including sterilization and threats against people trying to vote. If Hamer hadn't spoken up, no one would have known about it. And her speech is just one example. Look at feminist history. You've heard of the suffragettes. You had them here in Florida."

"Those crazy old maids?"

"They were savvy spinsters and married women, Jaudon. They're the reason we have the vote."

"How did men stop women from voting?"

"Like they did black Americans. When the suffragettes tried, they were turned away from the polls because men made registering a woman to vote a crime."

"You're talking ancient history."

"You said it in a nutshell, cutie-pie. His-story. We know what the men did since the beginning of time. We need to teach *her*-story."

Jaudon shrugged. "It's your revolution, not mine. Someday I'll finish my CPA. I'll keep running an honest, profitable store and go home to Berry at night. That's enough for me."

Allison waited until a line of commuters on their way home from Tampa left. "Okay, what's your story?"

"Story? I don't have a story."

"Of course you do. Tell me why you love Berry. She's such a gentle soul. She'll make a great healer."

"She's studying nursing, not trying to be a *traiteur*."

"Tell me about *traiteurs*."

"It's someone who heals through prayer. The Cajuns have them."

"Is Berry Cajun?"

"Her mother's people started out in Louisiana. Nobody handed the treatment prayers down to Berry, but she says it's in her blood. She thinks it's why she always wanted to be a nurse."

"Berry told me you two had no idea what to do. How did you become lovers?"

"Oh, it was like our hearts made an agreement early on." Jaudon's face grew hot. It embarrassed her to talk about what she and Berry did. She sent Allison to fill customer orders and stayed on the register for the rest of their shift to keep Allison quiet.

About a week later, Jaudon was studying when Allison came around the counter, swabbing the floor with a wet mop.

Allison put three items by the register with some cash.

"Thanks for the job. I can afford some supplies."

Jaudon dropped deodorant, toothpaste, and razor blades into a bag. "You're not planning on doing away with yourself, are you?"

"Suicide will never be on my agenda, but if it was, at least I'd smell good. I need to shave my hairy legs. I hoarded my last blade for my underarms but it's gone dull."

"You're the one scraping your armpits and legs and you think you're the feminist?"

Allison stopped dead, money in hand. She looked at Jaudon with widened eyes. "Who knows, you may be the real feminist here, and I'm in the throes of the patriarchy, following the boys' rules."

Jaudon gave a brusque nod of affirmation. "Doesn't Cullie have a razor?"

"She doesn't share."

So Cullie used a razor. Jaudon wasn't sure what to make of that.

She decided she liked Allison, but it was hard to be nice to her. The way she lived was poles apart from most people. She went in for such extreme opinions, talked so high-toned. It was in her personality to upset every applecart she passed. Like her or not, Allison spelled trouble.

"Yours isn't bad, but I'd get rid of it if it was up to me," Allison said, touching Jaudon's chin with a finger. "Why don't you?"

Jaudon jumped away. She knew this time her face was flushed with shame. "You're talking about my duck fluff? Why should I? Berry wants me to keep it."

"Oh, cutie-pie, if that's duck fluff, I'm Che Guevara."

"Who?" She was glad she knew how to control her temper, because at that very minute, she wanted to wallop Allison's butt. School kids had made her life hell enough; she didn't have to put up with comments about her body anymore. So she said, "Well, bless your little pea-pickin' feminist heart for speaking your mind." She tried for a sweet yet venomous smile, on the verge of telling Allison not to look a gift horse in the mouth—a job and a place to sleep were hers thanks to Jaudon.

Allison's remarks about her body were plain rude and she was offensive, crude, and nosy. She'd never hire a fugitive again, no matter who begged and pleaded. She had a mind to turn Allison in.

CHAPTER TWENTY-ONE

It was five weeks to the day Allison started working at the store that two men came stiff-legged, in reflective sunglasses, jackets, and long pants, to Jaudon's Beverage Bay. At first, Jaudon thought they were robbers, because they were on foot. They looked so out of place with their long sleeves and big hats in 80-plus degree heat. That was when she took note of the silver five-point badges. Did they find out about Pops's homemade liquor stored behind the commode wall?

"Good afternoon, sir. We're U.S. Marshals. Do you have an Allison Millar employed here? Or, I mean, ma'am."

The photograph shocked her. It was Allison to a tee before Gran transformed her. She tried not to show her fear. Pops taught her long ago to keep her mouth shut and her face shuttered around the police because of his liquor sales.

She shook her head. "No. Not my employee."

"But you recognized her."

She tried for a puzzled look. "She could be a customer? Not a regular."

"Do you mind if we look through the premises?"

"Help yourselves." She embarrassed herself with a nervous giggle. "To look around. Not to the premises."

The men hadn't waited for permission to move toward the shelving.

Allison was there somewhere. Jaudon's heart seemed to expand to fill her chest with pounding. From the corner of her eye she saw a dark shadow flit out the rear exit faster than greased lightning. The gravel crunched once before Allison, in tennis shoes, was on asphalt. One marshal looked up and at the exit, but turned away when the sound didn't repeat.

Jiminy. She caught her breath. Did the marshals know employees seldom worked alone here? Did they intend to search the other Bays or talk to Momma because she was the owner? Allison needed to go into hiding again. At least she'd moved into Cullie's rental just outside the city of Four Lakes north of Rainbow Gap.

The best, the sole thing Jaudon thought to do was act shocked, but otherwise normal. She prayed for some customers to arrive. Aw, heck. What if those marshals asked for the store schedule, read names from it? She'd tell them Allison, under her Texas name, called in sick, and flesh the tale out by saying she suspected it was one of her kids that got sick. Tell them she was always getting calls from the kids and asking to go home. There, they'd be convinced.

"She leaves me high and dry in the busy times," she would complain.

"We'll need the names and addresses of your female employees, ma'am."

"Not their private information."

"This is a matter of national security, ma'am. Privacy takes a backseat in this case."

"National security? My employees are decent Americans—"

The shorter marshal held his hand out, then folded his arms. He looked grim.

She got her box of employee information and handed it over. "Everybody currently working for us is in the front section." He handed it to his partner who took a small notebook from his pocket and copied with a quick hand.

It occurred to her to ask why they were there or they'd think she knew.

"Routine," was all the shorter cop managed.

Allison had had plenty of time to hide or catch a bus on busy Buffalo Road. "What else can I do for you?"

They returned the files. "Call us if you see this person or hear of her." He handed over a business card.

On their way out the man with the notebook stopped and said, "We got an anonymous tip that she works here. I see your wine and beer license is up to date, ma'am. Don't you try to sell any other spirits." He didn't wait for a response, but his heavy emphasis on the word license warned they were going to be watching.

Who in heck told on Allison?

When she got home, Momma was sitting on one of the old chairs she left at the house, fanning herself with a magazine, her oversized white straw purse on her lap. She had grown heavier in the last few years and her lap spread to either side of her.

Jaudon remembered how shook up she'd been after walking in on Allison's so-called class in her living room. Seeing Momma made her remember the animal desire, the panic, the regret and added another shock: Momma was aging. The Beverage Bays were her life and her constant attention to them was taking a big toll on her. The Vicker family had been prominent in Rainbow Gap long ago. A road out in the country was named after a great-grandfather; Momma wanted that name to be prominent again.

Momma held an index finger up to her temple, like she was trying to remember something.

"You okay, Momma?"

Momma looked startled. "Why shouldn't I be?" Her eyes shifted down, as if she'd dropped her memory on the floor. She met Jaudon's eyes, blinked and barked, "Answer me one thing, Daughter. Why do U.S. Marshals think we have a criminal working for us?"

The hairs on Jaudon's arms rose. "You think I know? They came to my store too."

"And your part-time help was there?"

"Was and wasn't."

"Who is she?"

"Some girl who came in looking for a job."

"White girl?"

"Yes." Their argument about Momma's old-fashioned hiring practices was ongoing. What Momma had said to Pops about Olive Ponder, which she said within earshot of Jaudon, was that she expected everyone had a prerogative to learn from their mistakes. Jaudon had sworn on the Bible Olive was not a mistake.

"You'll see," was Momma's hissed response.

Jaudon remembered thinking, *We have a race riot of our own, here, between Momma and me.*

This day Momma wanted to know, "So your hippie took off when the government showed up?"

"What hippie? If you mean my part-timer, she wasn't there when they left. I took over her work. The store's fine."

"It takes some doing to set federal agents on a person. If it gets out we employed a criminal, if such a thing is reported in the papers, we can say good-bye to our reputation. It's another mark against us. I know some people who won't patronize your Bay because of the other person you hired."

"Mrs. Ponder is doing a great job."

"The better customers are going elsewhere and we'll be serving the dregs. Next thing you know, they'll start robbing us."

"Momma, quit talking that way. We're bound to hire a lemon here and there, but Olive Ponder is not one of them."

"It pains me to write out her check. If you think I'm going to pay the hippie for time put in since her last wages, you have another think coming."

"You're being so unfair."

"I know your daddy made you a manager. I told him it was too soon, you're still a baby with who-knows-what-all wrong with you affecting your judgment. I want to clear any hires until you grow up."

"But, Momma, it wasn't the part-timer they were after, didn't look a thing like her."

"Why in heaven's name did she run?"

Jaudon shrugged, arms out, to show she was stymied.

"I'll be doing the hiring out of the office from here on in. You give me the applications and I'll fill the jobs."

"That's so harsh, Momma. I do everything I know to prove my worth to you. I'm studying management this year. I'll be more knowledgeable about business when I'm done than you and Pops combined. Besides, it's too much for you. You're wearing yourself out."

"You're talking out of your hat, child. When your brother gets out of the service, I expect him to train alongside me to take over and hiring is one of the jobs he'll learn first. This company will be appreciated more with a man at the helm. A man who'll be producing my heirs once he comes home and finds a decent girl to marry."

Momma's plans knocked the wind out of Jaudon. She was speechless. Bat didn't care about the business that was her own heart and soul or he'd be home doing his job. What did Momma want her to be, one of those women who wears white gloves to church and lunches in the department store restaurant, trading Jell-O mold recipes before going home to watch game shows and produce heirs?

"And don't you go running to your daddy about this. You came into a drop more of his Vicker blood than you have my Batson blood. It makes you as gullible as him. He won't be running the drivers much longer, as soon as Bat gets home."

"Bat wants to re-up, Momma. He wants to put in twenty years and get retirement pay before he comes home."

"He never told me. Don't you be carrying tales behind his back."

"He's afraid to tell you, Momma, but it's what he wants. He's fond of the service."

Momma sat there looking around and steaming, her face scrunched up with thinking. The confusion she observed earlier took over Momma's face. Without a pause, she was on about a new pet peeve.

"I want you to get those pictures off the wall, you hear? March on Washington for aborting babies. What's gotten into you? Mobilize *against* the war? Has Bat seen them? Lord A'mighty, where you get these ideas, I don't know. I'm sure Berry doesn't go in for this. Not with her Gran riding herd on her."

Nothing in the world was going to make Jaudon say they were Berry's posters, with Berry's ideas.

"I'd close up this place until Bat returns and have you move in with me to keep an eye on you, but I need to make a good impression on neighbors and business associates at gatherings I have there."

Stung, she said, "This is our home, Momma. Can't we decorate it as we please?"

"This is Vicker land. Your ancestors' home, child. You can live in it as long as you respect it. I don't call what I'm looking at respectful. I ought to be getting rent from the lot of you."

Momma's eyes grew warmer and her face relaxed, as if she'd heard herself say the word child. "I don't propose to be hard on you, Daughter, but your father let you run wild while I put the long hours into creating a future for us all. I may be your mother, but I'm your employer as well, which means I care about you twice as much. If you get yourself mawmucked up, I want you to tell me about it. Is being a manager too much for you with your studies?"

"I want to be a manager, Momma. Go look at my store. It's shipshape and you know it."

"As long as you understand the business comes first. And, by the way, no more shorts at work and get rid of your chambray vest—it's worn and stained. We're getting to be important in this community. I'm enforcing the dress code. The bright blue jackets make us stand out and look professional, not like one of those shameful go-go bars. Wear yours."

"But it gets so hot in there. I have to stand in the cooler some days to dry off the sweat." She wasn't giving up the shorts. Let Momma go ahead and fire her. There was no way to air condition a big open hangar.

"Don't stay in the cooler unless there are no customers."

She was tired of this. Most customers were willing to wait a couple of minutes before tooting their horns. "Of course not."

"Some people will take advantage and help themselves. I see it happen."

Jaudon folded her arms. "Are we going to get some of those convex mirrors to reflect the whole store?"

"What do you need them for? You have eyes in your head."

"I caught kids creeping in on foot. They take bottles of Coke or boxes of cookies out of the cases."

"You insist on opening those cases at delivery. I told you to keep them shut."

She spread her arms in frustration. "It's so much faster if the boxes are already open, Momma."

"And our inventory is safe from youngsters' hands if they can't open the cartons."

"Unless it's company policy, I'll do it my way."

"Don't look to me if you have shrinkage problems. It'll come out of your pay."

"Most places give a bonus for keeping down the shoplifting losses—you dock pay. No wonder some of the Bays can't keep adequate help."

The blank, searching expression returned to Momma's eyes. Her hands never rested. She gave her head a slight shake. "They're hiring at the 7-Eleven, Daughter." She hefted her considerable bottom up from the chair.

Where was the slim younger Momma she first knew? She pledged never to put on weight like Momma's.

Momma took Jaudon's chin in her hand and seemed to search her face. "Remember, you represent an upstanding business in this community and you need to fit in, not shame us."

After Momma drove off in her Cadillac, Jaudon wandered out to the tree house for the first time in months. She realized, for Momma, the Beverage Bays—and her children—were nothing more than a means to make money so she'd never be left wanting again. For Jaudon, it was the rhythm of work, of the store, that she loved. Rolling the door up at dawn, pulling it closed at night; catching freight off delivery trucks, building product endcaps, bantering with the vendors, emptying boxes and breaking them down, stocking the shelves, the coolers, and the freezer. She loved the chats with customers. She loved closing out the drawer, tallying sales, checking inventory, mopping the floors, sweeping the driveway. If she had nothing else in this world, if she lost Berry, she had her work. Momma wasn't going to take the Beverage Bay from her; she'd fight, fight dirty if she was compelled to do so.

It occurred to her that Pops and Bat were as spineless as they were because they were afraid to stand up to a force as strong as Momma. She chastised herself, and pledged to be more daring.

CHAPTER TWENTY-TWO

Berry found Jaudon in the tree house on their now-mildewed mattress. "What all are you doing, angel?"

"Fixin' to give up."

She crawled under the table and lay with Jaudon, holding and rocking her without another word. It didn't take Jaudon long to recount her mother's unpleasant visit.

"Take my posters down? And how else can Olive prove herself?" said Berry. "Is this the land of the free or what?"

"She's trying to protect the business, Berry. You know the new convenience stores cropping up everywhere are trying to lure our customers. We can't have a scandal at our drive-thrus."

"It's discrimination, plain and simple," Berry said, at the same time trying to calm herself. "Your momma won't hire non-whites as it is and she's getting finicky with women?"

"She doesn't want to lose the business of people with money."

"White customers."

"Sometimes I think you don't remember who my family is, Berry. The Vickers, Jaudons, and Batsons eked out a living in the strawberry fields or the canning plants or the phosphorous mines. Momma is the first businesswoman on that side of the family. She keeps to the timeworn ways, unbefitting as they may be, like making me look girly."

When it came to the way Momma treated Jaudon, Berry always turned as cross as a bag of weasels. She ran a finger above Jaudon's cheek. The growth was noticeable, but not very. Customers might see it in certain light. She knew Jaudon continued to be sensitive to the quick about this, and it might hinder her passion to succeed in business. That would be tragic.

"Your momma could be kinder."

"She's meaner than chicken poop."

Mad as she was, Berry drew on her scanty store of wisdom. "Goodness gracious, angel. Gran says that everyone, Momma included, is put in our lives for a reason. We have to serve our purpose in the time that we have."

"I have to forgive her again?"

"No, I do. It's a way of being kind to ourselves. Who gets hurt most by anger?"

Jaudon nodded. "You sound old as the hills when you say things like that, Berry."

Berry smiled. "I sound that way to me too when Gran's words come from my mouth. I think what we need to know is out there for the taking. I'm trying to learn to listen for it."

"Momma never listened. She's accused me in the past months of hiring from that pack of crazy feminists."

"You told her, didn't you, that they're my friends?"

"We don't need you in trouble too. Meanwhile, she's taking the hiring away from me."

"She doesn't trust you? Her own daughter?"

"I'm messed up. That's what she thinks."

Berry took a deep breath. "Will getting rid of your duck fluff change her attitude toward you?"

Jaudon's face flushed red. "Are you agreeing with Momma?" She grabbed Berry's wrist and thrust it away from her face. "'Cause if you are, I'll go get this taken care of tomorrow."

"Mother Nature put it there for a reason we aren't privy to."

"You know what? She made a mistake growing it on me. I wish people would stop treating me like a freak. Or I need to admit that I am a freak. You'd be better off without me."

"And your momma might think better of you if I wasn't around. I'm what's wrong with you. I should be taking Gran and moving out. I need to let you go."

"The hell you do!" Jaudon said.

"Language!"

"You eat your words. You're my good influence, according to Momma. I can't live without you, Berry Garland, and Gran's better to me than Momma. Don't go away. Please, Berry."

Berry shrank from her. She tried to twist her wrist out of Jaudon's grasp.

"Take it back," howled Jaudon, holding on.

Berry forgot to breathe. She wasn't able to breathe. "Jaudon, let go. Spider!"

A fully two-inch wolf spider dropped from the ceiling to the floor next to the mattress.

"Jaudon, do something!"

Jaudon scrambled backward out from under the table, sorrows forgotten. The spiders were a fact of life, but Berry never got used to these huge brown ones that kept down the earwig, fly, and mosquito populations in the tree house.

"Heck, you know they're not poisonous, Berr." She checked around her for signs of other spiders, always vigilant for the hourglass marking of deadly gray recluses.

"I saw somebody the day after she was bit, as itchy and red like she rolled around in poison ivy. She said it itched and burned worse than fire ants."

"Oh, for land's sake. If she carried on, it must have been one of those genteel high school hussies you were running with."

"They were not huss—"

Jaudon caught the spider in a Potato Stix can she kept for that purpose. She threatened Berry with it.

Berry shrieked. "Don't do that, Jaudon. You know I'm afraid to death of them."

Jaudon took the can to the entryway and shook it until the creature loped away, all eight legs, eight eyes, and wooly body.

Berry stood and pressed herself against Jaudon. "My hero. You're so kind to varmints."

"Hey, you're the vegetarian. They deserve to live."

Berry gave Jaudon a playful push out of her embrace. "You're learning." She was finished arguing; it wore her out. "You come on in the house, Jaudon. Gran's heating up her barbecue sauce from the other day to put on your frankfurters."

"Store bought buns?"

"Of course not. She mixed up a batch of cornbread and she's fixing greens too."

"What are we waiting for, Georgia gal?" Jaudon herded her out the tree house door. She'd give chase to Berry any day, way up to the Georgia border, or farther.

After dinner, Gran cleared them out of the kitchen to mash some guavas for jam. There were moments Gran was as bossy as Berry since recovering from her losses, thought Jaudon. They grabbed their homework and sat on either side of the cypress turned-leg table that had served generations of Florida Vickers. After a while, Berry realized that Jaudon was chewing on a pen, staring into space.

"What is it, angel?"

Jaudon took on a hound dog look and turned away. "She hasn't given up talking about Bat running the company someday. He never did tell her he didn't want to come home."

"All this because of Allison? You see? I make trouble for you, like you predicted."

Jaudon kept her head turned. Her face grew damp from tears. "You had nothing to do with it. The problem is I'm female. Momma thinks a company needs a man in charge."

"What is the matter with that woman? Doesn't she know she's a female?"

She was wrong to think it, but Berry wished Momma would find a bottomless sinkhole of her own. She and Eddie Dill were welcome to be hateful together from the spirit world. Because here it was, ignorant bigotry on their doorstep again. Didn't Jaudon's momma see the harm she was doing Jaudon?

Her stomach churned from distress. "I'll go talk to Momma," she offered.

Jaudon frowned vigorously.

"Or I'll ask Gran to talk to Momma, angel."

"Why? I'll still be me. Momma will still be her cross self. I need to remember she went hungry as a kid after her father died in the phosphate mine. Her momma had to support the whole family on nothing but her earnings at the strawberry plant. Until they replaced half the women with their machines."

"She doesn't need to be nervous about losing Pops to the mines. That can't be turning her sour."

"She gets worse and worse. If fear can make you so hard, I guess you never lose it."

"Yes," said Berry, thinking, *my poor castoff lover*. Jaudon's sadness about her mother had to be as heavy as her own about Ma and Pa never calling for her. She was as much of a castoff as Jaudon for that matter, though Jaudon's boyishness was the way she was made and her Pops sure loved her.

"I guess Momma was always obstinate. When the plant laid her off was when she got her allergy to eating strawberries. She quit high school and walked the five miles to work at the big produce stand they used to have up on Buffalo Road. It's where she learned to run a store. She refused to bring children into the world unless she could feed them, so Bat and me are lucky we got born at all. Having enough means everything to her."

"I don't care. Your momma needs to be dragged into the mid-twentieth darned century. She's insulting to you."

"Makes me want to grow out my hair so the people who think I'm a man will mistake me for a long-haired draft dodger."

Berry said with a grin, "You turn peace activist and the president will change his mind about war quicker than poop through a goose." She got up for colas and they took them outside to the porch before bed. Zefer followed.

The oaks were leafed out and made soft swishing sounds in the rising wind. Jaudon was just able to discern a pair of ducks on the ground below the pond bench, bills tucked under their wings, sleeping. Berry's arm was damp from humidity where she touched it.

The moonlight shone on the tree house. "You think the full moon brought this mess? Momma carrying on, me fighting with you."

Berry lay a hand on Jaudon's and squeezed, quietly laughing. "We'll know if the coyotes start howling."

There were nothing but frogs and the vibrating growls of a gator on the pond. Zefer sniffed around, squatted, and rejoined them.

They sat on the swing, holding hands, looking at the luminous clearing around the house.

"Moonlight is different from any other light," Berry whispered. "It's got this dim ash-colored glow like the light comes up from inside the earth—from within, not without."

Jaudon put a finger to her lips. "There's a truck stopped out on Eulalia Road."

Zefer growled. Berry held on to her collar.

Jaudon half stood and squinted toward the big pickup, a diesel. She strained for a sight of it like a scared rabbit on its hind legs. They heard it bump in and out of the ditch that lined Eulalia, then scrape through the ragged sow thistle, a new crop of pokeweed, scrub hickory, and spindly saplings before it stopped smack dab on Vicker property.

Two doors closed almost without sound. A flashlight shone through the dense scrub. Whispered cussing accompanied the sounds of people tripping over old stumps and storm-felled tree limbs. Clouds covered the moon and moved on as the winds picked up. Berry remembered the weatherman saying a tropical storm might graze them.

Jaudon's joints were achy, her sinuses throbbed from the change in atmospheric pressure. She reached inside the house and grabbed the shotgun from its rack where Bat hung it for their protection. She handed Berry a leash to hook up Zefer.

"Should I get Eddie Dill's pistol?" asked Berry. Over the years they'd used it for target practice and kept it in working condition.

In a hoarse whisper, Jaudon said, "The shotgun should do the trick."

She and Berry followed an eager Zefer along the porch and around to the back steps, heading toward the hammock that hid Gran's trailer.

"Who in the world?" Berry whispered, close behind Jaudon.

"It better not be Allison coming out of hiding. If so, I'm running her off. She's leading the cops directly to our land."

Berry spoke in a low voice. "But how did they find her?"

"Same way they found her at the store. Somebody's talking."

"I don't even know where she went, Jaudon. If Eddie Dill was alive I'd blame him for tracking her down. If it's her, let me talk before you do anything." She intended to give Allison—or whoever—a piece of her mind. The nerve of the woman; Allison already agreed Berry had done her duty by letting her stay, and overstay, in Gran's trailer. Berry's sense of responsibility was complicated by the fact they were friends.

They waited at the edge of the porch, shotgun extended. Moments later, Cullie strode out of the soggy woods, Allison hurrying behind, Kirby sniffing between them. Zefer whinnied and almost pulled Berry off the porch in her eagerness to reach her playmate Kirby. Cullie's flashlight was off and they were watching their footing, not the porch. Allison glanced their way, cried out, and grabbed Cullie's jacket. The first heavy drops of rain fell.

"Are those our heroic Amazon warriors, champing at the bit to save us from the forces of evil?" Cullie called over the plummeting rain.

The wind was strong enough to lift Allison's hair across her face. A growl of thunder sounded. The lightning took its time to smite the sky some distance away.

"Is that where you've been, Allison? Still at Cullie's?"

"No one knew. Her place is off the beaten track."

"And my little coconut was with us, but she wasn't telling."

"Why are you here, Allison?" Jaudon challenged, standing her ground in the downfall.

"The deputies, they're down the street from Cullie's. It's pure luck we drove home a roundabout way and saw them. We have no place to go. We need some sleep and we'll be gone."

Cullie stood to her full height. "I'm storing everything at my sister's, suiting up my gallant steed Kirby, and driving Allison cross-country in my sister's car. We need to go to Four Lakes to pick it up, but we're too tired to start tonight."

"Didn't you think the police might follow you here?"

Cullie picked up the dog and held her close. Berry saw both Cullie and Allison were bedraggled and rattled.

"There's no way, Jaudo. We sat in the Dairy Queen parking lot eating Dilly Bars and watching out for them. Kirby won for eating the most Dilly Bars."

Jaudon saw that Allison's slight, wet body was shaking despite the muggy heat. The rain was hot.

"Easy, jujube," said Cullie. "We're going to be okay."

Berry couldn't abide sending them away and looked at Jaudon.

Jaudon couldn't abide upsetting Berry.

"Jujube? You call her jujube, like the candy?"

"You're jealous that you didn't think to call Berry jujube first."

Berry tried to stay calm. "Cullie, is your truck well-hidden?"

"I checked," Allison said. "You can't see it from the road."

"But you can see the tracks, you yo-yos." The male voice was muffled by the dense growth of tall bushes and trees. "Put the gun down, young man."

At the sight of the two deputies, guns drawn, Jaudon froze.

Cullie didn't waste a minute. "These women haven't done anything, officer. They were asking us to leave. We'll be on our way."

Jaudon held on to the gun, loosely, and pointed at the ground, as if she was about to drop it. It wasn't loaded. She had a plan for getting rid of these cops while Berry and their friends escaped.

"We decide who broke the law. Put that gun down. Now," commanded the cop. Both officers wore rain jackets and plastic hat protectors.

She stopped planning and set the gun in front of her. Darn Allison and Cullie, didn't they know what was going to happen? She at least wasn't going to let the dog catchers take Kirby to the pound.

Berry was annoyed at Allison. She had people at home to help her. Times like this she'd love to have a ma, a pa on her side. It must make a difference to be brave when you had family in reserve. What privilege did she think she was entitled to, dragging trouble to their doorstep?

Gran's light went on. "You all right out there, Berry? Jaudon? Come on in out of that storm."

Wind drove the rain toward them. The ground was dissolving to muddy sand beneath their feet. Zefer sat on a step, her ears bent, as if she was trying to keep the rain out.

One of the deputies answered. "We're with the sheriff's office, ma'am. Please keep away from the windows and stay indoors."

Gran ignored him. "Berry? You there?"

"Leave it go, Gran. Do what the deputy says."

"Come along, folks, nice and easy. We'll take a ride to the office."

"Not us." Berry set her hands on her hips. Gran needed protection, and she'd stand up for her if she had to use Eddie Dill's pistol to do it. "We haven't done a thing."

"We'll talk about that at the station."

"You can't arrest us for protecting our home. We didn't know who was out here."

One of the big oaks creaked above them. Jaudon looked up at it, rain in her eyes. She'd all along meant to find the power saw and take the heavy limb down before a storm did it for her.

"So you know these..." He looked Allison and Cullie up and down. They were drenched, Allison's long skirt hanging slack, little waterfalls cascading from the brim of Cullie's bowler. "Flower people? They may put up with trash in Tampa, but out here in the county? Nuh-uh."

"You're saying I know them, not me." Berry walked toward the house and shouted, "Gran, call a lawyer."

"Wait up. Cullie, give me Kirby." Jaudon almost caught herself, but the words spilled out. She'd confirmed an association with the fugitives. "Gran can take care of her." She stooped for the shotgun. "Can't leave this out in the damp. My brother's in 'Nam. He'd be mad."

"Leave the gun on the ground, mister."

She stood up, legs wide, fury pumping into her every vein. "Stop calling me mister and leave my property. I'm taking the gun and our dogs and going inside. Shoot me if you want."

Berry and Zefer started for Kirby. Wind blew raindrops like warm bullets, pelting them. The palm fronds whipped at the air, the giant oak branch ready to rend away from its trunk. Gran screamed bloody murder from the window and Jaudon snatched up the gun.

In their distraction, visibility low, the deputies turned away from Allison and Cullie who dashed, carrying a dripping wet Kirby, to Jaudon's van. Allison knew the key was always in it. They were squealing onto the gravel road before the cops stopped struggling with Berry and Jaudon.

"Now we *are* taking you in," said the tall deputy, "for resisting arrest, aiding in the escape of a federal fugitive, and threatening a law enforcement officer with a firearm."

"We never did. You going to arrest Gran too, for calling a lawyer?"

He grabbed Jaudon by the upper arm and spun her toward the brick barbecue, handcuffs out, but he either didn't know his own strength, or didn't realize that Jaudon was less solid than she looked.

"Hey, Shrimp." The other deputy stepped between them. "She's just a kid. Back off and stay out of trouble this time."

She tried to catch her balance, but the thrust was so strong, the mud so slippery, she lost her balance and fell hard, pushing the center of her ear into the corner of the barbecue. The rusted grate flipped up and landed on her exposed neck, leaving a gash.

"*Jaudon.*" Berry hollered when Jaudon didn't move. In horror, she covered her mouth with one hand, watching blood surface from the gash. She tried to go to Jaudon, but the other deputy pulled her toward the road.

"I'm a nurse, leave me go. Her carotid artery might be cut." Was this happening because she abandoned the church's God for her own?

Jaudon couldn't tell what was going on. She had an instant, nauseating headache. The pain in her ear was quick, but monstrous. The tall deputy helped her stand and stay up. Berry's hand touched her neck and came away bloody.

"What's the matter?" The short deputy smirked and pointed at the side of her head. "Cut yourself shaving, mister?"

"Lay off, Shrimp," said the other deputy.

"Wait." She turned away from her deputy to a clump of grayish-green cudweed and vomited onto the wooly leaves. She held her head. The pain was calming down, but was there was a bug in her ear, or a pebble? She was wet to the skin and shuddering.

Berry yelled before they were put into the police car. "Call that lawyer, Gran."

Jaudon tried to shout, but her words came out feeble. "Don't tell Momma!"

She fell into the backseat on Berry. One of the deputies said, "We know the fugitive woman is a homosexual. From the looks of you"—he eyed Jaudon—"you are too. Is this your lady lover?"

"Their kind should be cannon fodder over in 'Nam," said the nasty partner.

"True. We ought to send you to fight in the jungle instead of our decent boys."

Berry was frightened, worried about Jaudon, peeved at these lawmen, but at last she was able to lean on the Great Spirit, bathe in its calm, and smile encouragement at her battered Jaudon. "Your neck stopped its bleeding," she told her. "It wasn't as bad as I feared."

Jaudon knew Berry was praying for them. They might be on the way to the sheriff's office in the path of a tropical storm, but that big tree limb was holding so far and Allison was for once—and she hoped like heck for all—rousted from Vicker land. They must be halfway to Cullie's sister's car, about to set out for the West Coast. She wished they'd take this ear pain with them.

❖

It was a nightmare: They sat wet and cold in the air conditioned sheriff's office. Jaudon had her arms folded on the table and her head down. A medic had come in and cleaned up her neck and ear, but it was all she could do not to scream with the ongoing pain. The deputies called in Momma and Gran and Pops.

Momma blew her top first at the deputies, then at Jaudon, and, when Berry told her she was to blame for befriending Allison, at Berry and Gran. Gran got up in Momma's face and told her off. If Jaudon had felt better, she would have cheered for Gran.

They were there until three in the morning. Initially, they tried to claim they didn't know anything or anyone involved, including Allison, but the shorter deputy reminded Jaudon that she knew their names.

"What in the world were you girls thinking?" demanded Momma.

"Now, Momma," Pops said. "Watch your blood pressure."

"They weren't thinking, Wayne and Jessamine," said Gran. "They were doing a good deed. Friends ask one another to help out and these two are generous to a fault."

The lawyer was behind closed doors with the sheriff himself. Momma and Pops left the room.

Every time Berry tried to speak, Gran took one hand and Jaudon the other, to silence her. Jaudon thought, *The truth is not what we need just now*.

Allison, Berry once told Jaudon, said being caught helped expose what was going on. Jaudon answered that Berry was welcome to risk her career and reputation if she wanted, but more was at stake. The state of Florida could jail them for being together the way they were. Momma would never forgive her for sullying the family name and business. Pops's heart might fail. Bat would come home to nothing. She'd be separated from Berry.

A phalanx of noise came down the hallway.

Jaudon saw Berry's hands shaking and steeled herself to show no more weakness. "That sounds like those antiwar demonstrators we passed on the way in."

"I recognize the chants—Rigo planned to be there. He can't have been arrested. He said his dad is volcanic when he's mad."

The protesters passed. They heard new voices.

"Is that Momma out in the hallway?" Jaudon stuck an index finger in her ear. "I can't make out what they're saying over this ringing."

"Shh." Berry leaned forward, listening. "She's arguing with the deputies. Telling them they're picking on us because they can't catch their bad girl."

Jaudon drummed her knees with the flats of her hands and swiped at her head to stop the buzzing. "They're going to be sorry they messed with Momma."

"She is boilin' mad. Your Pops is accusing them of beating on his baby girl."

Jaudon's headache was reviving her nausea. The buzzing sound seemed louder. She clenched her eyes shut against the light. It was their own fault if she dirtied their room. She swallowed hard.

Berry was looking at Jaudon's eyes. "Angel? You look poorly."

They were locked in, but not handcuffed. Berry moved closer to Jaudon.

"Keep away, Berry. You don't want them thinking that about us."

"No, you stay idle. Your eyes are funny. How hard did you hit your head?"

"My ear is what I hit."

"Isn't your ear attached to your head, silly? The emergency guy said it bled outside and in. Look at that, Gran—the bandage is red again and he told us to keep it dry. I'm mad enough to tear someone's head off."

Though her face was blurry to Jaudon, she watched Berry's struggle to banish her exasperation: the closed eyes, the slow expansion and deflation of her chest.

There were paper cups of water on the table. Berry and Gran used those along with Jaudon's back pocket bandana to clean off crusted blood from her face and chest.

"I don't like the looks of this ear."

"Me neither, Gran. We need to carry Jaudon to a doctor."

"Aw, heck, you two, I'll be fine." The dizziness hit again and she laid her head down. She was being growly. It was the pain, she decided.

Berry returned to reporting. "The lawyer's in the hallway, trying to calm your momma down."

After a period of murmuring, the door opened. It was the lawyer. "How bad are you hurt, Miss Vicker?"

Berry held up the bloody bandana. He looked at Jaudon.

She turned her uninjured ear to him. "Say that again?"

The lawyer yelled, the sound startling in the tiny room. "Are you hurt?"

"I'm queasy, to tell you the truth. There's a buzzing in my ear that won't quit and it hurts a mite."

"I'll get you released to go to the emergency room as quick as I can. Sit tight."

Berry put her arms around Jaudon and held her.

"I smell of barf," Jaudon said.

"Shh. Lean on me, angel."

As the attorney shut the door he raised his voice at the police. "Are you dingbats aware how badly my client is injured? She may have lost her hearing. Why didn't you call an ambulance? You'd think they were out pitching fits in the streets like the last group you pulled in. They were on their own property, protecting it. I'm going to sue your whole dang posse. Didn't you learn the error of your ways during the riots in '67?"

Berry said, "You have to admire lawyers. They get things done."

Gran made an unpleasant face. "I don't have to at all. We should have been at the hospital long ago."

Jaudon got off her chair and lay on the wood floor. The dizziness eased a bit.

Berry was cross-legged on the floor with Jaudon's head in her lap when the short officer came to release them. Jaudon refused an ambulance, but let him pull her up. She held the bloody bandana over her bandaged ear and shuffled along between Berry and Gran, behind Momma and Pops, not her jaunty self at all.

In the vestibule, the lawyer explained that Berry and Jaudon were not under arrest because the sheriff didn't have a shred of proof that the girls knew a federal warrant had been issued for Allison, or that they hid the fugitive, or intended to prevent Allison's arrest. They had nothing but a tip from an unnamed member of the public.

Berry thought this was the type of sneaky thing Eddie Dill used to do, hoping for a reward. Or maybe a jealous Lari. Was one of the newer women's group members an undercover cop? Had one of them told a disapproving husband? They talked about the need for silence, but she saw how dimwitted women could be around their men. Poor Gran, for one.

Allison was right—someone had been watching her from the woods.

After work the next day Jaudon poured iced tea and swallowed aspirin. She jumped when Berry appeared at her side. "I didn't hear you come in."

"Stop stirring for a minute, angel. That ear looks grisly. Hold up." Berry used a paper napkin to pat inside Jaudon's ear. "We're going back to the emergency room."

"But I'm tired."

"You've never been tired before in your life. You have an injury and maybe an infection and it's taking all your energy to fight it. No telling what else it'll do to you. I'll drive. Bring that tea with you."

"Jiminy, Berry. It's one thing after another. Is our whole life going to be this brambly?"

"You mean, perfect despite a few bumps in the road?" Berry hugged her. Ever since the ride in the deputies' car, she'd kept the calm of relying on the Great Spirit for longer and longer periods of time. "I am so happy every day, Jaudon, to be with you, studying what I want, living in your Pops's house, having friends. We need to stop the infection before it sneaks into your brain like a snake in a bird's nest or knocks out the rest of your hearing."

"Knock out my hearing? It better not. I need to hear my customers."

"And not your wife?" Berry was teasing, in her quiet, coy way.

Jaudon lifted her off the floor in a crushing embrace. "I love you, my Georgia gal. No way will I settle for not paying attention to you, if you have to bang me over the head with a rusty skillet to get my attention."

The hospital wasn't busy at that time on a weeknight. Jaudon was taken to an examining room and Berry went with her, telling the nurse they were best friends. Jaudon had suggested she claim kinship, at least cousin—she might need to hire on at the hospital someday—but Berry would not lie to save her soul. She imagined fighting to stay at Jaudon's side if she had to, but she would not lie. Her quiet, polite insistence did the trick.

They left two hours later with a referral. The ER physician gave Jaudon antibiotics. He didn't find signs of a fracture, but said she'd definitely been concussed. After a serious lecture, he called an ENT guy he knew. He would see her the next day. Against Momma's wishes, Pops always insisted the company provide health insurance because so many employees were relations of one sort or another.

"I don't have time to be seeing specialists," she said the next morning, although Olive was covering for her.

Berry *tsk*ed. "Neither do I. Now get in the van."

The specialist told them Jaudon had a ruptured eardrum, without a doubt caused by that fall against the concrete step. Bacteria had been able to quickly invade the middle ear and start the infection. He assured them the antibiotic was designed to clear that up and ruptured eardrums typically healed on their own. He sent them off with a follow-up appointment for a hearing test which Jaudon didn't intend to keep.

"I don't need some test to tell me whether I can hear or not. The pain isn't bad," she told Berry. "He said the rest was going to heal up, remember?"

"Jaudon, you can't hear out of that ear."

"Well, what are they going to do? Sew it up? They're not sticking anything in there. I'm a quick healer. Give it time. Nursing school makes you think we need to go to a doctor for every cut and sneeze."

Berry sunk her chin down. There was no arguing with her bullheaded beloved. She got that from Momma Vicker. From Pops she learned her cavalier way of ignoring her health. Jaudon always put Berry and the store before herself. There wasn't much for Berry to do other than pray for her. And for Allison and Cullie. She looked up. "The stars are out."

"What?"

She pointed skyward. "Stars." Her voice was louder than she meant it to be.

"Nothing wrong with my sight," said Jaudon in a huff.

Berry smiled, but thought, *This is going to be a trial for both of us.*

Chapter Twenty-three

When Jaudon and her headache arrived at the Beverage Bay the next morning, Rigo was waiting outside in a white shirt, tie, tropical weight trousers, shined shoes, and that outrageous curly head of red hair.

She was doing a lot better, but the buzzing and difficulty hearing persisted. "Rigo, we don't serve breakfast here. Or did you run out of ciggies?"

Rigo answered, "Actually, I was told there is no smoking on the job."

Her hearing was never going to improve. She was so nauseous that first day after their arrests she was glad that Berry had insisted on the emergency room. They hadn't yet picked up the van from Cullie's sister's place and Cullie's truck had been impounded. Berry took the bus to school.

She asked Rigo to repeat what he said and turned her normal ear toward him. "On what job? You don't need to work."

"It was either this or my father was going to sneak me into Cuba to give me experience on a plantation. He thinks the US is going to rescue his lands. He also thinks that because he's always worked like a dog, I should too."

She was setting up the cash register in anticipation of opening when she put two and two together. Cousin Cal had completed his military obligations and Jaudon found him dribs and drabs of hours at her store. But last week Cal found a full-time motorcycle repair job. "Wait—you're replacing Cal? You're working here?"

Rigo's words were muffled again and she leaned her head toward him.

"I interviewed with your mother yesterday. Definitely snowed her. Told her my last name is Italian, not Spanish."

"I didn't know you had it in you to act straight."

"You kidding? In my family?"

Jaudon had a good chuckle, imagining Rigo playing lumberjack or a quarterback.

"So Momma's plan to do the hiring ricocheted," she said, surprised at her enormous relief. She massaged her head with both hands. *This headache won't go on forever*, she assured herself, *not with Rigo here, making me laugh.*

"She informed me I was to report here when you do until I'm trained. My classes are at night this term, the same as yours, and I'm free weekend days."

As she showed Rigo how to operate their cash register, she realized what was bothering her. "How did you know Momma was hiring?"

"A little birdie told me you might have lost your help and weren't feeling so hot."

"Did the birdie have a name I might recognize?"

Rigo rounded up the loose paper clips on the counter and handed them to her. She pushed them down into an empty Band-Aid tin. "When I called to tell Berry I managed to avoid arrest—imagine being arrested for marching for peace—she gave me the rundown on your troubles, both with the cops and the store."

"I thought you were in that demonstration. We were there in the police station too."

"Berry told me. It wasn't possible to talk to you anyway."

"And Momma hired you with a criminal record?"

"I wasn't locked in the jailhouse. The cops wanted us off the street. They interviewed us and anyone under twenty-one had to have a parent take us home."

"Is this your father's way of punishing you, making you earn your living?"

Rigo's skin was a tawny shade, but with the heat of embarrassment, he flushed like a true redhead. He was saved by the entry of a car and fled to the driver's window. It was a gray-haired couple who came in once a week for their supply of pilsner. They kept Rigo chatting for a while.

He hustled to the counter and stopped at Jaudon's accusation. "So Berry put you up to this."

"Ah…"

"You are the worst liar, Rigo. I swear, you'd call a puddle an ocean if I wasn't looking at it."

"I needed a job, I swear."

"And Berry was looking for a bodyguard for me. What will you do if the police come again?"

"Get hold of Berry or your momma."

"Jiminy. Momma's in on this?"

"She told me you can't hear a thunder peal if it goes off on the side of your damaged ear. I have instructions from Berry to do all the ladder work and anything else that involves balance and heights."

"I see the doctor again next week. I expect it'll fix itself before I see him. If not, I'll wring Allison's and Cullie's scrawny feminist necks. I don't suppose you heard any news of them?"

"You think those women will take me, the male oppressor, into their confidence? No, I haven't picked up any news, but Berry asked some time ago if I might hide Allison. Oh, missy, I told her, you know I can't do that. My father's applying for his US citizenship. Bad enough I got caught in the demo. The US should want someone who's paying taxes on his smoke stores, but no, they're afraid Cubans are communists so they're giving him a hard time." Rigo rolled his shoulders and shook himself as if to be rid of these worries. "Thank God I didn't take Allison in, after what Berry told me happened at your place."

"Your father doesn't mind you working for a competitor?"

"You must be joking. Look what you sell." Rigo pulled out a pack of cigarillos, Corona and Dutch Masters tubes, and some Swisher Sweets cigars. "My father's a cigar snob. He won't let any of these in his store. I'll take you there sometime."

As they worked, it was plain people enjoyed Rigo. He managed to temper his queenliness. *We'll see how long that lasts*, she thought. She watched him carry one six-pack on each shoulder to a waiting driver, a woman, who tipped him with some coins. No wonder Momma hired him. She'd seen girls drool over his boyish charms; she was worried about some of the rougher men who came in because they were the ones Rigo seemed to warm to most.

They finished with the noon rush and sat behind the counter on two tobacco roller chairs Pops bought when one of the cigar factories closed. A fat fly circled their heads. Jaudon swatted at it when it passed her good ear. Rigo grabbed a spray can of insecticide and drowned it in the air.

"How's your home life since Allison got you two in hot water?"

"I wish, Rigo, feminism was never invented."

"Don't you want to be equal?"

"I'm equal enough—to men. It's those women Berry's involved with. They act all biggity if I come home and walk in on one of their get-togethers. It could be that the sight of me reminds them that Berry and I are an item. Berry says they were miffed when they found out Allison was family, as miffed as if she'd betrayed them."

"None of them are gay?"

"Cullie. And Lari of course."

"That bitch. She's in with them? I should have known."

"She doesn't come to meetings at our place anymore."

"So they don't know about you and Berry."

"They do, but don't want to. I'd love to walk in and give Berry a great big kiss on the lips in front of them to shock some sense into their heads."

"Why don't you, hon?"

"Aw, Rigo, I won't do that to Berry—they're her friends."

"What's their appeal for our Berry?"

"She doesn't care for some of the things men do—hitting women, fighting wars, cementing over farmland, and running everything. She thinks women might do a better job."

"So that's what feminism is about. I'm inclined to agree with her. But I can't abide the man-hating part. Some men treat women like tornados in a trailer park. Not me. To me, they're ladies."

"Berry says that's demeaning too. Treating women as if we're born fragile makes us think we can't do for ourselves. We're capable, she says, of sitting at a table without someone shoving a chair under our rear ends."

"Well, excuse me for my good manners. How do you live in the same house with so many rules?"

"I keep hoping she'll boomerang to her old self one of these days. We seem so far apart. Where's my innocent Berry? This women's politics thing is as strict as her family's old religion." Jaudon placed a hand over her ear to stop the buzzing—her hand came away wet. The ear continued leaking. Aw, heck, she thought. "I do love Berry for having principles and sticking to them."

Behind the shelving area, across the building from them, a jar crashed to the floor. It was so loud, Jaudon heard it over the buzzing. They looked at each other.

"Those darn kids."

She started to hustle over there, but Rigo stopped her. "Go look after your ear. This is my job now," he said.

Jaudon waited about fifteen seconds before following him.

"Easy, boy."

Rigo was skipping backward along the aisle and collided with her. Allison was pummeling him with their gear.

"Quit that," Jaudon called, propping Rigo up.

Cullie dropped her fists. She looked Rigo up and down. "Who *is* he?"

"What?" Jaudon strained to hear. "He works here. Let him alone."

She saw him wink, smile, and extend his pinkie finger, complete with sparkling ring. Cullie's eyebrows went up and, behind Allison, she copied him, down to the wink.

Allison asked, "How do you know he's not a plant?"

Rigo planted a hand on his hip, tapped his foot, and looked to the heavens. Once again, out of Allison's sight, Cullie did the same.

"Rigo is a close friend of ours. He belongs here." She emphasized the word *he*, to get Allison's goat.

By this time, Cullie and Rigo were mirroring each other's every move, as if dancing. They bumped shoulders and broke out laughing. Jaudon joined them.

"I loved this woman at first sight." Rigo snaked an arm around Cullie's shoulders. He turned to Allison. "And I'm here to protect Jaudon."

A black car with a tall antenna braked sharply, in the way of the city police. Allison and Cullie, dog in arms, snuck out of sight.

Jaudon's heart beat double time, but it was construction guys on break. She served them cold bottles of soda.

"Call if you need me," she told Rigo. He loved waiting on construction workers. By the rear exit, she found Allison and Cullie with a small selection of food.

Cullie gazed at her filthy white sneakers. "We wrecked my sister's car."

"Aw, heck, Cullie." What pitiful dopes, she thought, teary at their follies. She was tired of being mad at Allison and her heedless altruism. Cullie was too infatuated to be held responsible for her dumb decisions, if they were decisions at all, but she was drawn to Cullie and wanted to be friends. It was almost funny, the scrapes they got themselves and everyone around them into. Funny like slapstick humor.

Kirby licked Jaudon's hand. She petted her and found that Kirby was a lot cleaner than either Cullie or Allison.

Cullie pressed her lips into a straight line. "I feel about two cents."

"We're hungry," said Allison.

Cullie nodded so hard her bowler went askew.

"We've been drinking from yard hoses, washing at culverts. Our money is gone. We eat fallen fruit and what we find in restaurant trash, use gas station bathrooms or the woods."

"You two are a sad sight. Take what you need," Jaudon said. She would pay for the goods herself.

"Thanky, thanky." Cullie held her two thumbs up.

"How far did you go?"

"We never left the Panhandle because we stayed on the shore roads and didn't speed."

"You weren't spotted?"

Allison's face looked pinched. "No. We drove after dark and slept on beaches during the day. This happened in a speck of a town called, of all things, Panacea, where we heard there was a peace encampment. We were headed to the beach when the guy drove out of a side street toward the Coastal Highway fast as a rocket. There was a stop sign, for goodness sake."

"He hit the engine compartment. Destroyed it." Cullie clapped together the heels of her hands. "We wore our seat belts and the car spun around like a kid's toy top, blowing out the tires. If he'd hit a second later, good-bye Allison."

"Why did you resurface here? You should have left the state."

"How could we sneak out without wheels?" The dog grumbled in Cullie's arms, struggling to climb down. "The local yokel who hit us was driving a muddy flatbed pickup with big wheels and a motorcycle in the bed, but he turned out to be too nice to stay mad at."

Allison said, "He apologized dozens of times."

"He went so far as to leave his bike with a neighbor and load the car on his truck—the neighbor came out with a set of steel ramps and helped push the car on and chain it down. The driver gave us his insurance information and drove the car way over to my sister's place."

"We asked to be let off on Route 19 because we were too tired to face her. We did call though," Allison added.

"Sure had me feeling sheepish." Cullie buried her face in Kirby's fur.

"We walked and hitched from 19."

Jaudon's eyes were caught by the flapping sole of Cullie's sneaker. She tilted her head to one side, more exasperated than sympathetic at the moment. "So you have no place to stay, no car, no money." She took bandages and Mercurochrome from the shelf and handed them to Cullie. "Nothing to show for your trip but blisters. Too bad the police have your truck."

"It's just as well. The truck drives okay for around here, but we'd have to have a tow truck follow us across the whole US of A."

Allison was in tears. "I thought I exposed a terrible crime—it turns out *I'm* the criminal. I don't know where to turn."

Rigo came up behind Jaudon and spoke by her good ear. "May I suggest an unthinkable solution? It's old fashioned, but it's tried and true. Why don't you dress as a hippie boy, Allison? Cullie, you can pass as is. That way you could hitch or borrow enough for bus fare."

Allison raised her eyebrows in what appeared to be horror.

"I'm all for it, jujube." Cullie squeezed Allison to her. "It's worked before."

"Only in the movies."

Rigo brushed the wrinkles from his sleeves and pants.

Jaudon reassured Allison. "You don't have to do it forever."

"Did you quit the pool cleaners, Cullie? Do you have a paycheck coming?" Jaudon hoped she hadn't thrown away her job for Allison.

"I told them I had a family emergency. They'll hold my paycheck, but I don't dare pick it up. If I cash it the police might catch on." She smiled as if she wasn't worried. "It's not the greatest job. The best part was being butch and threatening to drown anyone who dared pee in a pool."

"It's time to ask your pals for loans," Rigo said. "And one of them should go buy your tickets so you can stay hidden until the last second before the bus leaves. You'll need food money too. After all, you're fighting their battles for them. I can help with clothes—I never throw anything out so I have some that should fit Allison."

"But my poor little coconut can't go on the bus."

"You'll find a way, Cullie." Jaudon was at the end of her rope; she needed to rid herself of Allison. Hands on her hips she glared at the two of them. Berry had to call her feminist pals tonight and drum up cash for Allison lickety-split. Jaudon was fine with the woman when she wasn't wreaking havoc, but Berry's unquestioning loyalty was inexplicable—was Allison sort of a mother for Berry?

"I might be able to dig up fake IDs. I'll bring clothes to the store tomorrow."

"Like hell you will, Rigo. Meet them at your college. You two put your food in this poke and hike as far away from me and Berry as you can before I manhandle you out of my store."

Allison's face was angry, but as she opened her mouth, Cullie straightened from her accustomed slump and raised one of Kirby's paws in a salute. "Much obliged," Cullie said. Jaudon pointed to the door, trying to make a tough face.

Rigo reached in his pants pocket. "Here's my car keys. I'm off in a while. Keep out of sight in the car. You can stay at my place tonight if you can stand to."

When they were alone, she asked Rigo, "Well, Mr. Good Samaritan, where in tarnation are you going to find fake IDs?"

"My dad has contacts. He helps out people who manage to come over on the boats."

"Isn't that plum handy?"

"Don't knock it. You'd do the same for your family."

"But you're doing it for two feminists who think you're no better than a flying roach, Rigo."

"Remember, I'm on their side, whether they want me or not. Didn't they pull at your heartstrings? Cullie's the kind to lay down her life for that belle of a rabble rouser who got herself in over her head. As a matter of fact, I'll feed and dress them, buy them a pet carrier, and front the money so they can leave town on the first bus that will take the dog."

"If you ask me, Cullie would lay down her life for the dog first. She reminds me of a big lost puppy herself. A very smart, resourceful puppy with a heart as big as the Gulf of Mexico. As far as I'm concerned, Allison's adventures, nutty as they seem, are rescuing Cullie somehow, not the other way around. It's the people looking for their way who latch on to the lost."

She'd have to chew on that for a while to figure if she was one of the lost.

Chapter Twenty-four

Early Spring 1974

Cullie showed up outside the hospital where Berry was tutoring a freshman nursing student. Cullie leaned on Berry and Jaudon's van, smoking. Kirby was on a leash at her feet. A luminously red cardinal dashed into the tree above them.

"You're back," said Berry and reached for a hug, surprised at how excited and relieved she was to see Cullie.

"I'm back." Cullie dropped the butt and ground it out with the heel of pair of scratched and otherwise wounded cowboy boots. She bent to hug Berry. "As desirable and available as ever."

"Available?"

"You don't think one woman is enough for me, do you?"

Berry thought she heard anguish through Cullie's teasing. "Where's Allison?"

Cullie's words came in a mutter. "Still on Birthday Mountain."

"On her women's land, like she wanted?"

"Like she wanted." Cullie didn't meet her eyes.

"We haven't heard a word from you in all this time. How did you two manage at last to cross the country?"

"Rigo put us on the bus to Atlanta and Allison's family loaned her money to buy a used car. They're embarrassed enough by her love life and politics to want to jump between her and trouble before it reflects on them. The Millars are pretty much big shots in political circles up in Atlanta. Republican circles."

"Why didn't you stay out there with her?"

"I guess I'm not a West Coast sort of person. Say, any chance of a ride to my truck? Providing you left it parked in the woods by your house."

It was very plain on Cullie's face that whatever happened out there caused her to grieve. Berry wanted to console her, but stopped herself. Was it consolation she wanted to give Cullie? Had she detected a little spark in herself that shouldn't be there?

"Jaudon and I got your truck from the police and took it to your sister's place."

Cullie met her eyes for the first time. "They took my truck? You paid the impound fees?" Cullie leapt to hug Berry. "I'll pay you back, and then I want you to adopt me. You're too good to just be my friends—I want you for family."

Berry laughed. "I missed you all over the place, Cullie." She stopped herself from grabbing another hug. In no way did she want to be attracted to Cullie. Most of all, she didn't want Jaudon, or worse, Cullie, to catch on that she might be.

"Your sister's isn't on the other side of the moon, Cullie."

"But that was nice of you." Cullie took out another cigarette. When she lifted her eyes to Berry's, over the light of the match, they looked stricken. "Allison hated for me to smoke, said I stank when I did. I'm never giving these up, they're my freedom."

Berry wanted her to be part of their little family. "Sure I'll give you a ride, but I'd rather you were our sister than our daughter." She wondered if she might have a blood sister somewhere and if she'd ever know. "We need to pick up Jaudon from the store on the way. I know she'll be glad to see you too."

"I missed my buddy Jaudo. Thanks for the ride. I came in at the bus station and hitched over here."

"Come on. Have you eaten?"

"Not hungry."

"Heart ache much?"

"If hurt was food, you could feed the world."

"You knew she wasn't the kind to settle down."

"She told me it was different with me. The whole trip west we talked about starting out new, about me finding work and her staying underground on women's land. There aren't many pools needing cleaning in the woods of the Pacific Northwest."

Berry nodded, sad for Cullie and her lost hopes.

"A letter from Allison's lawyer came a couple of weeks ago. He told her the police offered to drop the charges against her if she'd give testimony about the militants and drop her lawsuit. Since Allison knew nothing about the radicals except what their apartment looked like, she could do them no harm. Her little bit of savings was running out. She agreed. The government promised to pay her round-trip plane fare to testify. Last I heard, the lawyer was negotiating."

"Why didn't she come home with you?"

"She half moved into her ex-lover's cabin a couple of months ago. They built it together when they first got to the land. I stayed in our cabin and tried to fit in. It was kinda hard, knowing she was a few yards away and wanted me to share her, but that's the new way: loving someone doesn't mean you own them."

"Oh, Cullie. I'm so sorry," she said, and she was sorry at the same time she was glad Cullie had come home. She chided herself. The last thing Cullie needed was someone with a crush on her. *At least*, she told herself, *I'm learning I'm as vulnerable as Jaudon when it comes to having my head turned.*

"Like you said, she's not made to settle down. I think she wanted to, but when she had the option, she didn't want to anymore. That weasel she reunited with worked on her since the day we arrived. We didn't talk much recently."

"You'll find someone closer to home, Cullie. A nice Florida woman."

Cullie thrust her chin upward and declared, "My leetle dogolette is company enough for me."

"Honey, you surely do need someone. Most of us do."

"Allison will come visit if she has to travel east to testify."

Berry watched Cullie's hopeful face, but held off lest she say stinging words herself. "I'm not looking forward to that day. Allison taught us a heap, but I don't like her hurting you one single bit." She started the van. "We better get on the stick. Jaudon will worry if I'm late."

On the way, Cullie was earnest for a change. "There is one thing I learned out there. I loved Birthday Mountain. What a slick notion: women's land. If only it was here. We'd call it Birthday Mountain East."

Berry envisioned Gran's land, where the sinkhole was. It was swampy and snaky, supported dozens of wild hogs, and there was that mushroom smell part of the year. It might be a start until they found a permanent spot. She couldn't see anyone living more respectfully on that piece of property than starry-eyed feminists.

"Now wouldn't that be a sight for sore eyes," she told Cullie. "Imagine, a women's health center for the women living on and visiting women's land. I hope you'll look into it."

Cullie patted Kirby on the head. "A place for dogs to run. Smokers' land too, not like out West."

"They're the smart ones, Cullie, the nonsmokers."

"Exactly what Allison told me."

"She was correct about that, though." Cullie looked disgusted so Berry changed the subject. "Did they have a shelter there for women assaulted by their men?"

"They were talking about that. I don't believe anything is set up yet."

"What a wonderful time to be alive," Berry said. "We don't have to scrape a living from the land and can concentrate on making the world a better place."

"You're such a sweet-tempered woman, Berry. I hope Jaudon treats you like a princess."

"Oh, she does. I'm not always sweet, but I'm working on it. There's no one I'd rather spend my life with. She is completely at sea about my involvement with you women, though."

"Jaudon doesn't get feminism?"

"She will, but presently she has other fish to fry. Jaudon's old-fashioned. She thinks protesting the war is unpatriotic. To her, civil rights activism is rabble-rousing, though she believes in the cause. Of course, Jaudon also believes in the War of Northern Aggression rather than the Civil War, but at the same time, she's ashamed of the South for keeping slaves."

"My folks are both teachers," Cullie reminded her, "and taught us different, but that's not an unusual attitude in someone from a Southern family that worked its way up from almost nothing."

"And that's okay, because she's a fair employer. Down the line, working at a Beverage Bay may be a fine start for some women we'll be working with. Jaudon makes the job playful."

As they arrived, Jaudon was locking up. She slid the van's side door open when she saw Cullie up front.

"Whatchu doing here?" she asked. Cullie looked in bad shape. Berry cut her eyes at her in the rearview mirror. *Don't ask*, was how she interpreted the look.

Jaudon patted the dog. "Has Kirby taken well to traveling?"

"My leetle coconut's always ridden to work with me. She confided she's thinking of buying me a Cadillac, Jaudo. Turns out she loves to travel, but thought the bus lacked the proper amenities for royalty like herself." Cullie scratched Kirby's back until the dog's foot started thumping on its own.

"Who wants to buy you a Cadillac, Cullie?" Jaudon asked. The van was noisy.

Cullie grinned. "Why Kirby does. So I can chauffer her."

"Oh, you're such a joker. I believed you."

Berry liked how soft-hearted Cullie was about animals, the way Jaudon was. She was attracted to Jaudon's qualities in Cullie. Both hard workers, both tomboys, both strong and purposeful, they plucked at her heartstrings and lifted her spirits when she was with them.

"I'd like to have a dog at work," said Jaudon. "Once upon a time they didn't care if there was a dog on store property. All of a sudden one day the health department decided dogs are going to pee on the raisin bran or some darn thing."

"Kirby is trained now. Allison insisted. She's such a country girl dog, there was no need before. On the job, she stays in the company truck unless the customer falls in love with her, and a lot of them do. Kirby never barks, never soils the truck, hasn't bitten any rich people—though I tell her to go ahead and do it."

"Hey, maybe we could get Zefer to go after thieving kids at the store." Her curiosity was getting the better of her. She was about to ask where Allison was when Berry's eyes squinted at her in the mirror again. She shut up. So Cullie and Allison didn't work out. No surprise there.

At Four Lakes Cullie climbed down, hugged them both, and went to her truck, patting it with fondness as she grinned their way. Her sister's front yard was thick with ferns, and Cullie made her way through them toward a little yellow bungalow with Indian bedspreads for curtains. She turned and called, "Me and Kirby are Florida women. Make me recollect that if I'm ever of a mind to traipse across the country after a woman again."

Chapter Twenty-five

"Are you embarrassed to be seen with me, Berry? If you are I'll try to act different and use a razor on my face." Jaudon's voice came out flustered.

They were in bed, Toby on top of Berry's legs, kneading a clump of sheet. It was a Tuesday morning, their one late day this week. "Why on earth?"

"Momma's on a tear about it."

"Stop that down there, angel." Berry swatted at her hand. "I'm trying to think."

"You are a most beautiful individual from head to toe, my Georgia peach."

Would Momma ever stop tormenting Jaudon? Jaudon was hiding her face, her hands twisted tight together, but Berry saw it in her mind's eye. Open, like Pops's face, with his sturdy bones. She had no pictures of her own ma or pa. They all burned up in the sinkhole fire. Gran said she was a thorough mix of both parents, sugar and butter.

Now that Jaudon was grown, her long square jaw, full lower lip, and broad nose made her face interesting. With that always overgrown, seldom combed sandy hair and tanned skin, she could be one of the Beach Boys singers, surfing her days away. Instead, she was a woman who had to fit the mold if she wanted to get by in life, but Berry accepted that Jaudon needed to go her own way. She caressed Jaudon's cheek with her fingertips.

Berry silently pledged to do anything to protect her Jaudon from the schoolyard bullies who'd become her customers, business associates, employees, and from herself, because Jaudon continued to raise her fists as often as she joked her way out of belittling. She saw these so-called grownups bully in new ways and use Jaudon's gender against her. Rigo talked about passing as a straight man; Jaudon refused to pass as a normal woman. As strong and testy as she was, she was more vulnerable than any male, straight or not.

Even the feminists asked about Jaudon. Was she really all woman? What did Berry see in her? It made her fly off the handle every blessed time, close to shrieking in an effort to make them understand their insensitivity and how they browbeat a different-looking woman and lesbians with their dismissive distrust. They reminded her of the schoolgirls she used to pal around with.

They complained about how their men treated them and how frustrating it was to make men see what oppression does to women. Little by little, the straight women seemed to accept that they treated lesbians the same way men treated women, but insisted they needed to hide the lesbians in the movement to be taken seriously. Nationally, they saw what was being called the second wave of feminism catching on. Friends sent them political tracts and newsletters from New York, San Francisco, and Washington, DC.

Donna Skaggs had quoted Betty Friedan who called lesbians in the women's movement a *lavender menace* and a radical named Susan Brownmiller refuted that position, accusing Freidan of manufacturing a lavender herring.

Berry came home from their last meeting with stories to tell Jaudon.

"Lari sat the whole time with her eyes half closed, smiling her high-and-mighty smile, and pointed out that a huge percentage of the movement consists of what she called women loving women. Then Cullie added that she'd been in a gay women's consciousness raising group out West. She dropped to her knees, hands folded in supplication, and begged for us to start one here."

Jaudon was half reading a textbook, but she guffawed at Berry's description of Cullie's antics.

"I asked her, why should we segregate ourselves? We have scant leftover energy to spread around. Can you guess what Lari answered?"

Jaudon knew without thinking. "To meet other lesbians, why else?"

"That person peeves the life out of me, Jaudon, and not only because of the way she tested you, tested our love. Meanwhile, Cullie was there in her pool-boy clothes, stained shorts and a company polo shirt, looking every inch the classic example of a gal who makes the others suspicious. She told Lari and me that those straights are too worried about women like us in their midst and too interested in what we do when we're alone together."

"I told them we'd be stronger if all kinds of women bunched up and focused on women's health, but Lari and Cullie want dances and lesbian land and feel-good groups." She tilted her head the way she always did when she met an obstacle. "There's a gap in the women's movement, don't you think?"

"Tell me?" Jaudon rested on one elbow, watching her think.

"Women make up over half of this country. That's millions and millions of people. We should be able to make changes, but we're too divvied up. Some women are horrified that we want to be able to make our own decisions. They don't see what's in front of their noses, how men protect one another at the expense of women. Among feminists, there's a whole split between women who love men and women who love other women. Between poor women and women doing well. Between women of color and us pale faces. It shouldn't be so hard to close those gaps, but it is."

Jaudon could only take so many stories about Berry's crazy group. She snickered. "Here we are, Berry, in the heart of the gap—Rainbow Gap."

Smiling despite her agonizing, Berry said, "That's it, Jaudon. A rainbow of women. I don't know if the rainbow is a celebration of our bonds or a symbol of our differences."

"Which color are we, people like us?"

"All the colors, silly."

Jaudon flopped up beside her. "Then I'm glad to be in the Gap with you."

"The answer to your question is, I'm proud to be seen with you, angel, not embarrassed," Berry said, caressing Jaudon's cheeks again.

"I just can't see the sense to it, Berry. What difference does it make if one woman has more hair than another?"

Berry held her and stroked her hair. "No difference to me. You're right as rain."

"Just when life was starting to seem normal," said Jaudon.

"Because Cullie's home? Or because we know Allison stayed out West?"

"Hey," said Jaudon. "I was thinking it was Lari who tipped off the U.S. Marshals about Allison working in my store."

Berry nodded as she considered the possibility. "Out of jealousy?"

"Or cussedness?" said Jaudon. "Or because she's deranged?"

"We always blame Lari."

"Am I trying to cover up my own craziness? She seems to take up a lot of time and space and skulks in everywhere. I get a bad feeling in my bones when she's around. If she had a beef with Allison, ratting her out was a perfect way to drive her off."

"Lari may wish she was as much a mover and shaker as Allison Millar. We'll hear of Allison again someday. She'll write a book or lead a big protest or become Secretary of Health in Washington, DC"

"Lari's jealous of Allison for being gutsy and respected."

"It's not nice of me to think it, but I wish Lari was the one run out of town and Allison stayed with us."

Jaudon laughed. "As long as Allison doesn't plop down in our yard again and stopped telling me that she loved women who don't wear bras, even though she wears one."

"Did she?" Berry smoothed Jaudon's hair.

"Last time I saw her before she left she ran a hand up my back. I about died. She was checking for a strap. She told me Cullie wears one."

"Oh, hush up, who cares." It was true, though. Most people hated to see a woman without a bra. "You are my beautiful Jaudon Vicker and Allison had best keep her hands off you if we ever see her again."

"I can't help my hating how we're supposed to keep our bodies just so, Berry."

"I know, angel, it's awful hard." Berry interlaced her fingers with Jaudon's and told her how much Cullie missed Allison. "I know a little how she feels. Remember how nice the patients at my part-time job were when I left? I miss them all."

Jaudon did and remembered how that whole send-off party gave her hope that people got nicer as they aged.

A teacher at one of Berry's clinicals had recommended her to the ob-gyn clinic in Four Lakes. The clinic wanted her to start work the minute she graduated, so she resigned from the rehabilitation center where she'd worked almost four years in order to concentrate on the last weeks of school. The rehab patients and staff gave her a big good-bye party and insisted she bring Jaudon to meet them.

"The Bible tells me she's a sinner, Miss Jaudon, but your Berry is one of the nicest human beings I ever met," said a very old white woman sunk into a wheelchair, fiddling with her hearing aids.

Beside her, a black man who appeared even older banged his cane on the linoleum floor three times and pronounced, "The Lord gives us means to balance out our sins. Miss Berry won't have trouble getting by St. Peter."

Whispering behind her hand, the white woman said, "He's a reverend so he knows what he's talking about, colored or not." The woman gave her a firm nod and a wink despite Jaudon's grimace. There was thunder in her gut at the woman's comment, but the reverend was pressing the woman's hand between his own. This was neither time nor place to say anything.

The director of nursing had presented Berry with a sterling silver stethoscope charm engraved with her name. The memory, now, of the little celebration gave Jaudon an idea.

"Let's arrange for Cullie to have someplace to be for Memorial Day," she said. "She's fun, even with her heart broken. I'd like to let her know we want to be her friends."

"We can have a holiday picnic. I'll invite the other women too."

"Not Lari."

"Jaudon, we can't exclude any women. The community is too small. She can come, but no one can make me be nice to that home wrecker."

"She wants girls stacked up like cord wood."

"Don't tell me she's still a temptation." The thought of Allison's non-monogamy ideas frightened her. She hesitated to say anything and the impulse passed. Instead she got up and brought Jaudon's ear medications from the bathroom. She busied herself tending to the ear.

"Lari's about as tempting as a bucket of bait grubs," Jaudon told her.

"Then why not invite her?"

"She's strange. She goes after women who aren't free. And when she came after me, she pulled me in the way a cat goes to catnip. Is she that desperate for sex? Or is that part of this no monogamy deal? Ouch."

Berry was so startled by their similar wavelength her hand had slipped. "I'll go slower. I wonder if Lari's promiscuous because she smokes marijuana."

"Ouch."

"I'm sorry, angel." She needed to concentrate. "This has got to be done."

"It's not your fault." She wished it was possible to amputate that whole side of her head. "Are feminists inclined to take drugs, Berr?"

"From what I see at the hospital, people our age have a hankering for drugs."

"Okay, ask Lari over for the picnic and maybe we can study how to protect others from her."

CHAPTER TWENTY-SIX

We can't leave out the meat at a Memorial Day barbecue," Gran declared.

"Did you write the rule book for patriotic holidays?"

"Never mind the sass, pet. Not everyone is a vegetarian like you."

"I agree, Berry," Jaudon said. "We have to have ribs and hot dogs and hamburgers. That's what a barbecue is, for gosh sakes."

Berry frowned with concern. "You'll get takers for all of it, but the non-meat-eaters may find the smells offensive."

"The whole South smells of ribs on the 30th," said Gran. "There's no escaping it. You need to think of your kin as much as you do your ladies' lib friends." She sighed. "How your pa loved a party, especially a barbecue."

Berry stood immobile, listening hard, hoping for more. Over the years she saw Gran had been as shattered as she was by Ma and Pa's departure. She grasped the pain it must cause Gran to share memories of her daughter. Every scrap of information Gran revealed, Berry hoarded. At the public library she'd spent many hours perusing newspapers on microfiche for motorcycle accidents along Ma and Pa's planned route. They could be anywhere—or nowhere.

"We'll make a few salads." Gran patted spots on the table as if to show where the dishes belonged. "Grill the franks and shape the burgers. Your friends can bring their favorite holiday foods."

Jaudon watched Berry digest the new morsel about her parents, watched her wait for more, patient with her gran, yet tense, expectant. One thing that had changed since she first met Berry, Jaudon found, was that, while Berry would do a thing her way, she went about it nicely, so others weren't aware their own plans were scrapped along the way. Gran was close-mouthed about her son and daughter-in-law; Berry never pushed her, but stayed alert for the rare times Gran broke her silence.

Throwing a party was a first for Berry and Jaudon. The word picnic made them less nervous, but they were nervous nonetheless. Nervous no one would come, nervous of the guests spending the day arguing, nervous about having enough food and drink. Berry moved her lips in prayer as she flared a cloth over the sun-bleached picnic table in the yard. Jaudon put smaller tables on the porch and imagined Ollie the ancient alligator trundling up from Rainbow Lake at the smell of food.

When Mercie Lewis, the first guest, arrived, Berry spoke into Jaudon's good ear, "Y'all be sweet, angel."

Jaudon pulled a face. She'd already put several hours in at the store, which was extra busy on holidays, and was tired. Olive Ponder, whose family celebrated at noon, came in after to relieve Jaudon.

"You watch," she told Berry. "The women who show up will be more interested in the lesbians than the food. Lari will hold an orgy in Gran's room by the time they're through."

The tables were loaded. No one complained about the smells—there was such a variety of them. The women raved about Berry's potato salad or Gran's rice and field peas. The guests brought spring sweet corn on the cob to boil, slicing tomatoes, skillet cornbread, a salad made with candied pecans, biscuits and butter, and baked beans in a hot barbecue sauce. For dessert Jaudon bought key lime pies from the baker who supplied the Beverage Bays and Gran baked a lemon chess pie. Berry made gallon jars of sweet tea flavored with fresh strawberries and the mint she grew on the porch.

"This is our one year anniversary of graduation." Berry hugged her old classmates until they squealed. All of them had been excited about receiving their nursing caps at the traditional ceremony. Berry's fit as though it was meant to be there. Although they met throughout the year, this was their first social event just for fun.

Lari was all of a sudden there, in black, floating around the women as if she'd dropped down from the sky. Donna Skaggs carried a watermelon. Perfecta Maldonado had ferried Samantha O'Connell with her baby daughter. Three new women climbed out of a pickup cab where they had been pinched together to the point of uncontrollable giggles. Cullie, sneaking the words out of the corner of her mouth, predicted to Jaudon that at least two of the gigglers hoped to come out by midnight. They were way too excited for a picnic.

Zefer was in a happy tumult. She greeted every woman several times and almost knocked down Perfecta.

The women admired the blue concrete mermaid, stroking her and talking about their affection for mermaids. The peacocks watched from a distance, gobbling wildflowers as they went. By the side porch, Gran showed off her potted geraniums, which won first prize at the county fair, and the camellia, trimmed by Bat's friend John to an impeccable roundness.

Jaudon, juggling the ribs, franks, burgers, and catfish on the grill, followed Berry's movement from group to group. The women were awkward with one another as they ate, unused to socializing outside a meeting. Lari kept disappearing to the other side of the house to smoke with one or another of the women.

Cullie plopped boiled peanuts from the farm stand onto the picnic table and started eating them. "This is all I had time for," she said. "I had two pool emergencies, one over in Clearwater, the other in Apollo. Never fails at the holidays. The boss always sends me because I have no family. Ha! What does he call my sister? What about you all, aren't you my family too?" she asked, opening her arms to include the whole group.

Jaudon and Berry smiled at each other. "So, Cullie thinks of us as family," Berry said quietly.

Judy rushed to her with a plate piled high. "Poor Cullie. I'll bet you never had time for lunch."

Cullie immediately held a rib in one hand for Kirby to gnaw on and told Judy to set a date for their marriage.

"Are you proposing to me, you gallant? I'm not even gay."

"Ah, but, Judy, I'm a lesbian lothario, and there is no resisting me."

Mercie was next to Judy. Judy turned and flung herself into Mercie's arms, announcing that she and her husband had separated.

Judy cried a bit and explained. "He wants kids and I think it's a lousy idea. I don't believe the fertility goddess Astarte expected such a dense population. She needs to turn down her volume because we can't be procreating as much as the ancients did. We're using up the whole planet."

That was enough to start a conversation filled with sympathy and dissension, but not enough to halt the feast. Gran rang a weathered porch bell with gusto and the women stopped what they were doing to assemble for food. Cullie kept them laughing all the way into her third helping.

Perfecta fussed with the plenty on the picnic table, uncovering, arranging the dishes, organizing serving utensils. Lari seemed more interested in Mercie than in food; Cullie was the same with one of the gigglers, despite her proposal to Judy. Donna Skaggs and Samantha O'Connell stood as they ate, and seemed, like nuns in a schoolyard, to scan for misbehavior.

Jaudon expected the whole gathering to devolve into a meeting if she didn't intervene. She stood. "Let's have a moment of silence for our fighting soldiers on this Memorial Day."

Donna said, "My moment of silence is for the young men to come home from Vietnam."

Berry watched Jaudon strain to hear.

Judy said, "I pray for peace between all countries."

Jaudon's eyes were squeezed shut so tight Berry worried she was in pain. When she opened them, Jaudon asked, "Did you hear about Emmett Ponder?"

"Emmett?" said Berry. "Your assistant manager's son? Olive's baby boy?"

"Emmett. Missing in action. Olive told me today."

"He was a kid," said Berry. "Is a kid. I thought he was going to Florida State."

"That's what Olive wanted. Emmett got his girlfriend pregnant and joined the army because no one he worked for here at home paid enough to support him, her, and the baby."

Berry looked at the sky to hold in her sudden tears. Inside, she was railing at the Great Spirit for allowing such tragedy and waste. Momma Vicker had refused to hire Emmett, citing some rule about not hiring relatives of employees, though she'd always done it for her own family. "I don't understand why we have to fight. Can you imagine what Olive is going through? I hope the army will take care of his wife and child."

Jaudon said, "He fought for our country. That's what matters."

Judy put a hand on Jaudon's arm. "I can't believe you said that."

"Why not?" Jaudon remembered Judy was newly separated and told herself to give her some slack.

"It's horse pucky. That's why. The military-industrial complex profits from war. Kids like your friend's son don't give their lives, they lose their lives to feed it."

"What in hell's bells is the military-whatever complex?"

"It's a good old boy scheme where industry makes the guns and the military buys them."

"What's wrong with that?"

"For the gun manufacturers to make obscene profits, they need to sell obscene amounts of guns. They influence the government to make wars so they have a guaranteed market. It's so obvious, Jaudon."

Jaudon's face was pink. "Is that why the American Revolution happened? The War of Northern Aggression?"

Judy said, "The Civil War had an economic basis, like every other war when you come down to it. The Revolution too—remember taxation without representation? It's a slippery slope from tea to cotton to guns."

"Are you one of those Socialists?"

"Are you a throwback to Confederate slavery?"

"No, I am not, but you're talking like a Russian."

Berry stayed out of the fray, siding with Judy, but loving Jaudon for her willingness to speak of her convictions.

Judy's voice rose to the same volume as Jaudon's. "I am. I'm Russian American. My family came to America at the end of the nineteenth century to escape violence and anti-Semitism. American patriotism is strong in my family. My father lost his right hand to frostbite in the mountains of North Korea because he refused evacuation when his platoon was at half strength. He learned very fast to shoot with his left." Judy held her thumb and index finger like a pistol.

Jaudon's deep breath escaped as a sob. She cried and reached out her arms to Judy. "I'm sorry. I am so sorry."

They held on. Judy's set jaw weakened.

Jaudon leaned away, hands on her hips. "Wasn't Korea an honorable war? Didn't we all have to fight to stop Communism, to protect the American way of life?"

"It was supposed to be a fight between North and South Korea," Judy said. "Instead, it was the US fighting the cold war with the USSR. We used Korea. It's the same thing in North and South Vietnam. Can't we stop the killing? War is a horrible idea. Kids are being brutalized here for objecting and the North Vietnamese are doing worse to our kids over there. Look at us fighting about the fight. My husband and I fought from day one. I thought that was what marriage was like, because my parents fought too. Where's the sense?"

"Sense?" said Jaudon. "I can see the civil rights movement, but these so-called revolutionaries taking over colleges, making bombs, having sit-ins at Army recruiting stations? What makes these people tick? Why didn't their folks take straps to the whole bunch of Commie brats—these kids aren't going to solve anything. At least our soldiers are protecting us."

Judy sat at the picnic table, legs crossed, foot kicking in a rapid rhythm. "I can't believe the clash of cultures here. We must be mirroring the whole country. Look at the dogs. They know better than we do how to play."

Zefer and Kirby tussled over a peanut butter pie tin.

Mercie played chords on her guitar, and Perfecta, Samantha's baby in her arms, began a lullaby in Spanish.

Gran put her arms around Judy and Jaudon. "Let's make this a Memorial Day we want as a memorial. Come on, Jaudon, once the girls stop playing, hoist that phonograph out here before it's too buggy for dancing. And I want you and Judy to start the dancing."

Jaudon hooted. "Stereo, Gran. Phonographs went out before hi-fi did." She turned to Judy and bowed. "I'll return to claim that dance."

Gran helped pull and push the stereo speakers to the porch before excusing herself to lie down. Jaudon encouraged her to rejoin them when she was rested. She carried Bat's whole 45 rpm record collection, plus the swing bands on 33s that she and Berry collected. Cullie started as DJ, spinning fast songs to encourage them to dance. Jaudon jumped in front of Judy, stumbling. *This ear business*, she thought with a silent swear. She recovered her balance.

When the song ended, Judy said, "Go on. Dance with your girlfriend." Jaudon, in turn, handed Judy off to Mercie.

Cullie chose an old Karen Bliss 33 next, and played one of Berry's and Jaudon's favorites, "Always."

They hadn't danced in front of friends since that night at the crowded bar. The others watched their ballroom style, gradually joining them. This generation knew their parents' dances.

"Jaudon," Berry whispered when the dance brought them close, "this is better than the bar. I guess I'm my pa's daughter. Gran said he loved a party."

She held Berry more tightly, both overjoyed and pained for her. Berry was finding a little more of herself today, thanks to Gran Binyon.

"I could get used to this freedom," Jaudon said. "Can you imagine being able to dance together anytime?"

Berry thrust her chin high. "No, I can't, and it makes me stark raving mad that I can't. We can't at weddings or school proms. We need to make some big changes in this world."

"I don't need to, Berry. I'm dancing on top of the world with you this minute."

"More!" cried the other women. "Where's our disc jockey?"

"Dancin'," Cullie told them, with Perfecta on one side and Mercie on the other. Berry was glad Cullie didn't ask her to dance. She continued to be a little too drawn to her and knew from Jaudon's experience that acting on such a fleeting impulse was plain dumb.

Donna Skaggs danced by herself, boogie-woogying like a small girl lost in a big dream, while Samantha O'Connell bounced her infant to the music.

Jaudon did her sailor-on-a-gangplank walk and hurried to the turntable.

Berry stood with Judy and her friend, who were waiting to dance more, when a blast of disquiet rushed through her chest and abdomen. She turned, searching for its source. A diesel pickup truck started, and she listened to its lingering rumble as it pulled away. She caught sight of brake lights before they were obscured by trees and brush along the road. Who in the world was watching them?

❖

The rain came, as it did almost daily in summer months, like the bursting of a galactic water balloon. The downpour distracted Berry from the creepy truck. She encouraged everyone toward the house, but Jaudon started a new song, and the women, faces and arms raised to the deluge, danced with the fervor of prisoners freed from life sentences.

Jaudon played another three peppy numbers before the rain stopped, leaving a sultry heat. The women trooped to the porch, merry, dripping wet, shaking their wet clothing and hair. Cullie was drying her glasses when Berry conscripted her to help carry blankets and towels to them. Lari wiped down Mercie Lewis, then was kissing her. Judy Fish watched them for a moment with her friend, before they turned to hold each other close, swaying. Jaudon played a slow song by The Carpenters.

All of this was visible to any vehicle on Pineapple Trail, but the rutted sand and gravel road had less than a trickle of traffic when the sun was out, and even less when it turned to muck, so Jaudon wasn't worried.

Berry didn't tell her about the truck, which she'd never seen before. Was it a friend of the people in the single-wide trailer at the end of the Pineapple Trail? Or a service guy for the ranch house that faced Rainbow Lake, the silly people who were trying to keep a lawn alive? It was the same trepidation she'd experienced whenever Eddie Dill was around.

The mosquitoes massed at twilight. Perfecta and Samantha O'Connor left immediately. Their husbands had gone to other picnics.

Donna Skaggs sat in the red steel porch chair and cooled herself with the folding fan she always carried. "You can cut this humidity with a knife."

Berry thought to ask what she'd wondered for some time. "Donna, are you related to that kid Jimmy Neal Skaggs in the class behind ours?"

Donna glowered. "My family doesn't have anything to do with my little brother."

Zefer ran by, followed by short-legged Kirby. Cullie swooped in front of Donna and grabbed Kirby. "Your own brother? What the hell?"

Berry watched Donna. "Because he's gay?"

Donna said, "He shamed us."

"No." Cullie shook Kirby at Donna. "Shame on *you*. He's your blood."

Donna jammed the fan into her pocketbook. They followed her as she made haste to her car. Donna said, "It's one thing you and your friends being the way you are—and I may quit the group because of it—but Jimmy Neal's a man. And family."

"So you cut him out?" Berry asked.

Donna set her jaw and got in her car.

"Mi amiga," Cullie said, arms wide, "you have this so wrong. Think what your attitude does to Jimmy Neal."

"Our whole family hopes it helps straighten him out," Donna said through her open window.

Donna needed to give up her prejudice and Jimmy Neal needed to survive it, poor kid. Berry shut her eyes and blessed them both. "I have to admit, we may need our own group, Cullie."

"Ah, but this makes me want to stay in the group we have. Donna needs us to educate her."

Berry considered that. She gave Cullie's arm a quick squeeze. "Good idea."

The rest of the guests thanked Berry and Jaudon with lavish words as they rearranged transportation. Mercie was following Lari home. Judy and her friend made out in Judy's car before they drove away. Cullie stretched an arm across the passenger seat of her truck and pulled one of the giggling women inside. The woman blew kisses to her friends as she left, and the friends clapped and waved her on her way. Berry smiled. They considered Cullie a catch.

This pairing off was entirely unexpected. Berry and Jaudon watched the configurations with a pleased incredulousness as they gathered the damp towels and blankets, the leftover food, and the trash bag of picnic gear. Gran took charge of the kitchen while Berry started the laundry and Jaudon returned the stereo, records, and tables to their normal storage areas.

They were tired, but giddy with the success of the party. Gran finished up and went to bed. Berry was arranging items left behind to return to forgetful guests. Jaudon hugged her from behind, her hands on Berry's breasts, and burrowed through her hair to nuzzle her neck.

"Think what some of those women are doing together as we speak."

Berry wriggled to face Jaudon. She widened her eyes and lifted her eyebrows. "Tell me, angel. What are they up to?"

"Come on, I'm going to show you, my dazzling swamp flower. Want to go to Australia with me?"

With Jaudon's arm around her waist, Berry realized she did want what Jaudon had in mind. An invisible steam built up with this many women in one place and stirred her too. Jaudon seemed to feel the same as she stood before Berry, bedroom door closed, and insisted on undressing her, one garment at a time, running her hands over Berry's body, kissing her most vital spots until Berry begged to lie on the bed.

"Sometime can we try using that goop on me, from your self-help clinic? So I'm wet too?"

Berry grinned at her, rolled over, and took the tube from the night table. She warmed a big squirt of gel in her hands and applied it.

That got Jaudon going. She was relentless in her touches, but postponed releasing Berry. Somehow, her imagination had found time to come up with a few tricks. Jaudon had quite a knack for this.

They moved quietly and made no sounds out of respect for Gran. Jaudon was luxuriating in their prolonged ardor when she became aware that Berry had worked a hand between her thighs and up. Jaudon grabbed the edge of the mattress to hold back. She realized that Berry must be about bursting too. She swiveled around. They quickened their touches and, for the first time, had orgasms at the same time. Jaudon's love for Berry took her over. They held tight, as if to meld their flesh.

Berry thought their souls were merging. Making love with Jaudon was a mystical experience; each led the other to greater and greater heights. They fell asleep entangled, in every sense.

The next morning was cool and luscious with new buds quivering in slight breezes to open and leaves translucent with green light. They prepared for work and school with every expectation that life, success, and endless love awaited them.

They weren't able to start the van. This didn't shake them up. They laughed away such a tiny obstacle.

"Let me take a look under the hood," said Jaudon.

"Okay, but Gran will take us."

Jaudon opened her door as Berry picked up a tiny item from the ground. "We don't need a ride."

Jaudon squinted. "Is that a fuse?"

"It used to be. It's squashed. Who does such things? And why? I'll wring his scrawny neck, whoever he is."

"How did it get there?"

"And why is it broken?"

"We'll talk about it later—we're running late. Don't we have a spare fuse?"

They kept spares in the glove compartment and Jaudon fit in a new one. As they drove to the Beverage Bay they puzzled about it.

"It can't be intentional," Jaudon said. "We moved the van to make room for guest cars. It was out of sight. Did someone at the party disable it?"

Berry mentioned the pickup cruising by. "It was scary. I used to have the same reaction to Eddie Dill coming home."

"At least that would let the women off the hook. Who but you and me can find the fuse box in this thing, much less know which one to take out? You know it was manufactured practically before fuses were invented."

Berry drove up to the store and gave her a light push out of the van. She almost lost her balance, but caught the door frame and held on, trying to hide her stumble and disorientation.

"I'm so sorry, Jaudon. Are you okay? Call Olive or Rigo to cover for you."

"This always passes. You be careful and check the van before you drive it tonight." She'd worry about Berry but, for now, locked herself inside the store and waved, their signal she was safe.

Berry, as always, didn't leave until she saw Jaudon was inside. Her first class wasn't until eight a.m. She drove unhurried to campus under wispy clouds. Once there, she used a flashlight to check the engine compartment. Nothing looked out of place, though she wasn't convinced she'd notice the difference. She walked through a gentle drizzle to the automotive department and peered into the chair's office. Students were already out in the shop yelling over the whirring sounds of hydraulic tools. She showed him the crushed fuse.

"It's vandalism," he concluded, after going outside with her to check the van over. "No question about it. He knew to pull the starter fuse. Has somebody got it in for you, Miss Garland? I don't believe it. You're about the nicest person on campus. You better lock your doors from here on."

She said with some enmity, "If someone wants the van, they won't have a problem helping themselves." She showed him that the cargo doors didn't lock, at the same time chiding herself for speaking with anger.

"We can fix that up, Miss Garland. What year is this rig?"

On the way to class, she thought about how furious she was with whoever hobbled their van. And how furious she was with Donna Skaggs's family for disowning Jimmy Neal. Why were people cruel? She wished she understood. If she ever did, she could try to turn her anger to usefulness.

Chapter Twenty-seven

After the picnic, Gran decided she wanted to go out and find some fun of her own. She joined a group of people in their sixties and older who met early each morning to walk before the heat of the day. A luncheon group developed from that and soon she was taking bus trips to various parts of Florida. Gran was full of plans to see museums, state parks, natural wonders, and historic general stores, whetting Berry's appetite for travel and tempting Jaudon.

The demands of the store along with frequent bouts of exhaustion since her injury had interrupted school, and Jaudon was behind schedule. She supplemented her accounting and tax classes with management, auditing, business planning, marketing, beginning computers, communications, business psychology, and human resources.

On top of all that, she was having trouble at her Beverage Bay. A number of young hoodlums had taken to congregating in the sandlot down the street. They walked in to the Bay for soft drinks, candy, and gum, a practice that was discouraged because of vehicle dangers. Her warnings didn't stop them. She was sweeping glass from bottles smashed against the outside walls almost every morning. The entrance smelled of beer no matter how hard she scrubbed the concrete.

The hoodlums waited until Jaudon was on her own and had customers. She saw four or five of them at a time raiding the open storage areas. Jaudon needed quick access to the shelving so a blockade was out of the question. She reported the incidents to the police and Momma almost every time.

"Hey," Rigo shouted one day after the nearby schools let out. He raced outside to catch a kid of twelve or thirteen who ran with a quart bottle of beer. He snagged the child by his belt and snatched the beer.

Jaudon wondered how many times she'd missed a theft because they came in on the side of her busted ear. She watched the whole episode from the doorway. Rigo returned out of breath and tossed the beer to her.

She caught it. "Thanks."

"I'm paid time and a half for that, aren't I?"

"Haw-haw," she said. "I'll talk to Momma about it."

"Oh, no, you won't. Your momma will dock my pay for leaving the store."

Momma was inspecting Jaudon's store on a breezeless, boiling hot Saturday. Even the palms seemed wilted. At least once a month Momma visited each store, giving no warning. Pops no longer came with her as he was too busy arranging shipments and deliveries at the office.

Two cars waited for service and Rigo wasn't due for another half hour. Momma often pitched in to help at these times and she was there when a swarm of neighborhood boys burst into the store.

Jaudon knew their pattern well enough to rush at them. She smashed into one of the thieves and tripped another. Their cohorts reversed course and ran for the entrance, to be met by Momma and one of her legendary white straw purses. She used it on the first poor little thug like a Paul Bunyon-sized wood splitter. The kids were trapped between Momma and Jaudon.

"Jaudon," Momma shouted. "Bring those two over where I can keep an eye on the thieving vermin. Call the police."

Every time one tried to escape, he got a taste of the purse. One had bloody lips, another covered his face with his hands, but his shoulders shuddered as he cried.

"Tell the police who I am."

For once, the police arrived quickly. One of the boys, as he was led away with his hands cuffed behind his back, raised both middle fingers at Jaudon and her mother. Momma didn't lose any time reporting the gesture to his captor. The police were so deferential to Momma; Jaudon wondered what influence she had with the department.

Next it was her turn. Momma lit into her for the risk to her inventory and listened to nothing Jaudon said in her own defense.

"You think everything will be handed to you on a platter, like this job. Well, it won't, Daughter. I have a mind to turn you out to find your own way. See how you fare if I pull the silver spoon from your mouth."

"Why don't you fire me, Momma?" She wiped her nose with a cleaning rag she always carried at the store. She was, as usual, ashamed of crying, though she knew they were tears of anger. "I do a good job.

You know I do. You knew this was a risky area when you built here. Any manager would have her hands full."

"You are not any manager, Jaudon Vicker. You are my child. I expect you to do better than a cousin or a stranger off the street."

"That's why I don't give up on studying for tax preparation and CPA licenses, Momma."

"That's good, child, because one of these days you may need a job. I can't keep coming in here and rescuing my store. You need to build up your connections so the police come running when you call, as they do for me. You can't just run a store these days. You need to be a businesswoman, tough as nails and twice as sharp. Put on your Sunday go-to-meeting clothes and head to the Greater Turkey Creek Chamber of Commerce once a month."

"You want me to put every minute into the stores the way you do, but you're giving the business to Bat?"

"Bat is more presentable than you. He'll be a proud Vietnam veteran, and that gives a man status from the get go. Plus, he's a man, so everything will come easier to him. If you were ever a normal girl, I'd have kept you far from the stores to stay home and take care of your kids, but you weren't blessed like that and I'm trying to do my best by you."

"I should quit on the spot and walk out that door the way you give me no credit, Momma, but I love my work. I don't want to leave it. As soon as I have my licenses, if I have to go to chamber meetings, I will."

"Not the way you look today, you won't." Jaudon wore her usual shorts and summer shirt with a Beverage Bay jacket. The ink stains didn't scour out no matter how much she tried and there was a slit in her pants from a case cutter. "I have hopes you'll grow up one of these days. People won't stop if I put you in one of the better stores."

"I thought you put me here because it's a tough neighborhood."

"The store looks neat and tidy, but I don't know that you'd work out in another neighborhood, where the real money is." Momma's tone softened. She looked around the store. "This is a better match for you, Daughter. How did my baby girl turn into a man?"

She hated how squeaky her voice became when she was holding in tears. "Momma, I'm not a man."

Rigo arrived in his convertible, walking in on the harangue. Momma quieted down and was nice as pie to him. She pecked them both on their cheeks and rustled off in her brown taffeta. Girlish puffed sleeves looked incongruous on such a willful woman. Momma had gained more weight and the dress fabric stretched tight across her girdle.

She wiped at the spot on her cheek Momma kissed.

When they were alone in the store Rigo asked, "Did that woman make you cry again?"

She shrugged. "She cares more about the Bays than she cares about her kids. Bat's not her son—he's the future boss man, her poster boy brave veteran. She thinks he's the best thing since sliced bread and I'm lower than a bug's butt. I must be one of those people who should have been aborted to stop me from taking up human space."

"Aw, hon, come here." Rigo wrapped his solid, red-haired arms around her and patted her back like he was burping a baby. He smelled of his lime-scented shaving cream. "Your momma is as cold as a mother-in-law's heart, as my mother says."

"It doesn't matter how nice I keep the store, it's me she objects to, Rigo."

"You and your momma were not made for each other. Mother Nature could have done better."

Jaudon told him about the incident with the hoodlums.

"Did you tell her the cops won't help us?"

"She said that's my fault, for not getting to know them."

"Who does she want? Barbie or G.I. Joe? She can't have them both."

She poked him in the ribs. "G.I. Joe might be a good idea here when the county releases those boys from the slammer."

"Which will be today, if their records are clean."

They looked at each other with alarm.

"Listen," said Rigo. "What about Jimmy Neal? He's six-four, almost three hundred pounds, and not beefcake material, but he's not nellie either. He's been looking for work. I'll give him my wages to come stand guard. You know I don't need the money."

"I don't want the store sued if he hurts anybody."

"Never. I call him my Manatee Man. He's gentle and slow moving like manatees. Let me use the phone to call him. You can't be alone when the creeps are released."

"How come he's not drafted?"

"He's in college."

She hoped Jimmy Neal didn't act light in the loafers in public. Rigo, who she thought wore something to darken his eyelashes and outline his eyes, seemed more so all the time. How did gay guys do that? They talked alike, had the same bearing, used the same words and body language. She guessed it wasn't any different from, say, toughs on a street corner who had a language of their own, including how they moved and walked, or homemakers chatting when they picked up their children from school. She loved it, the way gay guys spoke and moved, and found herself taking on their mannerisms when she was around them.

Still, she walked a tightrope when Rigo was there. She feared customers saw through him, thought they were one of a kind, and half expected local guys to hurt him, or both of them. It was better than working with some man who wasn't family, though, and Momma was obstinate about hiring more men.

"Okay, send Jimmy Neal to Momma. You can give your wages to him if you want, but we'll pay him too because I need his help. I hope Momma doesn't become suspicious of you boys applying as soon as she tells me she's going to hire."

"Your Momma's suspicious no matter what, so with Olive Ponder as second-in-command, let's see if we can get away with making this an otherwise all-gay store."

CHAPTER TWENTY-EIGHT

They got together on a Tuesday evening at Samantha O'Connell's house, when most of them had at least part of the shift off. Berry had imagined a crowded apartment. It turned out that Samantha's husband was a contractor and had built a well-appointed, roomy place for his family. They weren't poor at all. Samantha had arranged for him to take the kids to the movies, but he had to work late so the kids were running wild in the house. They were on and off the women's laps, hungry for attention, excited to meet their mother's friends, and upset to miss the movies with Daddy. The living room smelled of milk and diapers. Daddy stormed into the house as they met, grabbed a beer, muttering about his work problems and cursing the group with his eyes. They had been discussing the lesbians in their midst. He couldn't have missed the gist of their conversation.

A women's equality demonstration was being planned by a larger group in Four Lakes. It was part of a celebration of women's suffrage and its goal was to bring attention to the lack of women in local politics.

Berry expected to go if she got time off work.

Judy Fish and Mercie Lewis were working nights at a Tampa hospital, so they planned to join the rally by Four Lakes City Hall. Perfecta had announced long ago her ambition to be a visiting nurse and arranged her schedule to be free. She was an experienced demonstrator and at the height of the Vietnam War had brought attention to the numbers of Hispanic kids who went to war to escape poverty only to be injured or killed.

Samantha's husband didn't want her to join the protest, not with a gang of what he called bull dykes. "It doesn't matter," Samantha told them.

"It doesn't matter?" Judy Fish said. "What do you mean, it doesn't matter? Of course it matters."

Each of them was in her twenties except Samantha, who had been let go from jobs each time her pregnancy became obvious. "I don't know how it matters if there's one less of you. It's not as if I can go anyway because of where I work."

Judy was always sheer energy and her new sexual relationship with the friend she brought to the picnic had not diminished that. Judy said, "Your husband is lording it over you and it doesn't matter? The fact that your employer objects is the point: men think we're less valuable than they are."

Donna Skaggs's testy voice rose above everyone else's. "This is a problem, but it's not the one you're talking about. I don't mind being seen with lesbians, but I worry what others will think."

"You're not making sense," said Cullie. "Not minding and worrying— don't they cancel each other out?"

"Others will think you're lucky to have so many friends," said Berry.

Lari showed up late, as usual. She brought her strange dimness with her, as if she stepped in front of the all the lights at once. Perfecta gave a small wave, the only greeting. The tension in the room increased.

"The way some of you dress," said Samantha, "I'd rather be buried in a croaker sack."

Mercie was sarcastic and accusing. "You're afraid, aren't you, that you'll be tarred by the same brush?"

"Well, I—" Donna started to say.

Mercie cut her off. "Do you think they're going to assume your family's from Africa because I'll be there?"

"Donna does have a point," said Samantha. "I hadn't thought of it, but if people thought I was one of you, I might lose my kids."

"Oh, for crying out loud," said Cullie. "You have the required male at home. What you should do is show up with him and your five kids. Show some real support."

Donna said, "Don't be snide, Cullie. We're in this together."

"Yeah." Cullie played with the unraveling straw safari hat she wore for work, rotating it in her hands faster and faster. "All but the lesbians."

"It's time for me to declare myself," Mercie said. "I have a new lover and she's a woman. So that's two reasons you won't want me to come."

Cullie threw her hat in the air and yelled, "Hot diggity."

Perfecta jumped up and put her arms around Mercie. "Hey, girl, I'm so happy for you."

Mercie told them she'd had a girlfriend in high school too.

Berry wasn't sure this merited a public announcement, but she smiled and leaned over to give Mercie a kiss on the cheek. Mercie pretended to be shy and sheepish, but her grin declared otherwise.

Donna said, "Some lesbians are all over each other in public. That's what we don't need. The bunch of you should act like you got some raising."

"When did you ever see that?" Judy asked. Her lover took her hand, as if to calm her down.

"At the picnic," declared Samantha.

"But, Samantha," Berry said, "the picnic was a private gathering."

"So how come that man in the truck was watching us?"

"You saw someone too?" Berry became more concerned.

"Bald, beard, smoking cigarettes, parked before the line of oaks north of your house."

"He didn't come up Pineapple Trail, did he?"

"No, but here's a gap in the growth where he was parked." The rainbow gap again, Berry thought. "You can see through to your front yard." Samantha sounded smug. "I checked it on my way home."

Once more, Berry thought about Allison's sense that she was being watched when she was in the trailer. Was this the watcher? Was there more than one? She breathed in, calling on the Great Spirit, breathed out, calmer. She needed wisdom, please.

"Maybe," Cullie said. "Maybe none of our kind should go to this event for the sake of our own safety." Cullie looked around at Judy and her girlfriend, the silent Lari, and Mercie. "It's a fact—this might be dangerous."

Berry knew Cullie was trying to protect them.

"Finally, a sensible comment," said Donna.

"You would think that way, Donna, the way you demean Jimmy Neal," said Berry.

"No, man," Lari muttered, from a corner of the room. "I mean, women. That's the voice of fear. We need to charge out there and do our thing."

"Easy for you to say," Samantha piped up. "You don't have a job to lose, and your family's footing the bills for college."

Lari shrugged. "Fear won't hack it. Perfecta made a difference out there on the antiwar lines."

"That may be true," said Perfecta, "but the danger was terrifying. The police, they kicked us in the abdomen. They jeered at us and told one another it was a cheap way to prevent us having babies. Me?" She opened her arms to indicate herself. "I can have no other babies. I'm injured inside."

Samantha's living room went silent, as if every woman there had been kicked. Berry reached for Perfecta's hand. Mercie, who had been strumming her guitar in the background, let it fall silent and said, "I've known gay people who've been beaten bad too, just walking down the street. Women and men."

"So," said Lari, in her nasal accent, "gay people, we can risk bar raids or beatings or hide in closets and rot—those are our choices?"

"This is why we need to work together," Berry said. "Stand together in public if that's what it takes. I'm terrified of risking my new job, but I'll go."

"How about this," Donna said. "No radical foolhardiness. We dress like ladies."

"Oh, no," said Cullie. "You honestly want *me* in church lady drag? Putting on white gloves may have worked for women's suffrage way back when—today no one will pay any attention to us if we don't cause a stir. Cameras need fascinating subjects like Kirby and me in our matching neckerchiefs to film, not a clump of ladies standing there with signs."

"Cameras?" Berry said. "What do you mean, cameras?"

Perfecta said, "The national leaders will send press releases to the newspapers, and to TV and radio stations. You can't make changes without publicity."

Berry's flutter became stronger. There was a sharp side to every knife. This must be what made Jaudon nervous for them; it would make anyone nervous. She dared someone to attack. She dared herself to stand up to authority. She never imagined having her picture in the paper, although she should have because Rigo told stories about gay bar raids. He said the police alerted the papers to further humiliate the patrons and some lost their jobs. A demonstration was not a good idea this early in her career, but the problem was serious and she wasn't closing her eyes to it. She might be dreaming, but she expected her new employers to agree with her.

She needed to talk with Jaudon about the rally. She didn't want to bite off more than she could chew. At the same time, she was hesitant to pile on more than Jaudon could tolerate. At her last appointment, the doctor told Jaudon she was facing permanent total hearing loss in the injured ear.

"Why don't you sue the county?" Rigo had said when they told him.

Jaudon, head down, said, "Momma says it would hurt business."

"I swear to God, Jaudon, if you don't get a lawyer on this, I'll drag you to one."

Berry wondered if Jaudon would go despite Momma.

The group kept arguing about how the members should present themselves at the demonstration. Mercie started a quiet folk tune.

"I hate to be a party pooper, amigas, but are we going to let men tell us how to dress at our own political rallies?" Cullie asked. "You're trying to dress to please again."

Berry had to smile. Cullie had learned a lot from Allison.

"It's silly," Berry said, "to pretend to be what we aren't. Samantha should show up with baby spit on her shoulder, Cullie should wear her pool boy shorts, Donna her largest cross necklace, and Mercie, your most colorful dashiki. If we're there to represent American women, shouldn't we look like them?"

"Yeah," said Judy, pointing to the Star of David on her necklace.

Berry thought that putting herself out there in public would be as much display as she could muster.

❖

As the day of the protest approached, Jaudon decided she didn't have a problem with Berry standing up for what she believed in. She considered going with her, to protect Berry, but she had the store to mind. She was going to stop worrying and enjoy the woman she loved.

Today she watched Berry shave her legs.

"It's all sorts of sexy, watching you, Berr, but I'll never get why you have to waste time scraping your legs. What do people care?" Jaudon had discovered cargo shorts and wore them at the store all the time. The pockets of her cargos held everything she needed: price gun, box cutter, dust rag, gloves for working in the cooler and freezer, price labels, pen, stamp for vendor deliveries, damaged cans, register tape. She clunked when she walked. Momma seemed to have lost interest in uniforms.

"I wear white hose, Jaudon. Our teachers criticized every little personal detail. Perish the thought someone doesn't brush her teeth." Berry grabbed a glob of shaving cream and planted it on the tip of Jaudon's nose.

Jaudon nabbed the whole can and squirted it at Berry's bottom. Berry swiped off a handful and covered Jaudon. They stumbled around each other in stitches until they had to stop to breathe.

They were in high spirits when Berry dropped her at the store. Momma had hired Jimmy Neal and he started work today.

"My worry," Jaudon said, "is whether Jimmy Neal Skaggs will be quick enough on the orders."

"Isn't the universe great, angel? The kid who bullied you is now protecting you."

"Small towns." She pretended to squirt more shaving cream at Berry.

She knew Berry, despite her antics, was as bothered about the upcoming demonstration as much as she was about solving women's problems. She listened to her worries, but had no advice. Gran did that, cheering Berry on, giving her safety instructions for the demonstration, dreaming up retorts to the women who were skittish about associating with gay girls.

Berry's group kept growing too, as more women read about the women's movement and heard their own dissatisfactions expressed by others. Jaudon didn't understand why, for example, they'd dutifully do the women's work at home when they wanted to do men's work.

Her shift started at six a.m. Jimmy Neal Skaggs was due to arrive at seven, when the summer school kids started hanging out to wait for their bus. She reviewed his application. Jimmy Neal had no criminal record and had experience working at a Tom Thumb convenience store. She would have hired him on the spot without Momma's supervision.

When she next looked up it was six forty-five and already the temperature was rising. The red and orange royal poinciana across the street led a cavalcade of flowers. In front of a small factory, a jacaranda tree was heavy with clustered purple blossoms, and a puff of clouds flew like pennants overhead.

The kids arrived at the bus stop, dragging their feet and satchels. It always surprised her how many failing students had to give up their summers to study. A few of them started toward the store when the great lumbering young man from the bar appeared, walking like an ungainly duck. He blocked the entryway. It was Jimmy Neal; she smiled in relief.

"Don't you need a car to shop at a Beverage Bay?" Jimmy Neal asked in a loud voice.

Jaudon's grin stretched her face. It wasn't exactly true, but she called out, "Yes, sirree."

"You heard the lady."

Lady. He couldn't have chosen a worse word, thought Jaudon.

The kids retreated, chorusing, "That's no lady."

Jimmy Neal started toward them. Jaudon had to stop from taking on the jerks herself.

The boys turned and walked toward the curb. Once in the driveway the smallest of them raised his middle finger in the air and yelled, "That's for the lesbo inside. Did she have to hire a moose to protect herself?"

Jimmy Neal caught her as she launched toward the kid.

"Don't let them see you upset, Miss Vicker. It makes them worse."

Jaudon knew that was true. She shook his hand in welcome. "Call me Jaudon," she said. Behind the counter she found his oversized blue jacket on which Momma had one of her cashiers stitch *Jimmy Neal*.

"Thank you."

"No, thank you for averting my catastrophe out there."

He shrugged and somehow twinkled his eyes at her. "My last job, I was a bouncer. This is child's play. Literally."

Jaudon started his training without delay, but they kept getting distracted, talking about this and that. He gave no sign that he remembered picking on her in school. Was he cowed because she was his boss? As far as she was concerned, he wasn't her tormentor anymore, so he had nothing to worry about from her. Jimmy Neal was almost as funny as Rigo. He joked with the customers. He wasn't fast, but he never shirked, moving along in a big man splay-footed way that was as comical as his one-liners. The Bay seemed brighter with Jimmy Neal there, the work easier.

At one point she asked, "Are you and Rigo...?"

Jimmy Neal, in what seemed to be his natural response to the world, did that eye twinkling thing again. "Wish me luck that it's not trifling-sized guys Rigo likes. I can't squeak into that category sideways."

CHAPTER TWENTY-NINE

They were on the porch swing when Cullie and her truck arrived in a cloud of dust and sand. Her pool cleaning route took her through Rainbow Gap. Developers had built a housing estate not five miles down the road from Pineapple Trail and half the houses had pools. One of the Culpepper cousins was a pool builder who always recommended Cullie to his customers.

Cullie spent half an hour or so drinking sweet tea on the porch with Berry and Jaudon, often pouring out her heart, this time about the giggler from the picnic and how she went back to her boyfriend.

"She didn't take to our way of life?" Berry asked.

"The ex-boyfriend harassed her so much she gave in to him. I don't understand the attraction to such a pest. You'd think God saw what he did wrong with Adam and corrected everything with Eve. Why he didn't improve on all the Adams to follow confounds me."

Jaudon was grateful for the distraction from ear pain and this everlasting headache.

"You stay in touch with Allison? I'd drop her like a pan of flaming okra," said Jaudon.

Cullie's face was a mix of embarrassment and pleasure. "I was waiting to tell you—she let that miserable weasel have one last chance. After that, Allison gave her the old heave-ho. What a fricking relief." She threw her arms wide. "Can you blame her when she can have a prize like me?"

"Cullie," said Berry with an affectionate laugh, "you are so full of it. You're the last person to brag on yourself."

"Seriously, the feds are flying Allison to Puerto Rico to testify. If she agrees to withdraw her suit, all her charges will be dropped."

"Why would anyone champion a bunch of bombers?" Jaudon asked.

"Ah, young grasshopper, there's where Allison's razor sharp mind comes into play."

Jaudon said, "Uh-oh."

"Allison isn't going to PR at all. She has to change planes in New York and plans to disappear in the crowds at LaGuardia and make her way to Florida in time for the demonstration."

"Oh boy," Jaudon said. "The bombers will be after her along with the marshals."

"No, her lawyer said the government wants to jail these Puerto Rican independence guys so bad they'll give in and take her deposition in Florida to avoid a delay."

Jaudon asked, "Why in heck didn't she stay in a hotel in Puerto Rico when she first went? Who wants to get mixed up with those Commies down there? They should be grateful the US protects them."

"I didn't understand either," said Cullie. "Allison explained how it all connects up. The island is so small, a lot of the groups help one another out. Crash pads, rallies—"

"Bombs," said Jaudon.

Berry took Jaudon's hand. "Allison's passionate about women's rights, not bombs."

"She wanted to show support from stateside women," said Cullie.

"I don't know why you have to be involved in her passion, Berry. You have your own."

Cullie teased her. "Who? You?"

Jaudon was sulky about the whole thing again. "Why do there have to be wars and protests about laws? Why do people fight about every little thing when we were promised World War II was the end of war? Skin colors are causing riots, women can't have abortions but they're not always supposed to have babies, you can't find peace in religion because everyone else's religion is wrong. Leave it be, is my opinion."

Berry squeezed her hand. "How in the world will Allison get here from New York?" she asked Cullie.

"That's what I'm worried about. I'm lucky they rehired me at work, but if I ask for more time off to drive up and fetch her, they'll can me. And I'd have to borrow the car I wrecked on my sister again."

"Why would you want to go?" asked Jaudon. "After what she did to you?"

Cullie grinned and shrugged.

"Because she's in love with Allison." Berry pointed at a wicker chair that had seen better days.

Cullie sat; Kirby clawed at the unraveling edge to climb into her lap, but Cullie leapt up again and paced to the steps, to the chair, stretched her arms out from her sides, and wailed. "What do I do?"

Kirby clawed at Jaudon's leg. "Pick up your mutt before she draws blood."

Cullie swept Kirby into her arms and stood her up to face her hosts. "Mutt? No one dares to address Kirby as a mutt. I'll have you know she has champions in her bloodline."

"She'll be the breakfast of champions if you don't stop her from tearing me and that chair to shreds," Jaudon said. "Are you really in love with that firebrand Allison, no if, ands, or buts?"

Berry clapped her hands, a joyful look on her face. "What other reason for Cullie to be all juberous to see her?"

"What is that, one of your Okefenokee Swamp words?"

"I never did live in that swamp, Cullie, and you know it."

"Near enough to be personal friends with Pogo."

"Are you looking for an introduction to Pogo, Cullie?"

"Okay, you two," said Jaudon. "Nothing wrong with being born in Georgia. Tell us more of your woes, Cullie."

"It may be hard to believe, my leetle friends, but Allison wants to be with me."

"Jiminy, how can she expect that?"

Berry said, "I'd be pleased to see her again, but she can't ask you of all people to be her welcoming committee, Cullie."

"*I'll* welcome the woman for you," said Jaudon. "I'll give her what for up one side and down the other."

"You might as well get used to her. She's not planning to leave any time soon." Cullie hugged Kirby to her.

"She's staying? Not visiting? That's terrific."

"Allison wants to talk with you some more, Berry, about starting up that women's clinic for lesbians and single women and migrant moms. She thinks this area is a natural with so much poverty."

Jaudon leaned forward. "I'll be dog. She's going to pull you in deeper, Berry."

Berry cut her eyes at Jaudon. "I wish you'd stop being so ornery."

In a fake wheedling voice, Cullie said, "Kirby's infatuated with her."

"Is there a human on earth that Kirby doesn't fall for?"

"Jaudon, Kirby's very discerning."

"That's why there's puppy spit all over me whenever she leaves?"

"Kirby dotes on you, even when you say insulting things about her."

Berry said, "I hope Allison understands we need to keep the demonstration low-key. She can run away—we're staying put."

"You might have a problem. There isn't any such thing as moderation and Allison Millar."

"Don't we know it."

"Momma warned she'll be hoppin' mad if she catches me out with those unpatriotic hippies."

Berry said, "We are not hippies. Or unpatriotic. Your momma should know me better."

"Aw, heck, Berry. That's how Momma thinks."

"Well, keep her away from Four Lakes during the march."

"March?" Jaudon reached over to the arm of Berry's chair. "It's a march now?"

Berry patted her hand. "If they approve the permit."

"Permit? What do you need a permit for?"

"You can't hold a march in any city without a police permit."

"Police? Why are you bringing the police in on this? I thought a few of you were planning to stand around baking in the sun with your signs."

This time it was Berry and Cullie who looked at each other.

"Don't you read the news, amiga?" Cullie said.

"I keep telling Momma we should sell newspapers, but she won't mess with returns. I like staying in the dark, to be honest with you. Why? What's wrong?"

"Wrong?" Cullie spread her arms wide. "Where have you been hiding out, Jaudon Vicker? Berry hasn't talked to you about what we're marching about? The things we're trying to correct? Equal Rights Amendment? Title IX? *Ms.* magazine? The Radical Feminists? Women's Equality Day? We have a lot of wrongs to fix and we're not very popular with the establishment."

"Jaudon works more than full-time. She's hardly home to follow the news and when she is, she's studying."

"I take TV breaks for *Sanford and Son* and *Chico and the Man*. That's about it." Jaudon smiled at Berry. "And Sunday mornings belong to us, but we're not talking about the wrongs of the world."

"I'll bet you're not," Cullie said, cracking a smile. "The march and rally won't be like the segregation protests," said Cullie. "Those were dangerous in the extreme. Protesters got killed."

"But you weren't there."

"I was. With my parents. I don't remember much. My father carried me and ran from the fire hoses. My mother was knocked down by the water. Two fellas picked her up by the elbows and rushed her to my father. She was soaked and scraped up, but I was fine."

"And you're going to one of these riots?"

"Jaudo, what a wild imagination. I bet you picture Berry smashing in a plate-glass window with her bare hands and running through the streets naked with a refrigerator in her arms."

Jaudon angled her thumbs down. "That's more your style, Cullie."

"At least I'd have Kirby to help me haul it."

Berry said, "Don't start me laughing, you two. Things have changed, Jaudon. The police have better training and women don't scare them much, so there's less violence. Not that we don't have reason to be violent."

"For what?"

Berry saw the anger in the knots of Jaudon's jaw muscles. They'd return to the subject another time, when they didn't have company.

She said, "How about some lunch? Gran has egg salad made up. Jaudon insists on Wonder Bread—that okay by you?"

"How about mustard? I'll eat anything with mustard on it," said Cullie.

Jaudon tried to push her anger away and join in the lunch fun. She didn't want this circus in her life: the war, civil rights, the feminists, the gay lib thing. All she asked was to spend her time loving Berry, Gran, Zefer, Toby, Rigo, Cullie, and the stores. She'd also appreciate being able to hear again.

CHAPTER THIRTY

June 1974

Allison Millar once again blasted her way into their midst like a meteor.

Jaudon was sorely disappointed when she saw her drive in and set the kickstand of a bunged up motorbike well away from the dry grasses in the front yard.

Berry ran out and hugged her. "I thought you loved the West Coast."

Allison's hair had grown out. "I got tired of mind games. And the rain and cold. Florida is the place for me."

Berry didn't ask if Cullie had anything to do with her return.

"You drove that rattletrap all the way from New York City?"

"Little old me did just that, Jaudon Vicker. Women can do anything. I didn't want the feds to be able to track me through the airlines."

Jaudon walked around the bike, studying it.

"I cashed in the unused part of my airline ticket in New York to pay for a train to Tampa. On the bus ride into the city to catch the train, I picked up a newspaper that someone left behind and found this little beauty in the want ads. As soon as I got into Manhattan, I found a pay phone and told the owner, a kid at NYU, if he had the paperwork ready, I'd pay him cash on the spot. It's a 1955 Adler 250cc, whatever that means. Somebody brought it over from Germany when it was new, but college guys have been selling it to one another ever since."

"Wasn't it scary, all by yourself?"

"I wanted to see more of the country, Berry. I stayed at women's land and found a women's clinic I toured for ideas."

Jaudon said, "The exhaust pipe is rusted." The light blue-green paint was worn off in spots. Allison's canvas rucksack was strapped to a rack behind the seat with rubber straps and hooks. It wasn't a real motorcycle; it was one of those little bikes they drove around on in Gulfport and Sarasota that sounded like someone shaking a can of dried beans.

"I have to sell it. I can't use a motorcycle to make home visits and give talks in the community. Before I left I applied for two jobs. Both called Cullie's phone and set up interview times. I have enough money from selling my car to buy a little buggy to get me around."

As much as she didn't approve of how Allison lived her life, Jaudon was mesmerized by the machine. "How much?" she asked.

"Jaudon?" Berry had a headlong attack of nerves. "You want to buy a motorcycle?"

"Why not? It's a little bitty one and can free up the van for you so you don't have to pick me up nights."

"It's not safe," said Berry. "I'd worry about you constantly with your balance as off kilter as it has been."

She'd forgotten about Berry's folks disappearing on their motorcycle. "It got Allison here in one piece, Berry. And it's not a big hog like your pa's. It's almost a bicycle with a motor."

"That's all true," said Allison. "It's economical and saves time and gas."

"I'll ride to work and never long distances."

"It makes me awful uneasy."

"At first." She put her arm around Berry. "You'll see, I'll always come home."

Berry tried to breathe away her scare. Jaudon wasn't her mother or father. Motorcycles did not equate to abandonment.

For years, Berry had watched Jaudon fall for big band love songs and new Beverage Bay equipment and for Berry herself. She saw that smiling-eyed longing again and, as always, could not bring herself to deny her. She contemplated the single seat on the bike. At least there was no question of riding along. "What will you take for it, Allison?" she asked.

Allison smoothed her hair the way she did when she acted as mediator for her squabbling group. She named a very low price, but of course the bike was antiquated.

"We can afford that, Jaudon."

"I promise I'll be extra careful, Berry. I bet I can learn to keep it in good repair too. Cousin Cal will give me lessons—after he finishes laughing at it."

Berry suggested Allison stay with them again since she'd sold her transportation. "I'll carry you where you need to be in the van until you buy a car, Allison. I can tell my honey isn't going to share her new toy."

"Fantastic," said Allison. "I can't wait to start making a crater in the consciousness of the women around here who think they're fine as is."

Jaudon took the bike to the tax office to register it. She rehabbed her little beauty after work and every day off under the instruction of Cousin Cal. That made it possible to avoid Berry's hurried meetings with her cohorts, the ringing phone, and drop-ins from their expanding contacts with other small groups around the region. Allison's arrival seemed to juice up the whole gang of women. Jaudon, when home, was distracted and nervous, worried about the phone's multiple-party line; she didn't want anyone listening in on the plans of these contrary women.

Berry was stressed enough without Jaudon picking fights.

"Why are you arguing with everything I say?" she asked Jaudon a few days before the demonstration. They were cleaning up after dinner.

"Me? That's what you're doing."

"See, you can't answer a question without turning it into a world war."

"It's that darn Allison," Jaudon said, scrubbing the iron skillet so hard sweat was stinging her eyes. "There is no way to ignore her, as much as I want to concentrate on you and on the store. What got into you, inviting her to stay in Gran's trailer again? Hasn't she brought us enough trouble?"

"You know it's only until she and Cullie work things out. That ought to take about three minutes."

Jaudon saw Berry's dander was up. She joked. "I think the first step may take three minutes. After that, close your eyes."

Berry shook her head, but she couldn't stop a smile.

"Aw, I love you, my glorious swamp flower." Jaudon pulled Berry into her arms, sudsy hands and all. The ringing in her ear turned to swing music at Berry's touch.

"Good. I was afraid that bike stole your affections away from me, angel mine." She flattened Jaudon's cowlick with the suds.

"I talked to your old mechanic at Cloud Christian today. He said it's a classic. I can put a double seat on it so we can both ride."

Berry laid a gentle hand on her chest. "If you don't mind, Jaudon, get yourself a big soft single seat. That bike is your baby. I don't see myself on the tail end of it. The seat it came with will torture your sweet parts." She trailed her hand between Jaudon's legs.

"Can you spare some tender loving care to those parts and put your worries to rest?"

"Oh, you," Berry said, her voice soft.

Gran was at bingo. There in the kitchen Jaudon reached under Berry's loose cotton shorts and rested the heel of her hand on Berry's spot. They might know all the body terms now, but Jaudon was partial to their own language. Berry interrupted her thought by unzipping Jaudon's fly front and imitating the rhythm of Jaudon's hand with her own. She loved when they both felt this together, the swirls of energy that wrapped around them and lingered for long minutes.

Until the phone rang.

Jaudon growled and nipped at Berry's neck. She stayed put until she heard Berry greet the caller with a cheerful voice.

In the garage to put a brighter bulb in the bike's headlight and bouncy from the brief encounter with Berry, Jaudon lit a citronella candle and thought she'd give the bike a name. Zoom, maybe, though it couldn't.

CHAPTER THIRTY-ONE

Berry was bored, overheated and her feet hurt. This was their third hour outside city hall. They shouted, chanted, waved signs and demanded to speak with the mayor. The city had never elected a female city council member. Also there were no Native American, Hispanic, or black representatives in local positions. Once they were represented, they'd have power to make more changes.

Judy Fish and her girlfriend Nina were there. Samantha O'Connor, who came despite her husband, brought her bright-eyed youngest. Perfecta Maldonado and Donna Skaggs displayed a homemade banner. Mercie showed up minus her new girlfriend—they hadn't worked out. Cullie and Jaudon were both at their jobs, but ready to post bail bonds.

The mayor didn't speak to the crowd. He had a young underling come outside to tell them the city didn't respond to unruly mobs filled with outside agitators.

From the sidewalk, a woman yelled, "He better agitate his chicken white butt out here or we'll show him how unruly these inside agitators can be."

The crowd, at least fifty or sixty strong, howled in approval. Up on the steps someone started a chant, "Chicken white butt/Get outta your rut!"

Both exhilarated and apprehensive, Berry joined in, shaking her sign in the air with the other women, but remembering the headlines reporting the arrests of thousands of anti-war protesters in DC. What were a few women to the police?

It was frustrating. Four Lakes was a testing ground for larger Southern cities. Respectable Donna Skaggs and other women had asked for appointments with the mayor and the city councilors repeatedly. Today

Berry found the courage to approach the mayor's secretary and ask to see the mayor. The secretary treated her as an annoyance, took down her name and contact information, but refused, as she had all the others, to set a time.

A few minutes before noon, two of the police officers who were standing around watching for trouble moved to the front door, blocking it. At noon, another officer wrapped a chain through the oversized door pulls and padlocked them.

Berry looked at Mercie beside her. The shock on her face reflected her own.

"I don't understand why we have to keep asking for the rights we ought to have," said Mercie as they moved with the crowd around the building. "I don't want to go through more messes like Selma and Watts, but if this mayor thinks women can't make big trouble, he's got another think coming."

At least half of the crowd surged around the side of the building to the parking lot. Several women tried to surround the mayor's car and were pushed away by city police.

Berry said, "Oh, Mercie, I hope the police have learned at least a little bit from the civil rights movement. But look at the street—they've brought in a line of highway patrolmen."

Lari was whiny. "What do these men think we're up to? We want to talk about inequality and punishing rapists and birth control."

Judy yelled to the police, "You better call out the National Guard. Women are dangerous to your status quo."

Perfecta took Judy's arm. "Shh, Judy. We need them on our side. They don't understand our problems are their problems."

"I hope this doesn't show up on the news," Berry said. "Jaudon has the radio going at the store constantly. I can see her come whipping up here on her scooter to save me."

Perfecta and Mercie both covered their mouths as they laughed. They all turned to watch new activity. The mayor stepped out a side door. Berry checked her white nurse's watch. It was lunchtime.

"Mayor Crum," cried Allison.

"She's going to get herself arrested," grumbled Lari.

Judy said, "Her lawyer will kill her for surfacing."

The mayor spoke, but without a mike. Berry strained to hear him.

Allison moved to the mayor with the stack of petitions outlining their demands that the city issue a proclamation supporting women's equality and instruct city departments to make hiring more representative of its population.

The mayor accepted the papers, turned, and handed them to a stone-faced police officer. Another officer forced a police car between the mayor and Allison and drove the mayor away.

Berry knew her pulse rate was soaring. She was light-headed from the sticky heat and hunger, and worried Jaudon was worrying about her. Perfecta mentioned her reddened face, motioned to Mercie, and they led her to a concrete bench under a fully leafed live oak that spread over the pavement. Mercie used a hat to fan her. A breeze off the big lake reached them.

"We did what we came for. Let's go home," Perfecta said.

Her voice weak, Berry reminded them that she was Allison's ride home.

"I'll go tell her." They watched as Perfecta tried to cross the lot to Allison, but was stopped by a police officer.

By this time the bulk of the demonstrators, sweaty and cranky, were massed tight in the parking lot behind city hall, denying access to a pizza delivery guy. Women crowded him with offers to pay for the pizza he'd never be able to deliver to officials inside city hall. He shrugged, took their money and retreated to his small car, driving with caution between the women. It was lunch hour and the crowd had grown.

Lari said, "I want to shoot these politicians with the biggest machine gun I can find."

In her black outfit, black bandana around her head, Lari appeared capable of that, thought Berry. "Who licked the red off your candy today?" she asked.

Lari's smirk got deeper, but her eyes had less light in them than usual.

Perfecta soothed Berry's damp brow with a cool hand. "We passed a restaurant with a big air-conditioning sign."

"I'm doing better," said Berry, queasy enough that she leaned away from the smell of meat-laden pizza. "Look at all these women who left work to join us. They want what we want. It's beautiful." She took her friends' hands.

Clouds swelled above them, some dark, some with undersides laundered white. They threatened to burst, but held off, shedding their swift shadows on the crowd of women.

Allison stood on a low cinder block wall. Though she wasn't tall, her head was above the crowd. She smoothed her hair.

"They're shutting us out of our own city hall," Allison roared. The women booed. "The mayor refuses to talk with his constituents. The police have been called to keep taxpaying citizens outside the offices of our government."

"Let us in! Let us in!" the crowd yelled.

"But wait," Allison shouted. "There's more than one way to enter city hall." Her words were met with questioning murmurs. "We can storm the doors or we can elect women to office. They'll have to let us in, won't they?"

She paused to let the idea sink in. "How many of you plan to vote for a female council member if we have one on the ballot?"

The response was universal applause.

"And for a female mayor?"

There was a short silence. There were open mouths, startled looks. One woman's deep voice sang the first words of Woody Guthrie's "This Land is Your Land." Others joined in.

When the song was done, Allison said, "I am declaring my candidacy for mayor today. Will you support me? Will you campaign with me?"

"Millar for Mayor!" was the rallying cry.

"Is there any chance she can win?" asked Mercie.

"Doesn't she have to live here?"

Berry said, "The election is two years off. She'll be living here with Cullie long enough to establish residency by that time."

"Is she with Cullie?"

"I predict she will be."

"Who's willing to run for city councilor?" A few hands were raised, Lari's among them, though she didn't live in Four Lakes either. Allison called them up front.

Berry stood and applauded until her hands hurt.

Allison said, "We need to go inside for the required paperwork."

"Let them in!"

The chief of police passed Berry. She heard him use the word *harpies*. Lari looked ready to spring at him. Berry grabbed her wrist. "Allison said it best. Electing women will be our best revenge."

"But so slow, Berry," said Mercie. "So slow."

"It's a stroke of luck for Allison that the voting age was lowered to eighteen, Berry. The kids will vote for her." Jaudon kept trying to be more accommodating about Berry's friendships. She got crabby, though, from the ear pain and not hearing well and Momma forever leaning on her about the store. Everything was an effort these days.

"We're registering young people to vote like all get out."

"I'm amazed that you find the time, my Georgia gal."

"Just an hour here and there on your late nights. There are more women than men in Four Lakes, but that may not help. Some of these women are such know-nothings it's not funny. They let their men tell them how to vote."

"Aw, heck. No wonder suffrage passed—men must have planned to use their wives as extra votes."

"Allison's going to try to balance that with old voters worried about their health and Social Security. They might like having a nurse in charge who has plans for a senior center. She has a chance of unseating Mayor Crum in the next election if she wins a city council seat this time around."

They hadn't been able to sit and talk for over a week. Gran brought them to Mudfoot's Fish Fry, the sole restaurant in downtown Rainbow Gap. This time of day the Spanish moss came close to lace trimmed in gold where the sun shone through. Jaudon had wanted to come here; it was a safe and homey place for her birthday dinner.

Mudfoot's brought in people statewide, it was that good. The big room, which held fourteen tables and booths, was empty when they got there in midafternoon. Jaudon's mouth watered at the leftover lunch smells of smoked mullet and deep-fried, seasoned batter. They marched across scuffed-up wooden floors to their favorite table away from the windows. The dining room was paneled and decorated with framed posters of long-ago fishing derbies. Checked oilcloth covered the jumble of square, rectangular, or oval tables. High up were gator heads, trophy fish, a long mural of a swamp, and another of parrots.

"I hear you're making your gator bites with chicken again, Mudfoot."

The owner, behind the serving window, was preparing his popular breading.

"You say that again and I'll make them out of you, Jaudo."

Jaudon yelped with glee. She, Pops, and Mudfoot had had an ongoing insult contest since she was in grade school.

Berry said, "I'm sticking with the butter sauce pasta, coleslaw, and hush puppies in peanut oil. I'll forgive you anything for your hush puppies—they're flat-cold good."

"I'd marry you for this coleslaw recipe," Gran told him.

Mudfoot winked. "You'll make a bigamist of me yet, Ida."

Once they had their sweet tea, Gran said, "Does Allison have any government experience?"

"What can a little city like Four Lakes want besides a master's degree in public health nursing and her work at county health departments?" Berry said with a fond smile.

"Goodness. I'd say she does. Oh, here he comes already."

Mudfoot delivered their platters of food. Gran took a bite of the slaw and gave a happy sigh as she patted her lips with a brown paper napkin.

"Isn't Mayor Crum up there a land developer?" Jaudon asked. "I don't think we need to keep land grabbers in office."

"You win the prize," said Berry. "All he knows about government is how to sign permit requests and convince the city to let him rip up the countryside."

Gran pointed a popcorn crawfish at Berry. "Is that all he's got going for him? Why, we'd beat him standing on our heads and whistling Dixie. It wouldn't take but a minute's thought to decide on Allison if I lived in Four Lakes." She dipped her crawfish in Mudfoot's special tartar sauce.

"Of course, Mayor Chicken Whitebutt has money to run a campaign."

That got Gran to chuckling.

Berry explained how the man got his name.

"The money does make a difference, doesn't it," Gran said.

"You can say that again," said Berry. "Your momma has a couple of stores in Four Lakes, doesn't she, Jaudon?"

"One east of town and another west. You're not thinking of asking Momma to donate? She'd sooner run herself than give money to a candidate."

"Now, there's a bad idea," said Gran. "Has your momma ever thought about running for office?"

"I'm not privy to what Momma's thinking, but she'd beat whoever she set out to beat come heck or high water."

Gran looked serious. "I believe it. No offense, but I don't know if I want Momma Vicker running any town."

"Or your life." Jaudon fingered her face. She caught herself doing that a lot to catch any new growth. She hadn't become less self-conscious about her looks, but she quit agonizing over them most of the time. "She won't listen to me about advertising the Beverage Bay as a convenience store. We have to start moving that way or lose business to major chains showing up here any day."

Berry said, "You're a real businesswoman, Jaudon." For some reason, Berry's eyes got wet when she mentioned such things. Her little friend Jaudon who was all grown up.

"Aw, heck, Berry, I'm a store clerk."

Gran's eyes were on Jaudon. "Nothing wrong with having a trade."

"I never thought of it being a trade. Working at the store is a sort of fun-and-games way to earn a living."

Gran said, "I expect one day you'll do CPA and tax work full-time, given your momma's plans."

"That fight isn't over yet, Gran. Momma will wake up and smell the roses one of these days. Bat's seen the world. What's in flyspeck Rainbow Gap for him?"

"Settle down and live happily ever after, like us?"

"With a military pension, Berry? I can't think he'll have the drive it takes to build a business. He doesn't have the instincts. I know he's my big brother and all, but he can be lazy."

Gran used a finger to clean her plate. "I discovered that myself. He leaves dirty dishes for the women to take care of. I find candy wrappers, bottle tops, and all manner of scraps everywhere he's been."

Earlier she told Berry to call ahead and make sure mango pie was for dessert. Mudfoot presented the pie with a citronella candle perched on top. "All's I found on short notice. Happy birthday, youngster," he said, and sat with them. They devoured the pie, lingering after Mudfoot returned to his kitchen while Jaudon and Gran downed coffee.

Jaudon's enthusiasm showed in her sweeping gestures. "This area is a goldmine. More people move here from the Midwest daily. I think the Bays can go beyond the idea of drive-thrus. Let the drive-thru part be a gas pump or two and while the cars are being gassed up, customers can come inside and pick up a quart of milk, a six-pack of beer, bread, and a candy bar. I guarantee more sales. Impulse buying they call it."

"It's the uniqueness of the drive-thru that attracts your customers, Jaudon," said Gran. "They're fond of staying in their cars and being waited on in their slippers, with a jacket over a nightgown or a T-shirt. Leastways, I know I do when I can afford it."

"The tourists and the new people stop at the drive-thrus too," Berry said. "They think they're quaint and scenic. You've seen them take pictures."

"Pictures don't make us money, Berry. They're more comfortable with a name they know from their own state. I have to find ways to bring them inside."

"There's six ways to Sunday to accomplish that, Jaudon. Start with a sale."

"Did you say sale? Momma won't allow it. We don't take coupons or food stamps either. She thinks that's giving handouts. You see what I mean? In her mind, Momma never did move out from behind her first counter at the roadside where she sold nothing but strawberries, cold pop, and candy bars. I'm so stymied I want to holler."

CHAPTER THIRTY-TWO

Later, Berry closed her eyes and considered this developing side of her lover. How did that eight-year-old grow up to scoot around on a motorbike and to have passions both for working in the store and for business planning, for taxes and accounting, for training and supervision? Berry considered herself a natural for a healing profession, but never predicted Jaudon's intense interest in business itself, not just the Beverage Bays. Had the blow to her head changed her? Was she becoming her unlovable momma? She expected Jaudon to be more of a Mudfoot. He ran his restaurant the way he always had, simply, with his original recipes and original style, one of the few surviving genuine fish camp restaurants.

Probably, Jaudon needed to try on the many ways of being Jaudon. Coming up was rough on her, but she fit—was born to—the Beverage Bays. She wasn't obligated to be as hard as Momma. She was a boss with a heart; once they got past Jaudon's difference, her employees became friends if they weren't already. All this talk about competition and gas pumps and changing the basic concept of the Bays—she suspected that was over-ambition talking. She had high hopes Jaudon would return to her roots before the Jaudon that Berry loved changed.

And if not? She herself was changing too, wasn't she? She planned on becoming a woman who saw blessings, not faults. Supported rather than discouraged. Whose bottom line was patience, kindness, acceptance, and lots of humor. She wanted to evolve into such a woman.

How? She wasn't making much progress. It was her fault that Allison had come into their lives, her fault Jaudon was roughed up by the cops and lost her hearing.

The next day she realized that she worked in a place that was a fit laboratory for making a silk purse out of a sow's ear. At least once a day her patience was tried by a ranting widow or a waiting room full of kids who needed a good walloping. What she found most upsetting were the mothers who let those kids run wild as leaves in a hurricane. The Beverage Bays were shaping her Jaudon, and what better place to mold herself than in a medical office?

It was about three thirty in the afternoon when she stopped herself from losing her cool, as Judy Fish would say, over a pesky patient who told the receptionists she was waiting too long to see one of the doctors. The back office LPN said, "It's a first visit, unscheduled, and late afternoon—of course the woman has to wait." They whispered in commiseration with each other.

She was shocked to see the name on the file was Larissa Hand. Were there two with the same name? She was Lari's age. The complaint was back pain and bleeding.

At the entry to the waiting room she called, "Miss Hand?" She led the way to an exam room. "Lari, what's wrong?"

Lari was not her usual neat self. Her hair was oily-looking and tangled, her black T-shirt stained, she reeked of tobacco and marijuana, and her black cutoff jeans sagged on her. A seam was torn. Her legs, full of red bumps and scratches, must be serving as happy hunting grounds for mosquitoes. Like Eddie Dill had, she looked as if she was spending too much time in the woods.

"These goddamn doctors are all the same," Lari said in a voice that broadcast throughout the open-plan office.

Berry recoiled at the loudness. This was Lari, wasn't it? Quiet Lari, always lurking, never speaking much above a whisper?

"They think my time is worth nothing," Lari said, "and theirs is gold. These men scheme to charge more while we wait and wait."

Lari leaned close to Berry and pushed the file folder to the floor. Moisture flew from her mouth along with a foul odor. "I got sent to Florida because the Southern pace was supposed to settle me. Well, it's slow here. Slower than slow."

What was making Lari act so strangely?

"Why did I have to fill out a hundred pages of paperwork? I want you to look at my back, Nurse Berry, that's all I'm asking." Lari used her title with heavy sarcasm.

"You do realize we're an obstetrics and gynecology practice?" Berry regretted the coldness in her words. She wanted to be home, on the rough old pond bench, breathing in the peace of the wildlife on the pond. The swallows would be skimming the water for mosquitoes, the long-legged birds would be high-stepping, beaks plunging for fish. Was the Great Spirit teaching Berry some lesson?

"My aunt's damn doctor won't see me at all today. No other office was willing to fit me in. I told the front desk I was friends with you and that homely gorilla you live with. Are you gyno people too good to look at my back instead of my crotch?"

She had a spell of nerves when, without warning, Lari pulled her T-shirt over her head and turned from Berry.

She saw patches of purple formed above and below what appeared to be a ragged puncture wound with bloody edges. "What were you doing when you first noticed it?"

"Trimming palm fronds in my aunt's yard. Mosquito bites itch, this burns. I can't sleep, it hurts too much to eat. Would you get someone in here who knows what they're doing, goddammit?"

"You've been scratching it."

"Of course I scratched the thing—it's itchy. It's too big for a tiny mosquito bite or a spider bite. Or skin cancer. You're not much of a nurse."

Berry was short of breath and scared as much as insulted. Lari's Wisconsin accent grew more nasal with every word. Had the demonstration left her unbalanced? Had her family sent her away for reasons other than college? In her gentlest manner she explained, "The scratching may have infected it, so it's swollen, that's all. I'll clean it up—"

"Not you. I want a doctor in here. People die from infections every day."

"Lari, what is it? Are you reacting to a drug?"

"I'm here for this itchy stingy thing." Lari raised an arm as if to strike her.

Berry stepped out of range. She'd tried not to hate Lari since the incident with Jaudon. Lari wasn't making her effort any easier. Allison had said Lari was acting off the wall these days.

"All right." Berry sighed and picked up the blood pressure cuff. "I need to finish some preliminaries."

Lari wrenched the cuff from her hand and hurled it onto the desk. "You don't need my blood pressure for a bug bite."

Now she wanted to knock Lari clean into next week and then some.

By this time Lari's face, always such a pale white, was very red, and her eyes seemed to protrude. Her hand rhythmically rapped on the desk. Lari reminded her of a pot on the stove about to commence a rolling boil. Lari was disturbed. She thought, *Of course the movement would draw mentally ill women. They must have a harder time than most.*

Berry clutched the file to her chest and hurried to the nearest doctor.

"I think I have an emergency for you, Dr. Gara." Berry was new enough at this to be nervous about her conclusion. She'd handled patients who declined routine vital signs at the rehab center and calmed agitated patients, but they were nothing like Lari. "The patient shows signs of dangerous high blood pressure but won't let me use the cuff, possible hyperthyroidism, a tendency to violence—and what may be an infected insect bite."

Dr. Gara looked at her, eyebrows raised.

Berry looked at the floor. "I know her outside of work, Doctor. She's strange, but I never saw her act like this."

"She frightened you, didn't she? Let's go."

She jogged to the room and opened the door, Dr. Gara close behind her. Lari was gone.

Berry headed for the waiting room and stopped at the sound of pounding on the bathroom door. She beckoned to the doctor and ran for the key to unlock the door. Lari yanked the door open and rushed into the room.

Dr. Gara tried to stop her. Lari grabbed the doctor's wrists and shoved her away, screaming at her. The two male doctors came running, took hold of Lari, and got her into an examining room. Dr. Gara, rubbing her wrists, joined them, picked up the phone and told reception to call 911.

Berry sat on a stool in another room down the hall, her clipboard shaking as she tried to catch up on her notes.

About half an hour later, Dr. Gara stopped by, wiping sweat from her forehead. "The patient calmed enough to remember being hit at the wound site by a falling palm frond. Fragments of thorn inside the wound caused infection. Very dangerous. You did well with a difficult patient."

The police spoke at length with Dr. Gara. Someone must have sedated Lari as she seemed to be sleeping when she was wheeled out to the ambulance. Berry spent the next hour dropping and forgetting things. On the way home, she went clear through a stop sign, never noticing it until she heard a screech of brakes and a horn.

The next day, a Saturday, the windows were so splashed with raindrops that the yard, through the wet glass, was a wavery green mess. She told Jaudon and Gran her story in bits and pieces as they worked together cleaning house and doing laundry. Rigo stopped by with a big bag of Chinese takeout for lunch and listened to Berry's story again, but she didn't use Lari's name.

"What are you worried about?" he asked.

"I was too scared of her to be compassionate. And I never learned about any palm tree infections in school. I'm not taking one more advanced class at Cloud Christian. There are too many gaps in my training. I'll bet there are better schools around."

"She sounds like her cheese went and slid off her cracker," was Gran's comment as she put her china cups and saucers on the table for oolong tea.

"Lari is bound and determined to ruffle every feather in this household," said Jaudon.

"Jaudon, no naming names. I told you her name in confidence."

"Rigo needs to know. What if Lari shows up at the bar acting nuts, Rigo? You can help her."

Berry hated herself at that moment. She'd betrayed a patient's trust out of insecurity, because she needed reassurance that she did everything as best she could. What if she'd made Lari leave for acting crazy? Lari could have died. If she faced the truth, she saw that she'd wanted to disclose Lari's name. There was comfort in company. How selfish she was; how far she needed to go to become a good person.

She needn't inflict her disappointment in herself on the people she loved. "It's not impossible that she wants to ruffle feathers," she said. "Or she could just plain be a very sick person who needs friends."

Jaudon berated herself too. If only she hadn't let Lari rile her in the first place. Lari must have sensed Jaudon was the soft underbelly of the family, the way to entangle herself with somebody else's happiness and ruin it in any way possible. "She's jealous of what we have. You're not going to be fired, Berry. You gave the kook everything you had."

Berry looked at her sideways and Jaudon realized she'd spoken with an edge of anger, though the anger was at herself. She remembered the few times Berry got so mad, how it made her feel sick. That didn't happen anymore. She needed to learn to control her own anger. She reached to touch Berry, to explain, but Berry turned away.

"It wasn't enough, Jaudon. It wasn't hardly enough."

For the first time, Berry skipped her Sunday afternoon woman's group. Dr. Gara had called to let her know Lari was about to be released from the hospital. She wasn't going to take the chance that Lari might show up.

She worried about her competence as a nurse when she went to the Monday lunch meeting at work. Each week the doctors chose a few cases to review with the staff. The first one they discussed was Larissa Hand.

"Berry. I hope you know that nothing you did triggered the patient's bizarre behavior," Dr. Gara said.

"How can I deal better with someone in such a state?"

"You can't at your current level of knowledge and experience. I checked the college program you attended and there was not an iota of course work in mental health. I'll be contacting the nursing program there and suggesting that they require classes on the subject if they want their students to get jobs."

"So she's mentally ill, not physically?"

"The patient was released, but later the police had her aunt commit her to the psych ward at Four Lakes General for evaluation."

Berry covered her mouth in shock. "I'm so sorry."

Dr. Gara leaned forward and assured her that she'd done well. She suggested that Berry have someone else see any patients she knew socially. It was better for both nurse and patient. "I contacted her regular physician over the weekend and learned that his office terminated services to her based on behavioral issues."

Berry wanted to say that she took Ms. Hand to the exam room because of the distress she was causing waiting patients and staff. That wasn't entirely true, she realized. She had been shaken and curious too.

Another of the partners said, "We'll bring in an expert to give training sessions. Every one of us needs to be able to recognize the symptoms of mental illness and to understand it so you can replace the alarm it inspires with empathy and confident know-how. Berry, call it a learning experience. Staying calm and asking for help were the correct steps to take. I'm sure you initially thought the patient was obnoxious." The doctor smiled. "She was, of course, but nothing is simple about mental health."

The meeting went on. Berry paid attention, but didn't take much in. She wanted to make something of herself—to do Gran proud. To do Ma and Pa proud if one or both of them showed up out of the blue. *There are miracles*, she told herself. Jaudon once suggested the idea of raising a kid might have panicked her fun-loving ma and pa. In that case, she was lucky to be alive at all, when getting rid of a baby back then was illegal, but possible. They ought to know she wasn't a burden to anyone at this late date. She'd take care of them when they got old.

Dr. Gara was asking her a question. She prodded herself away from her fairy tale.

By the time she drove home that evening, she began to accept that while she hadn't failed in the eyes of the doctors, and while it was fitting for Jaudon to be peeved at her for carrying on, she was disheartened at her lapse of compassion, understanding, and tolerance. She trusted the Great Spirit to teach her, but there was no end to what she needed to learn.

CHAPTER THIRTY-THREE

Hurricane season was passing without much activity. It was a cooler October than usual. A freak cold snap was expected for the next two nights and they were covering Gran's late summer seedlings with bedsheets tacked together by clothespins.

As she tried to spread a sheet across the chard and spinach, Berry kept dropping the pins and the fabric's edges. She hadn't recovered from her tailspin after the Lari incident, and was brooding, losing weight and her self-confidence, anxious about every blessed thing.

Jaudon missed Berry's playfulness and calm support like crazy. She kept trying to give Berry whatever she needed, but it didn't help—Berry was downright fearful.

"The doc said you did good," Jaudon reminded her once more. "What's got you all stirred up?"

The temperature was dropping and the air was calm, heading into the freeze. They decided to cover the old sago palm they loved. It was almost twice their height. Jaudon staggered as she pitched a blanket up over half of it from a ladder on one side while Berry struggled on her ladder to shroud it from the other side. Berry threw and threw, unsuccessfully. They both descended. Berry stood across from Jaudon, a doleful figure hugging the blanket to herself in the dusk.

"What is it, my sad swamp flower?"

Berry let her head drop toward a shoulder. "Disappointment, Jaudon. In myself."

"Because the sago tree has outgrown us and our blankets?"

"I try and try to at least tolerate the staff and every last patient, but sometimes, someone or some office procedure will stick in my craw. It doesn't take a Lari to set me off."

"I don't work in an office, but I come unglued—it's natural, Berry. Who doesn't go through it?"

"That's not how I want to be."

Berry ran up on the porch. She unfurled the blanket from there. Jaudon caught it and went up the ladder to attach it. Berry gave up and went inside. She let the door slam behind her. Berry never did that, and the loss of control filled Jaudon with heightened apprehension. Was Lari's mental illness caused by the women's movement? She wouldn't be surprised.

There was a stack of towels on the steps and she used them to cover the patches of fall flowers they'd planted since Momma and Pops had moved out. Momma had never cared about flowers, except to cut and sell. Berry loved her fall flowers: the reliable lavender-colored society garlic, the busy plumbagos filled with blue flowers, the red and purple bougainvillea growing by the house. Weeds, Momma called them. Berry took such pleasure in them. The gladiolas, daffodils, and other bulbs were well-protected underground.

Headlights went by on Eulalia Road. The vehicle inched away. She suspected trouble of some kind, but the engine sound faded. With Allison long since moved to Cullie's, Jaudon didn't expect any more trouble. The police wouldn't have a problem finding a city council candidate if they wanted her. Allison's lawyer had succeeded in arranging for her to give a deposition rather than go to Puerto Rico.

Enough had gone on in the past year that Jaudon was antsy. She went in the house and made sure all the doors were locked.

Berry was on the couch, worrying the hem of the old beige sweater Gran knitted so long ago it had shrunk too small to button. A healthy fire popped and sparked in the limestone fireplace. Gran had the house TV on and was red-faced with hilarity as she watched *All in the Family*. Berry watched too, though she told Jaudon some time ago she was aware Archie Bunker was an ignoramus.

Jaudon exhaled in relief when she saw Berry laugh. "I'm thinking it's time for you and me to run away and have some fun for a day, Berry."

Gran nodded her agreement.

"Let's go exploring once the weather warms up. I'll schedule coverage at the Bay. I reckon we'd enjoy a daytrip to some lake."

"That sounds peaceful," said Berry. "I could do with some peacefulness."

"I could do with some fishing. Hey, let's stop at a barbecue stand after and carry home dinner. We'll take Zefer. She's older and calm enough to stay put in the boat with us, don't you think?"

"After all, we can't work every minute," said Berry. Jaudon saw the excitement in Berry's eyes. "I'll hold her leash, Jaudon, if you row."

"That's a deal."

"Do you want to ask Allison and Cullie?"

The question jarred Jaudon. As harsh as she was about Allison, she'd come to understand that the so-called patriarchal government she'd been raised to love was the same government that took half her hearing. It made her so angry she didn't want to think about what happened. Allison stirred it all up every time she saw her. "I wanted time for the two of us."

"I do too. I don't know why I said that. Or it might be that I do know why. I want them to stay together always, the same as us. Wouldn't it be nice to have another couple to do things with once in a while?"

"What about Rigo and Jimmy Neal?"

"You know I love them to pieces, Jaudon. I need woman company too, for fun times, as much as meetings."

"Because I'm not that much of a woman, I guess."

Gran gave her a severe look. "Jaudon, if you don't stop acting like a hound dog that can't find the duck, I'll knock you so hard you'll see tomorrow today."

"Aw, heck, Berry, Gran, can't a person talk about her shortcomings without having more shortcomings pointed out to her?"

Gran said, "I'm trying to help build you up, not pick on you, Jaudon Vicker."

The TV advertisement ended and they sat watching in silence until Edith Bunker got Gran hysterical again by telling her doctor to take two aspirin and get some rest.

Berry said, "That's what we should do, Jaudon."

"What?" asked Gran.

"Take an antiworry pill and get some rest."

Berry said she wasn't as down in the dumps as she had been.

The threatened freeze never amounted to much. Jimmy Neal and Olive both needed hours at the store, so when the weather warmed up by the weekend, Berry and Jaudon were raring to go out on the small boat.

Gran said, "How about I make you girls a picnic lunch? My senior group went to Pleasant Grove Reservoir about a month ago—the reclaimed phosphate mine? The reservoir makes a nice clean lake. We saw wood ducks, bunny rabbits, one of those lacy-shawled anhinga birds, and egrets galore. It's brand new, just open to the public, so you might want to go before every family in Lecoats County and their shirttail cousins discover the place."

Jaudon popped up, saying to Berry, "I'll hose down Pops's skiff and hook it up to the boat trailer before we go, Berr." She hugged Gran and rushed out to clean the boat.

They left the house by eight a.m. Sunday after dousing themselves with sunscreen and a homemade lemon eucalyptus oil Gran swore kept bugs away. They applied it to Zefer's collar too, though she protested by hammering the kitchen rug a few times with her snout and throwing a sneezing fit.

Lines of fat oaks spread the length of Eulalia Road. Sun made the moss drapery sparkle this time of day and streamed slanted rays along their path, fashioning a dreamy light. Berry pictured this as the passage to heaven, if there was a heaven, and if there wasn't, the sight was heaven enough.

They rode with the van windows open to the morning cool. Zefer, all thirty-four pounds of her, sat on Berry's lap, head out the window.

"A whole day together," said Berry.

"No ornery patients or customers. No politics."

"We'll wash this dog soon as we hit home, Jaudon. Didn't you smell that she stinks on ice?"

"I was going to wash her, but I got busy."

"You needn't look so apologetic. I was too busy myself."

The skiff was a shallow nine-footer made out of composite materials. They wrestled it into the water. Jaudon almost went under, losing her footing as she pulled the boat out deeper, but got aboard with Berry's help. She rowed while Berry, shoulders bare above her halter top, settled in the stern. They both sat on red combination life saver/seat pads, and they put their picnic blanket under the flat bow for Zefer, who turned up her nose at it and jumped to stand on top of the bow, tongue lolling, leash hanging.

She rowed to the center of the reservoir. A gang of ducks paddled away from them. Otherwise there was no one on the water.

As if she was reading Jaudon's mind, Berry said, "Just mallards."

There was one car parked at the edge of the road and they heard very young children calling to parents in the woods.

Jaudon fished for a while, catching small ones and two legal bluegills before letting them go. By the time she put her rod away, she smelled almost as bad as Zefer.

"Phew. You need a dousing." Berry scooped up handfuls of water to splash on her.

"Berry, that's cold." She shook her head to empty the water from her ear. Zefer barked. When Berry didn't stop, Jaudon took the bait pail and filled it. Zefer nearly dropped them in the drink leaning against the gunwale and yipping in excitement. At one point she tried chasing her wiry tail, but the boat was too small for a decent chase.

Berry gave Jaudon a threatening grin, hands in the water.

"Berry, I'm soaked now. You stop or I'll slather bait slime on your sexy top."

Berry surrendered, laughing. "Nothing makes me happier than seeing you have fun."

Jaudon thought Berry's smiling eyes looked as warm as a mug of hot chocolate in last week's chill. She emptied the pail over the side.

The lake was surrounded by evergreens: tall, straight slash pines, their dark limbs reaching wide, bushy wax myrtles, and old longleaf and loblolly pines with top notches of greenery. Their shadows were still long over the lake, keeping the water clear and cool and the fish active. The air smelled of wood and warmed honey. The day was sunny, but the cooler nights took the sting out of the heat and by ten Jaudon guessed it was about seventy-five degrees, perfect to her mind. Without warning, a screen of white birds swept upward into the pines.

"This is glorious," said Berry. "Angel, I truly believe we live in the most beautiful place in the world."

"You won't catch me disagreeing."

"I wish I brought a fan though. As if—" Berry's sharp laugh made Jaudon look up. "As if a fan is any defense against Florida heat."

"A second ago you claimed you loved it here."

"I do, but occasionally I imagine the horror of air on fire. Don't you think that's what hell is?"

"Berry, you're overworked. Relax and don't be thinking about such matters. You know I don't believe in hell. Wasn't Georgia this hot?"

"Almost, but my memory says it's brighter here."

"It does get gosh awful hot, the sun."

"There are moments I believe the whole South is not survivable, Jaudon. How can a woman withstand winds that level buildings or tear trees from thousand-year seatings? From waters that would as soon drown us as feed the plants? Mother earth isn't the enemy—until she is."

"Mother Florida." Jaudon was thinking of Momma.

"Let's us someday go north far enough to see snow. We've never seen snow, Jaudon."

"We have in the movies." She rigged up some shade for Berry with a piece of tarp and fishing line.

She stretched out next to Berry against the stern, their legs under the center bench, heads propped on their seat cushions, Zefer on the bench itself. They held hands and took turns turning the pages of their paperback books. A jet from MacDill crossed the sky, leaving a streak of white contrail like skywriting in a language they didn't know.

There was something about Berry's light touch, both provocative and soft as a cat's belly fur. She squeezed closer and slid her hand up inside Berry's shorts.

"Jaudon," Berry said in a quiet voice which sounded, to Jaudon, a mix of shock and pleasure. Berry let her book fall open on her breasts.

Jaudon removed her hand. She played a tattoo on Berry's inner thigh.

Berry squealed and squirmed. "Angel. My angel."

Jaudon was too desirous to tease Berry for long. She found the elastic waist and half pulled the shorts down. Berry moved enough to open herself. She was so wet Jaudon's hand slid before it found its place again. In the full heat of the sun and the heat of herself Berry raised her knees, let them fall askew, and lifted herself to Jaudon's ever faster fingers. She slammed her bottom on the boat's bottom as she came.

Jaudon didn't stop. With two fingers inside Berry she was able to satisfy her again. Berry lay unmoving afterward, her breath slowing, while Jaudon adjusted her shorts and placed Berry's book on her chest.

The sun was straight overhead. Grinning too widely to speak, sopping up sweat from her forehead with Jaudon's bandana, Berry watched Jaudon row them to shore and maneuver the trailer down the ramp. They secured the skiff and ate their lunch at a picnic table in the shade. The new grass could not have looked more green.

"Key lime pie, Berry?"

"Mercy me. Gran must have got up before us to bake it."

No trails were established yet, so they walked the dog on the quiet pine needles, smiling at each other, holding hands in broad daylight. The small bunny Gran predicted was peering at them before scuttling under some brush.

Jaudon said, "I like this doing nothing kind of day."

"And nothing bad happening."

"Oh, I thought we were bad enough."

"You surely were, Ms. Vicker."

"All for a good cause." Hands on hips, she narrowed her eyes at Berry. "You're doing better?"

"It gives a body perspective, getting away from it all. We've run ourselves flatter than a gander's arch since we started college. I was so petrified of not passing every course and not measuring up at work, I never gave myself breathing space to build some confidence."

They reached the van and Jaudon opened the side door. Zefer jumped in. "You didn't let that stop you," said Jaudon. "You didn't let it show most of the time either."

Once in the van, Berry opened up more. "There was no need to burden you. Your plate was just as full. It seems I always teeter on the brink of failure. Do you think someone, like Eddie Dill, put a curse on me? As fast as I was running toward being an effective nurse and a decent person, my fears were chasing me down. I was on tenterhooks from second to second."

Jaudon started the van and tooled through the park. "What makes you think Eddie put a curse on you? Or knew how?"

"Because I walked away and left him in that sinkhole. Because he comes from people who did that sort of thing. Every time I remember that night I start trembling. The evening itself was a curse."

Jaudon hadn't seen Eddie go down, but the very thought of it made her claustrophobic. "You know there was nothing to be done for him, Berry. Remember, the firefighters and the police and the ambulance came and stood around shaking their heads. What were you going to do, grab hold of the truck and yank it onto solid ground while the sinkhole was active?"

"You know there's always someone haunting my life, Jaudon. First Ma and Pa leaving, next your bullies at school, Eddie Dill, Lari Hand. They're like flying curses, flittering their way into my mind when I'm not looking." She shook her shoulders to shrug off the scraped-raw sensation the thought of them gave her.

Jaudon worried that Berry was caught up in a nasty spiderweb and tangling worse with her struggle. As she did with upgrading the Beverage Bays, she tried and tried to puzzle out how to work Berry loose.

Berry said, "I've been thinking more about Eddie's death because Allison asked if Gran wanted to sell the Stinky Lane property for a women's free clinic, or for women's land. They could put up a few small cabins for women passing through who might be in trouble and need a place to stay."

What remained of the pleasure of the day ran out of Jaudon. She was aware of the ringing in her ear for the first time in hours. She stopped in the park roadway and looked at Berry's pretty, expectant face. "Aw, heck, Berry, that woman is unhinged. Does she think because she found a refuge here, we need to scoop up more troublemakers?"

"No, Jaudon." She put a hand on Jaudon's bare arm for emphasis. "She's thinking more like women in trouble than troublemakers."

Zefer stuck her nose between the seats and Berry scratched behind her ears.

"Same thing," Jaudon said, squeezing Berry's thigh, "when Allison Millar's involved. I'm enjoying my day and won't let her goofy pie-in-the-sky ideas bug me. Anyone who builds on Stinky Lane has got to be—"

"I know, I know. But if Gran lets down her guard for even one minute, the developers will find a way if Allison doesn't. Look at what they're doing over in Orlando. Walt Disney is destroying every bit of land he can buy. Gran wants to let her land be, but if women used it wisely..." She covered Jaudon's hand. "Gran once told me that the Seminoles believe all creatures and inanimate objects have spirits that are set free when we die or an object breaks. Eddie's spirit must be soaked into Gran's land."

Right before the exit from the park, Jaudon stopped and waited for a large tortoise to cross the road toward the reservoir. They watched it stump along, as if carrying the troubles of all the humans in Florida.

"Berry, that turtle's taking your curse away on its shell. When she finds water she'll drown the darn thing, guaranteed." She wasn't what she'd call lying, and she might have been telling the truth.

Chapter Thirty-four

Jaudon didn't want to upset Gran by bringing up about Berry's state of mind, the way she felt cursed. It was Cullie, with her font of common sense wisdom, who she'd like to mull things over with, but not in front of Allison. She went to Rigo. He was packing up his texts at the library carrel where they first met.

"You'd think," said Rigo, "it would be my father's people who wrote the book on curses and all that stuff, but every time I see my mom, she's the one who presses another stone on me. Some are for love, others for money and luck and protection. I have a whole box of them at my father's place and a list of their powers."

She followed Rigo to his off-campus apartment. Jimmy Neal had moved in and he lifted her in the air with a hug while she protested. Rigo worked at the Bay once a week. Jimmy Neal took all the hours available to keep himself in school.

Jimmy Neal said, "His mom even gives me dried lavender and peppermint sachets for calm and sleep."

"I smell the peppermint."

"I have a little bit of insomnia," said Jimmy Neal.

"No you don't. I keep you awake snoring like a stock car that dropped its muffler," Rigo said as he came out of the bedroom with a small wooden box. The three of them sat close together on the couch to examine the stones.

"I'll be," said Jaudon. "Those are too beautiful to touch."

"My mother loves this stuff. She reads the tarot and uses a Ouija board and says she's a psychic."

"And she's a showgirl?"

"Was. My father made her retire from that. Look, her list says malachite will protect a person." He held out an oval piece about an inch and a half long. It was made of wavy stripes in various shades of green.

Jaudon held it in her palm, skeptical. "You think this will undo a curse?"

"Onyx is another one," said Jimmy Neal. "Rigo gave me one of those to carry in my pocket."

"Does it work?"

"Jaudo, I don't believe in curses—don't ask me."

Jimmy Neal said, "What does it matter if it does or doesn't? It's a comfort to me to carry."

"Take that one, Jaudon."

She drew her hand away. "No, it's too precious, and your mother wants you to have it."

"Give it to Berry. Tell her to keep it with her always." He looked at his mother's list again and read aloud about malachite's healing and protective properties. "When those shadows come into her mind, Berry can rub a thumb on it or grip it tightly."

Jaudon slipped the rock into a buttoned pocket for safekeeping.

Rigo told her the news about Lari had hit the streets.

"What about her?"

"People know she fell apart and got thrown in the nuthouse."

"It could be she's not the only nut, Rigo."

"The feminists?"

"Berry's batch of them anyway. I never saw such arguing, but they're careful to stay off each other's toes. There's a lot of talk about men. The straight women defend them while the women who came out lambaste you guys but good. Meanwhile Berry, Judy, Mercie, and Allison are trying to pull the others together to work on big goals."

Jimmy Neal asked, "Didn't you say Lari took up with the Lewis woman?"

Rigo shook his head. "That was short-term. Lari came sniveling to me about Mercie turning tail after a few nights together. She didn't understand why she was dumped."

"Have you gone to see Lari?"

"I don't seek her out, Jaudo. Not after she pulled that stunt on you. Anything new about her?"

"Nope. She's disappeared."

"She was always strange," Rigo said. "I never thought she was crazy, but she smokes dope like it's going out of style."

"She is wild. We know that. A person can only be so wild before she goes off the deep end."

"And sharp-tongued enough to draw blood."

"Bowed up is what Gran called her when they met. The way a snake bows up his head before he strikes?"

Jimmy Neal wrung his big hands. "I don't know the woman, but should you abandon her? Being gay can make anyone mentally ill. Near did me in before I saw I was being lied to about loving guys being unnatural. Once I opened my eyes, it was as plain as the nose on my face."

Was that what was happening to Berry? Jaudon wanted to rush home and save her.

"I knew this guy who killed himself over it," Jimmy Neal told them. "If that's not a way of being sick, I don't know what is."

That spooked Jaudon more. "I have to go soon, guys."

"It's tough out there," said Rigo, as if he didn't hear her. "I know a dancer who got beaten up so badly he's never going to dance or walk normally again. At least he lived. He was at his neighborhood gas station, washing his windshield so the attendant didn't have to. Two men from the street where he lived walked by and called him a faggot. When he didn't answer, they started whaling on him. The cops came quickly, but the animals were twice his size and had already stomped on his feet."

"Why?" asked Jaudon.

"That's what I'm going to study, Jaudo. I want to pry open their brains and see if we can fix sick people. I'll find out what we do to bring violence on ourselves."

Jimmy Neal reached over Jaudon and grabbed Rigo's shirtfront. "I don't want to hear anything about us causing the violence, Professor Lunkhead."

"Yeah." Jaudon pulled Jimmy Neal's hands away from Rigo. "Why would we do that?"

"Sometimes people send signals and don't know it," Rigo explained.

"The signal is acting like a fag. Wearing mascara, for example," said Jimmy Neal, swiping his hand toward Rigo. "But being ourselves shouldn't be an invitation to half kill us."

"I want to know why we act like fags. Can't we be gay without carrying on? A lot of guys act straight. Those who don't—is it peer pressure? A way to belong?"

"What about me?" Jaudon was lost in all this conjecture. "I don't carry on. I was born looking this way, moving this way, and have been put down for both my whole life. The ear doctor is talking about a hearing aid. Won't that add to this sad package."

Rigo put an arm around her. "Hell, Jaudo, if I had your mother, I'd run quicker than a swamp rabbit away from her style. And who else was around for you to ape? Your Pops and Bat."

"I don't ape anyone."

"Poor choice of words, Bub," said Jimmy Neal. He always called Rigo Bub. "Jaudon endures enough grief over her androgyny."

"Okay, you don't copy them, but they're your role models."

"You're wrong, Rigo. My doc says I'm part boy because I have too much male hormone in me."

"That's not a gay thing. That's biology."

"It got me beat up and bullied as a kid. They were right. I turned out to be gay."

Jimmy Neal ducked his head. "I'll be guilty the rest of my life for being part of that. I was frightened when I kept falling for other little boys. I was trying to beat the queerness out of me when I whaled on people I thought were queer."

"You see why I need to study these subjects?" said Rigo. "There are hundreds of variations of such twisted thinking at the very least. I want to make the world better for you and us and Berry."

"That's what Berry says. She wants to leave the world a better place than she found it. She wants to do it through healing and feminism."

Jimmy Neal raised both arms as if he just won the gold. "Hell, yes. Women should be able to have abortions and men should be sterilized if they can't be responsible. No one on this planet has any business having more than two kids."

"My boyfriend is a feminist." Rigo held out a hand. "Here, Jaudon. Here's a black onyx ring my mother thought I needed when I turned twelve. I bet it fits you." Rigo slid it on her pinky finger. "Onyx will keep you strong and self-confident."

"That's neat—a superpower ring." She admired it on her hand and grinned at the gift. "Me strong like bull." She filled her lungs with air as she flexed her arm muscles.

"Exactly."

Jimmy Neal said, "You know I'll always protect you too, Jaudon."

She got up and shadowboxed.

"I think you created a monster out of her, Rigo."

"Hey, is there a stone to get rid of hair you don't want?"

Rigo sniggered. "Sure, it's called a pumice stone. It'll take a layer of skin with it if you're not careful."

Jaudon took a wide stance and moved across the wood floor on the balls of her feet, jabbing at Jimmy Neal. "Me Jane, you Tarzan." She fell on the couch, waving her arms about until the three of them were silly with giggles.

"It's clear that's the stone for you," Rigo told her.

This was what she needed: to be playful with friends. She decided to have fun with Rigo and Jimmy Neal a speck longer before she went home to give Berry the green stone. She didn't expect Berry's gloom to dissipate immediately, but she sure itched for it to scram soon.

CHAPTER THIRTY-FIVE

They sat on the porch eating Pop-Tarts with Rigo early on a Sunday morning the next June. Jimmy Neal's car didn't start so Rigo dropped him at the Bay and invited himself to Pineapple Trail for breakfast. A batch of mud hens swam in and out of the reeds down past the pond bench.

Jaudon had her eyes on Berry, smiling. "I don't know if it was your protection stone, Rigo, or returning to school that did it, but I'm tickled to death at how much lighter Berry's walking these days."

At the start of spring term, Berry began classes part-time to study psychology. She planned to keep on training to be a psych nurse.

Rigo said, "I'll take credit for the psych courses too, if you please. I'll be up onstage with you when they hand you your master's degree, bowing."

Berry broke open her Pop-Tart. "I can't imaging working long and hard enough to finish a master's, Rigo. I'd rather put the energy into my patients."

"Maybe your patients would benefit in the long run." He looked around. "Why isn't Gran making us her fried cornmeal mush? These Pop-Tarts are cardboard next to sorghum molasses on mush."

Jaudon flicked a balled up napkin at him. "Look who's talking. I do believe you have enough of these things in your cabinet to feed you and Jimmy Neal for a year."

"Why do you think I come over here?"

Berry did a little bounce in her seat. "Gran's off on a two-day bus trip over to Myrtle Beach. The Air Force is putting on a flight demonstration and she's hoping to admire in person the gold airplanes she saw in the paper. I'm delighted she's gotten so active."

"I wish she'd pass down some of her recipes to you," Rigo said.

"Oh, one of us could cook up a mess of fried mush if we weren't so busy."

"Berry's working as hard as Jimmy Neal between nursing and learning."

"It keeps them out of trouble," Rigo said.

"As long as you're taking responsibility for my new goal, Rigo, I'm having a problem with one of my psych assignments. And you know how I think you're a better teacher than the ones I have at school." Berry tried fluttering her eyelashes at him.

"Oh, hon, you have it all wrong." Rigo did a quick flutter too. "You have to practice to be this expert at batting your lashes. Meanwhile, let's take a look at your homework before I go in for my behavioral experiment."

"What're you messing with this time, Dr. Shrink?" asked Jaudon.

"We're testing tests."

Jaudon smacked her knee with a hand. "Jiminy, I'm so glad I'm running a store and not a psych lab."

"I hope to the good Lord above to skip statistics and experiments," Berry said.

"You'll do well in both once you take them. They're very useful for understanding the whole science. This one's to look at stress while taking tests."

"I can tell you the answer is yes," Jaudon said.

"Psych is in its infancy, Jaudo. I'm dying to move into psychobiology."

Jaudon raised an eyebrow.

"It's fascinating to the nth degree. We study how personality, behavior, and mental illness are related to biological, social, cultural, and environmental factors. Yes, we know testing causes stress, but is there a biological basis or do we learn to stress out? Can we reduce that through meds or some other brain stimulation? I want to help put that puzzle together."

"Can you stop making my head spin with all your learning?" said Jaudon.

Berry placed a hand on each side of Jaudon's head. "Is that better, dizzy-dumbbell?"

A small car passed the driveway. It braked, reversed, and turned in. The driver peered through her window.

"That's one of Allison's Four Lake buddies," Berry said.

"Judy's lover?" asked Jaudon.

"Her name's on the tip of my tongue." Berry looked at Rigo. "She's a rabid separatist."

"What the heck's a separatist?" asked Jaudon, a sharp edge to her tone.

"The way she's looking daggers at me, I think you can guess," said Rigo. "This is going to be fun."

"Rigo," said Berry.

"What? I said fun. I'll be good."

Jaudon decided to keep her mouth shut. Why did Berry's pals have to hate men so much?

"Nina, that's her name," said Berry.

Nina carried a sack to the edge of the porch and set it down. She spoke to no one but Berry. "Judy's trees are having an extra good year. She asked me to drop off these blood oranges for you and your...partner... before her ex-husband shows up and takes them for his new wife." She used the word *husband* with disgust.

"Thanks for bringing them." Berry waved the woman forward. "Come on up and set awhile. We're having a Pop-Tart breakfast. Want one?"

Rigo leaned over the bag and took an orange. "These look delicious. Mind if I help myself?" he asked as he dug into the peel with his thumb.

Jaudon hadn't heard what Rigo murmured, but she saw his vague and innocent expression. She held a bark of laughter at the sudden pinched look on the woman's face, as if they were forcing her to inspect their outhouse barrel.

"Yum, sweet. Thank you." Rigo, with great slow care, separated sections of orange and passed them to Berry and Jaudon. He offered one to the woman, but she went toward her car.

"I'll guess we won't be seeing you at the bar anytime soon," Rigo called to her.

"Sweet," Jaudon said. She pointed to her mouth. "Not our visitor."

Berry clucked. "Really, Rigo, you're one of the best people I know and she treated you like a poison snake."

Rigo hissed.

Their visitor slammed her car door and reversed fast toward Pineapple Trail.

Jaudon jumped up and thundered, "Stop!" but it was too late. As Cullie turned into their driveway, Nina, in Judy's pint-size buggy, smashed into Cullie's big pickup and bounced off the heavy bumper. Cullie stopped the truck with such suddenness a bunged up pool ladder flew out of the bed.

They jumped from the porch and ran toward the collision.

Cullie was out of the truck and looking in Nina's window.

"Is she okay?" called Rigo.

Cullie opened the car door and supported her as the woman hobbled out, all stooped over.

"I can't stand up straight." She was coughing and crying.

Berry already had a finger on Nina's wrist, eyes on her white watch.

Jaudon raced to the house to call an ambulance.

"How bad is the car? Why did Judy make me take her car?"

"If you have more oranges in the trunk," said Rigo, "they're juiced."

The woman cried out, frozen in place by pain. Berry wrapped a blanket around Nina and had Rigo support her.

Jaudon returned, out of breath.

"Listen," Berry said. "Here comes a siren already."

Jaudon didn't hear it yet. She told the woman, "The volunteer fire department isn't far."

Cullie sat cross-legged on the ground, Kirby in her arms. "I'm sorry. I wasn't going over five miles an hour into that turn. I know this sandy driveway. You have to drive slow."

Rigo asked, "How's your dog?"

"I don't know. My little coconut went flying from the seat like a hoppy toad off a lily pad. Nothing seems broken. I think she's traumatized. Of course I'm steady as a rock." Cullie held out her shaking hand.

Peahens and their peacock from down the road strutted into the yard, peering and pecking as they arrived. When a deputy sheriff braked to a stop on Pineapple Trail they fled in an awkward line into the undergrowth.

"Aw, heck," said Jaudon. "Not the police again. Trouble comes in threes. What's next?"

"You didn't call them?"

"No. This is private property—I didn't think I needed to. They must have heard about it from the dispatcher."

"What's wrong with the police coming?" Nina asked. "I was hit by a goddamn truck. I want to make a report."

Cullie looked at Nina, open-mouthed.

"Where's your sisterhood, Nina?" said Berry.

It was clear Nina was at fault, trying to speed away. Jaudon had watched the whole thing and Nina never once looked behind her. She rubbed her damaged ear. "As long as the cops don't hit *me* again. They've been here way too often."

Rigo retrieved the pool ladder.

The medics arrived and the deputy directed them around the wreck to Nina. As they checked her out she emitted short shrieks of pain. She looked at Rigo, not Cullie, as she said, "Don't think sisterhood will keep me from getting somebody to pay for this."

Rigo held his hands up, palms out, as if to ward off a threat.

"Be kind," said Berry. "Let's have some peace and compassion here. She's in pain and not thinking well. A crash like that, even going slowly, can compress the spine. I'll call Judy and have her meet you at the hospital, Nina."

"It hurts, it hurts," was Nina's reply.

Jaudon was irritated beyond endurance. "I hate to leave this party, but when I was inside my part-timer called in sick. The churches will be letting out any minute. I need to go to work until I arrange coverage."

The medics readied Nina for their ambulance. As they closed the double doors, Cullie muttered, "Don't forget to floss. Devil-woman."

Jaudon tried not to laugh. She hugged Berry. "You were terrific. I'll be home as soon as I can be. Do some of your breathing and praying while you work with Rigo, okay?" She rolled Zoom out of the garage.

"Hey," said the deputy, grabbing her handlebar. He wasn't one of the deputies that shopped at her Beverage Bay, but he had been at the house the night Cullie and Allison escaped. "Where do you think you're going? I need to take witness statements."

She stifled her fear and tried to act casual. "Don't worry, officer, I'll come by the station. I'm needed at my place of business."

"Most folks would rather stay out of the station, sir. You come in within the next twenty-four hours and give me your contact information now."

Sir again, she thought. Ashamed, fuming, aggrieved, she sat on her bike, hands on hips, as she gave him the information. As soon as they were done, she kicked Zoom to life without meeting anyone's eyes.

CHAPTER THIRTY-SIX

Allison didn't as much press Berry about Gran's land as induce her to dream what they could accomplish with it. She knew someone—of course, Jaudon said when Berry told her—who was a civil engineer. Allison inveigled her to walk the property.

Berry was working Saturday morning and able to take off Friday afternoon. It was a cool day.

Gran held Berry's arm to steady herself as they followed Allison and the engineer. "Mind your arms, girls. You don't want to end up brushing against swamp sumac."

The engineer stopped. "Is this where everything fell in?"

Gran clucked. "That's the place. Poor Eddie, he wasn't the worst man in the world."

Berry held her tongue.

Allison said, "We need to know what you might tell a developer about this acreage. Do they always put in streets and houses?"

The engineer pursed her lips, looking around. "You'll need a topographical survey for height and drainage patterns. Probably a soil evaluation and perc test. You need to consider if the soil in the leach area is permeable enough to support a septic system. What did you use here before?"

Gran grinned. "A barrel we emptied well into the marshland like everyone else outside Tampa. Remember that, pet?" Gran gestured east.

"Yes, I have a shadowy memory of Pa rolling the barrel farther into the marshy area for you. I can picture him gunked up with mud and muck, a straw hat pulled low down to protect him from mosquitoes. He wore high boots for the snakes. He was gone so long I was afraid he was lost."

Gran whooped. "You smelled him coming with that empty barrel. And you ran to your ma."

The engineer led them forward. "This is a remarkable piece of land for wildlife. Look at that little green heron, and the black ducks out on the scummy pond over there." She stood, arms folded, nodding. "I shouldn't say this since it's how I make a living, but I don't want to see it developed."

Gran clapped her hands without making a sound. "That's my vote too."

"We aren't talking about hundreds of homes or a shopping center," Allison said. "A small central lodge for cooking depending on how much money we raise. No hunting, no fishing, no electricity or phone."

The engineer kept her arms folded. "We can dig down seven to ten feet for rock and soil samples. If there's a problem, you might resolve it, but at quite a price. Is the site appropriate for road access, parking, storm water? Is it made up of the type of clay that shrinks in a drought or swells when it's wet? If so, you're going to see cracked foundations, sinkholes, and subsurface voids. Developers kill off what's natural to the land. The birds, deer, foxes, possums—all of them love the purple pokeweed berries. Trumpet vine sustains the hummingbirds. The moneymen don't care if a toxin kills a weed if there's money to be made. Small changes impact hundreds of wild things."

Allison asked, "We have to do all that to put in any structures at all?"

"To be legal, yes. I can tell you I trust some parts of the property more than others, but I wouldn't throw my life savings into any of it."

Allison turned to Gran. "You might want to sell this piece of land, Mrs. Binyon, to buy a smaller parcel, higher quality."

A rush of wings and cries went up. A number of pink-legged white ibis, beaks down curved and bright red, rose from the saw grass and landed way up on a line of scraggly swamp bay trees, making their soft *hah, hah, hah* sounds.

Berry said, "Must be an alligator returned to its nest." Allison, she thought, was welcome to try and persuade Gran to sell her land till the cows came in.

Gran said, "I know you're well-intentioned, Allison, and have the interests of womankind in mind, but this is family land and I intend to protect this little bit of land for the critters. You'd think humans never heard the word share. We're nothing but another breed of critter. Don't you think the Lord wants us to respect their right to a place to live? They don't have grocery stores or houses or cars. I don't have much to give this world, but I can offer this."

The engineer was smiling. Berry took Gran's hand.

"I see your point," said Allison. "It's what men do to women, isn't it? Take what they want from us, do what they want with us, expect us to survive on what they leave."

There was a splash somewhere behind them. Berry turned in time to see a gator tail disappear underwater in a small pond. Her shoulders tingled at the sense of another presence. Gran held her hand tighter. They both looked around for signs of life.

Songbirds sang and geese squawked in the leafy canopy. Gnats swarmed. No-see-ums bit. Sounds of something heavier moved away from them.

A wind came up. Berry said, "I'm all shivery, like a cow ran over my grave."

Gran turned toward the road. Behind them, dead tree branches creaked as they rubbed in the breeze. "Haints. Too many haints."

Allison looked to Berry, eyebrows raised.

"She means ghosts, Allison," Berry said. "Lost souls. Come on, it's time to leave."

Allison followed them toward the road. "You two have your own language. You speak country Southern."

"Have you had squatters on the land?" asked the engineer. "You might want to keep an eye out. Here and there, I'm seeing little signs of human activity."

"Upon my word, you can't keep them out," said Gran. "Poachers, people dumping their trash, others digging up young trees to sell by the side of the road to trailer tourists. Some of those city people, I swanee."

"It's worth protecting."

Allison raised a fist in the air. "Women as caretakers of the earth. What a concept."

Berry guided Gran across Eulalia Road. A volley of vehicles sped by, separating them from the engineer and Allison. When the road was empty, they saw Allison point up Stinky Lane.

"Did you see him?" Allison called.

"No. Who?"

The engineer crossed to them. "Ball cap, long hair, carrying a shotgun."

Berry looked at Gran. "I think you were dead on about haints. That could be Eddie Dill."

"What a foolish notion." Gran watched the land, eyes narrowed, and watched Allison who ran up the lane shouting, "Hey."

The engineer said, "She's crazy to run after someone with a gun."

"She is a little bit crazy. Allison. Allison!"

Allison was already out of sight.

"I'll turn her around," said Berry.

"No, Berry." Gran had a hand on her arm. "I don't know what makes that woman tick, but she wades into any danger she finds. You stay with me."

There was the sound of a shot. They looked that way. Another shot followed. Berry hotfooted Gran out of range up Pineapple Trail, the engineer after them at top speed.

"I don't want the police out here again, Gran."

"We have no choice, child. Your friend is in there. She might be hurt. Or the man with the gun might be a poacher."

They huddled together behind a fat old oak. The engineer said, "Here comes Allison. She's fast."

"Everybody's fast when they're being used for target practice."

Allison was panting. "I lost him, darn it."

"What about the gunshots, Allison?" asked Berry.

"Once I lost him I wanted out of the woods. Someone may be in there hunting."

The engineer said, "That wasn't a rifle. Those were pistol shots. Who hunts with a pistol?"

"You can use one for small game," Gran said. "Eddie used to bring home rabbits and such."

Berry made a face. "Ugh."

"I'll call the rangers, not the sheriff," said Gran. "As long as Allison here is safe. Those deputies seem scared of you harmless young women."

Allison, hands on her bent knees, catching her breath, said, "The last thing I want to be is harmless. The whole sheriff's department is afraid one day they're going to have to patrol with women—armed women—as we gain numbers and our demands are taken seriously."

"You, young lady," said Gran, "have a one-track mind."

"Isn't that what we need? Women who devote themselves to the cause?"

"I meant that as a compliment, Allison. I'll volunteer at your clinic or shelter. Find someplace that's already developed. As for having women in trouble camping out in this wild space, I think you see that dog won't hunt."

"You'll volunteer, Gran? That's great news," said Berry.

"If I live long enough for you to get this show on the road."

"Oh, you don't have to worry about that. I'm working on some grants," said Allison.

"What exactly are you planning?" asked the engineer.

"Two things," said Allison. "A place where women of any income can access health care, whether it be for birth control, STDs, cancer screenings, or information. And a place where women can stay for a while to hide from abusive men and misanthropic laws or to be with one another."

"You do realize," said the engineer, cocking an eyebrow, "that's the work of more than one lifetime."

❖

A wildlife officer came to Rainbow Gap and took Gran's report a few days later. He went over to Stinky Lane to look around.

Gran wasn't satisfied and complained at supper that night. "I'll bet look around is all he did. If they don't catch poachers red-handed, they don't sit there and wait till one comes along."

Berry said, "We'll call every time we suspect a trespasser. No ghost can shoot a gun."

"That we know." Jaudon grinned.

"You don't think Eddie survived that hole, do you?"

"Aw, heck, Gran, if anybody it would be Eddie, but that's an impossible if."

Jaudon wasn't so sure herself and the thought gave her a fright.

"I heard of a patient who did," said Berry. "I was talking to the scheduler at lunch one day. She used to work at the hospital in Emergency. A guy came in with multiple injuries. He was working alone on a construction site when the earth disappeared under him. The building materials he was working with fell in too and left him bruised and sore, but also created a breathable underground cave. He was able to wiggle his way to a storm drain and holler for help."

Gran sopped up the rest of her gravy with a bit of biscuit. "That was a darn lucky fella. No chance it happened twice in a hundred years, Berry."

"If not, who's out there?"

Jaudon saw Gran's nervous blink. "Allison's description fits a hundred guys around here. A friend of Eddie's who took over his hunting grounds?" She grinned. "Or one of those skunk apes."

Berry's voice grew high. "You have a thing about apes, my angel, but I don't think you'll find one shooting a gun over there."

Jaudon bantered with her as much to unspook herself as anything. "Why not?"

"Every time I hear a hoot owl, I think it's Eddie risen from the dead," said Gran.

"We need to post signs so whoever's in there doesn't injure himself and sue us, Gran. You have no insurance on that land."

Jaudon decided to tackle their doubts head on. "I can pick up some signs at the feed store and put them up Sunday. For the moment, I'm putting on my boots. Let's drive down to July Lake and backtrack to see where somebody might be creeping in and hiding. You coming with me, Berr?"

"I'll be darned if you're going alone."

"Leave it to the law, girls."

"The law's not going to do pea turkey squat. I'm tired of waiting on someone else to help us with every dinky thing."

"Agreed," Jaudon said. "We gave them a chance to either fish or cut bait. Let's get a move on while it's light out."

Berry held tight to Jaudon's arm as they went to the van. "Should we bring Bat's shotgun? Eddie Dill's pistol is missing. Bat took it one day and I keep meaning to look for where he put it."

Jaudon loved being Berry's protector. "I'm not planning on a gun battle, Georgia gal. Leave the shotgun home. I want to see what we can see and report straight to the wildlife people."

"Remember when we were small fry and used to go exploring, Jaudon? I'm reminded of those days."

In the van, turning onto Eulalia Road, Jaudon nodded so hard her neck cracked. She enjoyed the memories as much as she'd enjoyed making them. "Don't you wish we were discovering the world again? I wasn't scared of anything but school."

"Isn't that what we're doing, rediscovering our world? We're not seeing it like six-year-olds anymore. Where're you heading?"

"To the end of Gran's property line by the lake. We'll come around this way and you can be the lookout. I'll hug the edge of the road so these jackass snowbirds don't drive inside our cargo door."

Berry patted Jaudon's knee. "Language."

For a second, she was annoyed. She respected Berry's pet peeves, but hated watching her words. Even more, Jaudon loathed being annoyed with her one and only. She made a U-turn and slowed to ten mph.

Berry leaned out the window. Jaudon squinted into the woods as she drove.

"Nothing so far," said Berry.

"I wonder if he comes in though the July Lake development. Could be some retiree from up north who doesn't know any better."

"The railroad tracks are another way in."

"Kind of open there for a sneaky person, but I heard tales about people living under the trestle just north."

"What if we find your skunk ape?" asked Berry.

"Now you're being silly."

"I am. But how neat. We should have brought a camera."

Jaudon raised an eyebrow at her. "You've got your very own skunk ape, Berr."

Berry jostled her arm. "Don't be ridiculous, Jaudon. You're much too short to be a skunk ape."

Jaudon bellowed with laughter and gave Berry's thigh a light slap. It was a miracle how Berry took the sting out of everything, how Berry, who was darn near perfect, loved her as she was.

They rolled along several yards more. "Wait. Pull over, Jaudon."

Jaudon started. She hadn't realized how tense she was.

"Remember where we found that Shaker table for the tree house?"

"That you called a shaky table?" said Jaudon in her teasing voice.

Berry turned and stuck her tongue out. "You didn't know enough to correct me. So there."

"Eyes right, Georgia gal. I didn't know anything about anything outside Rainbow Gap, Florida. I expected the thing to shake, but it never did."

They laughed, bumping heads. Jaudon touched the back of Berry's neck, so vulnerable and appealing since Gran gave her this short, bouncy cut full of waves and a few curls. No more braid: here was Berry's grown-up style.

"This is the Shaker table spot. All the stuff that's been dumped made a permanent opening, and look, there's a path."

"Might be an animal trail, but for something taller than any animal I've seen."

"Can we leave the van here?"

"Let's take it home first." Jaudon knew she was being what Pops called a yeller dog.

Berry was already stepping out onto the shoulder. "Catch up with me."

"Aw, heck, Berry. Don't go in there by yourself."

"You're forgetting I lived on this land, Jaudon."

Jaudon took off, left the van, and raced her own fears to the path. Berry shouldn't have gone in without a firearm after the shots she talked about. She climbed down and walked fast, avoiding the mushy spots on the trail. Ahead, in a clearing, she saw Berry bend over to examine the ground.

"Berry," she said softly, careful not to startle her. She didn't know if she was more relieved to see Berry or to have made it this far herself.

"The undergrowth's tamped down through here."

They looked at each other.

"I haven't been here in forever. We better turn our pockets out to keep the ghosts from harming us.

"What are you saying?"

"It's a Georgia superstition."

Jaudon, arms folded, steeled herself. "I'll go first." She had too much stuff in her pockets to wear them inside out, but she went as far as to switch some of it around and left one emptied pocket to hang like a warning flag.

Berry slapped at her arms and face. "Mosquitoes find me tasty today."

A scrub jay dove at them, protective of its territory.

They pushed through branches bowed down with vines, air plants, and hanging mosses, thickets of low growing palmetto and ferns. A snowy egret lifted from a pool of water and flapped high into a tree. Bullfrogs warned them away. The land here was flat as a floor gradually starting a patient slope upward. The earth got drier after they passed between two old cypress trees, green moss clothing their hoopskirt-shaped trunks. They startled a white-tailed deer.

"This smells to the high heavens," said Berry.

Jaudon parted the bushes and recoiled. "Armadillo carcasses. Rabbit too."

"He's eating armadillo meat?"

"Ugh."

"Even Eddie didn't eat them, though he dried the shells to sell. Armadillos carry leprosy."

Jaudon moved away, holding her breath. "Can you catch leprosy by breathing the germs?"

Up on a hillock a flutter of green caught Berry's eye. Most of the cypress trees had trunks that were whole, but one had a wide gap between its aboveground roots. Inside was that flutter of green. She should have told Jaudon to go after the shotgun. She didn't like it in the house, what with her recent low moods, which was one reason she hadn't searched hard for Eddie's pistol. Still, a gun might come in handy about now.

"What is that?" she whispered.

Jaudon turned to her, a hand behind her good ear.

Berry tiptoed closer. Jaudon looked.

They walked toward the tree, stooped over, peeked inside. There was a green mat hanging at the opening, woven with palm fronds, moving each time a tiny breeze bumped it. Inside, a blanket, somewhat worse for the wear, covered padding.

"Someone's made a cozy campsite here."

Berry poked a cigarette butt with her toe. "Someone who smokes."

"Jiminy. Did Eddie Dill smoke?"

"No. His church didn't allow smoking, drinking, or cussing."

Jaudon raised the blanket. "This bedding is made of palm fronds over Spanish moss."

"I see that. What's behind there?"

Jaudon climbed inside. "It's another palm mat, with loops at the corners." She looked at the entrance to the hole. "Whoever it is carved wood pegs around the opening to seal it. Aw, heck, Berry. He's got a pistol hanging up in here."

"Must be the one Gran and I heard the day we came out with the engineer."

"We should take it."

"May I see it, Jaudon?"

Berry turned it this way and that. "I swear, that's Eddie Dill's pistol, the one I thought Bat misplaced. See? It has a gouge where his did." She checked for bullets, but the gun was empty.

"Now we know where his gun went, but who stole it?"

Berry walked around the tree, holding the gun. "There's a mirror hung on the tree and a half-rotted wood milk crate with stuff in it."

Jaudon went to look. "A hair brush?"

"With long dark hairs. We're not looking for Eddie, Jaudon. This is young hair. A woman's hair."

"Or a long-haired man."

"True. We better leave these things alone. They're someone's personal property." Berry made to close the box, but Jaudon stopped her.

"At the bottom, Berry, in the plastic box. See those packs of cigarettes and matchbooks? That's the kind Lari smokes."

"Is this where she disappeared?" Berry squinted to make out what was printed on the matches. "This is crazy. We need to get away from here."

"Finally, you're talking sense."

"It was your idea to look."

"It was my idea to drive by."

"The matches? They're from the bar Rigo took us to." Berry pulled her away from the box.

"Where Lari hangs out."

Berry tucked the gun under her blouse and they hurried home the way they came.

"Can you think of anything scarier than Lari with a pistol?"

CHAPTER THIRTY-SEVEN

B erry, honey, we need some sleep."

She was so darned tired and Berry was flouncing onto her sides or her belly or flipping her pillow every few minutes. This new thing with Lari—if it was Lari—was weighing them down and interfering with work.

Plump-sounding raindrops slugged at their roof and poured down the gutters.

"I'm trying, Jaudon." Berry plumped her pillow again. "I can't face tomorrow."

"Telling the doctor about Lari?"

"I'm full of guilt both ways. If I stay quiet she'll die in the swamp of giardia or another infection, if I turn her in she loses her freedom."

"Her freedom to what? Hunt down your beloved critters? Start a fire? Keep sneaking over here to spy on us?"

"If that was her, Jaudon."

"That was her all right. She can walk to Stinky Lane from her aunt's place without using Eulalia Road once."

"But why? She has everything, a nice car, her slick clothes. Did Eddie Dill's spirit get into her and take her over?"

Jaudon scoffed at her. She'd never been spooked on Vicker land before Lari. "We have our bottle tree and Rigo's protection stones."

"Oh, you. You're poking fun at me. At least we know it's not Eddie watching us from the woods, bless his tarnished soul."

"If he had one," Jaudon said.

"And if it didn't take Lari's over."

"You don't believe that, do you, Berry?"

"No. Yes. I don't know, angel. Some man in a noisy rig has been spotted. I've heard the truck idling on Eulalia and Samantha saw it, saw the driver. In her description, he sounded like a thousand men around here—including Eddie."

"Maybe one of his church friends? But why?"

In answer, Berry put her arms around Jaudon's firm, untapered waist from behind. Berry asked herself if she believed these demonic things she was saying. If so, she needed to exorcise them from her head. They were so ingrained in her. She grew up hearing sayings like: *Don't keep a chair rocking once you're up or you'll soon get sick* and *A howling dog is a sign of death.*

Then again, Zefer did howl half the night when Eddie died. She made herself think of the Great Spirit, made herself breathe deep as she could five times: five seconds in, five hold, five out.

Jaudon was lulled by Berry's sleepy embrace. Outside the window was a pure white half-moon on its back that gave no illumination.

Berry whispered, "The moon is only a pearly half disc watching us sail by."

She turned and kissed Berry until the air around them seemed to pulse with pleasure. Berry slept like she was in hibernation the rest of the night.

By seven a.m., Berry was at work. She wanted to catch Dr. Gara before patients started arriving.

"There isn't anything I can do, Berry," said the doctor, after a call to the hospital. "Miss Hand was released after observation. She should improve with medications, but it sounds as if she's not taking them. That's part of the illness, of course. Patients grow suspicious of the very medications that can help them."

Berry brought up the leprosy issue.

"That's not likely. You can try contacting the health department, Berry, to determine if there have been incidences. The other possibility is calling the police out there when you know she's on your grandmother's property." Dr. Gara smiled. "We can't go capture her and put her in a strait-jacket anymore."

"It's not okay to call the police on her. She can't help being sick."

"Now that's where you're wrong, Berry. She needs that medication. If she's not taking it, we're going to have to intervene."

She called Allison, who'd been hired by the Four Lakes Health Department.

"Poor Lari. I'll come by tonight," Allison said, "and we'll discuss strategies and an intervention. My coworkers will know what's done in these cases. Can you start the phone tree to round up the group at your place? We need to locate some help for Lari."

The day went by too quickly. At noon, she called Jaudon to tell her what Allison proposed.

"Aw, heck, Berry. I'll go over to Rigo's after work."

"It might be no one but Allison and me and Gran. I need you."

Figures, Jaudon thought, amused and aggravated when she got home and saw the driveway full of cars. The whole gang was there to work on a loving, feminist, communal way to help Lari.

Fists at her hips, she looked up and saw Cullie's truck creeping into the driveway at about the speed of dirt.

"I don't want to hit anyone else," said Cullie through her open window.

"Get out here and let's go find Lari."

"How? When no one else can?"

"I'll bet my bottom dollar some one of these women tried to reach her about the meeting hoping she'd show up and she's behind some brush watching, close enough to listen."

"If so, I'll hoist a root beer to you. That woman is scared."

"You won't get an argument from me, but what's she scared of?"

"Herself. She's scared of herself. And of us dashing lesbians. What'll we do if we find her?"

"Providing she doesn't shoot us…"

"Which is a big providing. We ought to call in an armored car."

She gave Cullie a playful shove. "You'll want the Marines next."

"At least as reinforcements." Cullie returned the shove with a laugh.

"Shh. Okay, here's the plan. Berry says Lari needs help. If we find her, we'll take her to the hospital. With any luck they'll keep her long enough to fix her this time."

"I can hear the women going on the warpath if Lari isn't given the appropriate care. I'll blame this plan on you and recommend we take away your lesbian badge."

Her fists came up and she play-growled. "Never. Berry will calm Allison down. This is the only kind solution they can come to in their meeting, but it'll take a lot longer."

Cullie lifted Kirby and put her in the truck, windows open. "I need to tell you this, Jaudo, before Lari kills us both."

Cullie funny was entertaining, but Cullie serious was commanding, thought Jaudon.

"I'll be remembering Berry's gran the next time I'm tempted to beat gay-hating parents over their hard heads, which I expect to happen at least a thousand times over the rest of my life. Gran might never understand gay love or understand that we don't have the rights of a field of peppers, but there's not a doubt in my mind that whatever you two do, that woman will be there for you. I wish Lari had that. I wish we all had that."

Jaudon was all warm inside. "Gran's a fine lady and she's raised a swell granddaughter. You couldn't stop Gran coming out here to track down Lari with us if we told her."

"What are we waiting for, you bowlegged slug?"

Bowlegged, thought Jaudon. *Am I bowlegged on top of everything else?*

Cullie inched one way and Jaudon tromped the other, her insides bubbling with trepidation. They circled around the house to enter the thick growth behind Gran's trailer. There was no sign of Lari.

Jaudon surveyed the land toward the pond. No one was on the old bench. She looked up.

Lari sat on the edge of the tree house deck, legs dangling, facing the house. "Of course," said Jaudon, gesturing for Cullie to look. She hadn't been up in the tree house for a long time. Lari must be using it, as well as the woods, for a hideout.

When they reached her, tears were rushing down Lari's mournful, exhausted-looking face. Skeletal, she wore a man's T-shirt. Jaudon saw bruises, scratches, scrapes, and the red circles of bug bites on her arms. Her black hair was braided, bits of leaves and twigs stuck to it. Her stained shorts were wet and her sneakers were sodden as well as torn. She was sockless.

Jaudon tried to imagine Lari's discomfort, sleeping in swampy land or under the rotting, leaky roof of the tree house. It was troubling, the way she looked, but she didn't find it in herself to have much sympathy for her. Oh, no, she thought. Some of Momma's coldness had settled in her own heart.

She held the ladder and Cullie climbed to put her hands on Lari's shoulders. "Hey, Lari," Cullie said. "Everyone's worried about you."

Lari peered around Cullie to see the Vicker house. She snorted mucus up her nose and wiped it off her lip. Her voice was a mere rasp. "Why didn't they invite me?"

"You've been out of touch, Lari. How were they supposed to invite you?"

Lari looked up at Cullie. "Oh," she said.

They eased her to her feet. She twitched, like she was about to bolt, but Cullie embraced and rocked her. "Let's find a way to put you together again."

Lari chanted in a dry voice, "I'm lost. I'm so lost." She let herself be guided down the ladder and to the van.

Jaudon drove, anxious to call Berry, while Cullie sat behind her holding Lari until they arrived at Tampa General. Kirby leaned on Lari's other side. They stayed with her while she signed herself in. Once Lari was taken to an examining room, Jaudon found a phone.

Jaudon heard the relief in Berry's voice and held the pay phone for Cullie to listen in. "I was going to go looking with Allison. The others wanted to let Lari be. Her freedom was most important to them, that she should be able to choose to die out there if that's what she wanted."

Cullie blew out a long breath through clenched teeth. "That's heartless, Berry."

"Allison used the same word: heartless. The others said we're putting her in the hands of patriarchal doctors who will rape Lari's mind. They have no understanding of female emotional problems. To tell you the truth, Jaudon, I think they're ill at ease with any mental illness."

Cullie muttered, "Or else they're egg-sucking dawgs."

"Be serious, Cullie. Either way, I know I'm on my true path, Jaudon, studying psychology. Doctors can help people with brain tumors or heart attacks or anything other than a mental illness."

"She seemed beyond sad," Jaudon said.

"That woman's gone through every known emotion these few weeks and experienced them more intensely than the rest of us ever will."

"You'll have to explain that to me someday."

With a laugh, Berry said, "As soon as I understand it, I will. Come on home so I can thank you properly." Jaudon snatched the phone away from Cullie.

Cullie's eyebrows waggled over her glasses.

Berry went on. "I'll tell the women your news. If Lari can't be well, at least she's warm and dry, and she'll be hydrated and nourished. Oh, and by the way, Jimmy Neal called. He's coming to work early tomorrow to talk to you. "

"Aw, heck, Berry. I hope he's not quitting."

Chapter Thirty-eight

She was jittery all day, waiting to hear why Jimmy Neal called. He wasn't scheduled until three p.m. and it didn't help that Momma had the inventory crew in for the second time that month. Had Momma forgotten the schedule? They hired the company quarterly, but two of them were working their way along the shelving, mouthing numbers and poking keys on their handheld machines. She didn't know what Momma was worried about. Her inventory was over, more often than not. It came down to Momma not trusting her as usual. If she lived forever, Jaudon thought, it was doubtful she could turn Momma around on that point.

Jimmy Neal rode in on his bicycle; Rigo usually drove him. She thought he could double as a circus bear on that thing. His face was wet with sweat—and were those tears?

"This sweat stings my eyes," he said, looking away. In front of the fan, he blotted his face with a tissue, blinking. As he tried to put his store jacket on he had trouble finding the opening to his sleeve.

She scrambled to the cooler and delivered a six-pack to a customer. When she returned, Jimmy Neal slid the counter chairs together to sit with her. He cleared his throat. She jounced from one leg to the other. When he patted the chair, she sat.

"I don't know whether to stay with him." He looked mournful as a hound.

"With Rigo?"

"I know he's better looking than I am. And more, uh, sociable, so I never expected him to be mine forever, though he promised forever. I'm head over heels with Rigo, Jaudon, and he says he loves me, though goodness knows why."

She patted his arm, ready to find Rigo and skin him alive if he put Jimmy Neal through hell.

"Rigo has hepatitis B."

"Oh." She was both relieved that Rigo wasn't breaking up with Jimmy Neal and concerned for him. "He's sick?"

"Yes and no. He's so yellow-looking and piddlin' he doesn't always make it to class, but he's close to scooping up that master's. He hurts in places it makes no sense to hurt. He can't keep anything down. He's not sick in bed or anything, but he went to the infirmary and they tested him. They sent him to a specialist."

"Jimmy Neal, Rigo needs you more than ever. Why in the devil are you thinking about leaving?"

"Do you know anything about Hep B?"

She rubbed her ear. "I guess not."

"It's an infection. You catch it from someone's blood or spit or whatever fluids."

"How did he do that?"

"Sex with a guy who was infected, I guess."

"But how—?"

"Don't ask."

"He cheated on you."

"We're not married. We can do what we want. But I don't go outside, Jaudo. Rigo is everything I need in a man."

"And he sees other guys." She made a face. "That's crummy."

Jimmy Neal looked at her. "Do I stay with him? I know it's a selfish thought, but what if he infects me? I don't want to protect myself against Rigo of all people, but I'll have to. Who'll hire an infected nurse? There's no reason they shouldn't as long as I use normal precautions, but if they knew—it might be a problem. Can someone work in a food store when you catch it?"

She couldn't help herself, she grimaced. Did this mean she had to fire Rigo?

She said, "We don't test, Jimmy Neal. And you know how careful we are about cleanliness. That's why there's a sink behind the office. But tell me this, you're not jealous when he goes out?"

"Of course I am and I don't know if I can live with that the rest of my life either." He sniffled. "Or the rest of the week." He looked at her again. "You know?"

She remembered her own panicked jealousy about Berry straying. Rigo helped her, and she wanted to help his lover, but how? Were guys this different from women? No, there was her quick lust for Lari, once.

Now she knew she was susceptible, she'd never be caught off guard again. Weren't men able to stop themselves?

"Rigo is my dream husband, Jaudo. I can't give him up. I'm what he needs, but he craves his excitement."

She checked: no one was in the driveway, the inventory crew had waved good-bye. Jimmy Neal sat behind the counter. She put her arms around him and patted his fleshy back.

"There, there," she said. "Did you tell him you're upset?"

"I have no call to object. He set the terms when we got serious about each other. He doesn't see sexual restraint as realistic. We'll talk about it when we're older, he told me. I'm such a sissy for not being able to handle this." His tears broke through and soaked into her T-shirt. "I don't want to share him, but I don't want to go through this pain every time he goes out."

"I'm the same about Berry. If someone else touches her, I'll cut their hands off."

"There are no good choices. I wish I was a lesbian. You girls aren't as flighty as pretty men."

She wondered if he was right and pulled away when a car drove in, followed by another and another. She looked at the new oversized watch Berry gave her for her birthday, enthralled as always by its digital glow. "Factory shift change. Pull yourself together. Momma tells me work is the best medicine."

They got busy. During the rush, she heard Jimmy Neal's sighs from clear across the store.

"You can't be sighing like that at home, Jimmy Neal. It can drive a body crazy."

They were restocking the cooler when he did it again. "I guess I do sigh loud. I'll quit it as of this second. What if I lost weight? Do you think Rigo would stay home with me if I got smaller?"

She didn't want to say the wrong thing. "He might work harder at keeping you home. Can you imagine being as lean as Rigo since he started working out? Or if you had his muscles?"

"And his stellar coloring."

"Nothing wrong with your coloring, Jimmy Neal. You'd look great with a tan."

"I don't know where I'd find the time to lie on the beach for a tan plus go to the gym at the Y."

She realized she was desperate for Jimmy Neal and Rigo to work out, the way Berry wanted Cullie and Allison to make it, as if the survival of other couples assured her own with Berry. "Haven't you ever seen bodybuilders at the beach? Go join a muscle club."

"I can't pay their fees. And that's another thing. Rigo won't let me pay rent. If I left him, there goes school…" The sniffing began again, but stopped when a car drove in. "Who knows if getting skinny solves anything."

She hung out while he searched for the pricing gun and loaded it with tape. "There is," he said, "a bodybuilding team at school."

"Well, shut my mouth. That's your answer."

"The school offers a weight-lifting class for phys ed credits."

"If Rigo goes for new men, nobody would be newer than you."

"I wouldn't be new forever."

"Men will be after you like ducklings trailing their mothers into a pond. You have those long lashes and bright blue eyes. You're blond. You're tall. Heck, you have this smooth almost-hairless body. Guys will catch on once they're not distracted by your weight. You won't be as dependent on Rigo."

"You think I can make him jealous?"

"I bet it'll be harder for him to share you. He's such a vain boy."

That got a yearning look out of Jimmy Neal. "He surely is."

"Uh-oh. Here comes Momma. Go dust some shelves. Or no, go fill the ice cream. We had a delivery today."

"Thanks, Jaudon. It never occurred to me that it isn't Rigo who needs to change."

His gratitude warmed her.

Momma didn't park; she drove in and stopped the Caddy at the sales counter.

"Momma?" When had Momma's hair turned all gray?

Without a word, Momma handed her a sheet of paper.

It was a shopping list. "Momma, what is this? You don't shop at the Bays. You always go to the Winn-Dixie."

Her mother blinked at her and retrieved the list. "Daughter, if a customer comes in and hands you a list of puppies she is considering buying, I want you to bring her those puppies."

She stammered yes, confused and sort of frightened. This was strange behavior. Was it a test? There was an acrid unwashed smell coming from inside the car. Was that Momma?

As she spoke, Momma's hands floated over the steering wheel, stopping to pick at it here and there. "Customer service, Daughter. Unless you understand customer service you might as well marry and give me grandchildren."

With that, her mother drove out. Jaudon didn't know what to say when Jimmy Neal returned.

"Is everything all right, Jaudo? You look spooked."

"Momma was real strange."

She was grateful he didn't ridicule Momma. "What did she say?"
She told him.

"How old is your mother?"

"Momma married late and had Bat and me in her middle and late thirties. She's closing in on sixty."

Jimmy Neal reached down to scratch his ankle. "Darned skeeters are picking on me today." He aahed in relief. "I think your mother might want to be checked out by a doctor. Does she have one?"

"She's always said she doesn't have time for doctors. Claims they don't know a lick more than anyone with sense."

"And I thought I had problems." Jimmy Neal shook his head. "Was it a stroke?"

"Momma doesn't put up with trifles like strokes."

"Has she fallen and hit her head?"

"Not that I know of." She was horrified at the thought. "Momma might not be a pleasant person, but she's a towering old oak, she's always there."

"Strong winds take down trees, Jaudon. Rocks fall."

"I guess strokes are tropical storms inside us."

"That's one way to put it."

"And rocks fall apart into pebbles and sand." It disturbed her to think of Momma in pieces on the ground, although in anger and hurt, she'd wished her worse often enough.

Jimmy Neal looked solemn and sympathetic.

"I'll ask Berry about Momma, talk to Pops and suggest seeing a doctor. But what about Rigo? Will he be okay?"

"He's lucky in a way. He has acute hepatitis B. His doctor told him eat well, drink loads of fluids, and no alcohol or drugs. I checked one of my textbooks. Some people heal on their own in a few months. He has to report new symptoms and have blood tests to see if his liver is doing okay. The doc gave him a box of condoms and a good talking to so he doesn't infect any girlfriends. Rigo teases me about being his best girlfriend."

"At least this spurred you to get healthy and slim down."

He started one of his loud sighs, stopped himself, and made the sign for zipping his lips. "You wait and see. I'm going to change."

CHAPTER THIRTY-NINE

Darn that Rigo," said Berry. "Boys are so careless. You have no idea how many women come in with one infection or another that their men brought home."

"Married guys?" Jaudon asked.

"Married men go with guys too. It's a real eye-opener for the wives. Jimmy Neal's practical to be careful. He has to insist on condoms. They both do. Jimmy Neal doesn't need to worry about working as a nurse, though. We have a nurse who has the same virus and she can do everything the rest of us do. We're trained in universal precautions."

They were on their way to Cullie and Allison's place. She wore her best Hawaiian shirt. She took her eyes from the road to look at Berry in her pretty shorts and a cotton embroidered blouse with tiny sleeves, her dark hair short and gleaming. She'd even applied light pink lipstick. "I wanted to tell you about Momma too."

"What's wrong?"

"Don't get riled up, Berry. It might be nothing." She was riled up herself and didn't want to ruin the evening with friends by making Berry upset too. She had to let her know, though, or alarm her for certain.

After she heard Jaudon out on the subject of Momma's changed behavior, Berry's response came slowly. "Have you talked to your father?"

"I wanted to see what you thought first." She grinned. "Isn't that why I married a nurse?"

Berry smiled but was silent. Jaudon peeked at her again and saw the patient look of exasperation.

"You're going to tell me to hustle her to a doctor."

"I'm trying to think what breed of doctor, Jaudon. Give me a minute. Why don't you bring her to our office? We can refer from there."

"You sound so professional, Georgia gal." She suspected she wasn't as smart as Berry, though Berry told her more than once they were both smart at different things.

"Professional the way you sound about the Beverage Bays."

Jaudon reached for Berry's hand and brought it to her lips. "Are you sure we can't turn around and go home?"

"Why," Berry said, giving Jaudon's hand several light kisses too. "Did you have other plans for us at home?"

Jaudon had embarrassed herself and answered with a shrug and a grin.

Berry's nerves were jangling. She giggled in excitement like she used to as a grade-schooler. "I think this is our first grown-up dinner party, Jaudon."

"I'd never think to organize a dinner party. People show up at our place, invited or not."

"Which is Rigo, most of the time,"

"And Cullie. Don't forget Lari. I don't guess we'll see so much of her anymore."

"This is confidential, Jaudon, and don't you dare blab it to Rigo. Lari's aunt's started to see Dr. Gara. A lot of the women's doctors around here don't take Medicare so she's been traveling up to Four Lakes. Apparently, Lari recommended us to her."

"There's a surprise. Do you hear news of Lari?"

"You're still interested?"

Jaudon laughed at the raised eyebrow. "Not *that* way, Berry."

"Her aunt says the medications are a miracle. She flew up to Minnesota to take Lari to her parents. Lari's supposed to be like a new person."

"I'm darned glad she's being a new person up there and not here." She paused. "You know I will regret that minute, those seconds, for the rest of my life. It's the one time I was almost glad to see Momma arrive at the store—seeing her stopped me in my tracks. It was this lightning surge through me, Berry, it wasn't from love. I'm not trying to sidestep the blame, because *I* did it—no one else."

"She put herself in your path."

"She was nothing but an object, a magnet."

"You didn't go looking for her."

"I didn't resist her. It happened so fast I had no idea there was a force I should resist." Jaudon was thoughtful. "I guess I might be a little bit off to have such an urge take me over, a man's weakness."

"No." Berry's voice was firm. "It's those all-powerful hormones. We're going to make love more. A lot more. I'll satisfy your appetite, Jaudon, wait and see."

She glanced at Berry's face, saw the slight elfin smile, and had to take a deep breath to calm herself. What a beautiful woman Berry was. In their first years as lovers Berry was shy and playful. Lately, Jaudon saw a new smoldering in Berry's smile.

What, worried Berry, did she know of seduction? She determined to heighten her allure for Jaudon. She'd ask Rigo how. He knew about such mysteries.

"I'm sorry to be the one to break the news, Jaudon," she said. "Her aunt told me Lari's coming down to finish school at the beginning of next term. She missed too many classes to graduate and can't transfer the credits she does have."

Jaudon wrinkled her nose. "Trouble finds us, Berry. Did that ever occur to you too?" She pulled on the lobe of her ear to stop it ringing, not that pulling or pinching or anything else ever worked.

"Gran says it's life. The older we get, the more troubles we'll see. She advised me against the word trouble and told me to say challenges, or blessings, since they test our mettle and bring out the best in us."

"I need to think about that one."

"If you greet trouble with a smile, it takes the sting out, according to Gran. She wants to turn around the way I think about Ma and Pa. She thinks I should smile every time they come into my mind and sooner or later I'll stop being sad."

"Berry." Jaudon gripped her hand. "That's genius. Why didn't I ever think of that? It'll turn into a habit."

"I'll link the memories with my smile and my spirits will lift."

"It'll lift my spirits, knowing you're happier." She squeezed Berry's thigh.

Was that true? Berry thought she was a mirror image of the whole state of Florida, all that wild, angry evil churning inside her like the teeming live things run riot beneath playgrounds and churches and careful lawns. Florida was a bridge of twigs over one big sinkhole, yet the bridge held, so far it held. She began to believe her parents left for some reason other than herself, but wasn't convinced. Had she been a savage infant? Did they think she'd be a handful or too expensive to raise? Did they fear tantrums, malevolence, truancy—what? What was inside her that might erupt again?

Jaudon said, "I hate to hear Lari's coming back. I dasn't be nice to her. She might take it the wrong way."

Berry thought her eyes must be turning greener than springtime. She stroked Jaudon's knee to keep from saying anything when what she wanted was to load Bat's shotgun against Lari. She pictured Lari on a gurney, torn, bloody, dead and gone, shook her head and forced a new picture: Lari in

Wisconsin, wearing bright clothing, holding hands with her true mate as they walked along a lakeshore. With that image in mind, Berry was able to say, "You leave that piece of trouble to me, Jaudon."

"I'll be glad to. Allison, though, she better not break Cullie's soft heart."

"Allison told me you were worried about that. You can't say Cullie didn't know who she was falling for."

"She's too loopy about Allison to see straight."

"At least Allison is with her. And has this," said Berry, looking around the gated town house development called Orangewood Grove. "Cullie's come up in the world."

Jaudon punched in the code to open the gate and parked in a visitor space.

"Busman's holiday," she said. "Look at that swimming pool. I can't believe we have friends in this ritzy neighborhood."

They were admiring the lighted walkways, the underwater glow of the pool, and the manicured landscaping when Cullie came to the door, Kirby under one arm.

"Howdy, howdy, howdy," said Cullie.

"Do you clean the pool?" Jaudon asked by way of a greeting.

Cullie half laughed, half groaned as Berry hugged her. "Do you know how many people ask me that when they see the company sign on my truck outside? As a matter of fact, it's how I found this place. They knocked a chunk off our rent because they needed a pool person."

Berry said, "This is one of those awful new condominiums that are gobbling up land."

Cullie cackled and rubbed Kirby's paws together. "Aren't we evil? We're serving displaced wildlife for dinner with pie made of toxic withered pecans from abandoned orchards for dessert."

"I can't wait," Berry countered.

Cullie led them inside and set Kirby down. The dog sniffed their ankles and trotted off.

The furniture was scant, some of it the cast-offs Cullie had accumulated in her cabin, covered with Allison's Indian throws and crocheted afghans.

"You did a nice job decorating, Cullie."

Cullie snorted. "If you have a yen for Early 4th Century Modern."

"Jiminy, Cull. This place is classy—the whole house is air conditioned?"

Cullie stopped and joshed her. "This house is the Taj Mahal by my standards. It's also a nice address for my ambitious Allison. The developer can't sell more than half the units, so he's renting them."

"But it's so nice. Why aren't they selling?"

"They're overpriced, Berry. He's going to wait out the market. He plans to lure buyers who want investment properties. Meanwhile, we're living lives of luxury."

"What will happen to you and Allison when this one sells?"

"Oh, Allison will already be mayor and I'll be a cop. We'll buy one of those houses in the historic district."

"A cop?" Jaudon asked, stopping short. "Cullie Culpepper, a cop?" She put her hands on her hips. "Did I misread you? I don't see it, Cull. What's got into you?"

Cullie swiveled toward them, beaming, both hands pumping in the shape of pistols. "I wanted to be a cop since I was a babe in arms." She guided them through the kitchen, the lanai, the bedroom turned into offices. "At the civil rights demonstrations, even a child could see there were better ways to treat people."

Berry said, "And here I thought you were a peace-lover."

"Good grief, child. Cops keep the peace. They used to be called peace officers, remember? With Allison on the city council, she's twisting arms to make Four Lakes one of the first in the state to let women be real cops, not sworn clerks. Four Lakes is forward thinking in some ways—they've hired black deputies since the 1950s." Cullie stood taller and straighter. "I'm shooting for top cop someday."

Jaudon had her hands stuffed in her pockets, trying not to be intimidated by so much ambition. "The two of you are going to run this town soon."

Berry said, "That was good horse sense on Allison's part, starting out as a councilor."

"I told her to start small because taking the mayoral job away from Crum will take time."

They were in a hallway. Political signs covered the walls: Allison's election campaign, Shirley Chisholm's presidential campaign, a Sisters Unite poster, and flyers for gay pride and lesbian events around the country. "I don't believe any politician should be in office more than two terms."

"Our ex-President Nixon, to be specific," called Allison.

Cullie led them into Allison's studio. Allison sat at a drafting table, spraying a sheet of paper. They peered at the piece—it was a colored-pencil drawing of a doe and her fawn. Allison had drawn them in fantastical colors, with large beseeching eyes, and the forest around them was colored so like the animals' fur, they were almost absorbed by their background.

Jaudon was unsettled.

Berry gave a murmur of distress. "They look so lost."

"That's the idea," Allison said, rising. "They're losing their forests. Some have never seen a human before or a hunter. Who knows what colors animals see—why not these?"

Cullie put an arm around Allison's shoulders. "My deep and darling thinker. It spills into everything she does."

Allison started down the stairs. "Dinner should be ready, if you put the dumplings in, Cullie."

"I sure did."

"Smells great," Berry and Jaudon said together.

Kirby was seated in a pink bed at the far end of the kitchen.

"Please bring them drinks, Cullie."

"I reckon I can do that for you, my little jujube." Cullie nuzzled Allison's neck.

Jaudon rolled her eyes every time Cullie used jujube as an endearment. She hadn't learned to lip-read many words, but that was one of them.

Allison looked at Cullie, her face stern, eyes narrowed.

Cullie said, "Mea culpa, I used *my* again. I know I don't own you. No kidding, I know."

Jaudon looked to Berry for an explanation. Berry smiled her I'll-tell-you-later smile.

Cullie, pink in the face, offered them wine, but they both asked for sweet tea. "Allison's the tippler in this family. I join her to bring out the wild sex kitten in her."

Allison lifted her head and laughed. Jaudon thought she heard a quiet titter out of Berry.

While their hosts were in the kitchen, Berry looked at more drawings, these over the dining room buffet. How did they live with such eerie pictures all around them? They were dark in mood, but filled with exacting detail and pleasant colors. They were both fascinating and disturbing. What did they say about Allison?

"You're very good, Allison."

"Thank you, Berry. I'm torn between art and politics—too many passions. Life's too short." Allison hurried to the kitchen.

She turned to Jaudon and asked, "Should we be living in a modern home with new furniture?"

"Heck, no," said Jaudon. "We're genuine Old Florida people. We'd hate it. Leastways, I would."

Berry nodded. "It's so closed off from everything. A gate. Refrigerated air. I'd hate living like a caged animal."

"We might sweat, but it's good Southern sweat. How does Cullie stand it here?"

Cullie, with great slow care, carried a full-to-the-tip glass pitcher of sweet tea and returned to the kitchen. The table was set with matching plates and silverware with wooden handles. Berry admired both.

Allison held up a dish. "These are stoneware. I bought them from a woman potter in California."

"Kirby, the dancing girls don't come on until after dinner." Kirby danced with her front paws up as Cullie brought in a large covered ceramic pot. She had to sidestep the dog all the way to the table.

Allison lifted the cover and sniffed. "Perfect every time. We cooked it since dawn in one of those new Crock-Pots. You prepare the food and let it simmer all day."

"Or night," said Cullie. "I fix oatmeal for the week in the slow cooker."

Allison filled Jaudon's plate.

Her mouth watered. "Is that white beans and rice? I love white beans and rice. And dumplings. Did you give it Cajun spicing?"

Cullie said, "Jaudo, think who you're talking to. It's my Big Ma Ma's personal recipe and she's as Cajun as they come. I left out the sausage for Berry's sake."

"Thank you. I was worried when I saw that pot."

Cullie spooned dinner onto Berry's plate. "We didn't think you'd appreciate gator stew."

"That's a load off my mind." Berry pretended to swipe her forehead with the back of her hand.

Allison said, "Don't you dare bring alligator meat into this house. It's bad enough you order it in restaurants."

Jaudon made a chortling sound and poked Cullie's shoulder with a fist. "You and me ought to go to Mudfoot's Fish Fry sometime, Cullie. He makes real fine gator bites."

"My whole family used to go down there about once a year. It was a real special occasion."

Kirby gave an eager yap.

"No gator bites today, princess. If you behave, I'll let you lick my plate clean."

Plain as day, Berry was trying to hide a look of distaste. She was such a lady, Jaudon thought, warmed despite the chilled air.

Allison engaged Berry in talk about strategies for serving the health care needs of female migrant workers. As always, Berry listened hard while Allison, with her greater experience and understanding of the way the world worked, waved her hands about and devised game plans. Each was as committed to her beliefs as the other; every once in a while Berry, with quiet certainty, made suggestions that stopped Allison in her tracks and led her to rethink some theory or action she was espousing.

Jaudon and Cullie reminisced about growing up in the area, by turns excited about how much they had in common and angry about most of the changes.

"Used to be, every orange was picked and shipped. Nowadays, people are letting them fall, not sweeping them up."

"They want to sell the orchards and walk away with fists full of money."

"Or the taxes are so high they can't afford to keep their family land, much less pay help to care for it."

Berry watched them. Another memory returned to her. Ma and Pa carrying bushel baskets of damaged oranges home to Gran's trailer. They worked in season as orange pickers. They could still be picking, but out in California. She wanted to visit California as much as she'd wanted to as a child. She smiled at the memory of Ma and Pa presenting the oranges to Gran as if they'd discovered hidden treasure.

Gran was onto something when she said to turn her focus to the best memories of Ma and Pa; she found herself grinning. "Look at those two cute codgers we love, Allison. Chewing the fat."

"Aren't they adorable?"

Jaudon tried not to smile.

Cullie leaned toward her. "Did you hear Judy broke up with that crazy driver who slammed into my truck?"

Allison shook her finger. "No gossiping, Cullie."

Jaudon wanted to ask if Allison thought she was Cullie's momma.

"It's not gossip, Allison. Everyone knows Judy had to give up. That woman of hers had more problems than a math book. She's trying to sue the car maker for not making a substantially safe product."

Jaudon winked at her. She was glad to see Cullie stand up to Allison.

Cullie went on talking. "Judy was ferociously against Nina suing someone for her own mistake. Nina flew off the handle. She's now threatening to go after Judy for breach of promise. I can't wait to be a witness in both trials."

Allison's outcry was a lament. "Judy never promised Nina anything."

"Poor Judy," said Berry. "Who can we introduce her to that's nice?"

Allison teased her. "What a matchmaker you are, Berry."

Berry had embarrassed herself in her excitement. "Judy's a great person. I want her to be happy."

"You know who else is single?" said Cullie. She was polishing the lenses of her glasses with a shirttail.

"Lari?" Jaudon wrinkled her nose.

"No. Mercie Lewis."

"Mercie and Judy? Two very strong women. Let's ask them to dinner." Berry chided Allison. "Don't you know you can't be that bald about it?"

Cullie spoke up for Allison. "Why the heck not? It won't do a lick of good to shroud our intentions in mystery and murk." She lifted Kirby to her lap.

"Not with guests at the table, Cullie," said Allison.

Cullie set Kirby on the floor and snuck her a bit of food. "We can double date with them. We can get Donna Skaggs to chaperone us frolicsome lesbians."

Jaudon put her fork and napkin down. "That was so fine I could rub it in my hair."

"Now there's an expression we didn't use in my family," said Allison.

"My Pops is known to say it after every exceptional feed. 'Course, he doesn't have all that much hair." She offered to do the dishes. Allison declined and reminded them that the place had come with an automatic dishwasher. They moved out onto the screened lanai, Kirby's toenails clicking across the tiles.

"How is it, being on the city council?" Jaudon asked. "I suspect I'd tell them to take a walk as soon as they started squabbling like a barnyard full of chickens."

"Don't tempt me, but I have to admit being involved is also exciting. I'm helping to shape this city. The other woman councilor is opposite from me politically. Two of the men are very cool so we're a block and keep the old guard and Mayor Crum from doing more damage than they have. Parliamentary rules keep the council from brawling too much."

Berry asked, "What about you, Cullie? Won't working as a policewoman be a tough row for a woman to hoe?"

"I don't know if I have the grit to stand up to guys who won't want me there. I do know we want to change what's wrong in this town. I won't spend all my time locking up criminals either. There's this new/old concept called community policing, making friends with neighborhoods, being approachable. I want to be involved in that. Another thing I want to concentrate on is the way women are treated by too many policemen and judges. Do you know how very often the courts heave a black or poor woman in jail for defending herself against an attacker?"

Jaudon said, "That makes me mad. Let's put some girl power on the streets."

"Woman power."

Allison made no sense to Jaudon. "Woman, girl, a word won't change the world." Allison looked hurt. Jaudon glanced at Berry who again signaled her to drop it.

Cullie threw ice on the fire. "You bet we need female cops."

Berry's hands were folded on her lap. She realized that Cullie hadn't lit one cigarette. Had she quit for Allison's sake? "Aren't your new lives a complete turnaround for both of you?"

Allison smiled at Cullie. "I'm a retired radical, grateful not to be arrested by the likes of Cullie. Running from authority wastes time, energy, and lives. If I was poor, I'd be in prison, not doing the world a bit of good."

Jaudon said, "Must be the soft Florida air coming in from the Gulf. The heat melts the edges off you."

"It does. I adore Florida. I'm in vacation mode all the time."

"But you work so hard," Berry said.

"Coming down here, I learned that protesting isn't all that effective. The newspapers and TV either ignore us or sensationalize our actions to increase ad revenue. I come by more publicity in a week as a city councilor than we accumulated for our whole demonstration with lots less effort. This, for me is a vacation. To change things I have to work my way into positions of power. Modest positions first, like a spider spinning a web. That way I catch vermin before they do more harm and I spin my web bigger and bigger."

"Is that a good thing? Spiders can be poisonous." Jaudon couldn't shake her suspicion of Allison.

Berry drew her shoulders back and bared her teeth. "And threatening."

Cullie held up her hands in mock fright. "My jujube doesn't have plans to poison anyone. Though she could scare them off a yard or two with her big whip." She gritted her teeth. "*This* jujube, not *my* jujube. Sorry."

Cullie apologized way too much, thought Jaudon.

Allison said, "I'm meeting a lot of people, learning what this piece of the world is in need of, and making voters aware that they want change. I need to build a case for solutions. We don't have to settle for an outpost on Stinky Lane for women's health care and safe space. There are deep pockets in this county, and deep purses. We're going to have a very accessible community-supported visible presence that will serve women's health needs, from birth to death. There are towns across the country establishing shelters to keep women safe. We can't do that with volunteers only. So I'm learning to play the games: bureaucracy, politics, rules and regs and laws and power."

"Looks as if our Little Miss Clitzpah is making a dent," said Jaudon, all the while ready to pull Allison's soapbox out from under her and smash it to splinters.

Cullie stood. "We need to play some fun games. Not political games. I bought Uno, brand-new on the market, from a customer who's the Florida distributor."

When Cullie returned with the games, Kirby jumped into her lap and tromped in three complete circles before curling up. Jaudon, too, realized that Cullie hadn't had one cigarette while they were there and remembered Cullie claiming that smoking was her freedom.

Allison relaxed on the lounger and gave Cullie a big smile. "This woman is a crazy game nut."

Cullie reached to touch Allison's arm. "And this woman never has time to play."

"Tonight, I do," Allison said.

Cullie kissed the air, saying, "This will go down in history. Let me get my tape recorder. Order up the all-lesbian chorus, the dancing femmes, declare a lesbian holiday."

Jaudon watched Allison through the evening. She liked her lighthearted side and gave Cullie full credit for it.

They laughed so hard learning to play that they never finished the game before Jaudon and Berry yawned in unison and Allison sent them home. She insisted they take what was left of dinner with them, saying, "You go out and buy yourselves a Crock-Pot. Your Gran will love you for it."

It was one of those heavy humid nights when you expected the air to burst into tears it was so full of moisture. After an evening with another loving couple, Berry was in a hurry to take Jaudon to bed and planned to tease her all the way home.

Other than the sound of an unmuffled car engine traveling fast, there was silence outside the front door of the condo.

Cullie stood in the doorway and spoke in a soft voice. "Drive safe, dear little lesbians. Don't fall off the turning planet."

CHAPTER FORTY

Zefer had her chin on Rigo's thigh. "You know I adore your pancakes, Gran, but my appetite has diminished radically."

Gran left the stove and sat with them at the table. "I don't care for the way you're looking, young man. Turn sideways and you'd disappear."

Berry exchanged a chagrined glance with Jaudon. Rigo was more disheveled than usual. He scratched his stubble. It shone copper-red in the light from the kitchen window.

"I have to keep my girlish figure, don't I?"

The phone rang.

"That's my ride, pet. I'm going with the seniors to the museum."

"The art museum in St. Pete?" asked Rigo, perking up from what seemed to be complete despondency.

"We already got our culture there last year. This museum is fun: the Circus Hall of Fame over in Sarasota."

As soon as Gran was out the door, Jaudon, petrified Rigo was dying of liver disease, said, "Tell us."

From the expression on Rigo's face Berry imagined what he looked like as a kid suffering a dressing down.

He took a deep breath. "I was at the park."

"Which park?"

"Ballast Point. A lot of guys go over there to get together."

"You mean…?" Jaudon was unable to hide the sneer of distaste that took over her face.

"I do mean. Where else can we go? Anyway, I got busted by an undercover cop."

"No." Jaudon punched him in the upper arm. Hard. "What is the matter with you, Rigo, you jerk."

Berry handed him tissues and he blotted the tears from his eyes.

"I called Jimmy Neal, but he didn't have bail money. The banks were closed. I asked him to call my father's attorney and tell the attorney to keep his mouth shut."

"I'd be so mad," said Jaudon. "I might call your father, your mother, and your first grade teacher."

"Did he keep quiet?" Berry asked.

"Of course not. The lawyer's job is to protect my father. I got bonded out, but my dad closed my bank account. He's not paying rent on my apartment starting next month. No more tuition payments. I'm destitute. The lawyer let me know my father never wants to see his *maricon* son again."

"What about your car?" asked Berry. The crabbed unworthy part of her thought he might deserve it for playing the field when he had a fine man at home.

"Thank God he gave that to me as a gift for high school graduation. I've put up a for sale flyer at school. I'll trade it for a clunker, find us a cheaper apartment, and finish my master's on time despite my father. You may have a dinner guest on occasion."

"I can give you more hours at the store, Rigo. Momma can put you on at one of the other stores too."

Berry said, "You and Jimmy Neal are welcome to join us for meals anytime."

Under his curly red mop Rigo gave a self-assured grin. Berry breathed and let her bad feelings go. She'd love to plop a bright white toddler's sailor cap on his head and cuddle him.

Jaudon no longer itched to punch his good-looking face, but she wanted this be a lesson to him that would keep him home with Jimmy Neal, who deserved better. She'd punch his father's face instead if she ever got an opportunity.

Rigo bowed to Berry. "I hoped you'd say that."

"Momma is bad enough, but disowning a kid?" Jaudon's jaw clenched. "Make my life difficult, sure. Break up the family? Never. You must feel like the last pea at pea-time."

Berry said, "I've a mind to ask Gran to call your father and give him what for. Be a good boy and eat your pancakes." Berry pushed the sorghum syrup to him. "You used to be nothing but an appetite on two feet."

Rigo slipped a pancake to Zefer.

"Rigo," Berry said with an admonishing scowl.

"Is your father some kind of a religious crackpot?" asked Jaudon.

"No. It's his culture. To him men are by definition heterosexual which makes me not a man and not a son. It's also this damned gay liberation movement, excuse my Spanish, Berry. It's got everybody up in arms about us. You should hear my father rage when they talk about gay people on TV, or, God forbid, interview one of us. Though I guess I won't have the pleasure of hearing his rants from here on."

"I don't understand what those city people are trying to do with their marches and riots," Jaudon said. "Shine a light on us so we're rooted out and beat up?"

"That's a fact. It doesn't have anything to do with gays here in the sticks. Leave me out of it." Rigo pushed his plate away and laid his head on the kitchen table. "Don't we have enough trouble without a bunch of spoiled brats stirring up more? They can have their equal rights. All I want is a regular everyday life."

Berry and Jaudon moved their chairs and made a circle of their arms around him.

"My father." Rigo gulped for air. "You hear about these things happening, but not my Papi."

"What about your mother?" Berry asked, praying his mother stayed in his corner. Would she have lost Ma and Pa for loving Jaudon? Gran would have put her foot down to stop that.

"She threatened to divorce him if he cut me off. He hit her. I got between them and that's when he ordered me out of the house. I told the bastard to hit me, a man, not my mother. You know what he said?"

Jaudon by this time was crying with him. She rubbed the onyx ring Rigo had given her. "I know his words exactly. He told you you're not a man, just like Momma tells me I'm not a woman."

"But you are, Rigo," said Berry. "You're more of a man than someone who rejects his own child."

"I didn't leave until my mother got away from him. He accused her of turning me gay for the same old reasons."

Berry rubbed his cold hand between her own. "Her gay friends must have been a sore spot between them since day one."

"While I blocked his way, she ran upstairs to her bedroom. I went after her and locked us in. She pulled out suitcases and packed like a maniac. We went down the back stairs and took off for the banks. She was desperate to withdraw every cent from the two accounts he'd given her access to, and she'd saved cash for years in a safe deposit box he didn't know about."

He lifted his head and drew a handkerchief from his pocket. "This was a long time coming. He started hitting Mom the past year or so. It seemed that, the older he got, the more narrow-minded and suspicious he was. He was a charmer when he was young, but Mom's long been disenchanted with him."

"I'd burn his darned house down," Jaudon said. "With him in it."

Rigo smiled. "I approve of how you think, Jaudo. Mom's left for Miami. To the freedom of the Atlantic Ocean, as she called it. We were in the parking lot of the First National Bank of Tampa when she kissed me good-bye. She called me her full-blooded American man. She wants me to move to Miami."

"No." Jaudon clung to him.

Rigo's Adam's apple bobbed up and down a few times, like he was swallowing a sob. "Absolutely not. I won't leave Jimmy Neal. Or," he said, looking in their eyes, "my best friends in the world."

Berry's eyes were inflamed with unshed tears. "My two castaways. Maybe I'm here for no reason other than to love you both. And Gran."

Rigo managed a small laugh. "I'll take every bit of love you can spare me."

"You might be here to love Jimmy Neal."

"You're close to sounding like a preacher lady, Berry," said Jaudon.

She covered her mouth with her hand. "I'm sorry if I sounded preachy. No, that's not quite true. I want you to be as devoted to Jimmy Neal as he is to you. As I am to Jaudon."

"Guys don't work that way, Berry."

"You're convinced about that?" Jaudon tried to keep the rankling out of her voice. "I think Jimmy Neal might work that way."

"I'm tempted to set him free so he can find someone who can be everything he needs. I'll move over to Miami with my mom, stay high, and have constant wild sex."

"You don't have the sense God gave a Billy goat."

"Yes, I do, Jaudo, because that must be my totem animal, the Billy goat."

Jaudon didn't think she heard him right. "Totem animal?"

Berry said, "It's your life to do with what you want, Rigo. This is your wake-up call. If you don't settle down, guaranteed, you'll get sick."

"Darlings, I *am* sick." He told them about his diagnosis. Neither let on that they already knew. "So you can stop your carping."

"Don't be peeved at me for telling you the truth, Rigo. Your spirit is trying to open your eyes."

"To show me I've always loved the wrong men for the wrong reasons, including my father?"

Rigo looked furious enough to take their heads off. He said, "Is there ever a wrong reason to love?" He slammed the table flat-handed and stood. Zefer barked the whole time Rigo strode to the front door. Rigo flung it open and left.

They looked at each other.

"Redheads."

"No," Berry said, rising and running after him. "He's a destroyed little boy with no idea how to use his precious life except to throw it away. We better see if we can stop him from doing anything dumb."

"Like what?" asked Jaudon.

"Like hurt himself."

"Not Rigo. He enjoys his life too much. He has plans."

"People under extreme stress aren't the same as their usual selves."

They called Zefer and jumped into the van. Rigo's car squealed onto Eulalia Road.

The van's engine cranked and ground, cranked and ground.

Jaudon got out and kick started Zoom. That boy was not going to mess himself up if she had anything to do with it. She sped around an idling truck parked just south of Pineapple Trail and turned onto Route 60 two vehicles behind Rigo, who for once wasn't driving like he was in a race with time. She smiled as she realized Rigo had to be careful: his father was no longer paying his speeding tickets.

By the time they hit Tampa she saw Berry behind her. The van must have come to its senses and decided to help. Berry passed her.

Rigo led them to the harbor. He pulled into a parking lot, got out, and went to sit on a piling above the docks. Pleasure boats came and went. Jaudon turned off her engine and glided to the van in silence. She lifted Zoom into the van and joined Berry.

"It was the fuse that's always blowing," Berry whispered into Jaudon's good ear. "Thanks for putting new ones in the glove box. It was also my fuse blowing. It set Rigo off."

"You spoke true, Berry."

They waited and watched. Berry reached over and stopped Jaudon from rubbing the space above her upper lip, a quirk that, she assumed, grew out of her self-consciousness.

"His parents have a stormy marriage," Berry said in a soft voice.

"I know. Do you think that's that why he can't settle down?"

"He's young, Jaudon."

"We're as young as he is."

Berry reached for her hand. "Some people need a lot of Laris."

Jaudon hung her head, lips compressed till they hurt.

"He told me once he didn't want to live like his mother and father," Berry said. "He may be running less from Jimmy Neal than from settling down."

After almost an hour, Rigo got in his car. He was oblivious to them as they followed his Camaro to the Skyway Bridge.

"Uh-oh," said Jaudon. She realized she was rubbing the stone on her pinky ring to protect Rigo. "Talk about cutting off your nose to spite your face. He'd punish his father by killing himself?"

Rigo pulled over before the bridge and sat again, engine running.

"Should we call the police?" Jaudon asked.

Berry's silence was always a sign of her tension. "Not yet—that might rattle him more. It would be best if he works this out himself. Meanwhile, we're on empty."

They crossed the highway against traffic and stopped at the nearest gas station. Jaudon watched Rigo's car and willed the pump to ding faster as it raced through the gallons.

Rigo drove onto the bridge. His brake lights came on as he reached the highest point.

"Berry," she said and stopped the pump before hitting the ten dollars she'd prepaid. She ran to her seat. "Go! Go!" she said.

Berry's heart beat hard, but she didn't start the van. Zefer panted, her head between their seats. Jaudon strained to see Rigo's car.

His brake lights cut off and Rigo drove forward, increased his speed, and made a U-turn at the other side of the bridge. If he saw their van as he passed the gas station, he didn't acknowledge them. Berry pulled onto the road.

"Is he going to do it somewhere else? We'll never catch up to him—he's upped his speed," said Jaudon, leaning forward to will the van faster.

"Did he figure out a better place than this bridge?"

"How can you be so calm, Berry? I'm white-knuckling this thing."

A sense of peace came over her. "I think he's going to be okay."

When they cruised by Rigo's apartment, his car was parked outside.

"Aw, jiminy, Berry, he's packing to leave."

"I'd rather have faith Rigo discovered where he belongs and went on home."

CHAPTER FORTY-ONE

Berry knew no one who believed in what she believed. Jaudon came closest, but wasn't big-hearted toward people, the way Berry tried to be, and she didn't blame Jaudon after she'd been treated like a freak of nature all her life. Jaudon shared Berry's love of animals and her complete respect for the land and for living things—other than fish. It was wrong to hunt them for sport. She imagined the panic and pain that must come with the hook, the human handling, the time spent out of water before Jaudon let them go. Berry announced last weekend she wasn't going in the boat anymore if Jaudon took her bait and tackle. In any case, Jaudon found little time for it, nor did she seem to miss it.

At age twenty-four Berry doubted she was any further advanced spiritually than she had been at eighteen or twelve. She'd stopped using the term Great Spirit for a while because she couldn't get used to it—she started to use it again because it came closest to what she understood. If you couldn't connect with your faith because of its name, what good was it? She was more convinced than ever that naming, making religious laws, envisioning faith as a Santa Claus figure in the sky, were incompatible with spirituality. Organized religion, to her, was a lazy way of celebrating life, but it seemed the concept of a Great Spirit—which could be nothing more than her own will to honor and caretake all of creation—was passed to her through her ancestors.

Whatever energy governed the world didn't need a name. Berry did though. It was human nature to name the unknown, to give it a recognizable shape. How many years would she struggle with this?

Other people believed without question; they didn't have to reinvent the wheel. She shrank from religions that were all about earthly judgment;

it wasn't up to her to judge. She chaffed at prim Protestantism; those denominations didn't seem to have room for people who got out of line or had their own ideas of deity and prayer. She didn't want to be Catholic, with their real estate and expensive pomp that she would turn into bread and housing for the whole world. Judaism was out for her because the men thanked their God that they were not women. Muslim women had to cover up because men didn't control their lusts. Buddhism was appealing for its emphasis on serenity and oneness, yet throughout history, women were treated as inferiors in most sects. For all the religious study she did in college, she continued to fit nowhere.

Cullie told them not to let the chaos of the world keep them awake, but what about the chaos of the soul? Just that morning, she'd gone to her knees before an azalea bush so big and abundant with yellow blossoms she wanted to melt into it and stay in that heaven forever. There was chaos, but there was also this ecstasy of faith she could not, would not, deny.

Washing dishes, Berry struggled aloud to explain her quandary to Jaudon. "I don't accept that there's nothing. I want so bad for there to be something…"

Jaudon took Berry in her arms. "You're a dreamer, Berry. Could be it's not up to a person when she can do this spiritual thing right. Could be the way to get there is to put one foot in front of the other." A few minutes later Jaudon got a call from one of the Beverage Bays and took off on her cycle to solve a problem.

She thought of Jaudon's words about putting one foot in front of the other as she led an old woman to an examining room.

"We haven't seen you in a couple of years," she told Mrs. Fossler.

Mrs. Fossler smiled. She had a few teeth left. "Had no reason to. I'm strong as an ox and fit as a fiddle." She wheezed at her joke.

"No health problems?"

Mrs. Fossler tapped her ear. "My hearing."

"Is that why you came in today?"

Lizzetta Fossler was eighty-nine. Looking at her and her health history, she could be as young as seventy-five.

"I can't lift this arm, child."

"Did you fall on it?"

"Never."

"Lift a heavy object?"

"Can't help but do that." She wheezed again. "'Course, anymore, I can't lift a finger."

"You're right-handed?"

"I was."

"May I examine your upper arm?"

"Be my guest. It's not doing me any good."

There was a well-defined lump there. She noted it on the chart and helped her change into a gown.

"No one came with you today?"

"My great-grandson dropped me off. I gave him fifty cents to go snare himself a crumb to eat while he waits. He'll buy smokes, the sassy rascal."

The doctor called Berry in later to start a referral for a biopsy of the growth. By the time they were done the great-grandson was in the waiting room, smoking. He leapt up to help his grandmother, first squeezing the glowing tobacco into an ashtray and depositing the stub into his shirt pocket.

"Doc says maybe cancer," Mrs. Fossler shouted to the boy. He looked at Berry with obvious alarm in his eyes.

"Makes me no never mind," said his great-grandmother with a chuckle. "Thank you, Lord. I will at last join you in your heavenly home. Come on, Junior. If it comes back cancer, I have things to take care of before I go."

How did anyone accept the possibility of cancer or death with such grace and humor? It was hard enough to do that in everyday life.

She wanted to find a way to be like Mrs. Fossler.

No, she thought, disgusted with herself. Who was she, Berry Garland, to think she could know where she fit in this vast universe? Why did she think she was so important that she should be privy to what others conjectured, but no human knew for sure?

Jaudon, so practical, knew her dreamer: if it took forever, she needed to put one foot in front of the other till she got where she was supposed to go.

CHAPTER FORTY-TWO

Halloween is in the air," Berry said as they went to their vehicles before work. "Even with Lari gone, this land is full of strange stories."

Jaudon nodded. She was looking at their neglected tree house. She needed to trim the branches slapping and scratching at it.

Berry came to her side and held her hand. "It's only supposed to gust up to twenty-one mph here today, but Eloise may hit the Panhandle hard."

Jaudon looked at the sky. "We've been lucky this year. Eloise may not be the last we see of hurricane season. I hope the tree house can hang on till I get up there with hammer and nails."

The paint was faded and mossy, the roof full of fallen fronds and branches. A large fern was growing up there. Jaudon was saddened by the sight of her childhood refuge and promised herself once again that she'd clean it, shore it up, and paint it.

The best thing to come of that tree house was Berry. She loved the delicate hand in hers, a bit roughened by gardening and repairs and constant washing at the clinic. What was she without Berry? A hoarse-voiced, mannish Southern Cracker working at a mom and pop business her Momma built up and now was running into the ground. She gave up being mad about it. As long as Berry stuck with her, none of that mattered.

Berry looked at Jaudon, not the tree house. To her, Jaudon's mix of feminine and masculine created a handsome androgyny. She found the sunshine on Jaudon's short light hair irresistible. She wanted to touch the shine of her all the time. Jaudon's wiry muscles sent a flush through her whole body. The way Jaudon stood with her legs wide, firmly planted, her insolent walk, her commanding gestures—every move a challenge to detractors—she could not love her more.

As for her own weaknesses, she shucked them off whenever she was strong enough. The Great Spirit caught them and incinerated them to ashes.

They parted for the day, Berry babying the van, Jaudon inseparable from her noisy bike.

Pops stopped to see her at the store during the slow time of the afternoon. He paced and shook Eloise's fringe of rain off his trucker's cap while Jaudon waited on a customer.

"What's got you so fidgety, Pops?" He was making her nervous.

Momma insisted that Pops wear suits and ties, but today he was in his work clothes, red-faced, disheveled and scrawny—when had he lost all that weight? What hair he had left was unwashed and uncombed. From the expression on his face, she expected him to tell her Momma said she was fired or had to give up their homestead.

His speech was way too loud and distinct since her ear injury, like he was spitting words. "It's your Momma, Jaudon. She's been so forgetful of late and walking and talking like a drunk woman. She gave in and let me take her to the doctor's. He gave us her test results when we saw him today."

Somebody might have thrown a bucket of ice water at her middle, Jaudon went so cold. "Did she have a heart attack or something?"

"Not exactly. He called it post-stroke dementia which, as near as I can tell, means she's been having small strokes all along, so small I didn't know. Add them up and they wiped out parts of her good, solid brain."

"She's lost her marbles?"

"She'll look up from her desk, stare at me, at the room, and tell me she wants to go to her office. Daughter, she does this when she's already in her office. She's taken to calling me Daddy, like she did her father. Or she'll be driving the Cadillac and we'll be way the heck down Turkey Creek Road, she'll turn east onto 60 and drive us halfway to Mulberry. I'll ask where she's going and she'll try and cover by saying she's looking for more places to put stores. Or she'll arrange for a drop ship of women's fancy blouses to all the Bays when we don't sell clothes, meaning to order one for herself."

Was it that night—the night she touched Lari and the cereal boxes fell on Momma's head? Did her one lapse cause this too? She didn't know whether to say anything—Pops might not know about that part of the incident and Momma had acted unhurt. She dismissed the thought for the moment.

She was unnerved because of Momma's condition, but more so because it was plain that Pops was fear struck. She'd always thought she inherited his courage; to see it fail shook her up. She'd never before seen her father scared of anything but Momma.

"Did you tell Bat yet?"

"I made a family emergency call to the Army. When Bat called, I told him he needs to ask for a discharge, because Momma wants him to come home and take over the business."

Jaudon looked away at this news.

"I know, Daughter. If your momma was a beach, she wouldn't appreciate the sand." His laugh wasn't as hearty as normal.

"Why, Pops? Why is Momma so flinty toward me?"

Pops folded his arms.

"No, Pops. Don't stand there and take her side. I need to know. Has she always had a little bit of dementia? Does that make her so cold?"

"I'm thinking, Daughter. Give me a minute."

She opened a carton of cigarettes for shelving while he thought. Rain blew in through the exit door. She'd have Jimmy Neal keep that mopped up when he came in. The cigarettes were half put away when Pops spoke.

"Growing up, your momma had nothing. The first Batsons to settle the Florida frontier were cowmen, and never rose higher than that. The Vicker boys built the house and hung on to their patch of land. Momma should have been born a Vicker, with her drive. How ambition chose her I don't know, because the rest of the Batsons worked just enough to insure they had hooch and fishing poles.

"Momma wasn't born to be lazy and self-indulgent. She hated going without. She hated being a poor nobody Cracker who was looked down on by everyone in Rainbow Gap including those with dark skins. It galled her. She didn't have good looks or talent, but she did have determination. You got that from her.

"I was sideswiped by her iron will first hand. She decided to marry a Vicker. We weren't rich, but we had property and held our heads high as a hard-working clan. I was her age and Momma set her sights on me. I never had a chance." He smiled.

There was so much she wanted to ask. Did Momma make him happy? Why did he let himself fall into her net? Why was Momma so disappointed in her and Bat?

"She made these stores from nothing, Daughter. My trucking jobs just about kept us in milk and bread, but your momma squeezed every dime till it bled pennies, then used those pennies to make another dime. It took all she had to rise this high and I'm afraid the effort took her mind."

He lifted his arms as if in surrender to Momma's voracious will and to a world so hard it ate up the frail creatures that brooked it. "There was nothing left for love, Jaudon. You have to understand that she showed she cared for you and your brother with her accomplishments, by what she's given you."

"It's kind of sad, isn't it, Pops?"

He nodded. "She gave you all she had. Meanwhile, Bat and I don't have your head for business. With him staying and staying in the service, I'd sell the whole lot of Bays, get by on interest income, and take care of Momma, but you live for these stores."

"Sorry to say, Pops, Bat's hopeless. He doesn't want what Momma can give him. He loves being in the service. It's Momma, without the out-of-nowhere, unpredictable disapproval. They make his decisions for him. They pay him and feed him and tell him what to wear. I love my brother and I might hire him part-time, or as a driver, because he's my brother, but I wouldn't let him manage one Bay."

"You don't have to worry about it. I begged him to come home and help his old man. He refused."

Even Pops went to Bat before he came to her. Bitter, she was compelled to ask, "How is Momma? Aside from her memory."

"That's it, Daughter. You don't know to look at her that anything's wrong. It took the accountant to spot it because his father's in a nursing home with a condition like your momma's."

"I tried to persuade Momma to let me do her book work." She didn't hide her annoyance. "I was afraid she was messing up."

"Jaudon, your momma had no idea. It wasn't her habit to be making bad decisions the way she has been for a while, but I didn't know what to do. I never thought she might have taken ill."

Her poor Pops. She reached for his hand. "Bat always joked Momma wasn't right in the head. I'll hazard a guess her mind's been going for a long time."

"He's wrong about that, Daughter. I'm the one who married her and watched her build a business. She was smart as a whip. But he did speak the almighty truth when he said to me that you're who I want. Said you've got the Batson brain for business."

"Bat said that?" Her eyes filled up with tears. "My brother Bat?" She was going to write and tell him thank you. No, knowing her batty brother, he'd deny he ever said it.

"Yes, he did, and I agree with him. Your momma fears you'll bring ruin on the family, looking the way you do and living as man and wife with Berry, but people don't care about that as much as she thinks."

Her pleasure at Bat's compliment flamed into rage at Momma. She swallowed it out of care for her being so sick.

Pops went on. "Bat told me to tell your momma that Jaudon's to take over. If it's not working out, he'll leave the service. Bat wants you to have that chance. He assured her that you'll see to it that Momma and me will live a life of ease and plenty."

The tears came again. Had she heard correctly? Was her hearing worse than she realized? Pops put his powerful arms around her.

"I never knew Bat thought that about me," she said. Over Pops's shoulder, she looked out at her store, heard the rain slow to a tapping on its metal roof. It was neat, clean, made them money, had low inventory losses; it was a perfect thing. Did she have it in her in fact to succeed at keeping all the stores running as well? For the first time it occurred to her that the years of name-calling, tears, and rejection she'd lived through so far might have made her strong enough to handle running a business.

She asked, "That's what Bat and you want? For me to take over? I'm not even twenty-five, but I know the stores like nobody's business. And I will for certain take care of the whole family."

A surge of anxiety hit her hard enough to stop her tears. She sat hard on the stack of milk crates. "Will you stay in charge of the warehouse and the trucks, Pops?"

"Honey, your momma's going to need some full-time care and I want to be the one to give it if she lives another forty years."

She bit her lower lip. *What does he see in Momma that keeps him so devoted?* "That's one thing Momma never let me in on, scheduling deliveries, supervising drivers. All I know is store level and how to keep the books."

"Your cousin Cal was in transport in the service, same as Bat. You know he's been working at that motorbike shop, but they can't meet payroll half the time. Cal's coming to work with us. I'll train him and give him all the guidance he needs.

"The doc said your momma will require routine and she'll have to be kept busy. I figure I'll take her around to the stores and warehouse every day so she can keep tabs on things. You'll let the crews know to agree to whatever she says, but not to carry anything out without your say-so. Will that be interfering too much?"

"Oh, no, Pops, I'll be grateful for the help, to tell you the truth. And I'll make Olive Ponder manager here if she wants it. She hasn't heard anything more about her MIA son; this will keep her mind occupied."

"You're a kind soul, Daughter. I shouldn't joke with your momma sick like she is and Mrs. Ponder hurting, but darn, I imagine we better skip this store when we make our rounds. Seeing a dark-skinned lady in full charge might send Momma screaming into the strawberry fields in the moonlight, stark nekkid."

Jaudon laughed with him. She missed her Pops since Momma put him in the new house.

With a poke in the upper arm, she grinned at him, teasing him by stealing two of his expressions. "I'll shoulder the load for you, Pops, and do you proud."

Pops squeezed her to him again. "I swear, there's no better child on earth than you, Miss Jaudon Vicker. There's just enough of the devil in you to be my child."

Did Pops truly love his shaggy daughter, she wondered, or was he being grateful she agreed to pick up the load? She wasn't about to take on his private liquor business, but she'd speak with him about that later.

Pops asked her to stop by the new house as soon as possible. He sounded desperate.

CHAPTER FORTY-THREE

Jaudon worked late that night and gave Berry the news the next morning, her voice raspier than usual from shedding a few tears.

"Well, that explains an awful lot about your momma. That rigid way she thinks, the way she bosses people around, her lack of compassion for her own children."

"She is difficult." Jaudon was cautious of being cruel despite how Momma treated her. She'd cried for Momma's sudden decline, but also for the two decades of mistreatment Momma inflicted on her, and in utter relief at this unshackling. Today she was all rabbity. She wanted both to hide out in the woods until everything came around normal, and to hurry up taking over the stores. They planned a visit to see Momma Sunday.

Berry kept her hand on Jaudon's shoulder as they drove to Momma's house past the rare bursts of brightness from creamy loquat flowers, and the purple, orange, and yellow leaves of the sassafras.

Jaudon said, "I've been thinking about poor Momma. What in the world am I without her and her great gift of the business she never intended to give me? What other job could I do where being me doesn't matter?"

Berry squeezed her shoulder. "Plenty." She hoped the war between Jaudon and Momma might be ending. How would it have been between her and her own ma? She hoped not this stormy.

Jaudon gave a disgusted snicker. "Packing strawberries?"

The visit to Momma was grimmer than either of them imagined.

Pops said, "Your Momma's gotten some worse all of the sudden. The doc says it's six of one, half a dozen of the other whether people go downhill real quick or not."

Berry was stunned to see Pops Vicker shuffling, a grizzly, shattered man. Jaudon was pale and sweaty-looking. She yearned to take Jaudon's hand, to give her comfort and strength, and settled for standing so close their arms touched. She knew the day he'd stopped at Jaudon's store was the last time Jaudon was ever going to see the Pops she'd always cherished.

When they entered the den, Momma was napping on her recliner.

"Momma, Jaudon's here."

Momma's eyes snapped open. She looked like her usual self. Jaudon was certain her father, the doctor, both got it all wrong.

"Why, Jaudon, you came to visit! My own daughter. Look, Bat," she said to Jaudon, "how pretty she is, smiling and ladylike. Come hug your momma." Momma stretched her arms toward Berry.

Berry looked at Jaudon. The horrified hurt in Jaudon's eyes made Berry recoil from Momma's arms. At that moment she wished Jaudon's hearing had declined in both ears.

"She gets confused," Pops muttered. Berry saw that Jaudon didn't hear him.

Berry blinked away tears. Everyone loses parents; she'd lost hers earlier than most, but the open wound of Momma wasn't any less for Jaudon.

Jaudon folded her arms tight across her chest. She wasn't going to let Momma make her ashamed about how she turned out anymore. As a matter of fact, at times she had a smidgeon of pride about herself. This was an eye-opener: growing up proved to be a matter of wrestling your demons. In Berry's case, evil spirits. For Allison, it was the wrongs of the world. When it came to herself and Momma, it was waiting out the demon of being so different from each other.

They didn't stay long after that. Pops had his hands full. He walked them to the door and pressed a check into Jaudon's hand.

Jaudon reminded Pops of what she'd always promised: she'd take care of the business, from accounting to store coverage to dressing up for the dreaded chamber meetings. "The chamber will have to put up with who I am, Pops. Berry will help me find a nice pair of slacks and I have a good white shirt. Besides, there's other ways into the business community," she said, thinking of Rigo's long-ago words about the loyalty of gay people and also of Olive, who, with the addition of Emmett's wife to the crew, brought in more African Americans. Jaudon's increasing grasp of Spanish helped too. "You'll see, results speak louder than lipstick."

She looked at the check and thrust it at Pops. "I can't take this much money. Are you sure you didn't put in too many zeros?"

Pop said, "Yes, Daughter. Vacations are few and far between in our business. I raided the store account to sign one last check on it. Shop for a dependable car. We can call it a company car and take a deduction. Go off somewhere for a couple of weeks to break it in. Or fly someplace you've always wanted to go, far from our hurricanes. We never took you kids anywhere, Jaudon. Go have some fun."

"We don't have any business living high on the hog like that, Pops."

"Your Momma made us a bucket of money, Daughter. You don't see it because she squirrels it away."

"You'll need it for Momma's care, Pops."

"The health insurance we've been carrying despite her squawking at every payment? Don't worry, if you don't make us another dime in profit, we'll be okay."

The thought of a vacation, of traveling away from Rainbow Gap, scared the bejesus out of Jaudon more than ever, with her hearing problem. Plus people were used to how she looked around here. In a strange place she'd be running the gauntlet of stares and kids' barbed questions and the torture of being reminded she was different every step of the way.

"How can I leave the stores?" she asked Pops. "And, Berry, I can't recall a time since we've been grown when we spent more than a day together without work or school between us."

She saw the delight on Berry's face and knew she wasn't going to refuse her this pleasure. If Pops faced Momma failing, she determined to face the perils of leaving Rainbow Gap.

"I hope we get along," said Berry, teasing now.

"This may be the last chance we get to have so much time off."

"Oh, no. I want to see places with you. The Grand Canyon, Mardi Gras, Allison's Oregon, New York City, the White House. You'd better get a very comfortable car because we'll put lots of miles on it."

Jaudon didn't want to think about all that. "I suppose we don't want the Bays represented by a nasty van and a foreign scooter," she said, making her first decision as the new boss of the whole company. "I never thought of that before. I won't buy a Cadillac. How about a Buick? I've been admiring a new Electra that comes through for wine."

Pops frowned in the way she knew meant he was pondering. "You're a CPA—you know you can write off the whole trip if you stop to visit some stores along the way. I'll try not to bankrupt us before you return. Berry, I'm counting on you to keep Jaudon from coming up with wild ideas. The Beverage Bays may be old-fashioned, but there's nothing wrong with that. People want tried and true."

"I won't abandon the foundation, Pops, but don't you think a show of ambition—advertising, weekly sales—will keep us competitive?"

He scratched his chin. "I'd say a little bit of that won't hurt. Remember, you don't want to get too big for your britches, Daughter. Momma's first principle is: don't lose money."

"I think I'll make myself a big sign to always remind me. Meanwhile, if we go away, would you look in on Gran sometimes? She'll be all alone except for Zefer and Toby and there's been someone hanging around, stopping to watch the place from the road."

Pops's eyebrows shot up. "You know I'll get over there every chance I get. Me and your momma can drive by on our rounds starting tomorrow. We'll visit too. You gals are away all day."

"That'll make both of us feel better." She turned to Berry. "We'll see what we can sell the van for, and take out a loan to buy you something to run around in."

"A loan? That sounds so grown up it's scary, Jaudon."

She smiled in agreement, but her mood was solemn, more so than high school graduation, her promotion to store manager, or earning the letters CPA after her name. "I wasn't planning on growing up this soon either."

Pops hugged them both.

"Don't y'all dare have a hurricane while we're away," said Berry.

They stepped outside and Pops went to Momma, where he belonged.

Rejection, wrenching sadness, excitement about her Beverage Bays, love for Pops, confusion, filled her up and sped around her insides—her own personal storm cell. Momma used to say a Bible line to her and Bat when they were being hellions, as she called them, though Jaudon realized that's how kids acted and there was nothing wrong with it. The line was something to do with putting aside childish things.

"You know," said Berry, "we both lost our mommas early on."

Jaudon looked at her, "We did?"

"I'm surprised I never thought of it before, that we never talked about it. I lost mine to Pa's motorcycle dreams, yours to Momma's obsession with status."

"Bat once told me how lucky we were compared to you being motherless."

"I used to think that too."

"And I wished our momma would take off like yours." She groaned at how unfunny life was, and imagined Berry vanishing in front of her very eyes into a fine mist she tried to capture. Her heart, her heart survived losing Momma's love, but wouldn't survive losing Berry. She might as well lay it on a rock and smash it with a sledgehammer. What could she do? Nothing, she told herself. It wasn't her fault she never really had someone to mother her, and it wouldn't be her fault if Berry disappeared too. Whoever, whatever she lost, in the end she, Jaudon, was the one with that sledgehammer, she was the one with the say-so over her heart and soul.

Berry looked at Momma's symmetrical, precisely trimmed trees and thought of her ma and pa. They'd given her this life. It was about a week ago when the Great Spirit told her to stop tugging at them, to leave them be. She decided since then to get on with things, blossom where they planted her, honor them and their crazy love by how she lived. Aloud, she said, "Who knows where life leads anyone?"

Jaudon pictured their pond bench and two little girls reading books side by side, unaware of what's ahead of them. As she looked, they dissipated, little ghosts of themselves, a long time ago.

In her determined, obtuse way, she said, "I'm not going anywhere." She didn't for one minute regret leaving her heart in Berry's careful hands. It took a load off her to know this time she was no needy infant. It was her decision to make, her heart to offer, to give, to protect. She wondered if she was up to it and determined to be up to it. If nothing else, she had Momma's grit.

"Good." Berry took her hand. "Good. It leads nowhere but vacation—with you. I'd love to see Oregon just once. Bat's friend John and Allison both say it's heaven on earth. Cullie says there are a lot of people like us there, but you decide, Jaudon. I want to be with you, wherever you are."

"Is it cold there?"

"There are such things as coats, Jaudon. Maybe between me and a Tampa Spartans jacket you'd be warm enough."

"A Spartans jacket? For me?" She'd coveted those jackets as a kid while listening to games in the tree house.

"I imagine we can afford one for our trip."

She closed her eyes and imagined the tree house as it was this morning when she held Berry's hand.

Offered up to the sky by its mother tree it looked forlorn. Clouds scudded past it, too hurried to pause; breezes buffeted it, as if Jaudon's little castle in the air was in their way. Neglect worked fast in Florida's damp heat. The plywood was warped, the ladder missing a rung. The wolf spiders must be mammoth by now, battling for mildewed space with one another and with generations of baby snakes lengthening by the day, grown snakes robbing birds' nests in the higher branches of the old oak. She wanted to keep up her tattered shelter. Why not use this vacation to fix it, expand it.

Or was that a pitiful excuse to get out of traveling? Jaudon never once pictured herself away from the Beverage Bays, way out West. It might as well be the moon. But if going made her Berry happy, she wanted to be the first one on that airplane.

The old tree house would be there when they came home.

About the Author

Lee Lynch is the namesake and first recipient of The Golden Crown Literary Society Lee Lynch Classic Award for her novel *The Swashbuckler*. Among other honors, she has received the James Duggins Mid-Career Award in Writing, has been inducted into the Saints and Sinners Literary Hall of Fame, is a three-time Lammy finalist, earned an Alice B. Reader Award, and is the winner of three additional Goldies. She is a GCLS Trailblazer.

Bold Strokes Books has also published *An American Queer, The Raid, Beggar of Love*, and *Sweet Creek* and has made Lynch's backlist available, including The Morton River Valley Trilogy and her short story collections. Lynch's long-running column, "The Amazon Trail," appears nationally. Her short stories can be found in many anthologies.

Originally from Queens, New York, she resides in the Pacific Northwest with her wife, Elaine Mulligan Lynch.

Books Available from Bold Strokes Books

18 Months by Samantha Boyette. Alissa Reeves has only had two girlfriends and they've both gone missing. Now it's up to her to find out why. (978-1-62639-804-7)

Arrested Hearts by Holly Stratimore. A reckless cop who hates her life and a health nut who is afraid to die might be a perfect combination for love. (978-1-62639-809-2)

Capturing Jessica by Jane Hardee. Hyperrealist sculptor Michael tries desperately to conceal the love she holds for best friend, Jess, unaware Jess's feelings for her are changing. (978-1-62639-836-8)

Counting to Zero by AJ Quinn. NSA agent Emma Thorpe and computer hacker Paxton James must learn to trust each other as they work to stop a threat clock that's rapidly counting down to zero. (978-1-62639-783-5)

Courageous Love by KC Richardson. Two women fight a devastating disease, and their own demons, while trying to fall in love. (978-1-62639-797-2)

One More Reason to Leave Orlando by Missouri Vaun. Nash Wiley thought a threesome sounded exotic and exciting, but as it turns out the reality of sleeping with two women at the same time is just really complicated. (978-1-62639-703-3E)

Pathogen by Jessica L. Webb. Can Dr. Kate Morrison navigate a deadly virus and the threat of bioterrorism, as well as her new relationship with Sergeant Andy Wyles and her own troubled past? (978-1-62639-833-7)

Rainbow Gap by Lee Lynch. Jaudon Vickers and Berry Garland, polar opposites, dream and love in this tale of lesbian lives set in Central Florida against the tapestry of societal change and the Vietnam War. (978-1-62639-799-6)

Steel and Promise by Alexa Black. Lady Nivrai's cruel desires and modified body make most of the galaxy fear her, but courtesan Cailyn Derys soon discovers the real monsters are the ones without the claws. (978-1-62639-805-4)

Swelter by D. Jackson Leigh. Teal Giovanni's mistake shines an unwanted spotlight on a small Texas ranch where August Reese is secluded until she can testify against a powerful drug kingpin. (978-1-62639-795-8)

Without Justice by Carsen Taite. Cade Kelly and Emily Sinclair must battle each other in the pursuit of justice, but can they fight their undeniable attraction outside the walls of the courtroom? (978-1-62639-560-2)

21 Questions by Mason Dixon. To find love, start by asking the right questions. (978-1-62639-724-8)

A Palette for Love by Charlotte Greene. When newly minted Ph.D. Chloé Devereaux returns to New Orleans, she doesn't expect her new job, and her powerful employer—Amelia Winters—to be so appealing. (978-1-62639-758-3)

By the Dark of Her Eyes by Cameron MacElvee. When Brenna Taylor inherits a decrepit property haunted by tormented ghosts, Alejandra Santana must not only restore Brenna's house and property but also save her soul. (978-1-62639-834-4)

Cash Braddock by Ashley Bartlett. Cash Braddock just wants to hang with her cat, fall in love, and deal drugs. What's the problem with that? (978-1-62639-706-4)

Death by Cocktail Straw by Missouri Vaun. She just wanted to meet girls, but an outing at the local lesbian bar goes comically off the rails, landing Nash Wiley and her best pal in the ER. (978-1-62639-702-6)

Gravity by Juliann Rich. How can Ellie Engebretsen, Olympic ski jumping hopeful with her eye on the gold, soar through the air when all she feels like doing is falling hard for Kate Moreau, her greatest competitor and the girl of her dreams? (978-1-62639-483-4)

Lone Ranger by VK Powell. Reporter Emma Ferguson stirs up a thirty-year-old mystery that threatens Park Ranger Carter West's family and jeopardizes any hope for a relationship between the two women. (978-1-62639-767-5)

Love on Call by Radclyffe. Ex-Army medic Glenn Archer and recent LA transplant Mariana Mateo fight their mutual desire in the face of past losses as they work together in the Rivers Community Hospital ER. (978-1-62639-843-6)

Never Enough by Robyn Nyx. Can two women put aside their pasts to find love before it's too late? (978-1-62639-629-6)

Two Souls by Kathleen Knowles. Can love blossom in the wake of tragedy? (978-1-62639-641-8)

Camp Rewind by Meghan O'Brien. A summer camp for grown-ups becomes the site of an unlikely romance between a shy, introverted divorcee and one of the Internet's most infamous cultural critics—who attends undercover. (978-1-62639-793-4)

Cross Purposes by Gina L. Dartt. In pursuit of a lost Acadian treasure, three women must not only work out the clues, but also the complicated tangle of emotion and attraction developing between them. (978-1-62639-713-2)

Imperfect Truth by C.A. Popovich. Can an imperfect truth stand in the way of love? (978-1-62639-787-3)

Life in Death by M. Ullrich. Sometimes the devastating end is your only chance for a new beginning. (978-1-62639-773-6)

Love on Liberty by MJ Williamz. Hearts collide when politics clash. (978-1-62639-639-5)

Serious Potential by Maggie Cummings. Pro golfer Tracy Allen plans to forget her ex during a visit to Bay West, a lesbian condo community in NYC, but when she meets Dr. Jennifer Betsy, she gets more than she bargained for. (978-1-62639-633-3)

Smoldering Desires by C.E. Knipes. Evan McGarrity has found the man of his dreams in Sebastian Tantalos. When an old boyfriend from Sebastian's past enters the picture, Evan must fight for the man he loves. (978-1-62639-714-9)

Taste by Kris Bryant. Accomplished chef Taryn has walked away from her promising career in the city's top restaurant to devote her life to her five-year-old daughter and is content until Ki Blake comes along. (978-1-62639-718-7)

The Second Wave by Jean Copeland. Can star-crossed lovers have a second chance after decades apart, or does the love of a lifetime only happen once? (978-1-62639-830-6)

Valley of Fire by Missouri Vaun. Taken captive in a desert outpost after their small aircraft is hijacked, Ava and her captivating passenger discover things about each other and themselves that will change them both forever. (978-1-62639-496-4)

Milton Keynes UK
Ingram Content Group UK Ltd.
UKHW011301151123
432621UK00001B/129